D1347741

This book should be returned to any branch of the
Lancashire County Library on or before the date

GBL

BURNLEY CAMPUS

01282 682273

-7 OCT 2016

1 2 JUL 2012

LANCASHIRE LIBRARY
BURNLEY

1 4 AUG 2012

STA

3/16

3 0 JUL 2016

2 8 SEP 2018

Lancashire County Library
Bowran Street
Preston PR1 2UX

Lancashire
County Council

www.lancashire.gov.uk/libraries

LANCASHIRE COUNTY LIBRARY

3011812383819 9

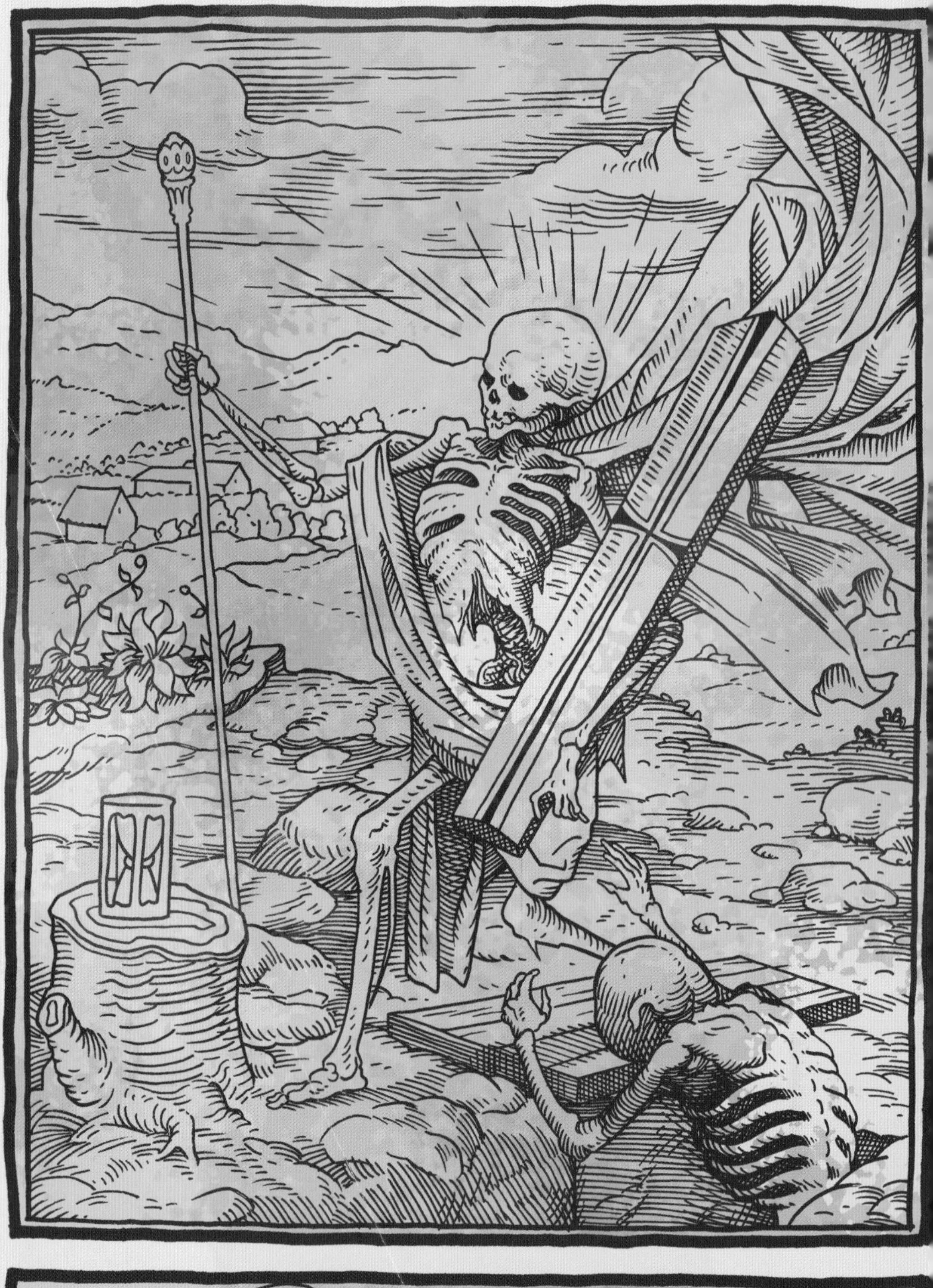

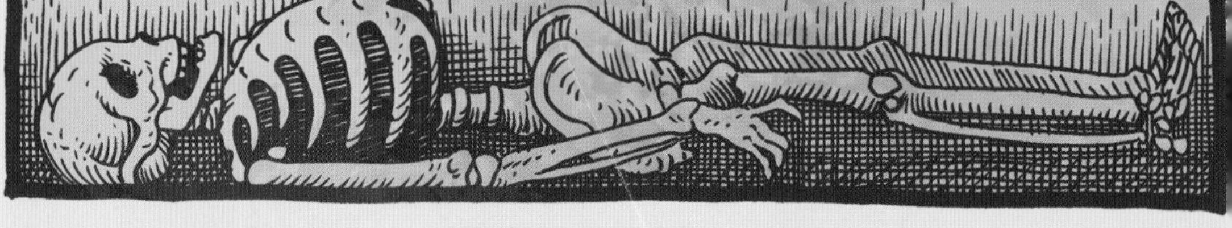

BALTIMORE™
THE PLAGUE SHIPS

VOLUME ONE

Story by
MIKE MIGNOLA
CHRISTOPHER GOLDEN

Art by
BEN STENBECK

Colors by
DAVE STEWART

Letters by
CLEM ROBINS

Cover Art by
MIKE MIGNOLA with **DAVE STEWART**

Editor **SCOTT ALLIE**
Associate Editor **SAMANTHA ROBERTSON**
Assistant Editor **DANIEL CHABON**
Collection Designer **AMY ARENDTS**
Publisher **MIKE RICHARDSON**

DARK HORSE BOOKS®

For William Hope Hodgson, who had a lot to say about wrecked ships and fungus.
—Mike Mignola

For Gene Colan, the first person to show me that comics could be creepy.
—Christopher Golden

For Danny Cox and Action Man.
—Ben Stenbeck

Neil Hankerson *Executive Vice President* • Tom Weddle *Chief Financial Officer* • Randy Stradley *Vice President of Publishing* • Michael Martens *Vice President of Book Trade Sales* • Anita Nelson *Vice President of Business Affairs* • Micha Hershman *Vice President of Marketing* • David Scroggy *Vice President of Product Development* • Dale LaFountain *Vice President of Information Technology* • Darlene Vogel *Senior Director of Print, Design, and Production* • Ken Lizzi *General Counsel* • Davey Estrada *Editorial Director* • Scott Allie *Senior Managing Editor* • Chris Warner *Senior Books Editor* • Diana Schutz *Executive Editor* • Cary Grazzini *Director of Print and Development* • Lia Ribacchi *Art Director* • Cara Niece *Director of Scheduling*

Special thanks to Jason Hvam and Pasquale Ruggiero

DarkHorse.com

Published by Dark Horse Books
A division of Dark Horse Comics, Inc.
10956 SE Main Street
Milwaukie, OR 97222

First paperback edition: December 2011
ISBN 978-1-59582-677-0

1   3   5   7   9   10   8   6   4   2

Printed at Midas Printing International, Ltd., Huizhou, China

Baltimore: The Plague Ships © 2010, 2011 Mike Mignola and Christopher Golden. Dark Horse Books® and the Dark Horse logo are registered trademarks of Dark Horse Comics, Inc. All rights reserved. No portion of this publication may be reproduced or transmitted, in any form or by any means, without the express written permission of Dark Horse Comics, Inc. Names, characters, places, and incidents featured in this publication either are the product of the author's imagination or are used fictitiously. Any resemblance to actual persons (living or dead), events, institutions, or locales, without satiric intent, is coincidental.

This volume collects the *Baltimore: The Plague Ships* comic-book series, issues #1–#5, published by Dark Horse Comics.

BACK FROM THE DEAD

by
JOE HILL

1.

LET'S PLAY AN ASSOCIATIVE GAME. Clear your head. I'll drop a word on you, and you say the first thing that comes to mind. Or, if you're reading this graphic novel on a crowded train, you can just whisper to yourself. Ready? Here goes:

Comics.

Mm-hm. You said "Superman," right? Or was it "Batman"? Maybe, just *maybe*, you said, "capes." (Okay, sure, a couple of you out there replied with something ridiculous, like, "onward," just to show how original you are, but trust me, everyone else thought of superheroes.)

I don't know how old you are—you might be fifteen or you might be fifty—but the odds are that the comics you were raised on featured men in ill-advised tights, battling psychotic grotesqueries in the name of truth, justice, and a possible Saturday-morning cartoon. I love cape stories myself, always have. Superman and Batman are more than great characters; they are icons and archetypes, and their stories inform us about ourselves and our historical moment.

Yet we are not too far removed from a period in time when comics were known not

for their masked titans, but for their decaying fiends; when they were famous, not for stories of superpowered heroism, but supernatural perversions; not for displays of idealized sacrifice, but for *human* sacrifice. There was a time, except when, if we were to play my associative word game, you might've responded to the word "comics" with "horror," or "crime," or "torture," or . . .

. . . tragically . . .

. . . "delinquency." (And yes, probably a few smartasses would've replied with "onward" or some other word that has no relationship to my prompt. But then every generation has its share of smartasses. I have occasionally been accused of being one myself, even by the cowriter of this very comic, Christopher Golden.)

I'm not going to use this space to rehash what happened to horror comics in the 1950s: psychiatrist Fredric Wertham's unscientific study purporting to show a connection between horror comics and sadistic behavior among boys, the shameless kangaroo court put together by Senator Kefauver to attack the comic-book industry (and free speech itself), the creation of the Comics Code, which shoved artists and writers into a superhero-shaped coffin and buried them alive under six feet of hysterical repression. If you want to read about it, I recommend a book titled *The Ten-Cent Plague* by David Hajdu, which methodically documents the effort to eradicate the disease of horror comics in the name of public health . . . the first skirmish in a tiresome culture war that continues to this day.[1]

No, my point is this: if they weren't in such a rush to strangle the life out of the horror comics, the repression brigade might've learned a very valuable lesson from them. The departed—especially those who have suffered a cruel and unjust death—have a nasty way of opening their

---

[1] When an outraged parent writes their newspaper to claim *Grand Theft Auto* or Eminem went and turned their child into a sulky, arrogant teenager, remember two things: (1) children turn into sulky, arrogant teenagers all on their own, without any assist from popular culture, and (2) the irate parent is repeating all the same arguments that were made against horror comics, Elvis, motorcycle movies, and (I shit you not) the hula hoop.

eyes and clawing their way out of the soil the moment you turn your back on 'em.

Somewhere in here, when no one was paying attention, horror comics came back from the dead, baby. *Hellboy. Hack/Slash. 30 Days of Night. The Goon. The Walking Dead.*

Baltimore.

Last but not least, *Baltimore.* Unapologetically: *Baltimore.*

2.

Let's say we turned my associative game around. Let's say you suggested a word, and I had to reply, honestly, with the first thing that came into my mind. And then you said, "fun."

My response would depend somewhat on when we played. If this were the fall of 2005, I would've said, "League," thinking of Alan Moore's *League of Extraordinary Gentlemen.* If this were the winter of 2007, I would've said, "Y," mindful of Brian Vaughan's game-changing comic, *Y: The Last Man.* No matter when we played—this year or twenty-five years ago—I probably would have answered with the title of a comic book. They have a lifelong hold on me I can't explain and don't understand. They light up all the pleasure circuits . . . especially the darker comics, those stories of desperate stands against a tide of infection, madness, and the damned.

Here, in the last frozen days of 2010, my high of choice is *Baltimore: The Plague Ships,* one of the most energetic and inventive works on the aforementioned list of remarkable new horror comics.

Plague Ships expands on a story begun in *Baltimore; or, The Steadfast Tin Soldier and the Vampire,* an illustrated novel by Christopher Golden and Mike Mignola, which was itself a thunderous war machine of a book, a relentless bombardment of action and ideas.[2] But don't worry if you haven't read the novel. This comic is not a sequel, but rather a companion, a second doorway into the same shadowy crypt. It introduces us to the grim, tireless, and really exceptionally well-armed Lord Henry Baltimore, and in less than twelve gruesome, violent, and brain-busting pages, his quest to destroy the king vampire named Haigus is *our* quest . . . and never mind that death sits on Lord Baltimore's shoulder "for those who ally themselves with him." We'll have to take our chances.

We can skip the plot summary; for Christ's sake, you're about to read the thing. Suffice it to say that *Plague Ships* moves forward with the ferocity and drive of its unstoppable protagonist, and throws at you all the visual horrors you would expect of *Hellboy* creator Mike Mignola, and all the mad, stomach-churning concepts that are the stock-in-trade of novelist Christopher Golden. Their vision is made complete by the muscular line work of artist Ben Stenbeck and the moody, chilling colors of Dave Stewart. I could mount a five-thousand-word argument to intellectually defend the excitement I feel for *Plague Ships.* I could drone on about how it operates as a fusion work, blending horror with the sensibility of steampunk sci-fi, to make a new genre (splattersteam?). I could discuss its playful riffs on classic nineteenth-century genre tropes (haunted islands, archaic submarines, Poe's red death).

But truthfully, my response to *Plague Ships* was something I felt more in my nerve endings; it was visceral, not intellectual. Stenbeck, Stewart, Golden, and Mignola had me by the third panel of page 4.

Max really should've run.

Okay. One more word-association game. I get to pick this time.

Ready?

Onward.

Joe Hill
New Hampshire
December 2010

---

[2]It was also, on the level of production design, the most beautiful-looking wide-release novel published in 2007, in any genre. Seriously—this bastard had the quality and beauty of a one-hundred-dollar limited edition. If every hardcover was such a pleasure to read and hold, the e-book industry would be nowheresville.

CHAPTER ONE

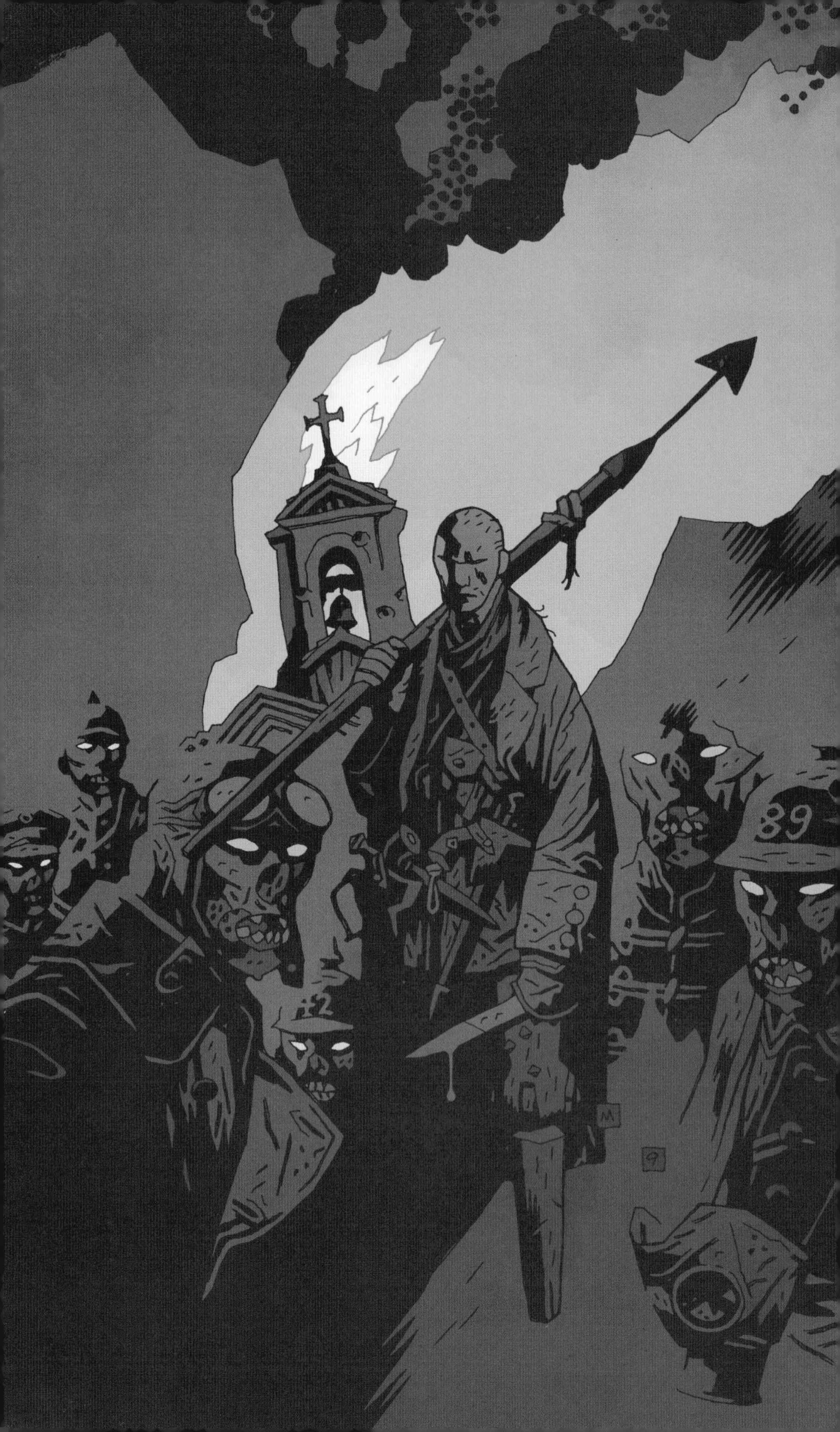

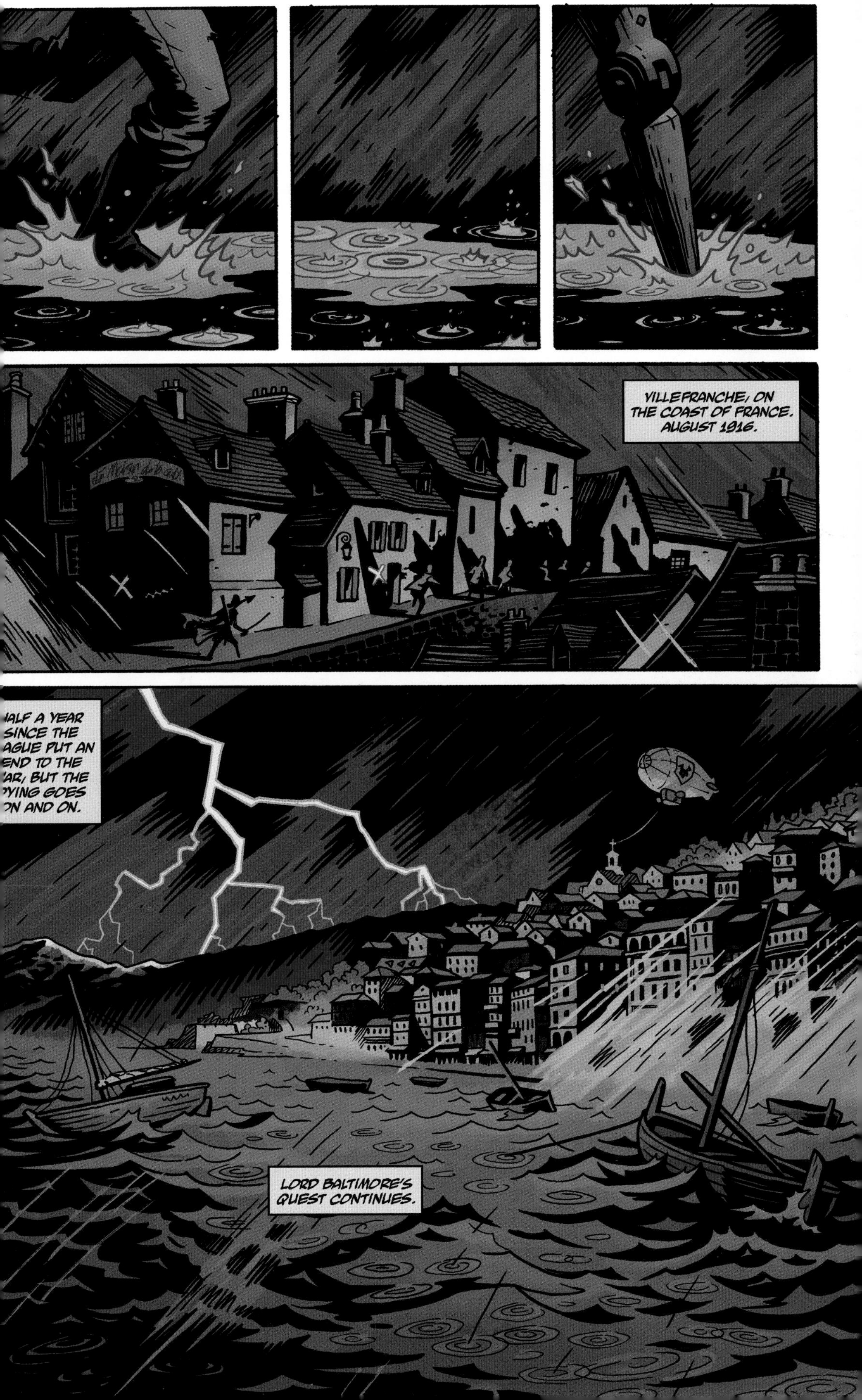
VILLEFRANCHE, ON THE COAST OF FRANCE. AUGUST 1916.
HALF A YEAR SINCE THE PLAGUE PUT AN END TO THE WAR, BUT THE DYING GOES ON AND ON.
LORD BALTIMORE'S QUEST CONTINUES.

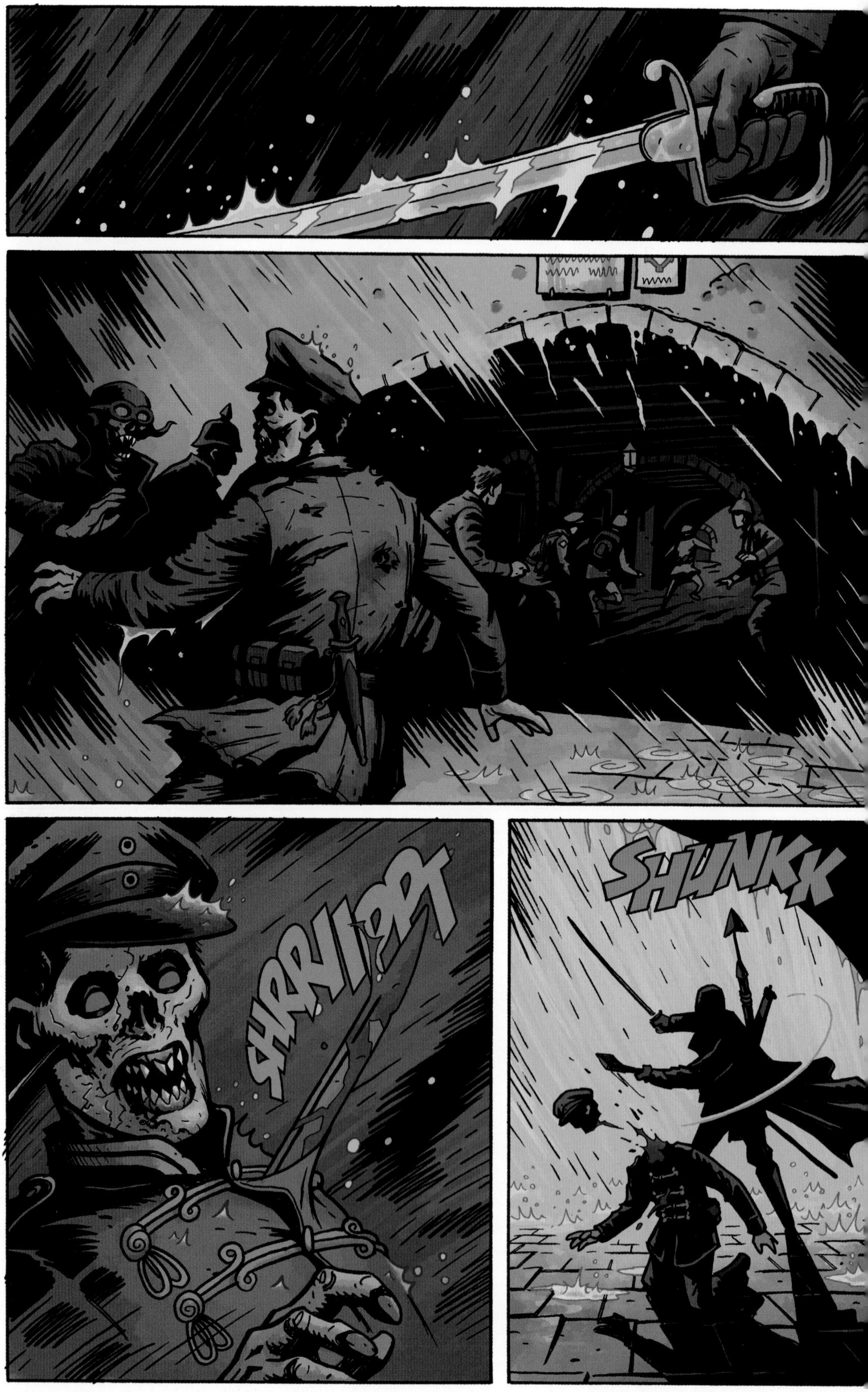
SHRRIPPT
SHUNKK

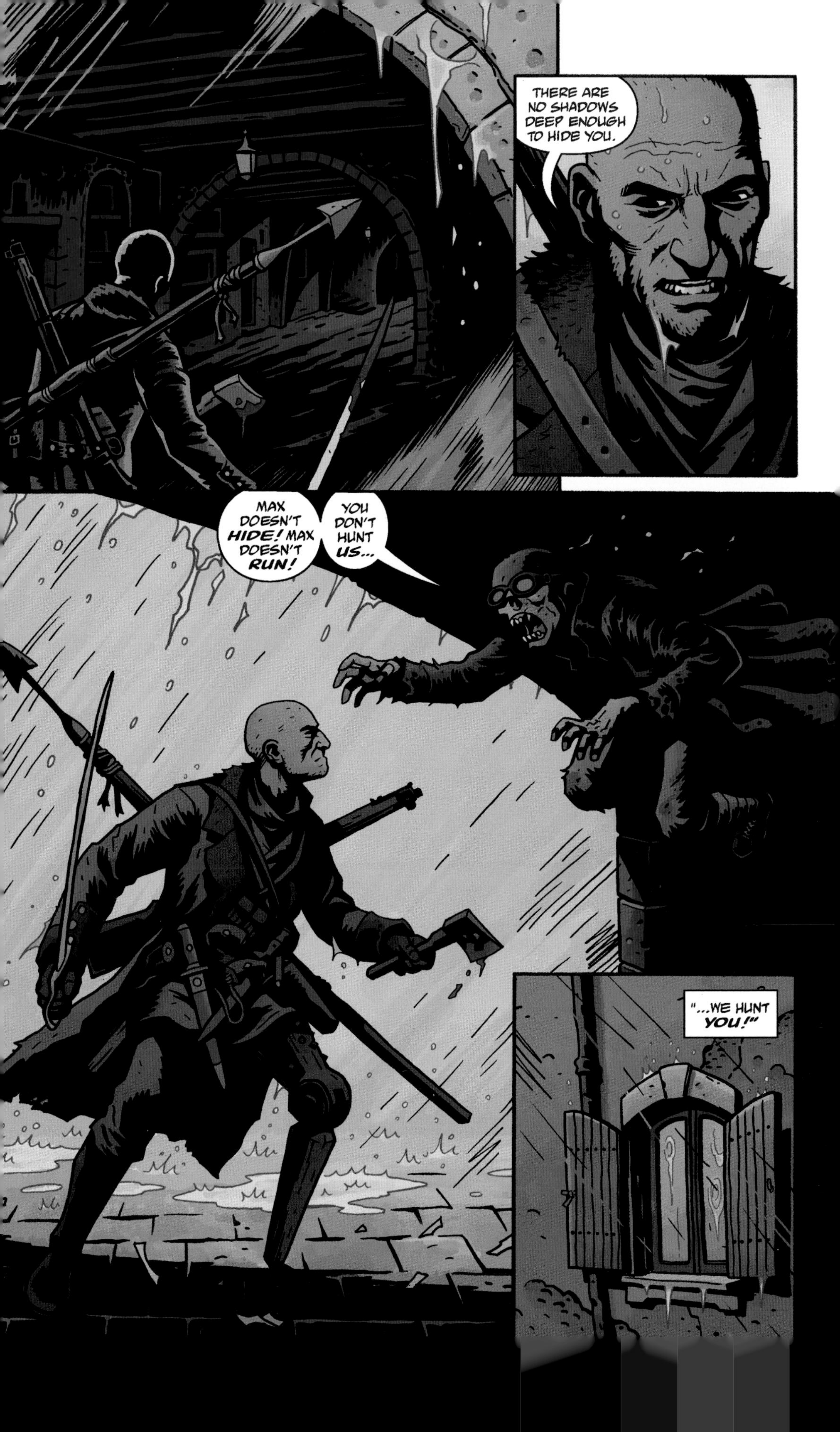
THERE ARE NO SHADOWS DEEP ENOUGH TO HIDE YOU.
MAX DOESN'T HIDE! MAX DOESN'T RUN!
YOU DON'T HUNT US...
"...WE HUNT YOU!"

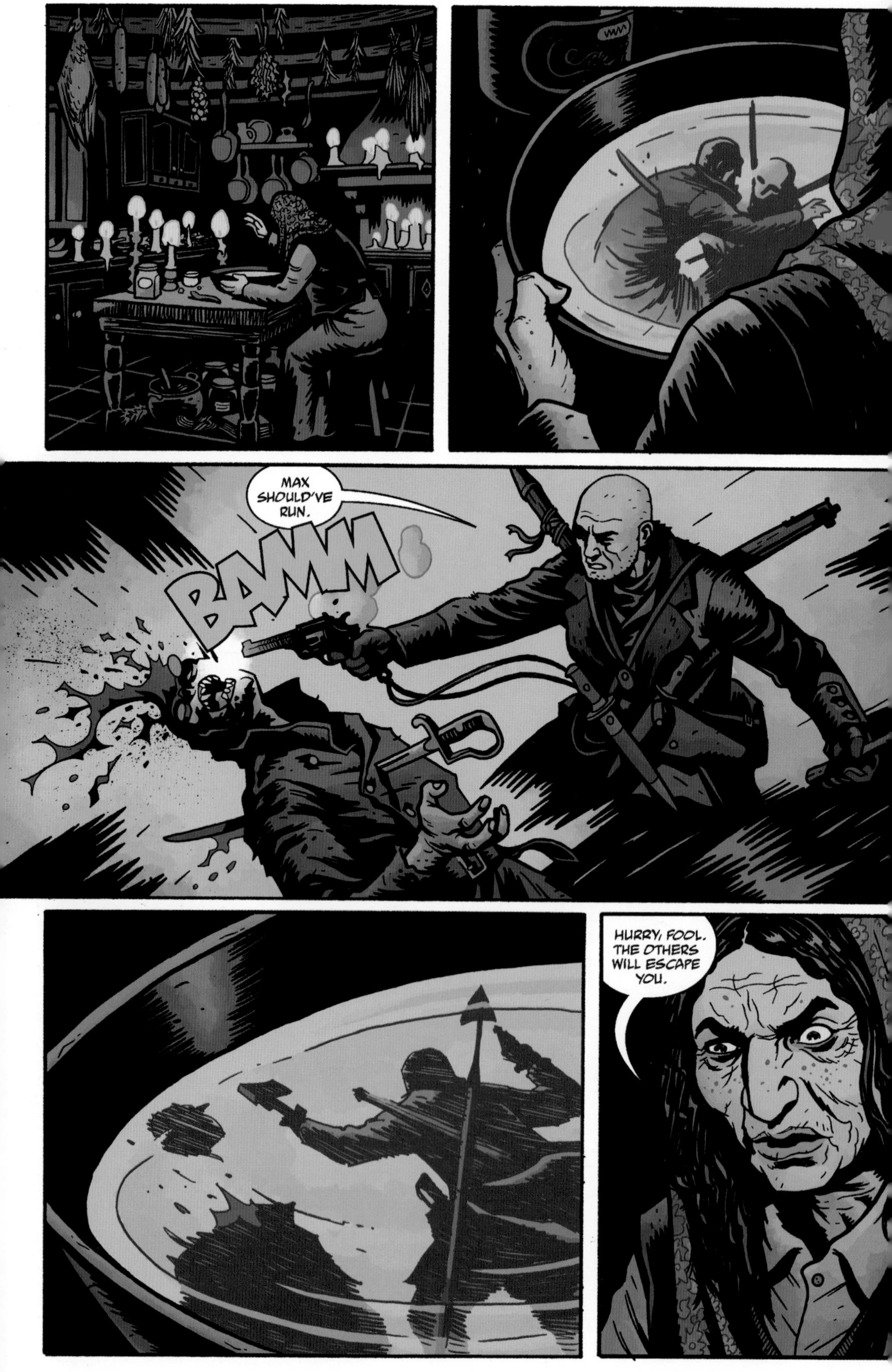
MAX SHOULD'VE RUN.
BAMM
HURRY, FOOL. THE OTHERS WILL ESCAPE YOU.

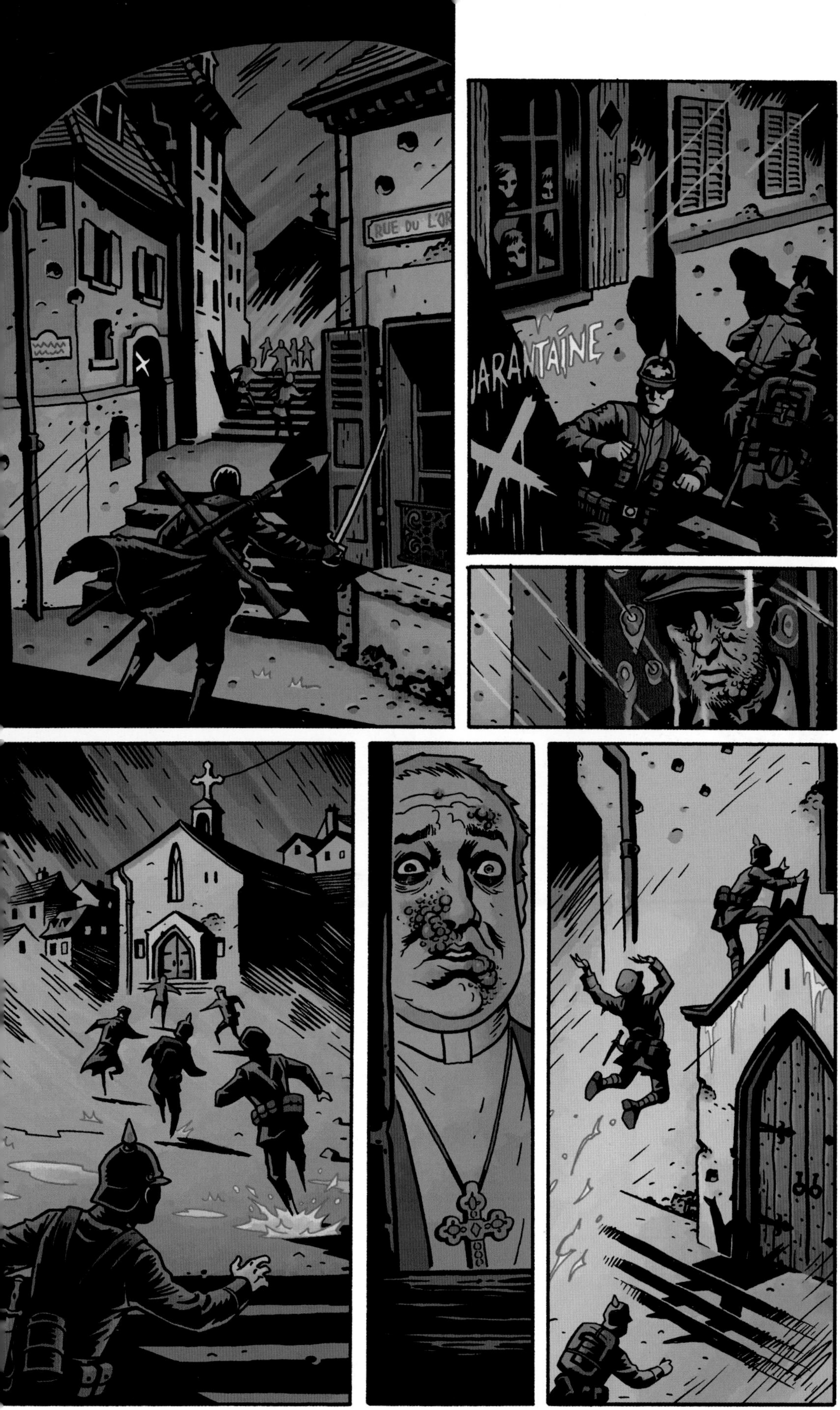
RUE DU L'OR
ARANTAINE

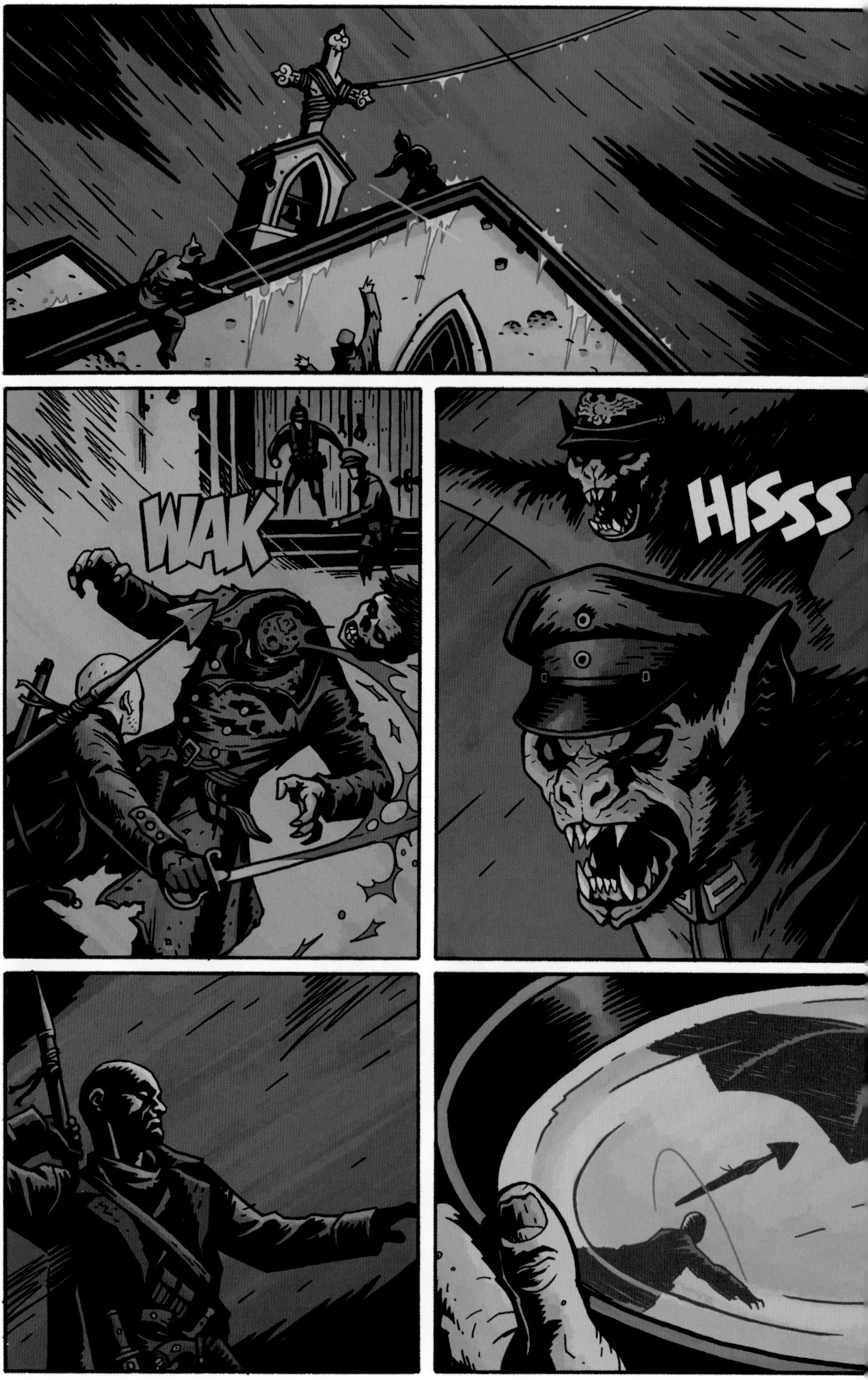
WAK
HISSS

SKREEE

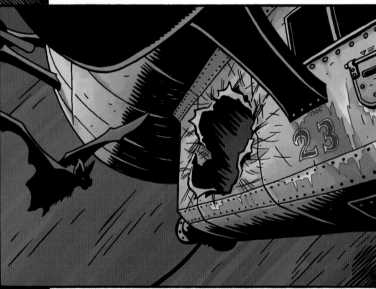

NO, DAMN YOU! NOT UNTIL YOU TELL ME WHERE HE IS!

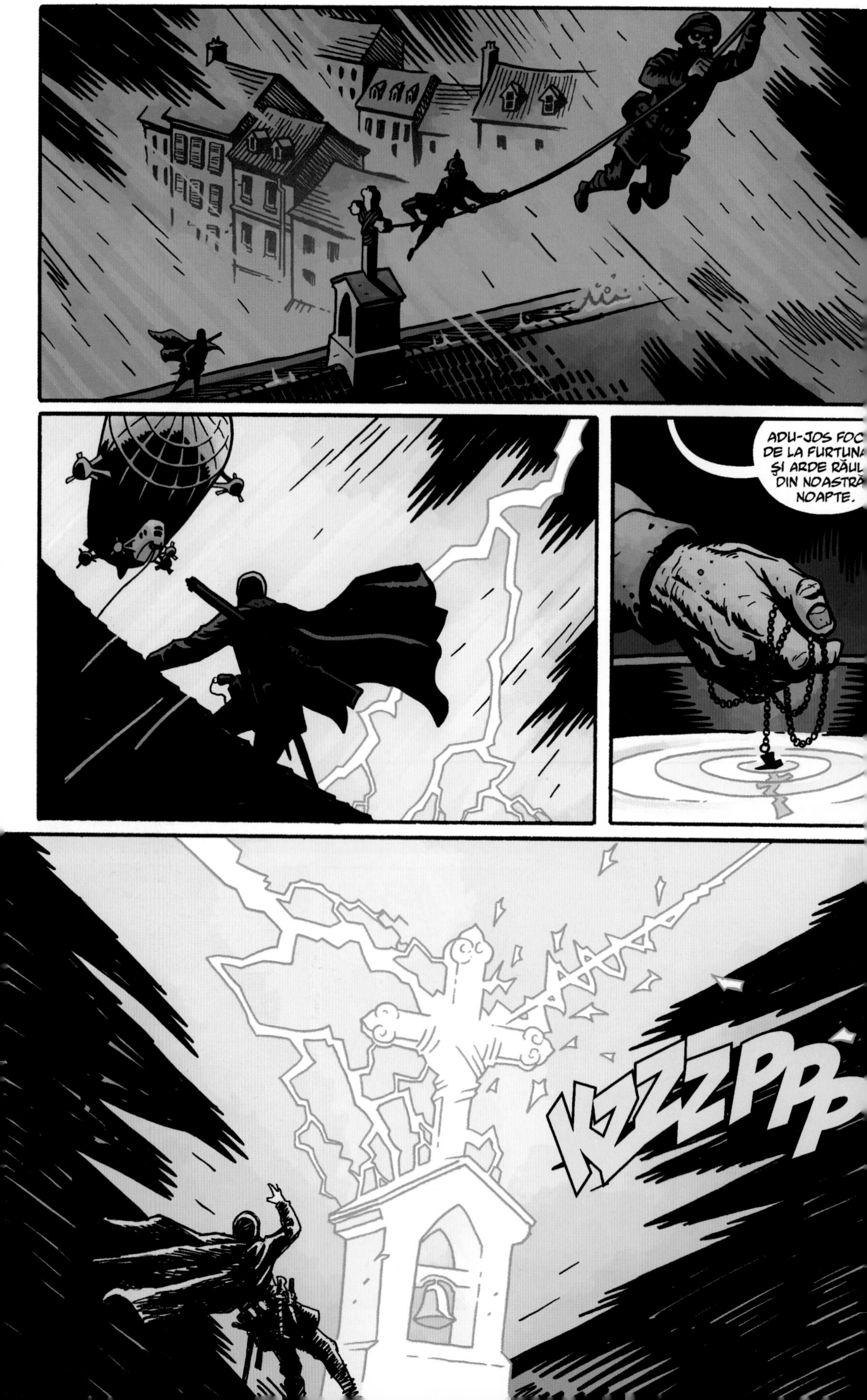
ADU-JOS FOC DE LA FURTUNA ŞI ARDE RĂUL DIN NOASTRĂ NOAPTE.
KZZZPPP

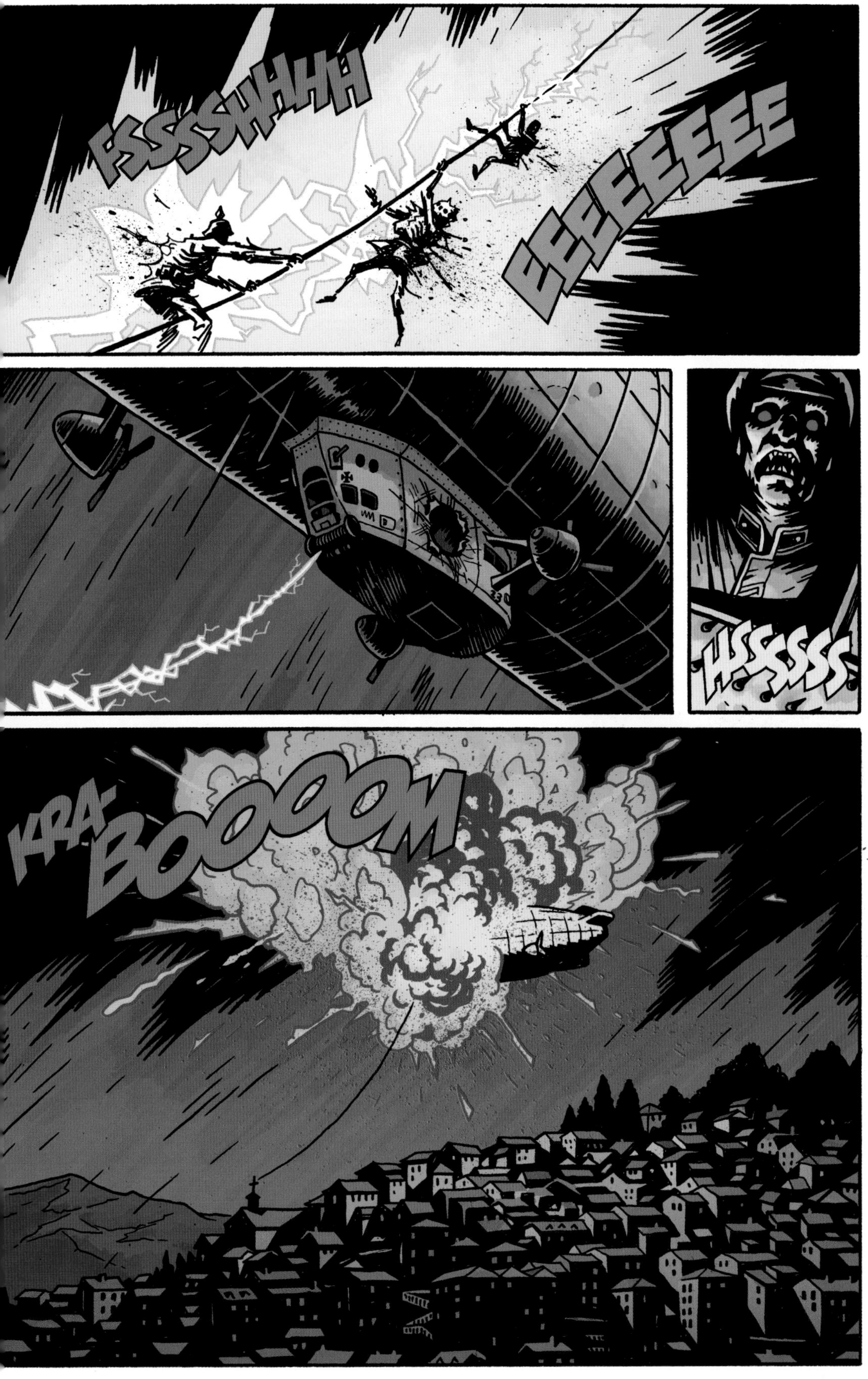
FSSSSHHHH
EEEEEEEEE
HSSSSS
KRA-BOOOOOM

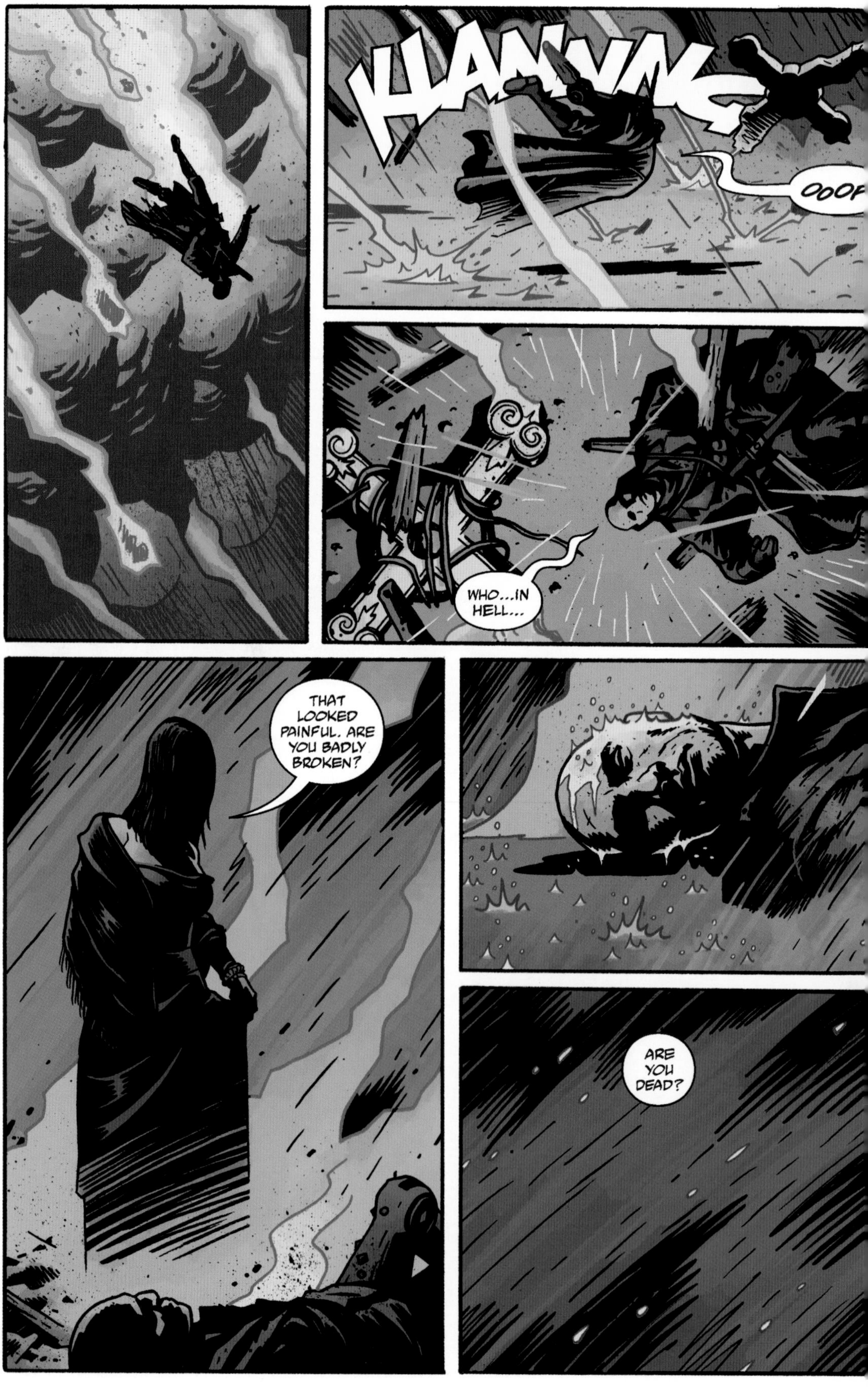
KLANNNG
OOOF
WHO...IN HELL...
THAT LOOKED PAINFUL. ARE YOU BADLY BROKEN?
ARE YOU DEAD?

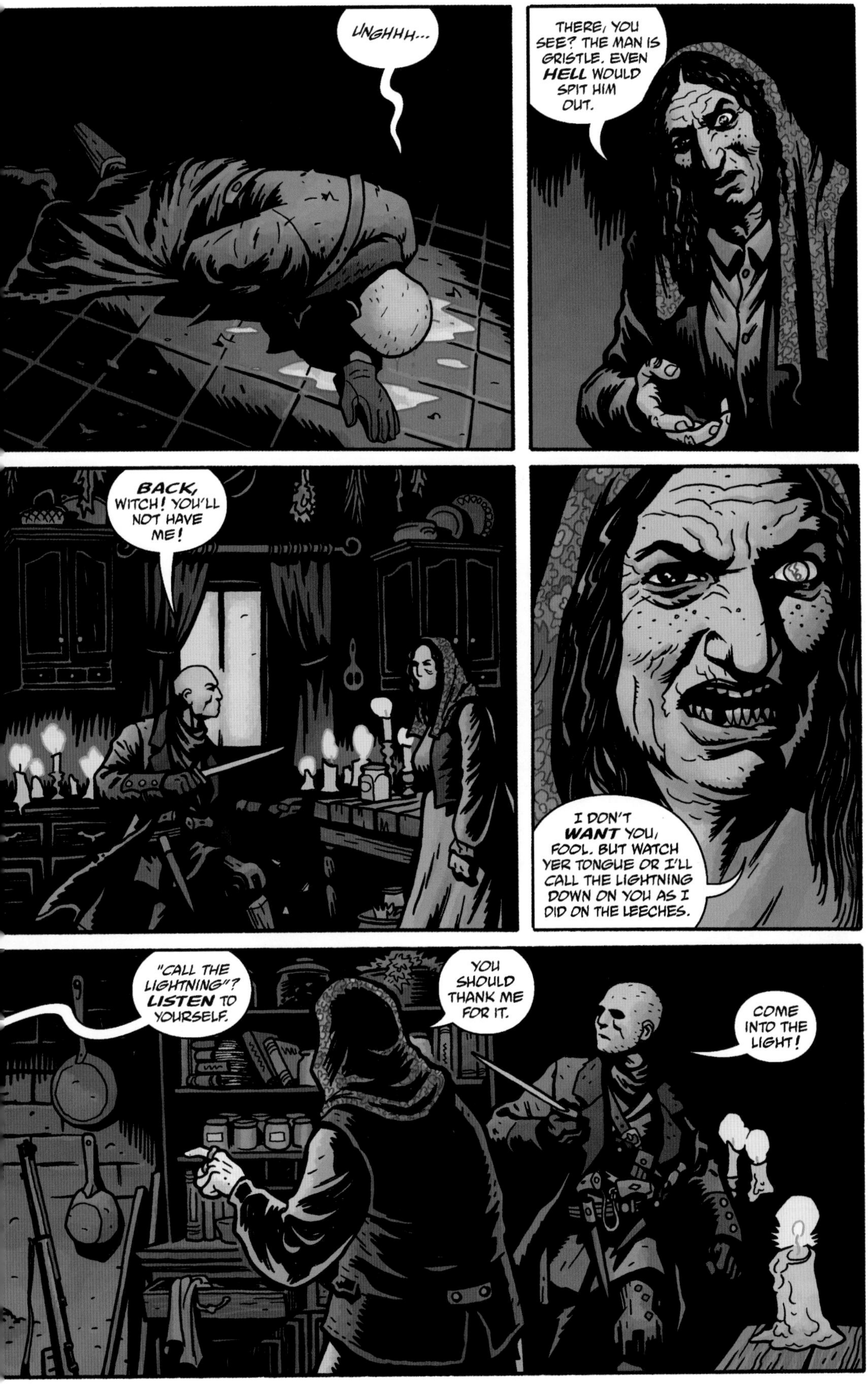
UNGHHH...
THERE, YOU SEE? THE MAN IS GRISTLE. EVEN HELL WOULD SPIT HIM OUT.
BACK, WITCH! YOU'LL NOT HAVE ME!
I DON'T WANT YOU, FOOL. BUT WATCH YER TONGUE OR I'LL CALL THE LIGHTNING DOWN ON YOU AS I DID ON THE LEECHES.
"CALL THE LIGHTNING"? LISTEN TO YOURSELF.
YOU SHOULD THANK ME FOR IT.
COME INTO THE LIGHT!

PLEASE, SIR, PUT THE BLADE AWAY. MY GRANDMOTHER MEANS YOU NO HARM.

WHO ARE YOU, GIRL? ANOTHER WITCH?

MY NAME IS VANESSA KALDERAS. AS FOR WITCHERY, DON'T LET GRANDMOTHER FOOL YOU. SHE CAN NO MORE CALL THE LIGHTNING THAN--

HUSH YOUR MOUTH, GIRL.

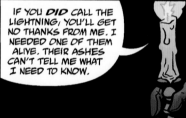

IF YOU *DID* CALL THE LIGHTNING, YOU'LL GET NO THANKS FROM ME. I NEEDED ONE OF THEM ALIVE. THEIR ASHES CAN'T TELL ME WHAT I NEED TO KNOW.

I CAN SEE YOU WE A GENTLEMAN ONC BUT YOU'VE OBVIOUSLY LOS YOUR MANNERS. KEPT THEM FR *ESCAPING*

THEY WOULDN'T HAVE ESCAPED.

ALF THE TOWN IS DEAD OR DYING OF PLAGUE AND HEY'VE BEEN FEEDING OFF WHAT'S LEFT FROM THE ADOWS. I WOULDN'T WANT EVEN **ONE** OF THEM LEFT ALIVE.

IF YOU COULD HAVE KILLED THEM YOURSELF, WHY DID YOU WAIT WHILE SO MANY DIED?

KILL **ONE**, THEY MAKE **TWO MORE**. THE OLDER ONES HIDE THEMSELVES. ONLY WHEN YOU FLUSHED THEM OUT COULD I BE SURE TO GET AT THE OLD ONES. THE **SMART** ONES.

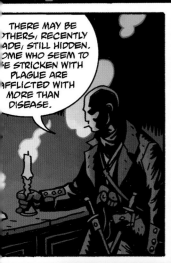

THERE MAY BE OTHERS, RECENTLY MADE, STILL HIDDEN. OME WHO SEEM TO E STRICKEN WITH PLAGUE ARE FFLICTED WITH MORE THAN DISEASE.

QUARANTAÍNE

THE STRAGGLERS WILL POSE NO DIFFICULTY.

WHAT WILL OU DO NOW, ITHOUT THE FORMATION YOU OUGHT?

CONTINUE MY HUNT.

I PURSUE A PARTICULAR VAMPIRE, ONE OF THE OLD ONES, SOMETIMES CALLED **HAIGUS**. YOU WOULD KNOW HIM BY THE LONG SCAR HERE AND BY THE ABSENCE OF HIS RIGHT EYE.

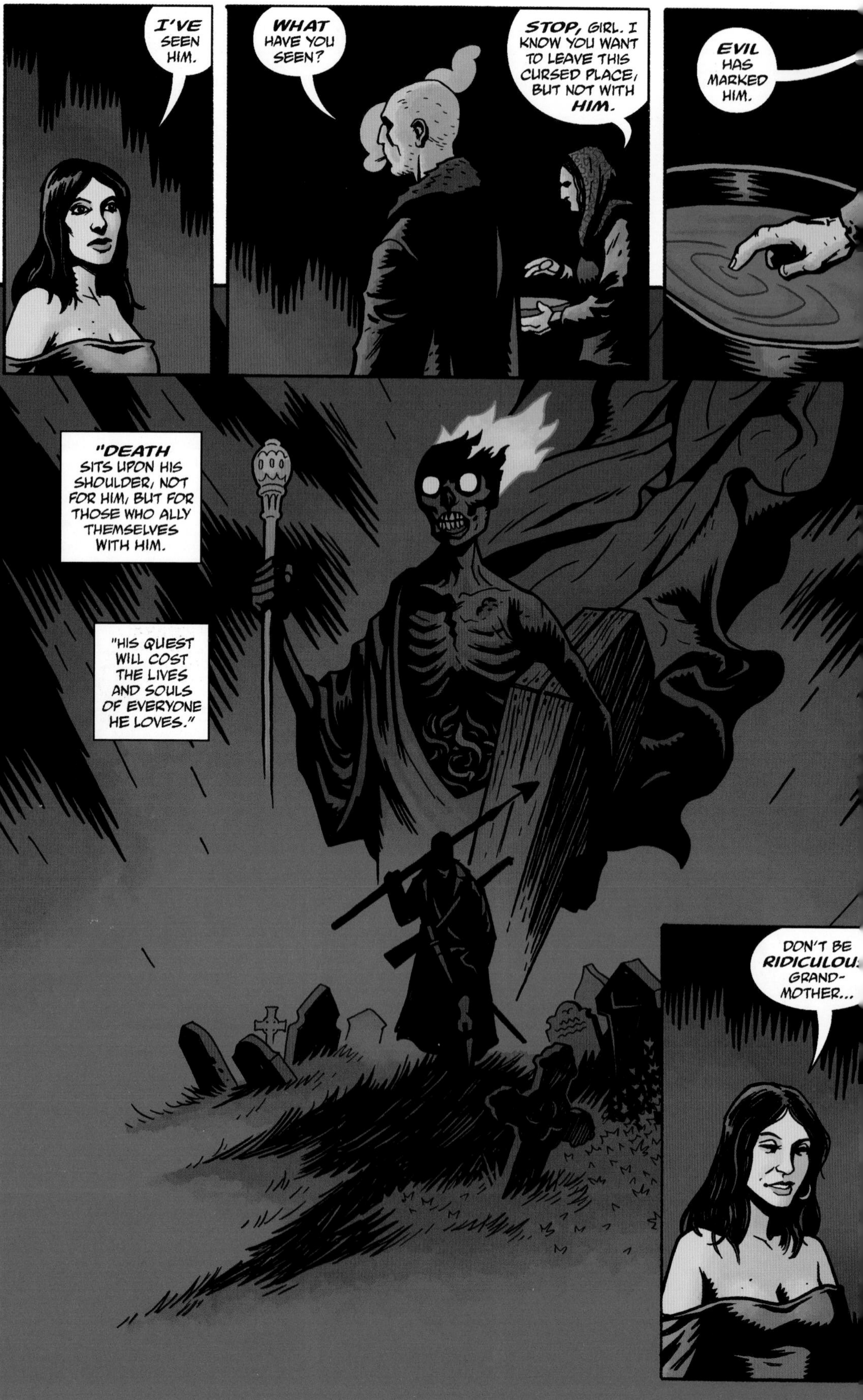
I'VE SEEN HIM.
WHAT HAVE YOU SEEN?
STOP, GIRL. I KNOW YOU WANT TO LEAVE THIS CURSED PLACE, BUT NOT WITH HIM.
EVIL HAS MARKED HIM.
"DEATH SITS UPON HIS SHOULDER, NOT FOR HIM, BUT FOR THOSE WHO ALLY THEMSELVES WITH HIM.
"HIS QUEST WILL COST THE LIVES AND SOULS OF EVERYONE HE LOVES."
DON'T BE RIDICULOU GRAND-MOTHER...

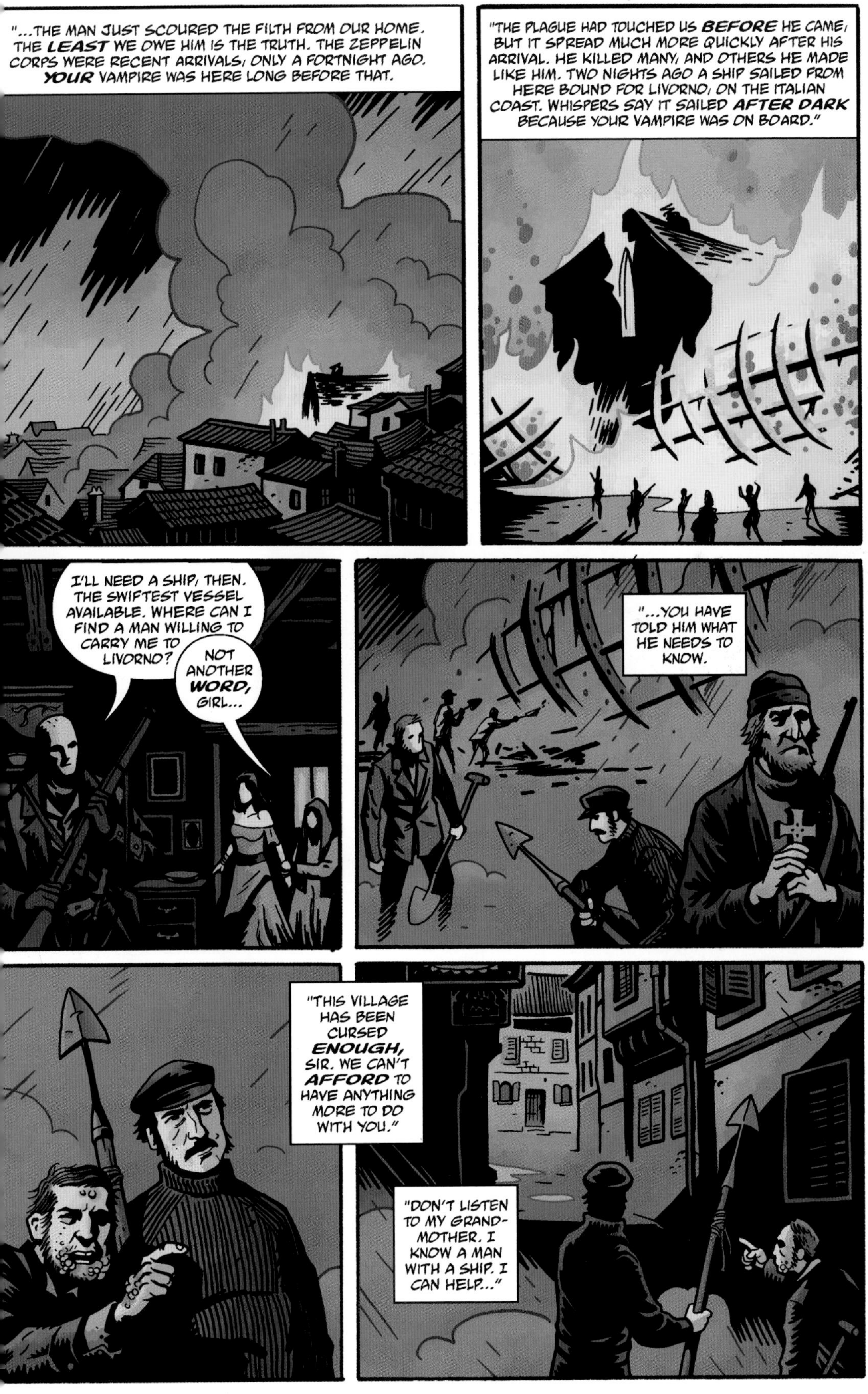
"...THE MAN JUST SCOURED THE FILTH FROM OUR HOME. THE LEAST WE OWE HIM IS THE TRUTH. THE ZEPPELIN CORPS WERE RECENT ARRIVALS, ONLY A FORTNIGHT AGO. YOUR VAMPIRE WAS HERE LONG BEFORE THAT.
"THE PLAGUE HAD TOUCHED US BEFORE HE CAME, BUT IT SPREAD MUCH MORE QUICKLY AFTER HIS ARRIVAL. HE KILLED MANY, AND OTHERS HE MADE LIKE HIM. TWO NIGHTS AGO A SHIP SAILED FROM HERE BOUND FOR LIVORNO, ON THE ITALIAN COAST. WHISPERS SAY IT SAILED AFTER DARK BECAUSE YOUR VAMPIRE WAS ON BOARD."
I'LL NEED A SHIP, THEN. THE SWIFTEST VESSEL AVAILABLE. WHERE CAN I FIND A MAN WILLING TO CARRY ME TO LIVORNO?
NOT ANOTHER WORD, GIRL...
"...YOU HAVE TOLD HIM WHAT HE NEEDS TO KNOW.
"THIS VILLAGE HAS BEEN CURSED ENOUGH, SIR. WE CAN'T AFFORD TO HAVE ANYTHING MORE TO DO WITH YOU."
"DON'T LISTEN TO MY GRAND-MOTHER. I KNOW A MAN WITH A SHIP. I CAN HELP..."

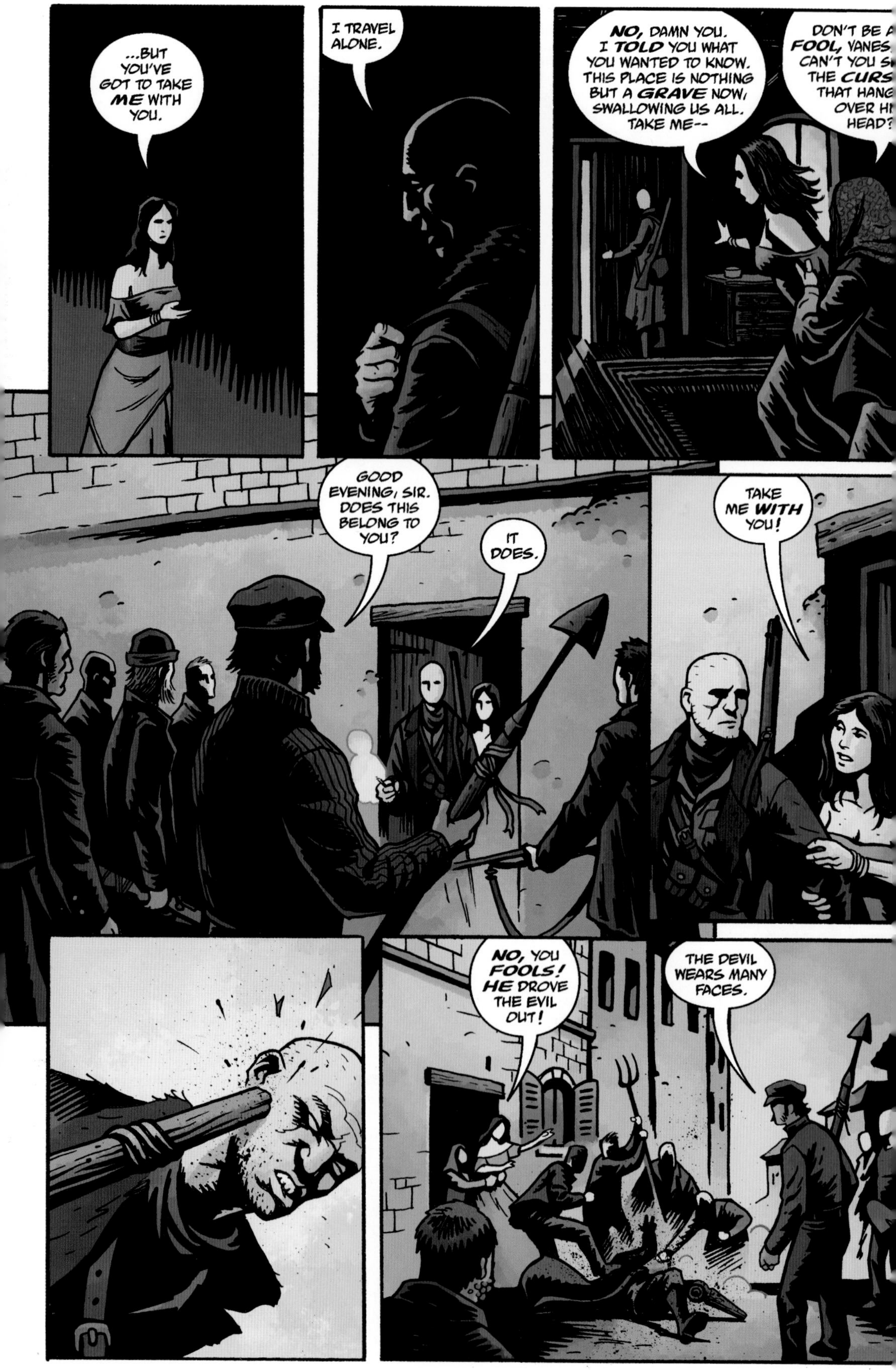
...BUT YOU'VE GOT TO TAKE ME WITH YOU.
I TRAVEL ALONE.
NO, DAMN YOU. I TOLD YOU WHAT YOU WANTED TO KNOW. THIS PLACE IS NOTHING BUT A GRAVE NOW, SWALLOWING US ALL. TAKE ME--
DON'T BE A FOOL, VANES CAN'T YOU S THE CURS THAT HANG OVER HI HEAD?
GOOD EVENING, SIR. DOES THIS BELONG TO YOU?
IT DOES.
TAKE ME WITH YOU!
NO, YOU FOOLS! HE DROVE THE EVIL OUT!
THE DEVIL WEARS MANY FACES.

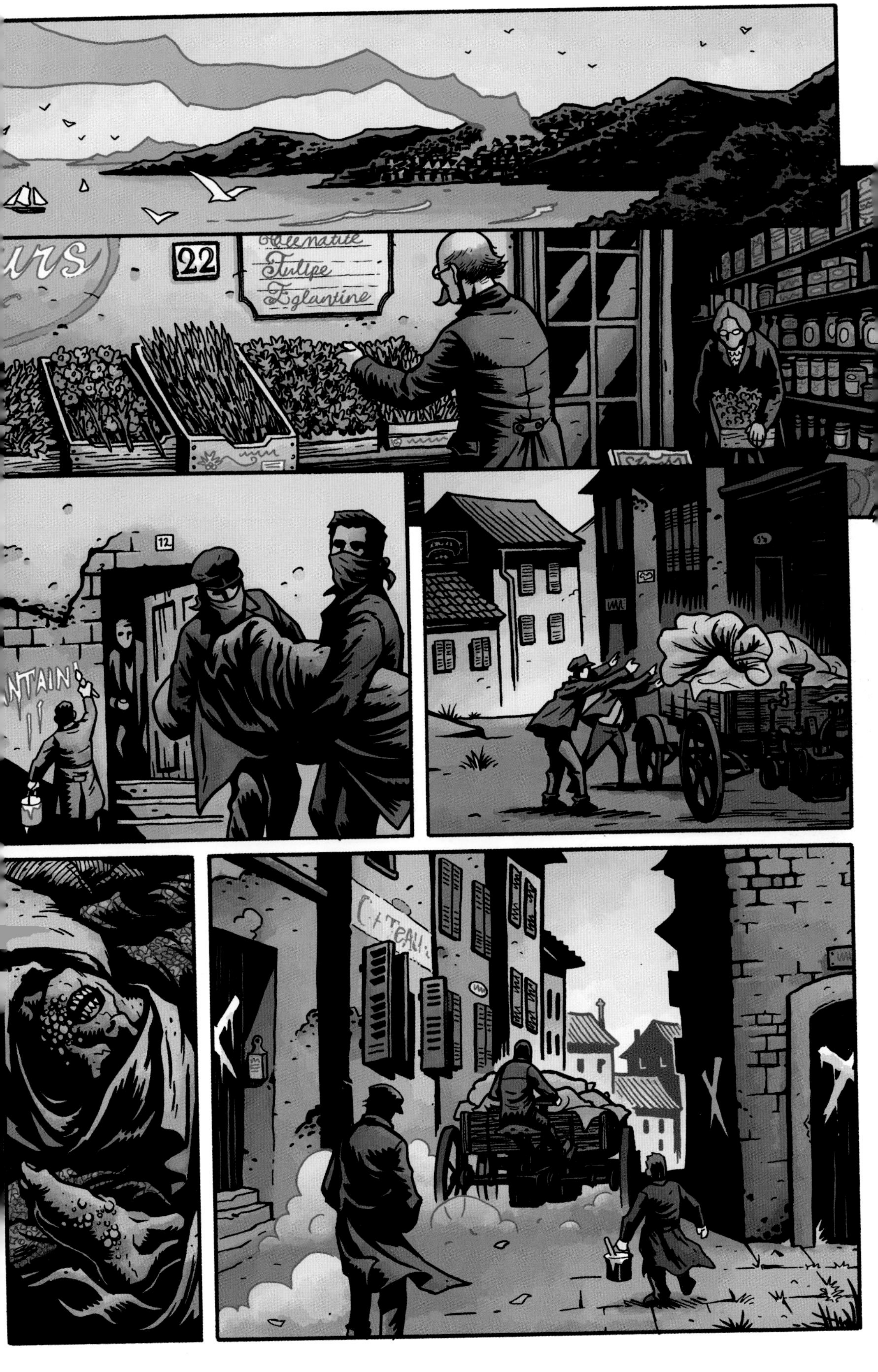

22
Tulipe
Eglantine
12

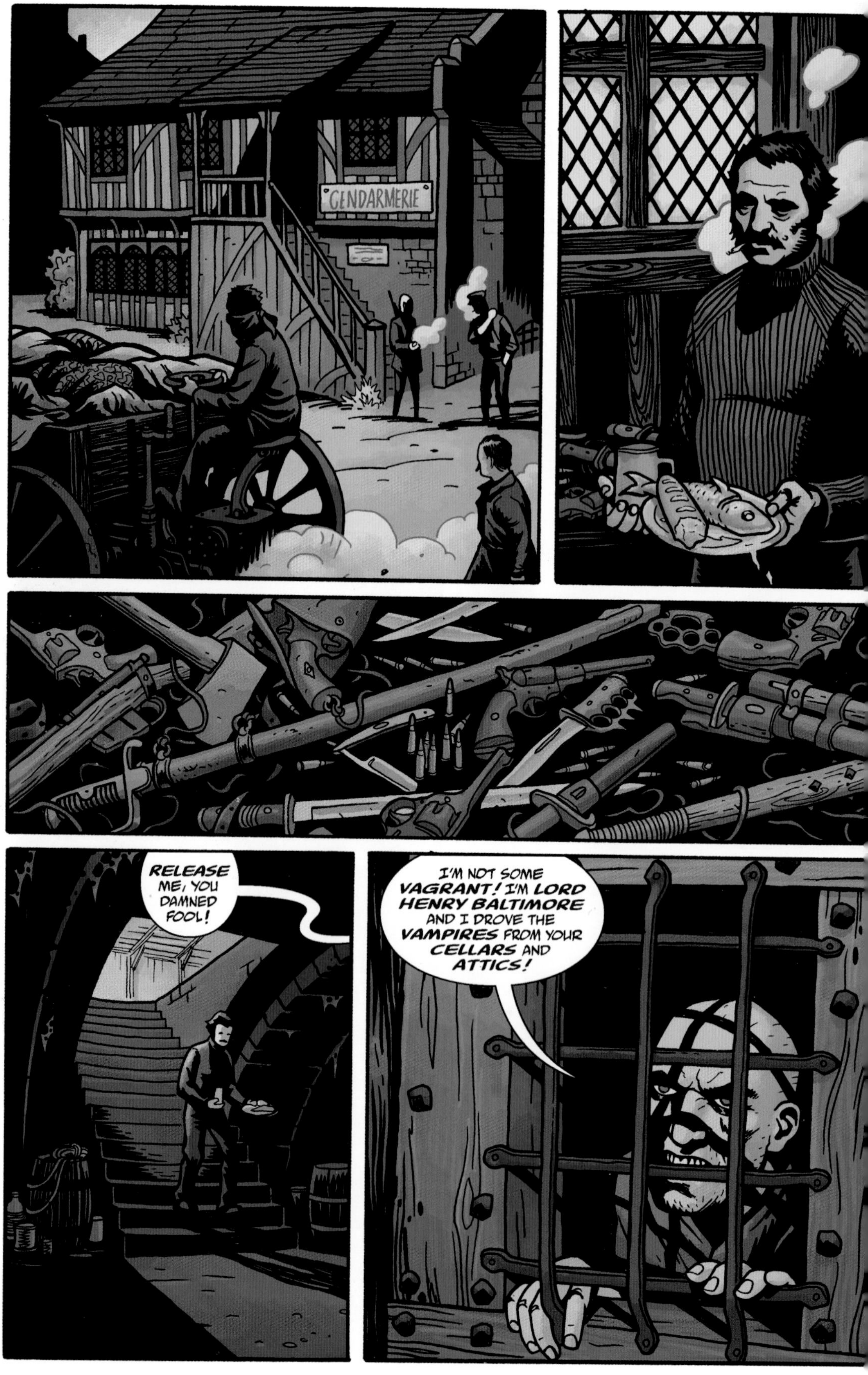
GENDARMERIE
RELEASE ME, YOU DAMNED FOOL!
I'M NOT SOME VAGRANT! I'M LORD HENRY BALTIMORE AND I DROVE THE VAMPIRES FROM YOUR CELLARS AND ATTICS!

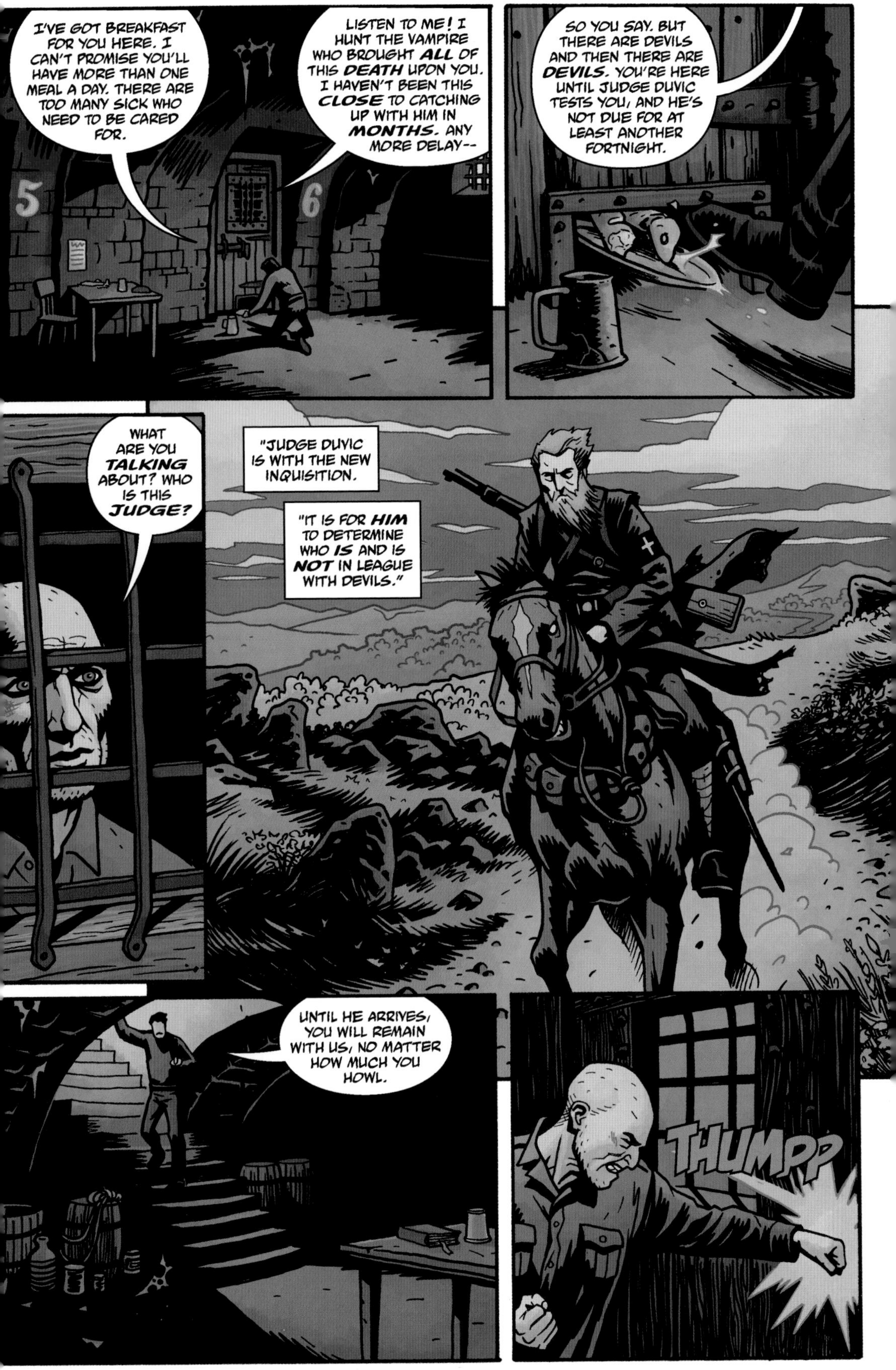
I'VE GOT BREAKFAST FOR YOU HERE. I CAN'T PROMISE YOU'LL HAVE MORE THAN ONE MEAL A DAY. THERE ARE TOO MANY SICK WHO NEED TO BE CARED FOR.
5
6
LISTEN TO ME! I HUNT THE VAMPIRE WHO BROUGHT ALL OF THIS DEATH UPON YOU. I HAVEN'T BEEN THIS CLOSE TO CATCHING UP WITH HIM IN MONTHS. ANY MORE DELAY--
SO YOU SAY. BUT THERE ARE DEVILS AND THEN THERE ARE DEVILS. YOU'RE HERE UNTIL JUDGE DUVIC TESTS YOU, AND HE'S NOT DUE FOR AT LEAST ANOTHER FORTNIGHT.
WHAT ARE YOU TALKING ABOUT? WHO IS THIS JUDGE?
"JUDGE DUVIC IS WITH THE NEW INQUISITION.
"IT IS FOR HIM TO DETERMINE WHO IS AND IS NOT IN LEAGUE WITH DEVILS."
UNTIL HE ARRIVES, YOU WILL REMAIN WITH US, NO MATTER HOW MUCH YOU HOWL.
THUMPP

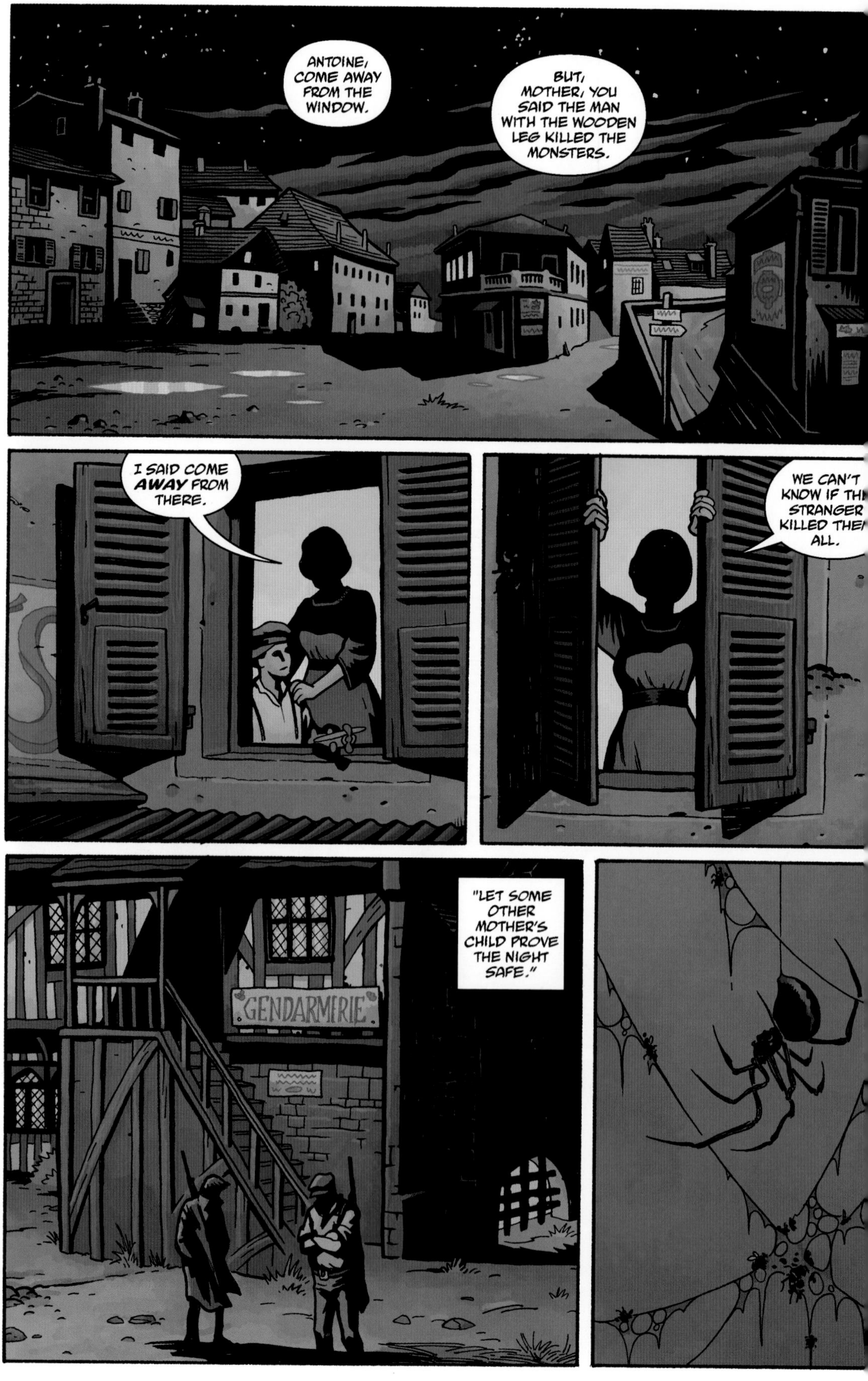
ANTOINE, COME AWAY FROM THE WINDOW.
BUT, MOTHER, YOU SAID THE MAN WITH THE WOODEN LEG KILLED THE MONSTERS.
I SAID COME AWAY FROM THERE.
WE CAN'T KNOW IF TH STRANGER KILLED THE ALL.
GENDARMERIE
"LET SOME OTHER MOTHER'S CHILD PROVE THE NIGHT SAFE."

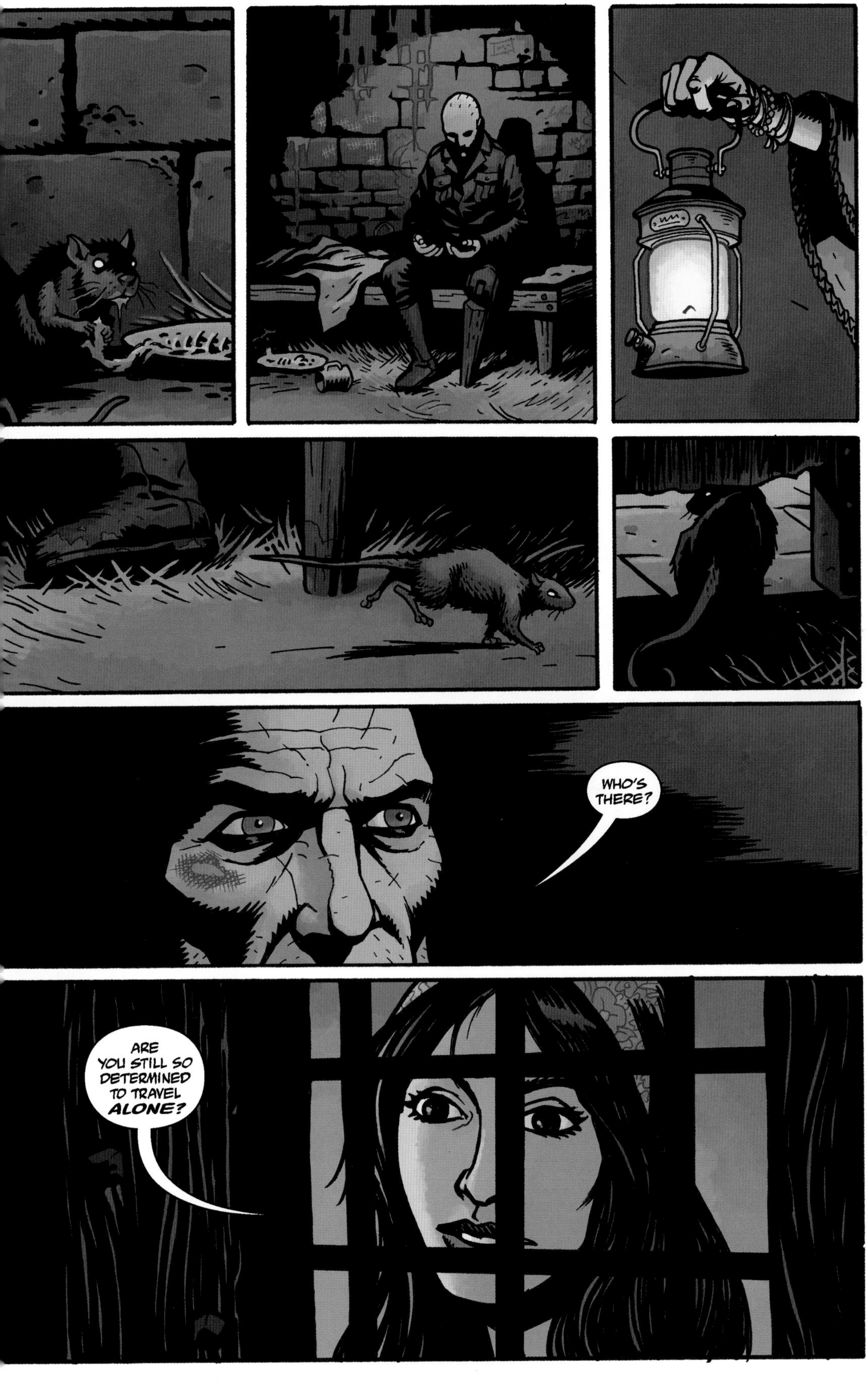
WHO'S THERE?
ARE YOU STILL SO DETERMINED TO TRAVEL ALONE?

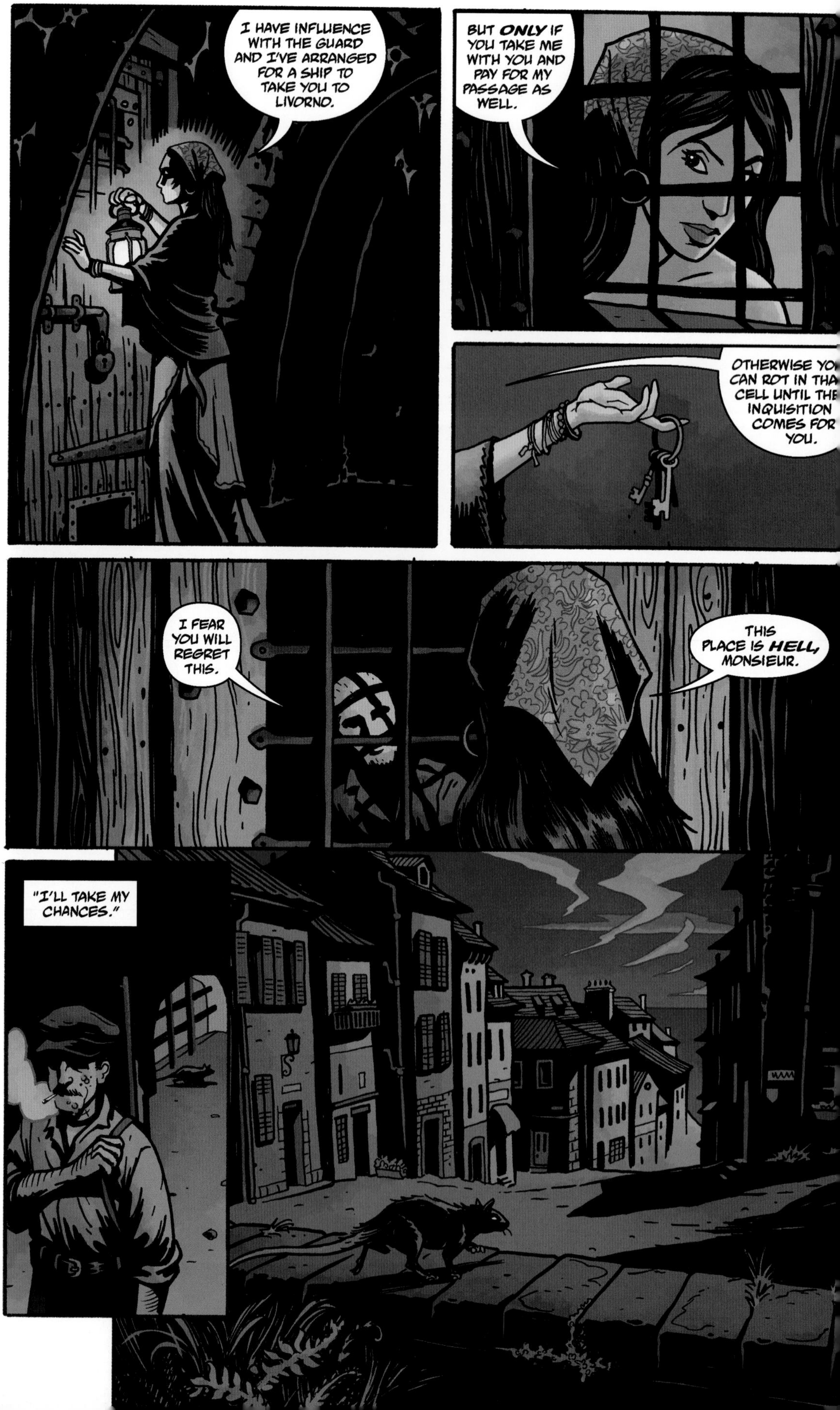
I HAVE INFLUENCE WITH THE GUARD AND I'VE ARRANGED FOR A SHIP TO TAKE YOU TO LIVORNO.
BUT ONLY IF YOU TAKE ME WITH YOU AND PAY FOR MY PASSAGE AS WELL.
OTHERWISE YOU CAN ROT IN THAT CELL UNTIL THE INQUISITION COMES FOR YOU.
I FEAR YOU WILL REGRET THIS.
THIS PLACE IS HELL, MONSIEUR.
"I'LL TAKE MY CHANCES."

CHAPTER TWO

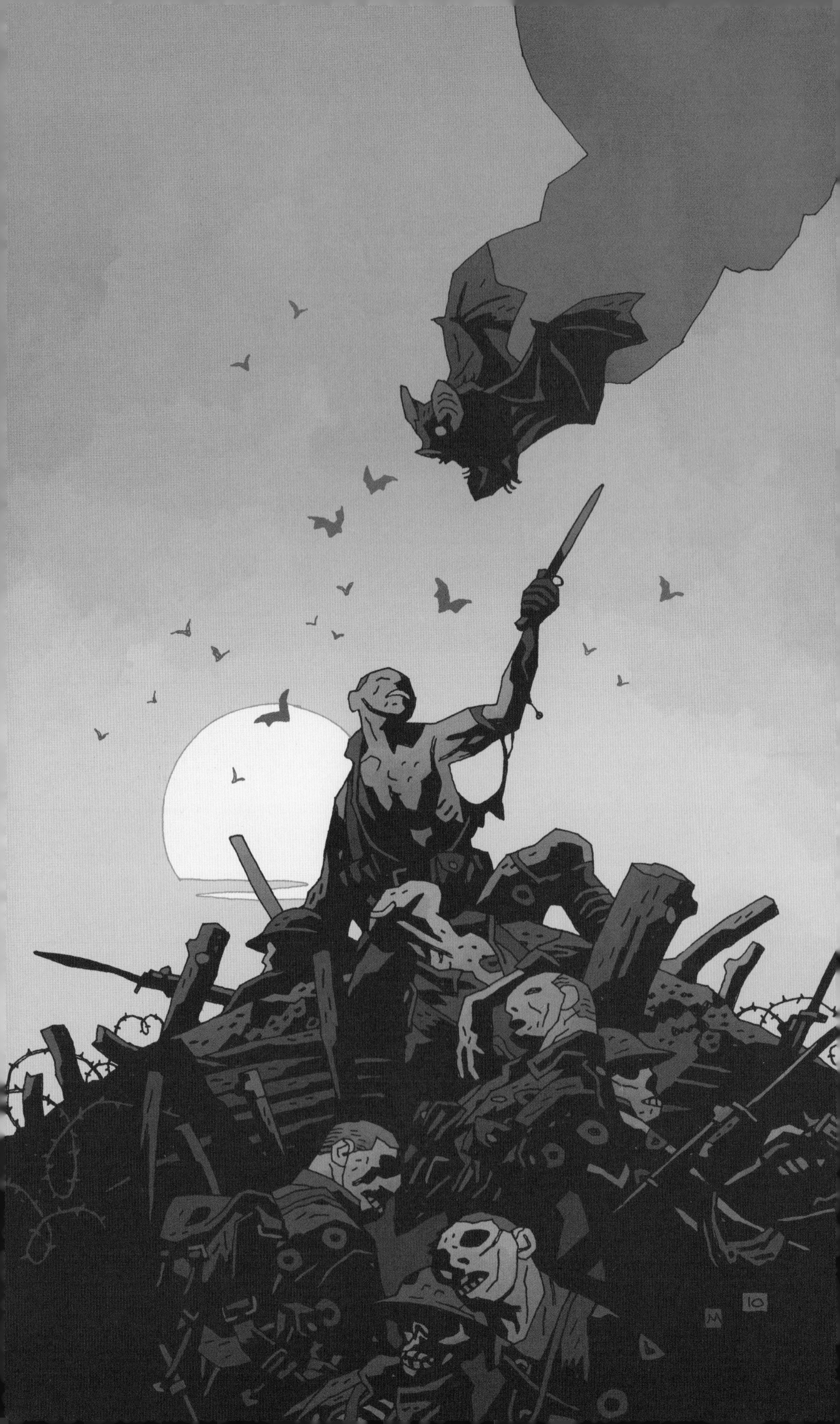

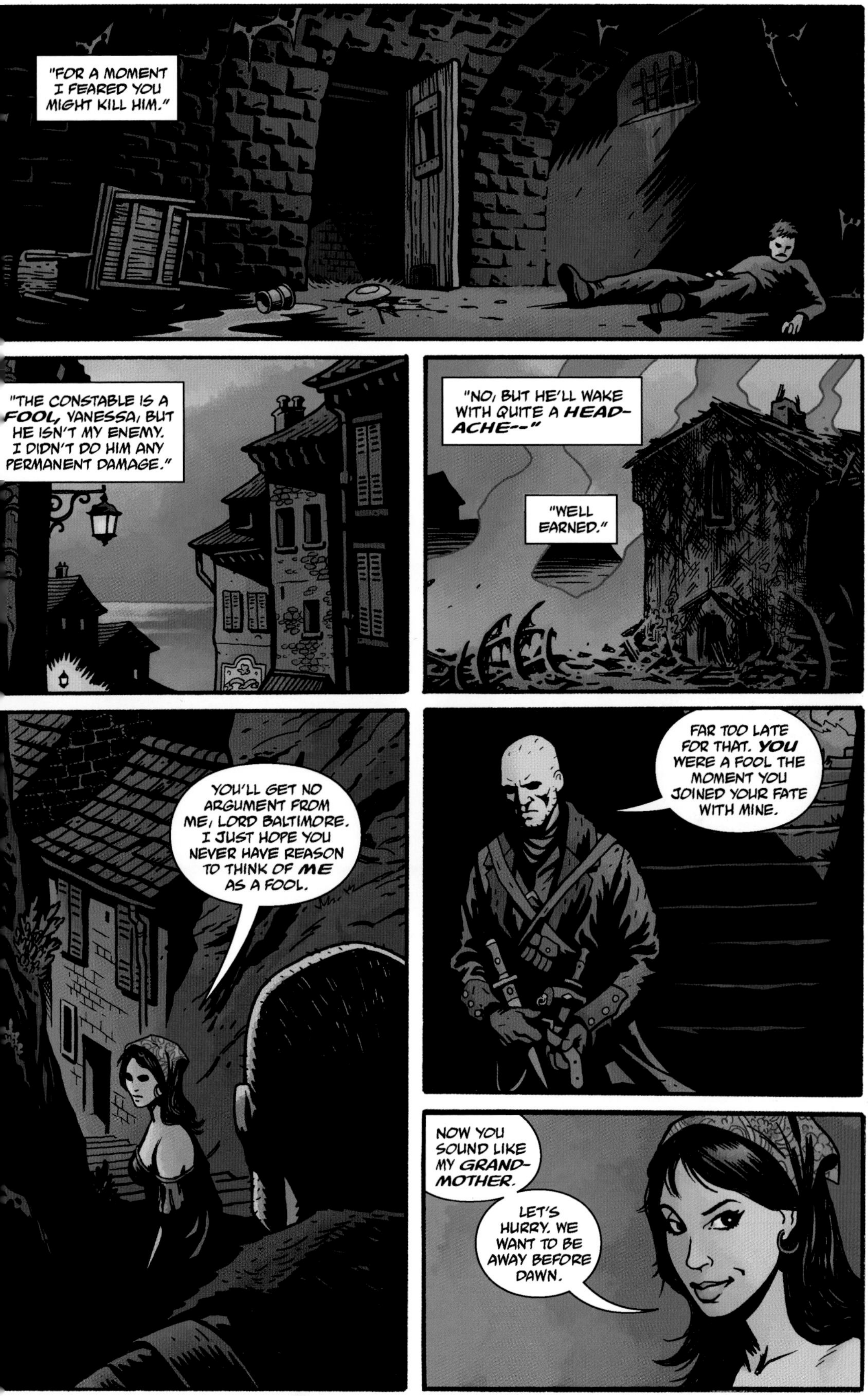

"FOR A MOMENT I FEARED YOU MIGHT KILL HIM."
"THE CONSTABLE IS A FOOL, VANESSA, BUT HE ISN'T MY ENEMY. I DIDN'T DO HIM ANY PERMANENT DAMAGE."
"NO, BUT HE'LL WAKE WITH QUITE A HEAD-ACHE--"
"WELL EARNED."
YOU'LL GET NO ARGUMENT FROM ME, LORD BALTIMORE. I JUST HOPE YOU NEVER HAVE REASON TO THINK OF ME AS A FOOL.
FAR TOO LATE FOR THAT. YOU WERE A FOOL THE MOMENT YOU JOINED YOUR FATE WITH MINE.
NOW YOU SOUND LIKE MY GRAND-MOTHER.
LET'S HURRY. WE WANT TO BE AWAY BEFORE DAWN.

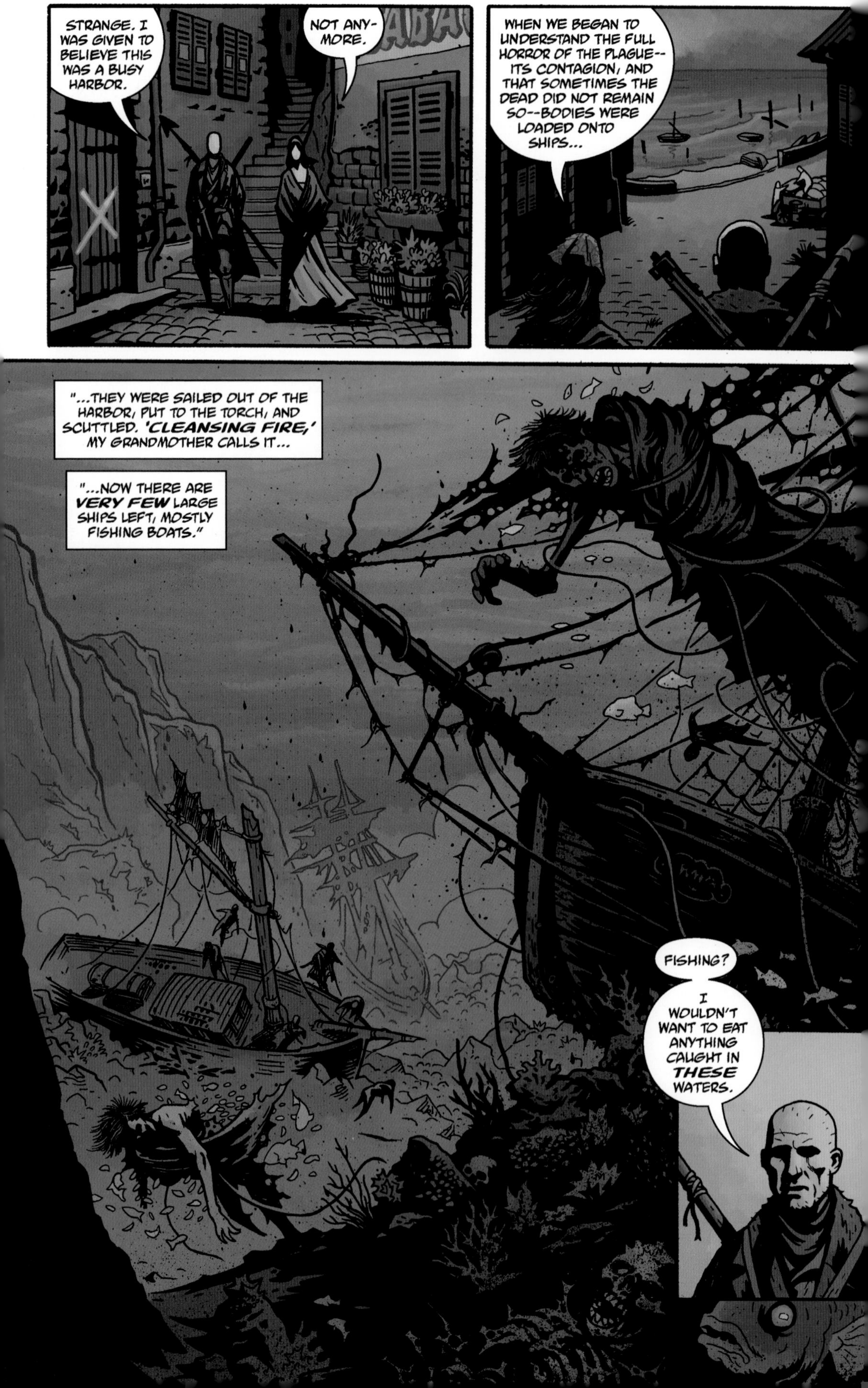
STRANGE. I WAS GIVEN TO BELIEVE THIS WAS A BUSY HARBOR.
NOT ANY-MORE.
WHEN WE BEGAN TO UNDERSTAND THE FULL HORROR OF THE PLAGUE-- ITS CONTAGION, AND THAT SOMETIMES THE DEAD DID NOT REMAIN SO--BODIES WERE LOADED ONTO SHIPS...
"...THEY WERE SAILED OUT OF THE HARBOR, PUT TO THE TORCH, AND SCUTTLED. *'CLEANSING FIRE,'* MY GRANDMOTHER CALLS IT...
"...NOW THERE ARE ***VERY FEW*** LARGE SHIPS LEFT, MOSTLY FISHING BOATS."
FISHING?
I WOULDN'T WANT TO EAT ANYTHING CAUGHT IN ***THESE*** WATERS.

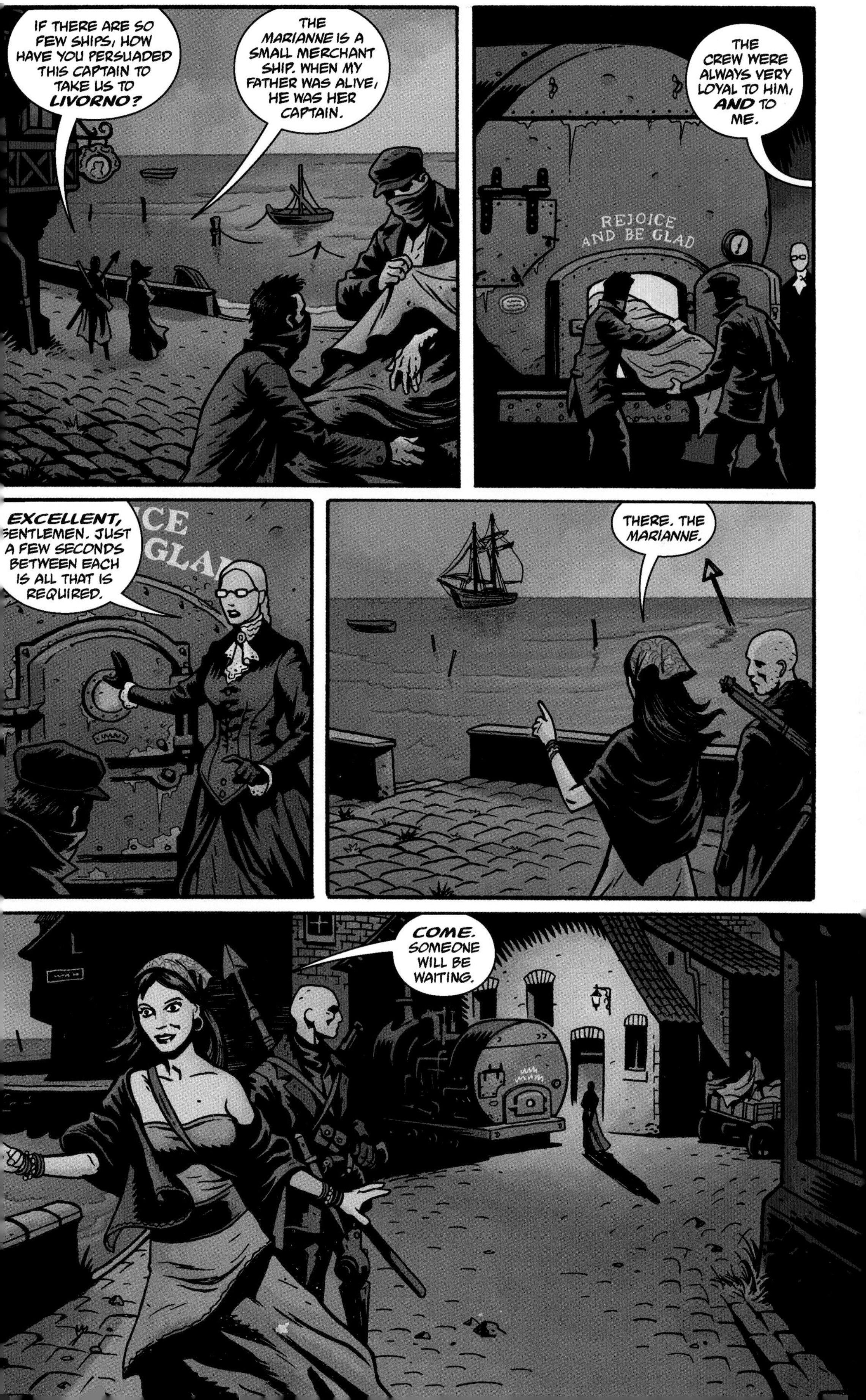

IF THERE ARE SO FEW SHIPS, HOW HAVE YOU PERSUADED THIS CAPTAIN TO TAKE US TO LIVORNO?
THE MARIANNE IS A SMALL MERCHANT SHIP. WHEN MY FATHER WAS ALIVE, HE WAS HER CAPTAIN.
THE CREW WERE ALWAYS VERY LOYAL TO HIM, AND TO ME.
REJOICE AND BE GLAD
EXCELLENT, GENTLEMEN. JUST A FEW SECONDS BETWEEN EACH IS ALL THAT IS REQUIRED.
THERE. THE MARIANNE.
COME. SOMEONE WILL BE WAITING.

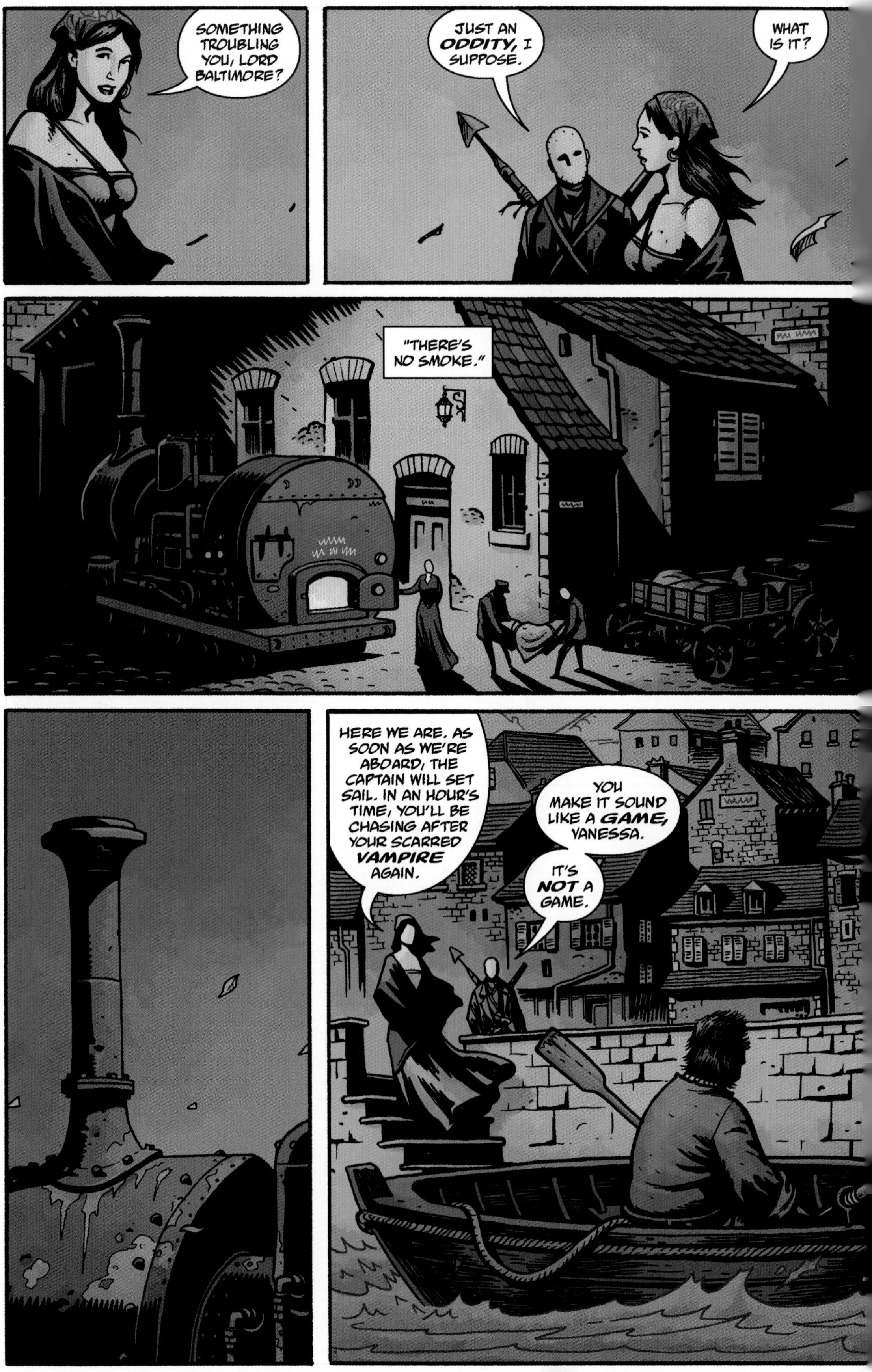
SOMETHING TROUBLING YOU, LORD BALTIMORE?
JUST AN *ODDITY,* I SUPPOSE.
WHAT IS IT?
"THERE'S NO SMOKE."
HERE WE ARE. AS SOON AS WE'RE ABOARD, THE CAPTAIN WILL SET SAIL. IN AN HOUR'S TIME, YOU'LL BE CHASING AFTER YOUR SCARRED *VAMPIRE* AGAIN.
YOU MAKE IT SOUND LIKE A *GAME,* VANESSA.
IT'S *NOT* A GAME.

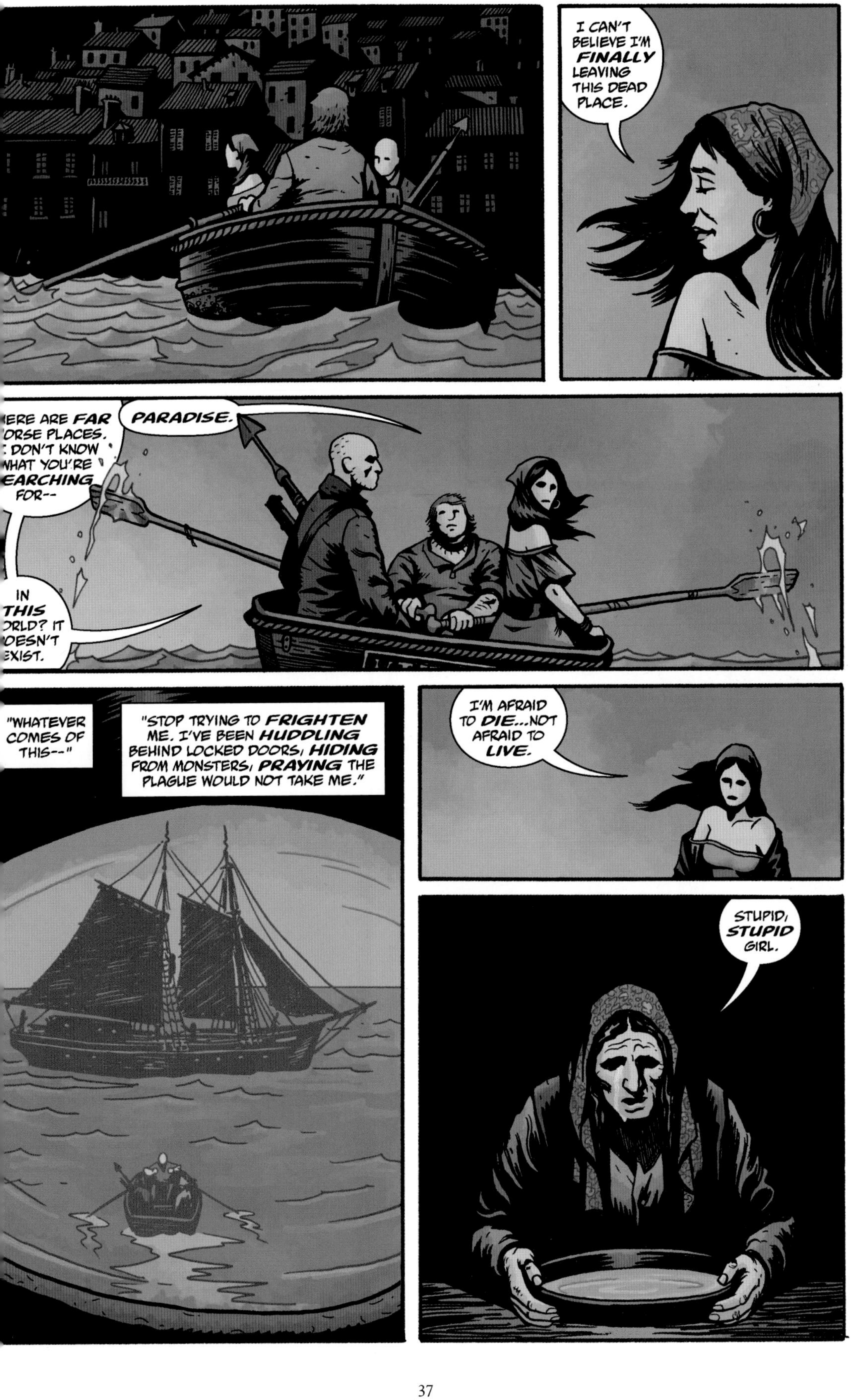
I CAN'T BELIEVE I'M FINALLY LEAVING THIS DEAD PLACE.
PARADISE.
ERE ARE FAR ORSE PLACES. DON'T KNOW HAT YOU'RE EARCHING FOR--
IN THIS ORLD? IT OESN'T XIST.
"WHATEVER COMES OF THIS--"
"STOP TRYING TO FRIGHTEN ME. I'VE BEEN HUDDLING BEHIND LOCKED DOORS, HIDING FROM MONSTERS, PRAYING THE PLAGUE WOULD NOT TAKE ME."
I'M AFRAID TO DIE...NOT AFRAID TO LIVE.
STUPID, STUPID GIRL.

...NO NEED, SIR. WE DO THIS FOR VANESSA, NOT FOR *PAYMENT.*

THERE'S *EVERY* NEED, CAPTAIN. YOU'RE A MERCHANT SHIP MAKING A TRIP WITH *PASSENGERS* INSTEAD OF CARGO.

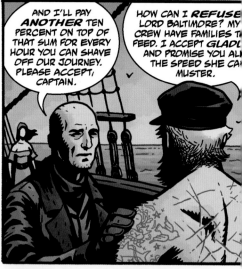

AND I'LL PAY *ANOTHER* TEN PERCENT ON TOP OF THAT SUM FOR EVERY HOUR YOU CAN SHAVE OFF OUR JOURNEY. PLEASE ACCEPT, CAPTAIN.

HOW CAN I *REFUSE* LORD BALTIMORE? MY CREW HAVE FAMILIES TO FEED. I ACCEPT *GLADL[Y]* AND PROMISE YOU AL[L] THE SPEED SHE CA[N] MUSTER.

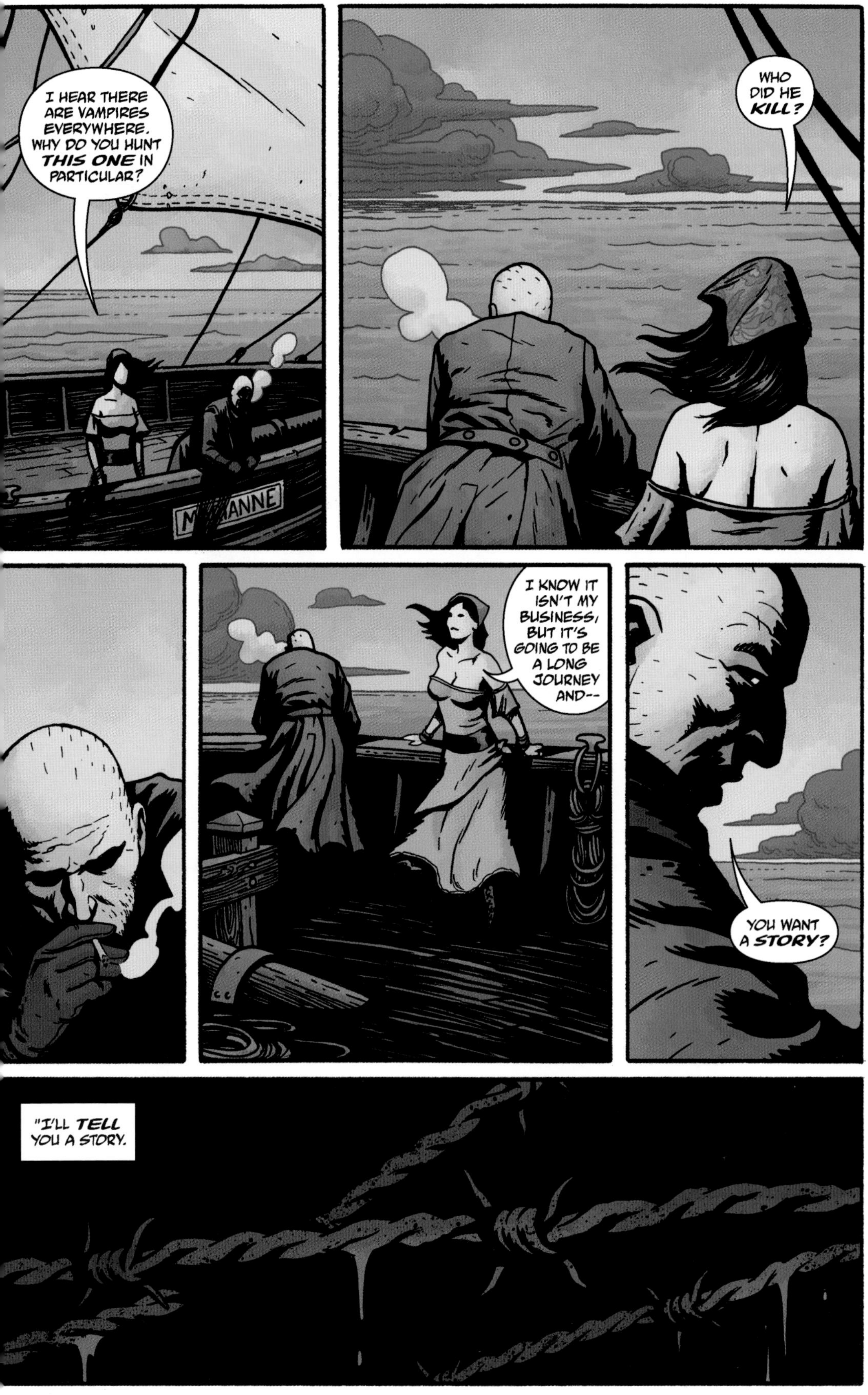
I HEAR THERE ARE VAMPIRES EVERYWHERE. WHY DO YOU HUNT THIS ONE IN PARTICULAR?
M—ANNE
WHO DID HE KILL?
I KNOW IT ISN'T MY BUSINESS, BUT IT'S GOING TO BE A LONG JOURNEY AND--
YOU WANT A STORY?
"I'LL TELL YOU A STORY.

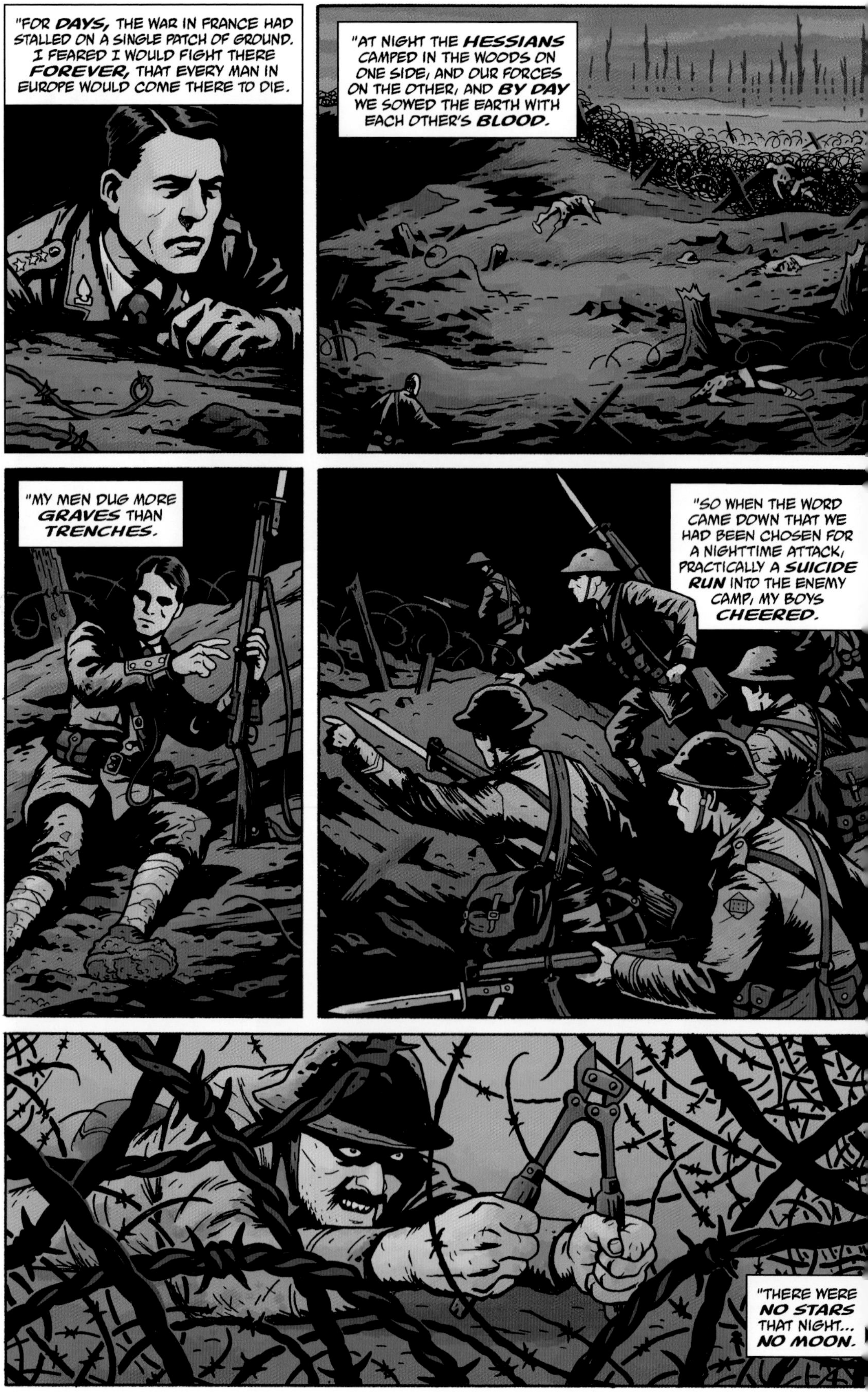
"FOR DAYS, THE WAR IN FRANCE HAD STALLED ON A SINGLE PATCH OF GROUND. I FEARED I WOULD FIGHT THERE FOREVER, THAT EVERY MAN IN EUROPE WOULD COME THERE TO DIE.
"AT NIGHT THE HESSIANS CAMPED IN THE WOODS ON ONE SIDE, AND OUR FORCES ON THE OTHER, AND BY DAY WE SOWED THE EARTH WITH EACH OTHER'S BLOOD.
"MY MEN DUG MORE GRAVES THAN TRENCHES.
"SO WHEN THE WORD CAME DOWN THAT WE HAD BEEN CHOSEN FOR A NIGHTTIME ATTACK, PRACTICALLY A SUICIDE RUN INTO THE ENEMY CAMP, MY BOYS CHEERED.
"THERE WERE NO STARS THAT NIGHT... NO MOON.

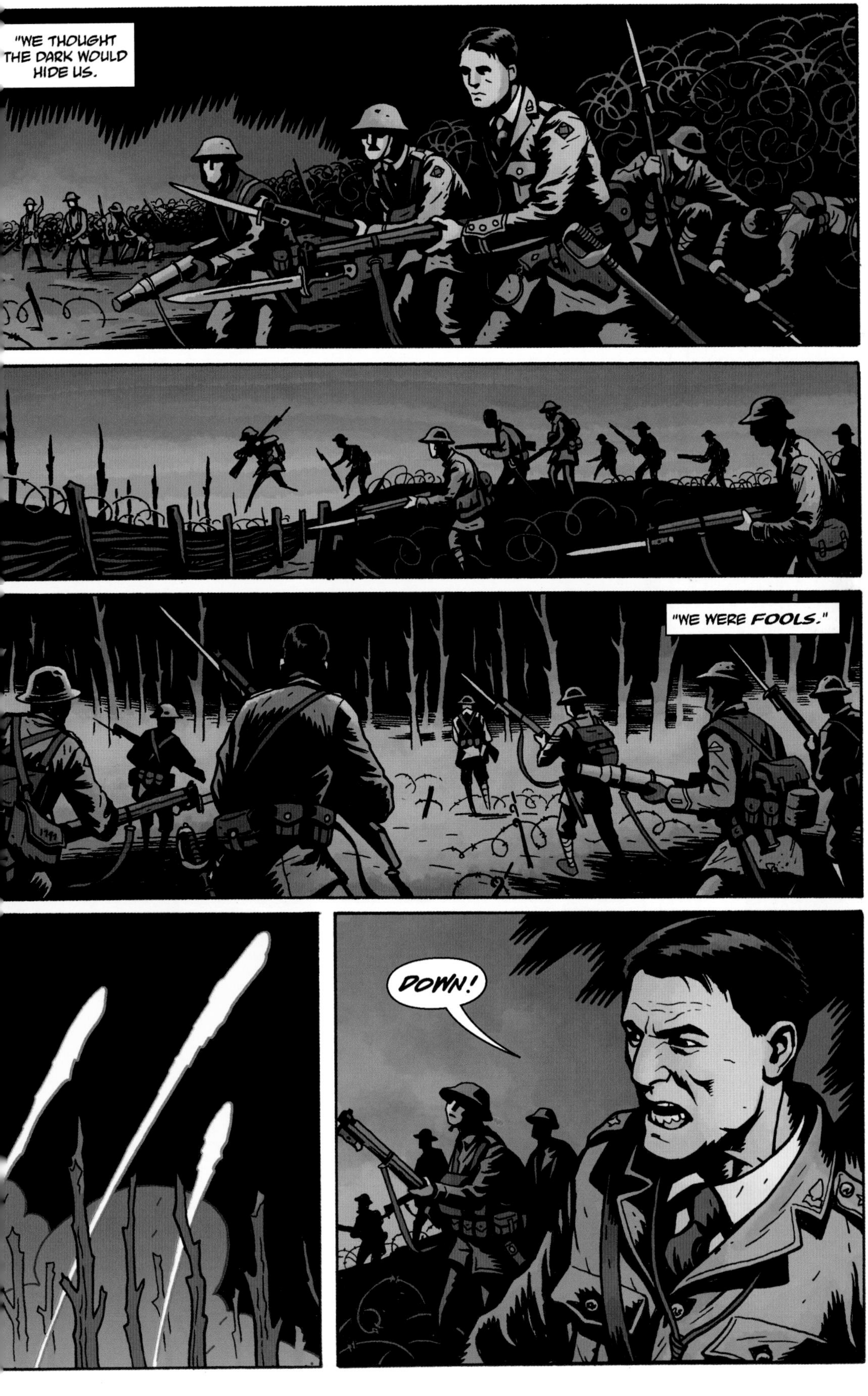
"WE THOUGHT THE DARK WOULD HIDE US.
"WE WERE FOOLS."
DOWN!

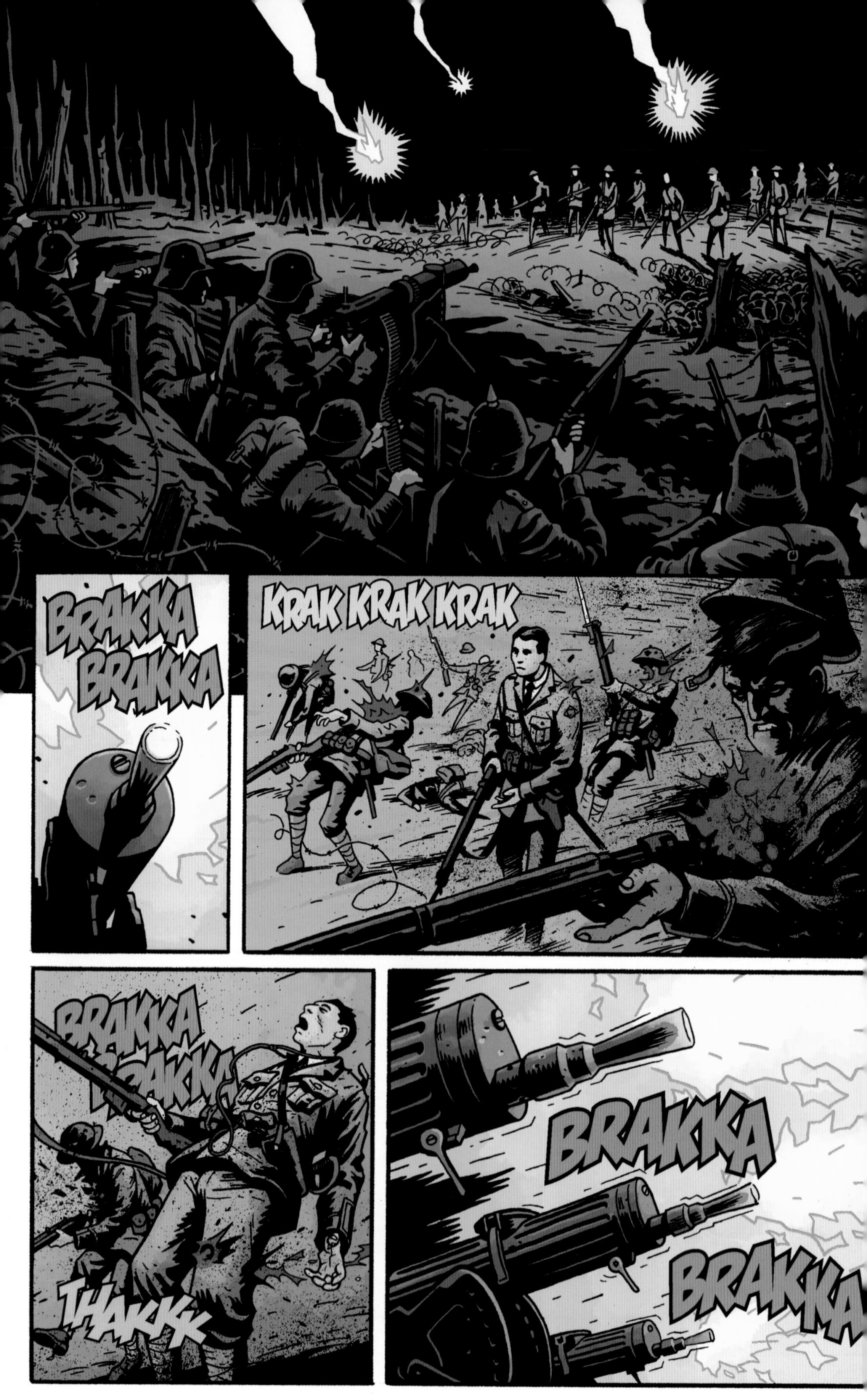
BRAKKA BRAKKA
KRAK KRAK KRAK
BRAKKA BRAKKA
THAKKK
BRAKKA
BRAKKA

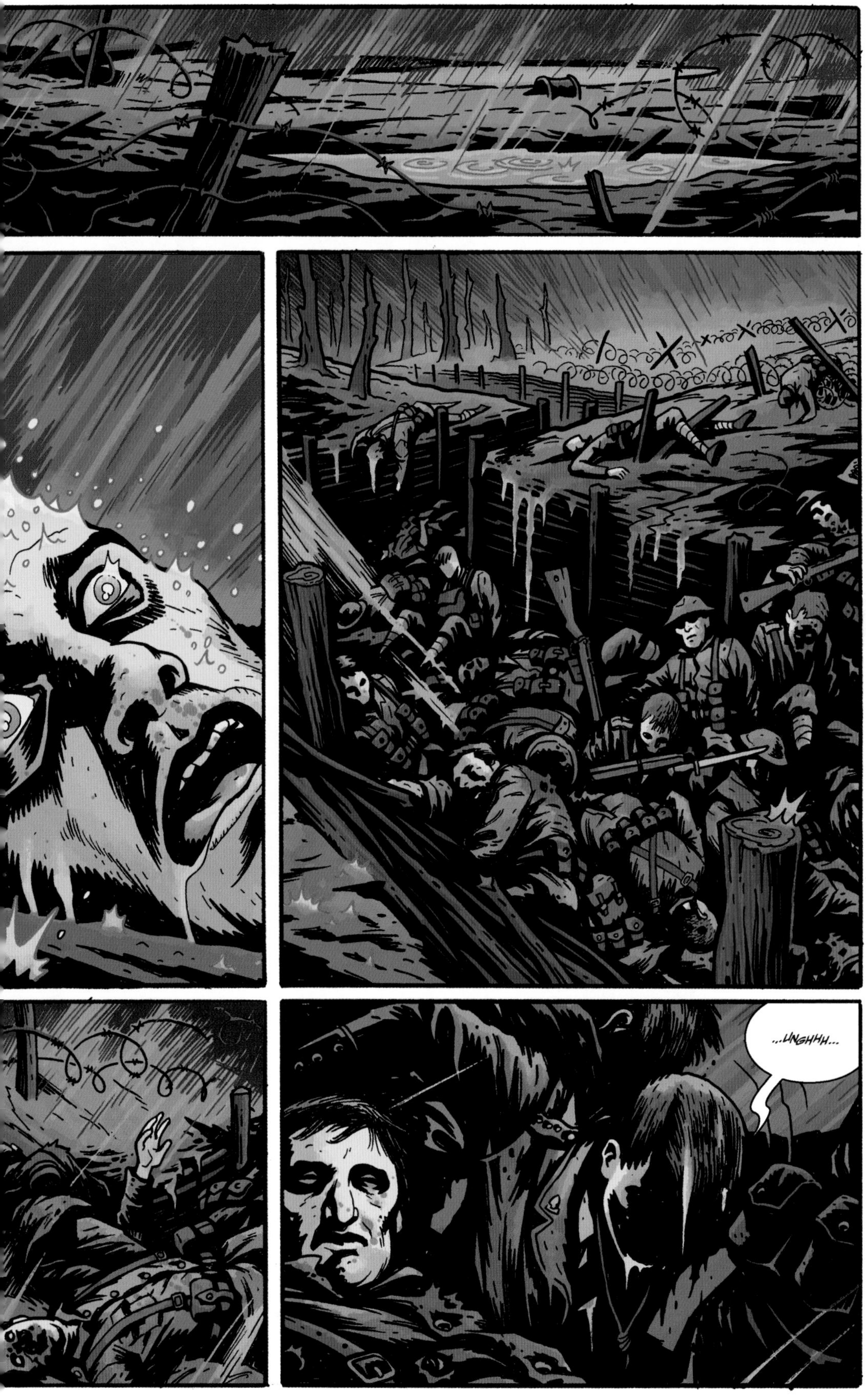
...UNGHHH...

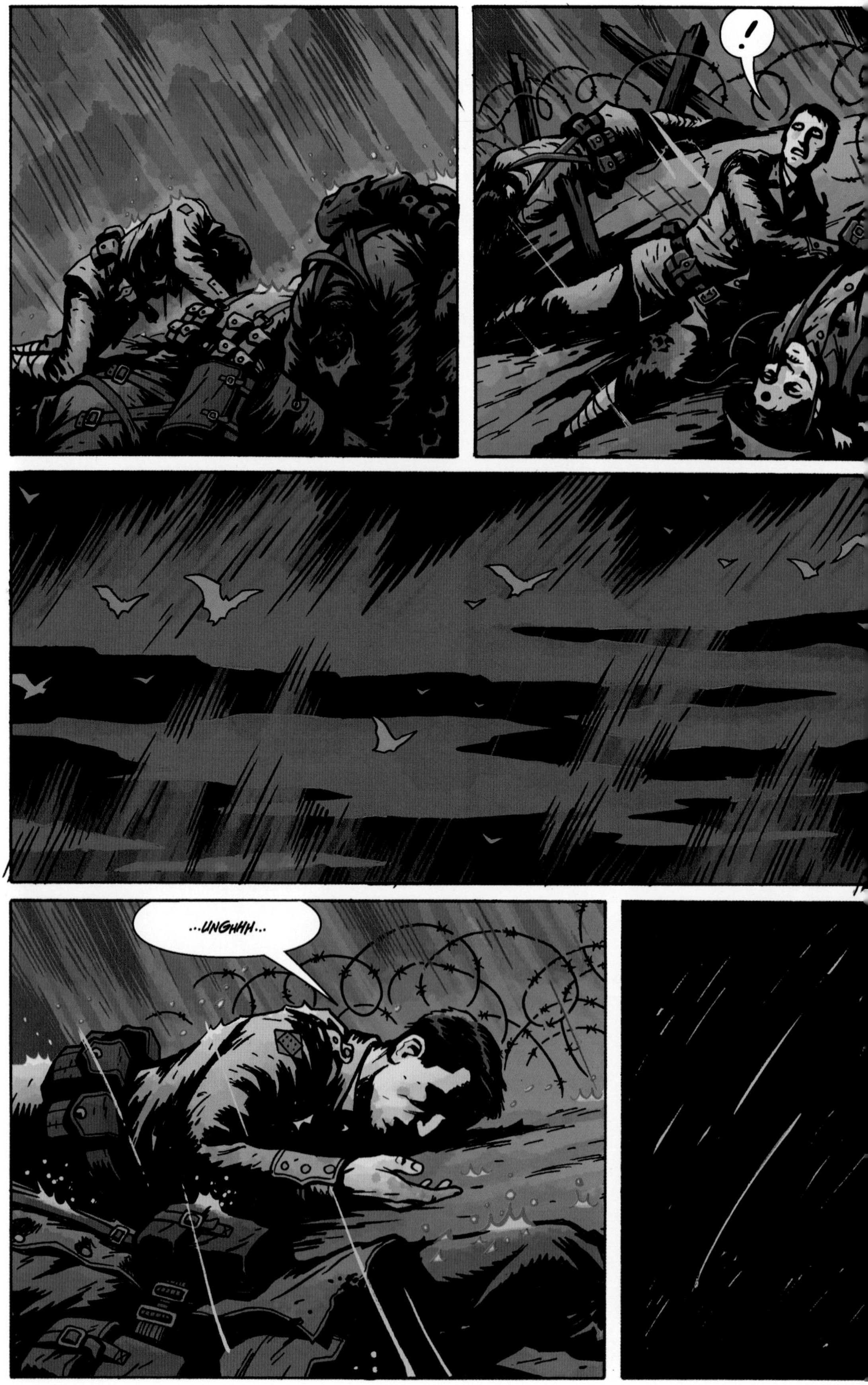
!
...UNGHHH...

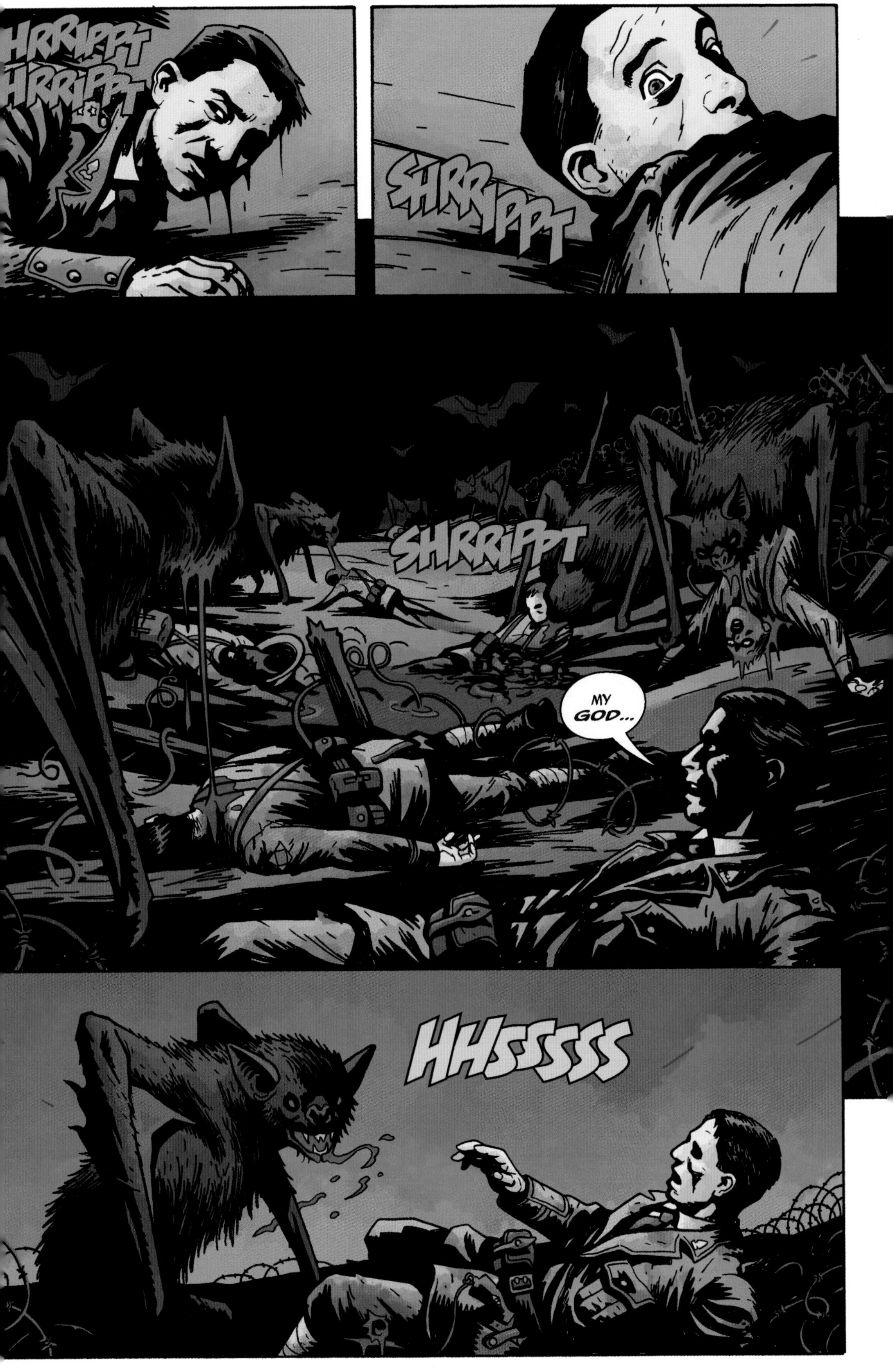
HRRIPPT
HRRIPPT
SHRRIPPT
SHRRIPPT
MY GOD...
HHSSSSS

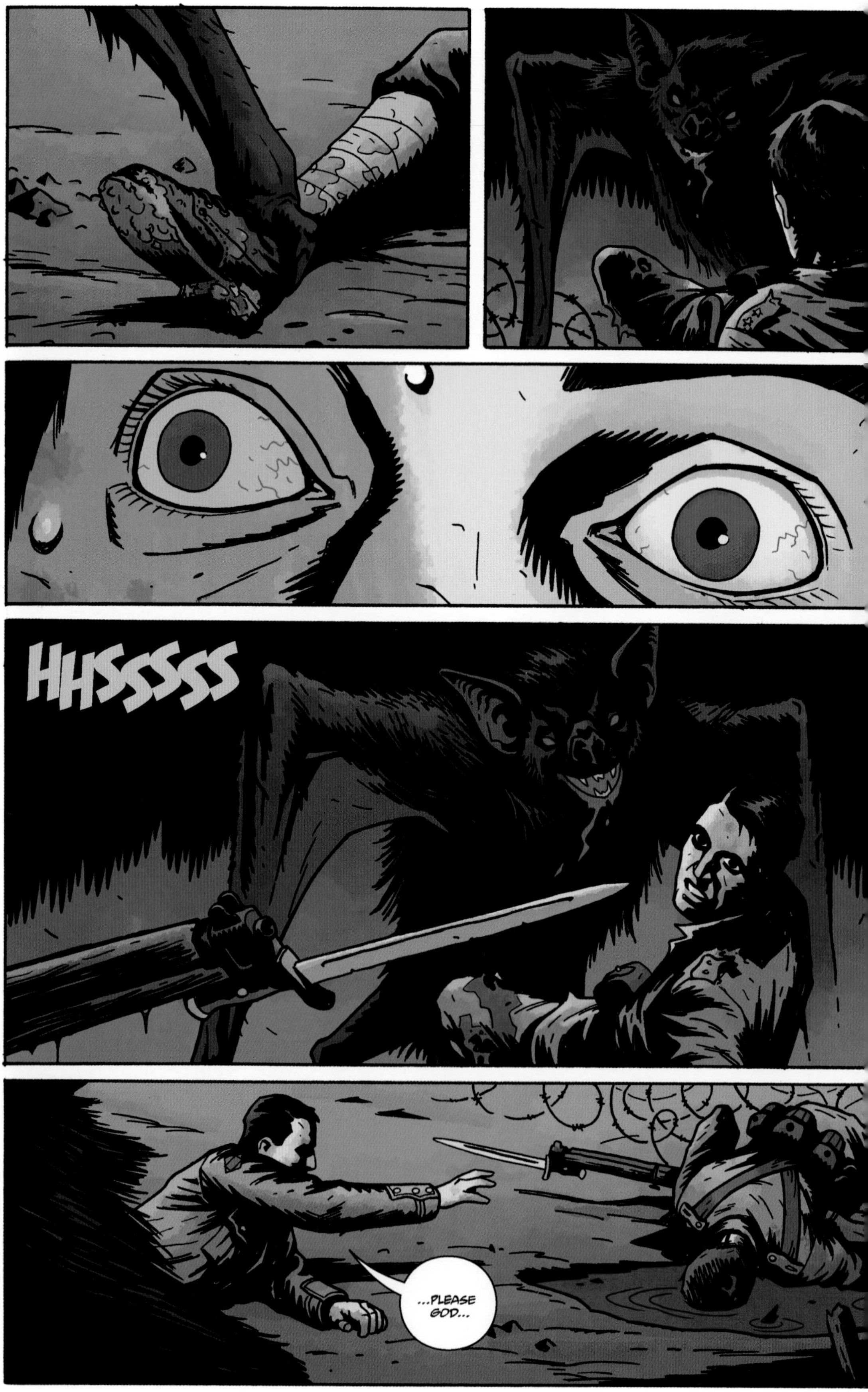
HHSSSSS
...PLEASE GOD...

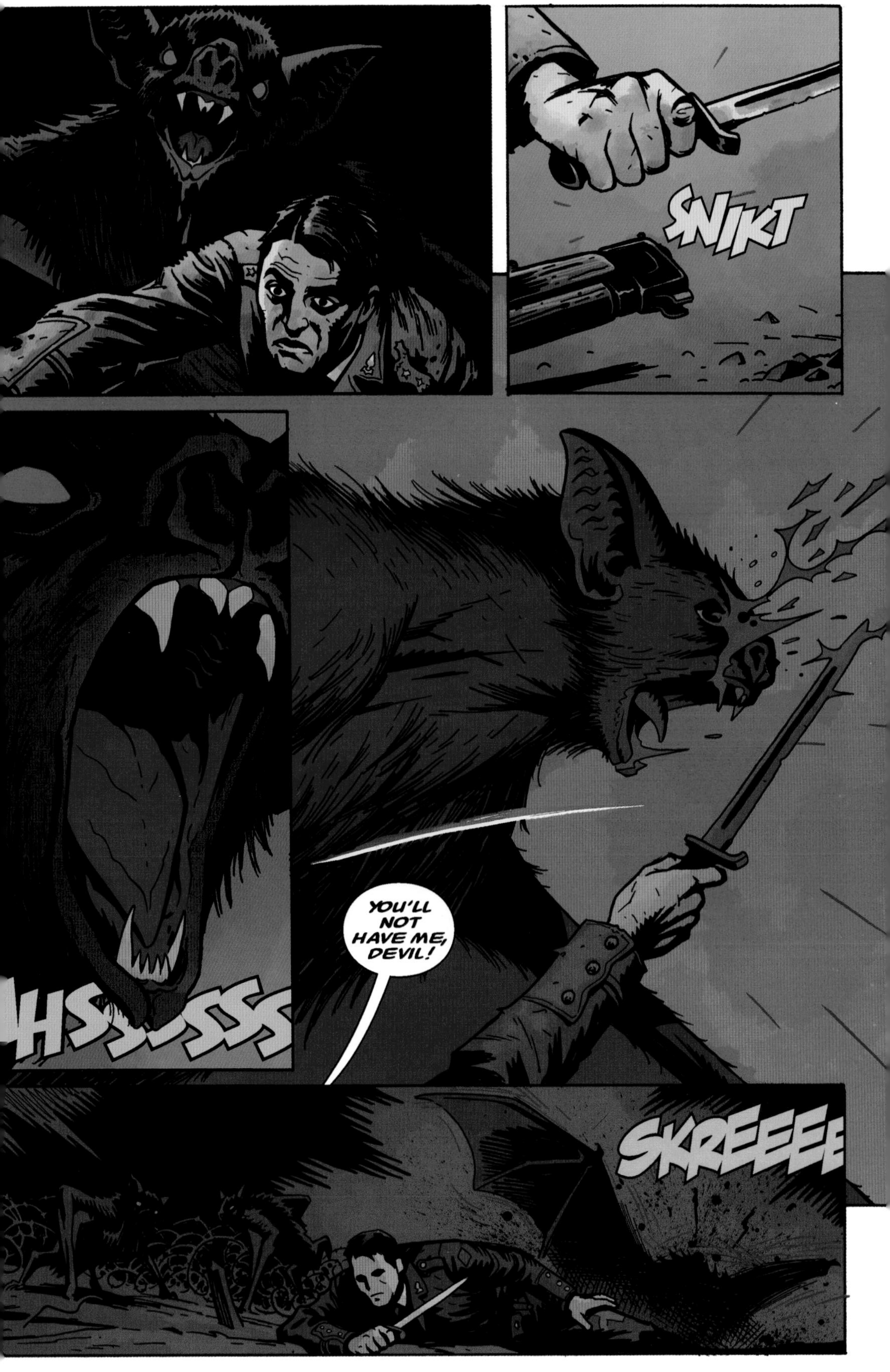
SNIKT
HSSSSSS
YOU'LL NOT HAVE ME, DEVIL!
SKREEEE

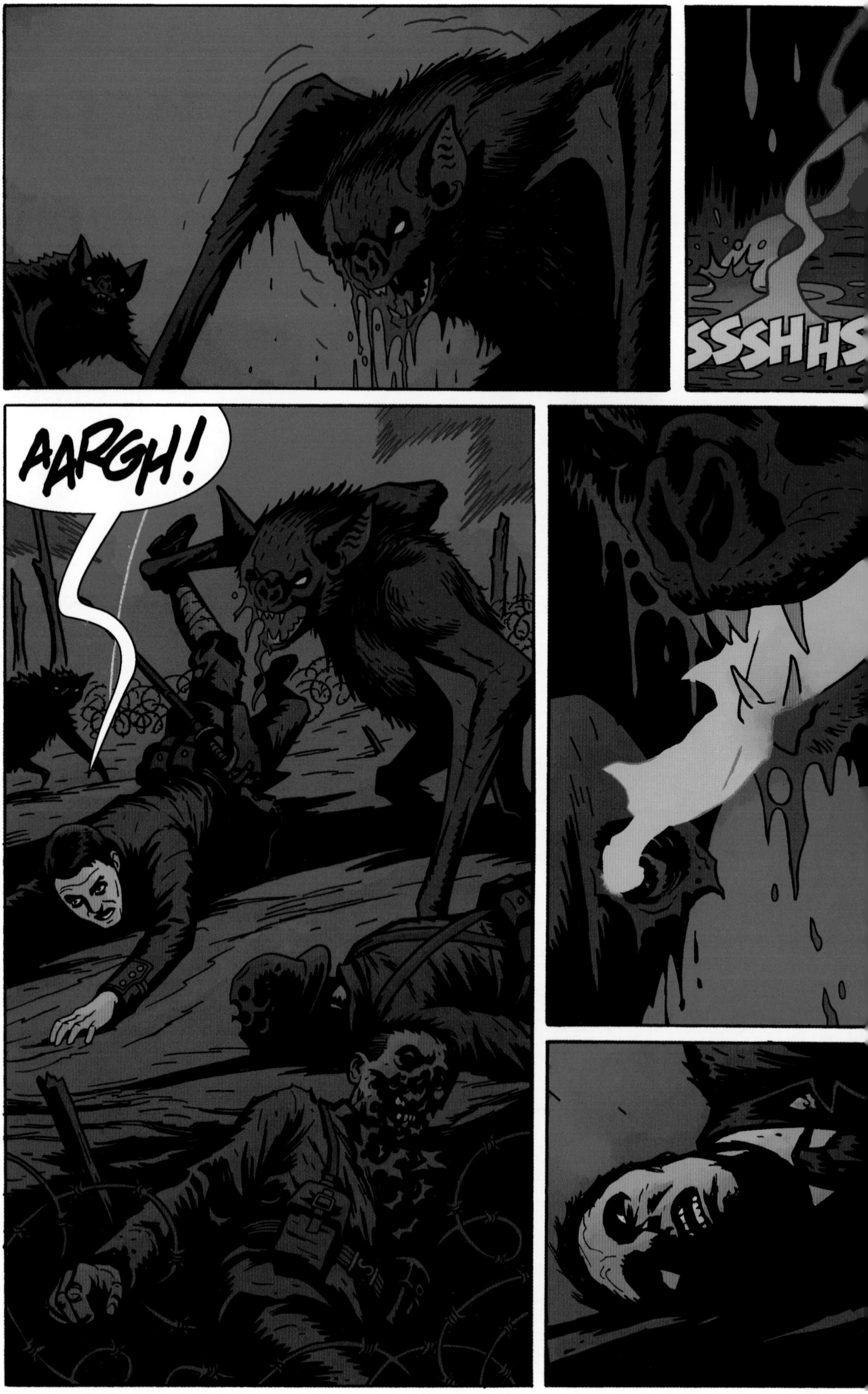
SSSHHS
AARGH!

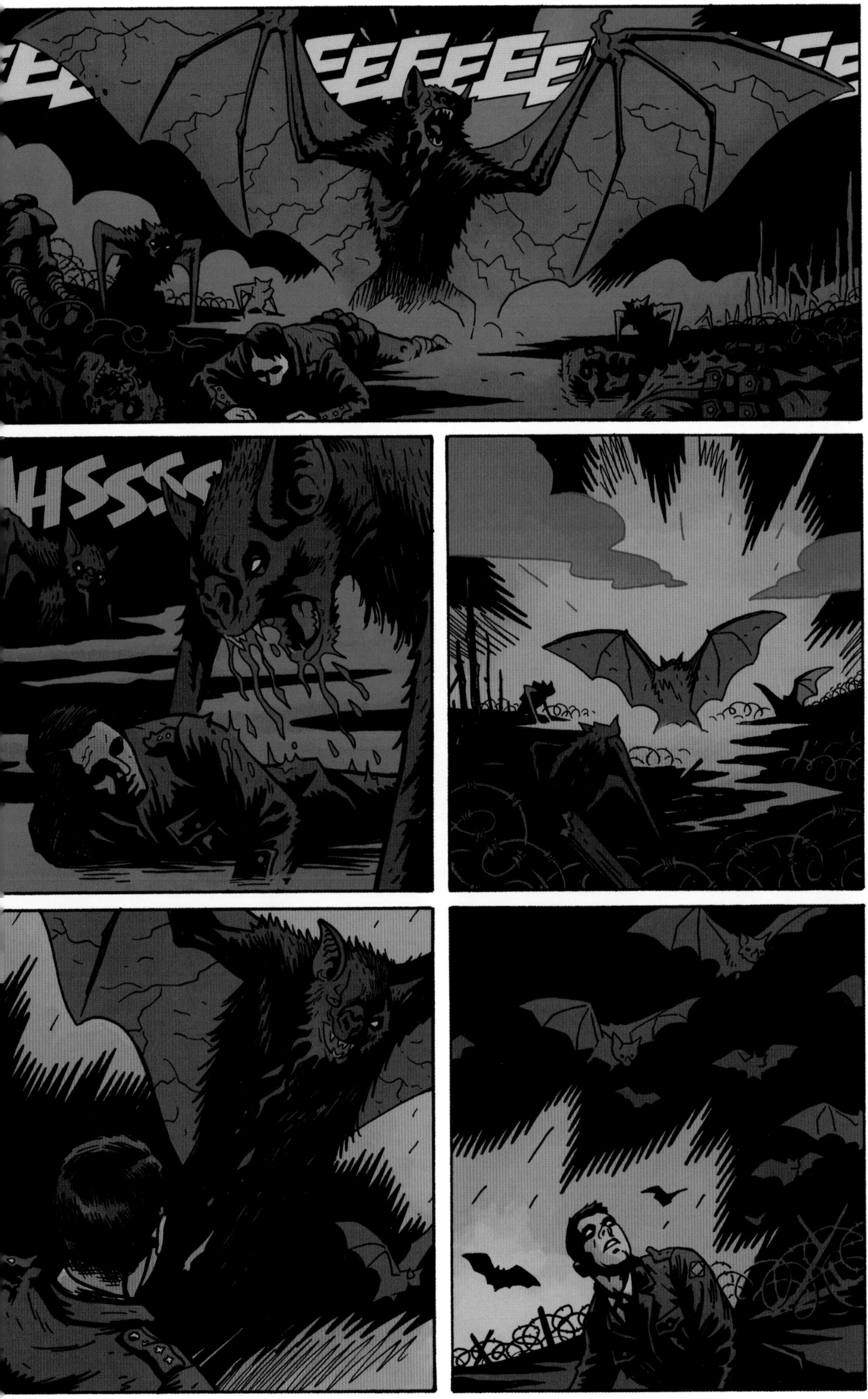
EEEEEE
HSSS

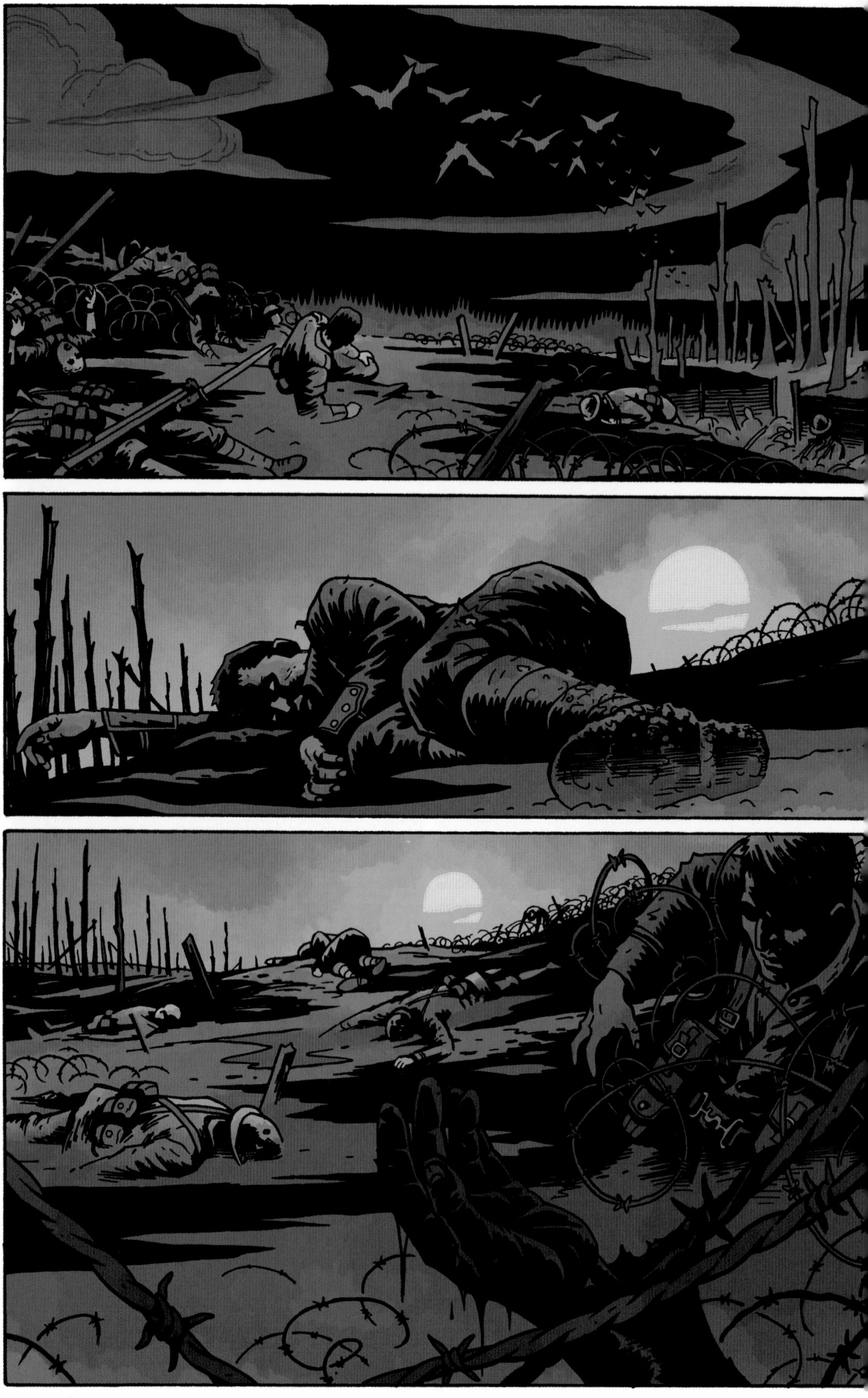

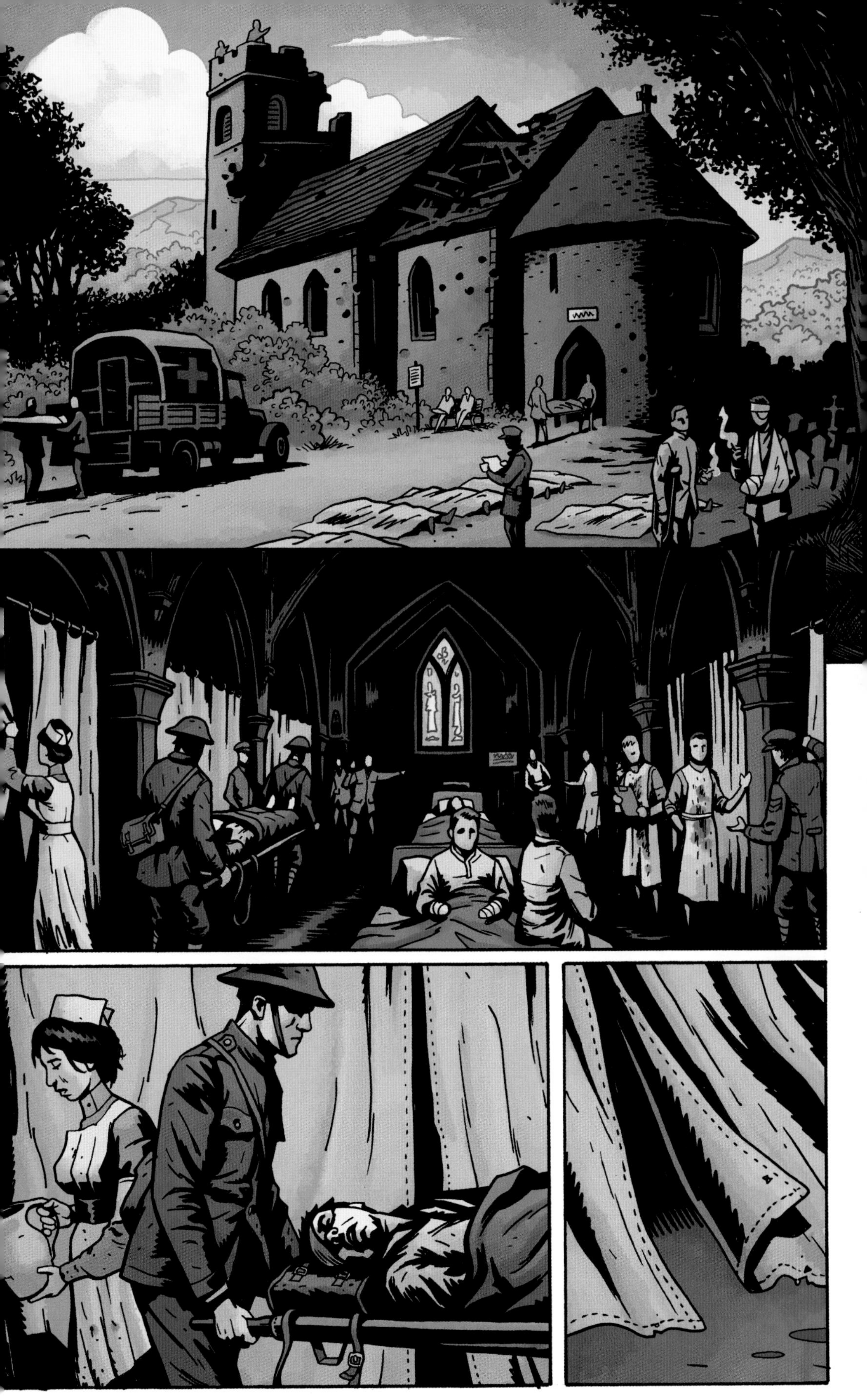

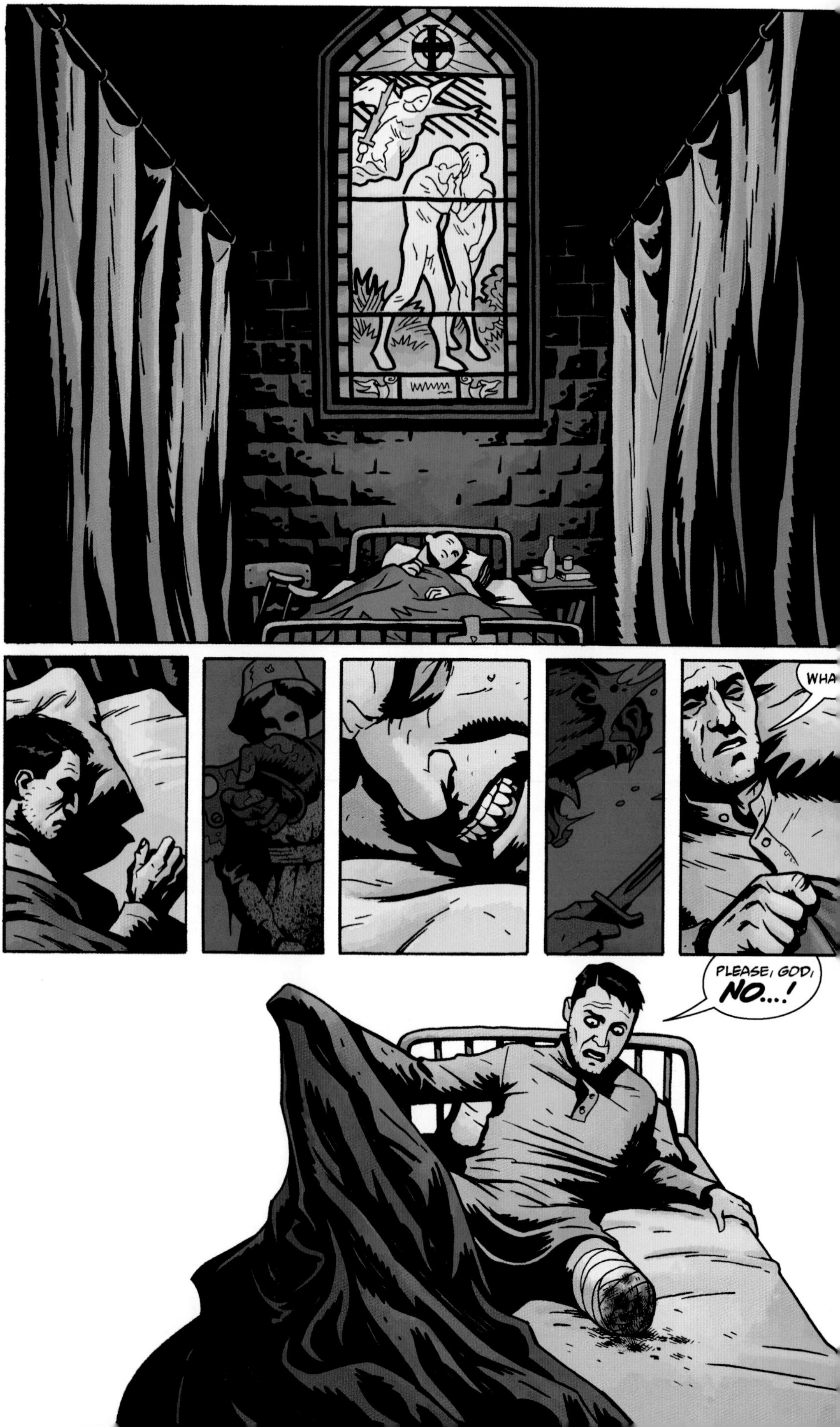
WHA
PLEASE, GOD, NO...!

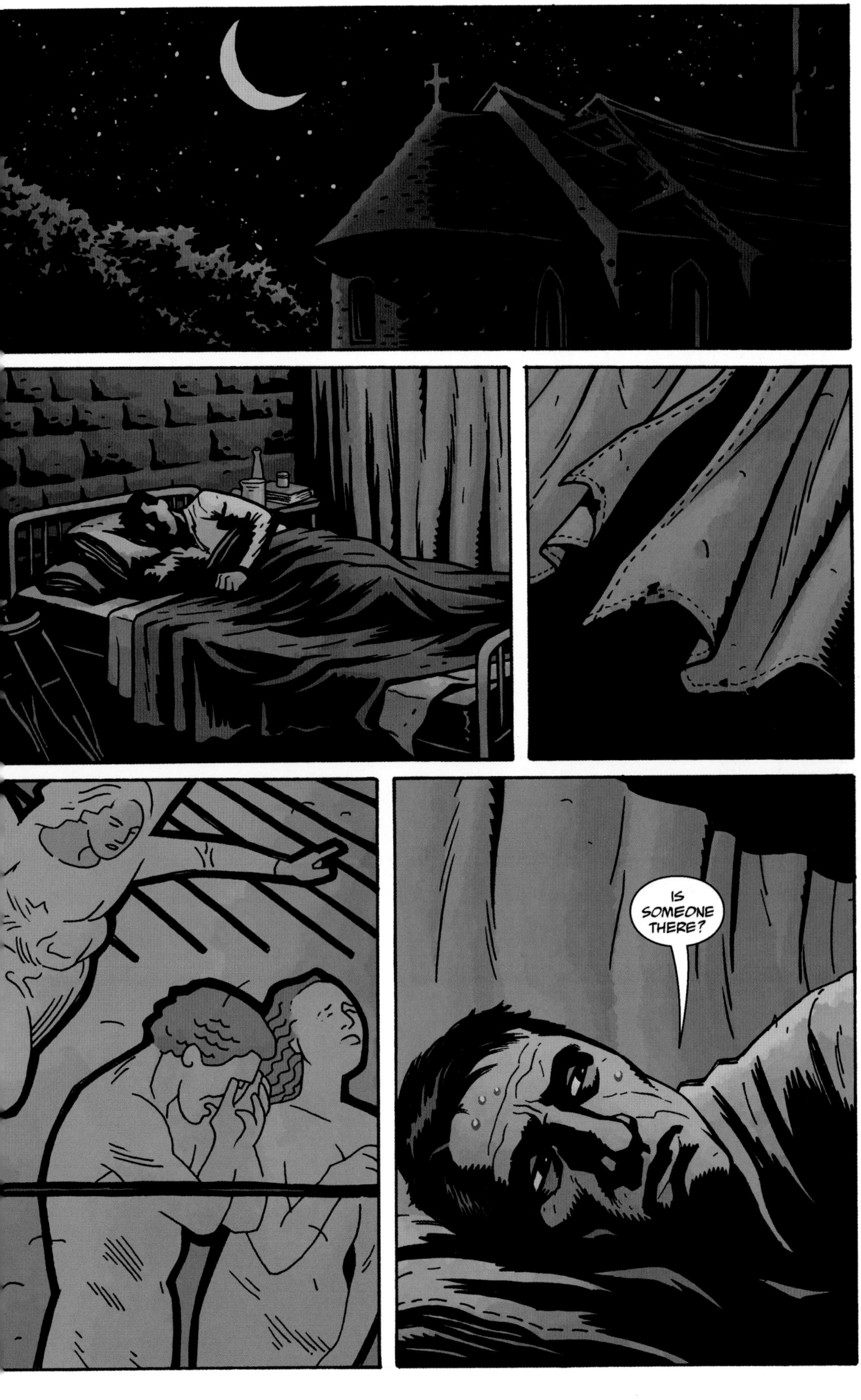
IS SOMEONE THERE?

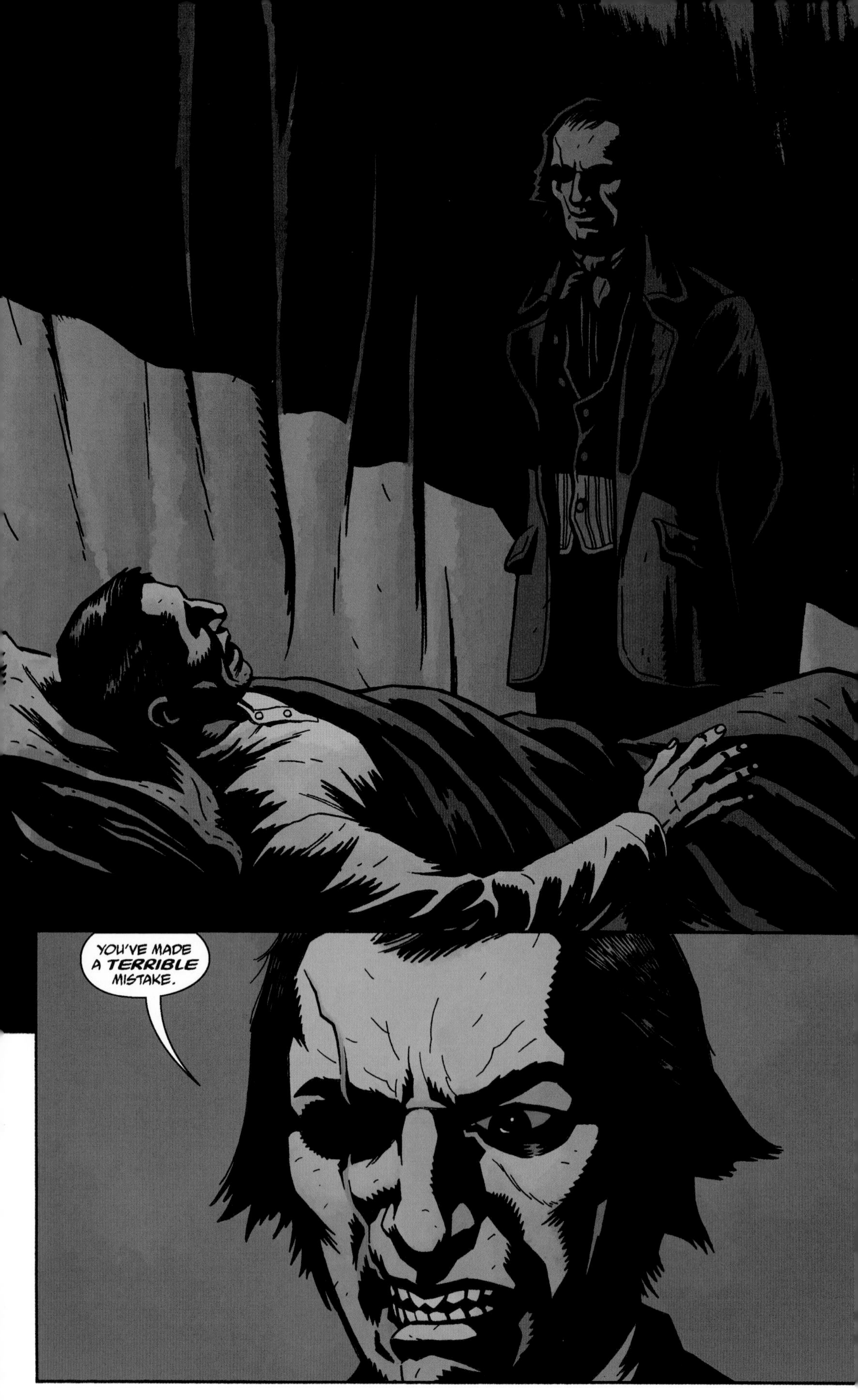
YOU'VE MADE A **TERRIBLE** MISTAKE.

CHAPTER THREE

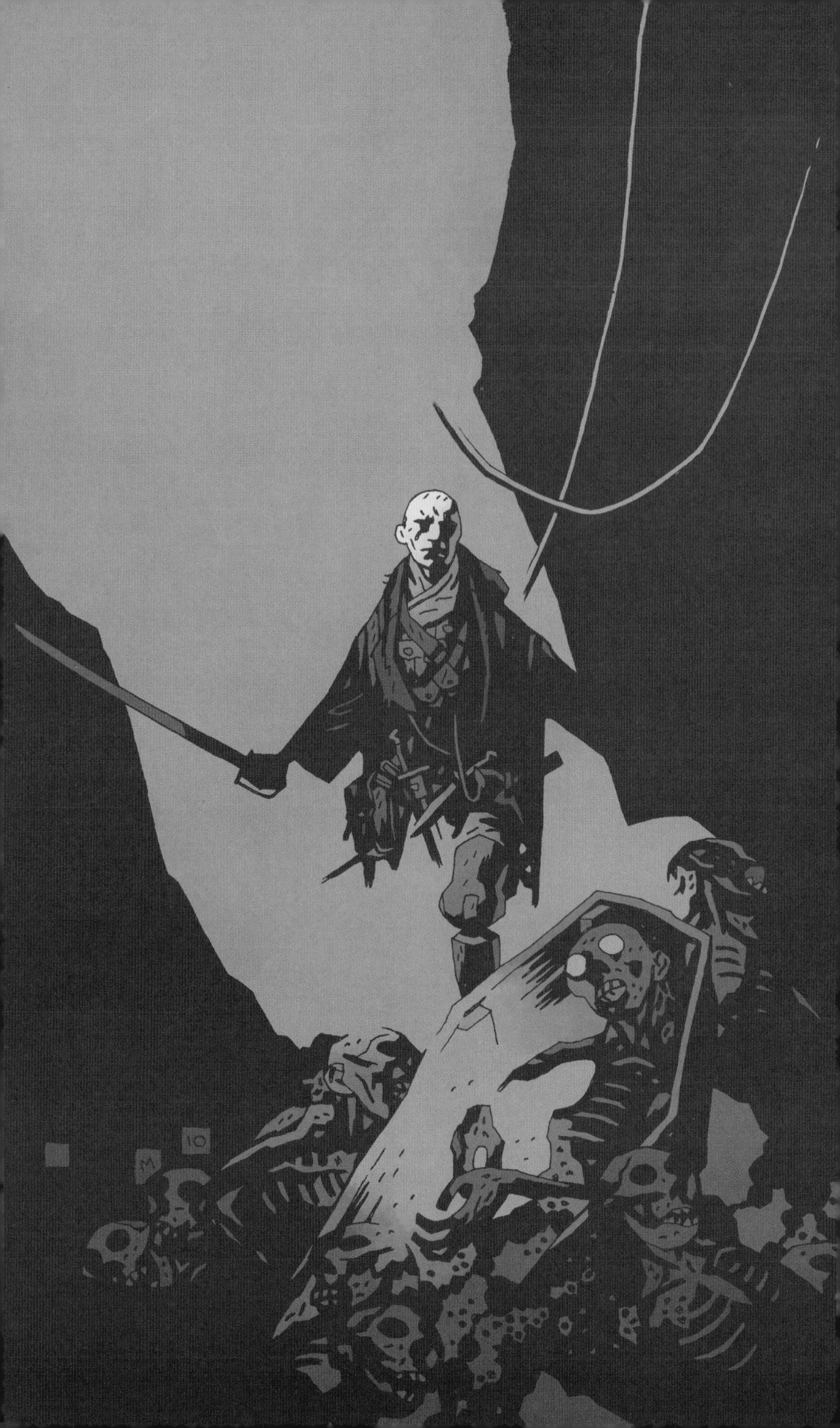

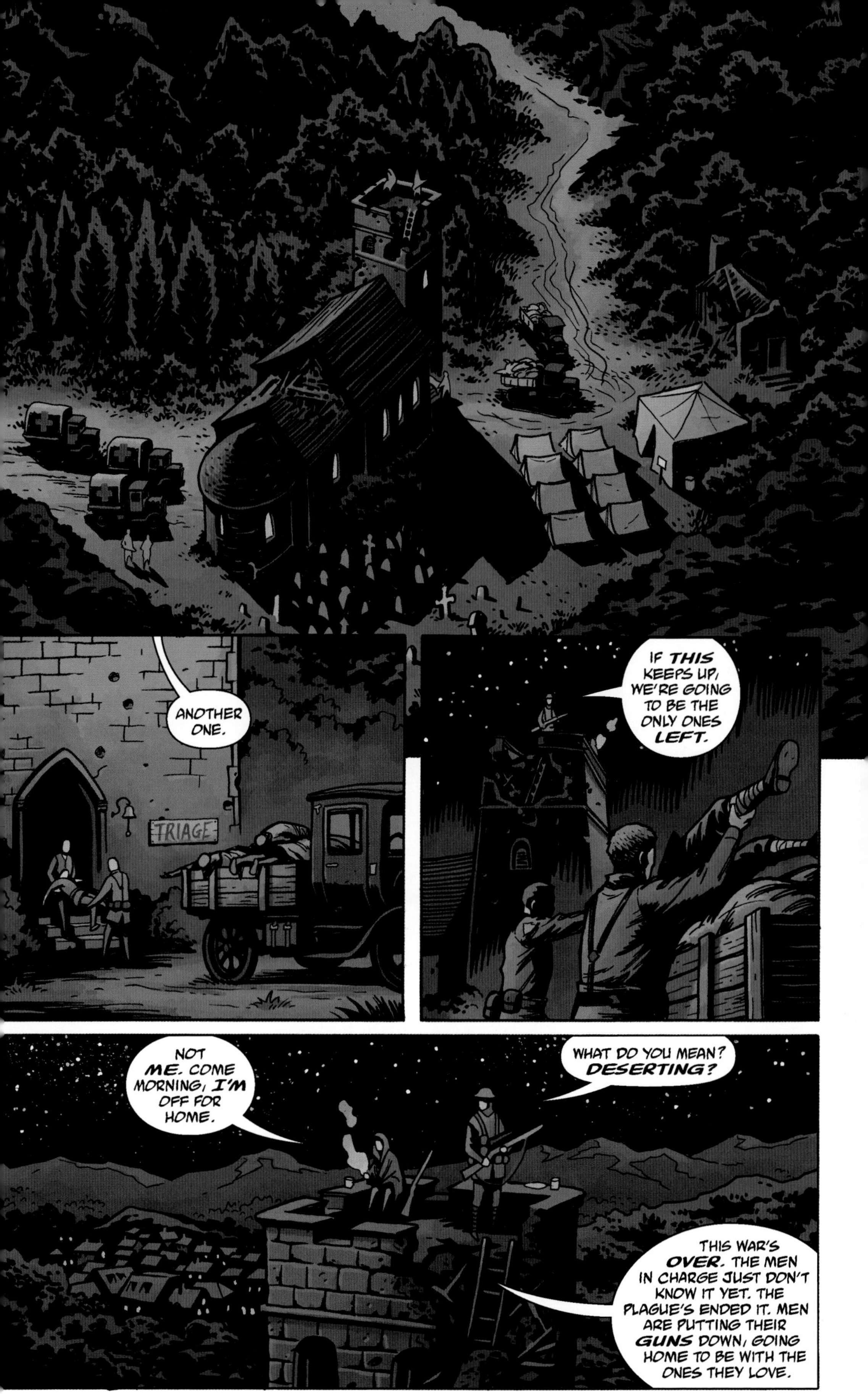
TRIAGE
ANOTHER ONE.
IF THIS KEEPS UP, WE'RE GOING TO BE THE ONLY ONES LEFT.
NOT ME. COME MORNING, I'M OFF FOR HOME.
WHAT DO YOU MEAN? DESERTING?
THIS WAR'S OVER. THE MEN IN CHARGE JUST DON'T KNOW IT YET. THE PLAGUE'S ENDED IT. MEN ARE PUTTING THEIR GUNS DOWN, GOING HOME TO BE WITH THE ONES THEY LOVE.

OR TO *DIE* WITH THEM.

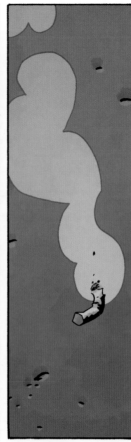

WHEN YOU GO FROM HERE, YOU MUST *REMEMBER* THIS.

HOW CAN YOU *BE* HERE? HOW IS IT YOU WEAR THE FACE OF A MAN?

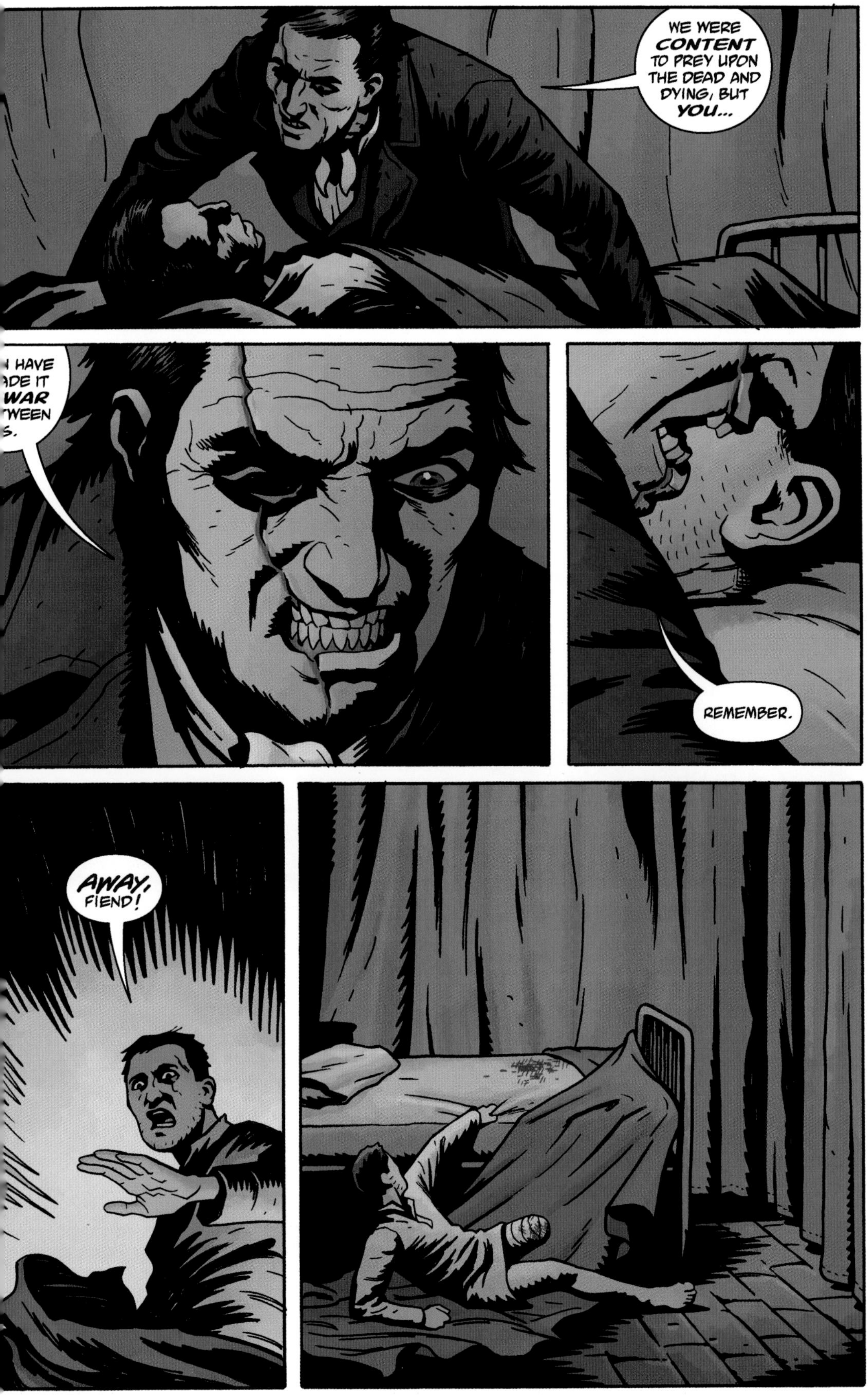
WE WERE CONTENT TO PREY UPON THE DEAD AND DYING, BUT YOU...
N HAVE ADE IT WAR TWEEN S.
REMEMBER.
AWAY, FIEND!

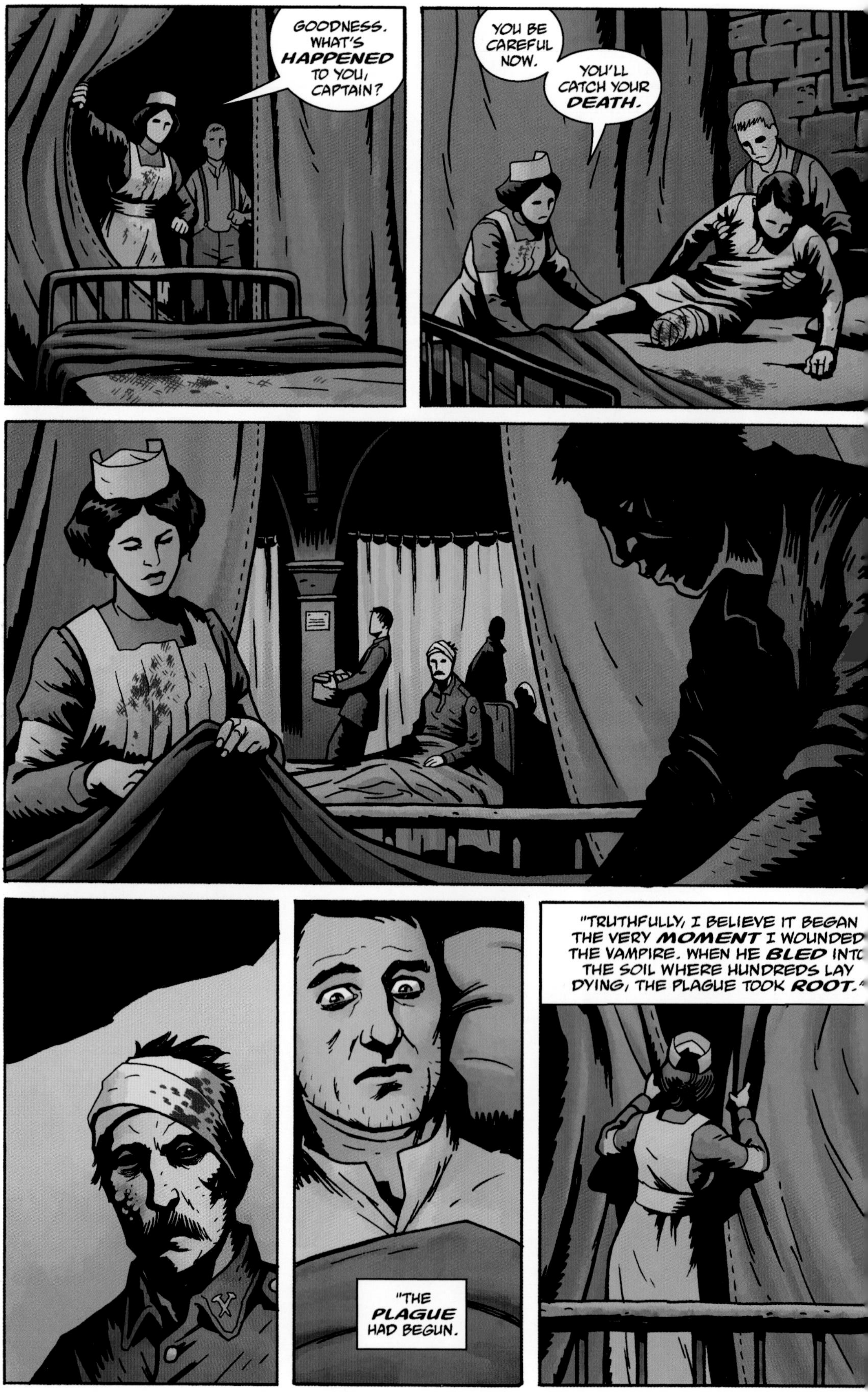
GOODNESS. WHAT'S HAPPENED TO YOU, CAPTAIN?
YOU BE CAREFUL NOW.
YOU'LL CATCH YOUR DEATH.
"THE PLAGUE HAD BEGUN.
"TRUTHFULLY, I BELIEVE IT BEGAN THE VERY MOMENT I WOUNDED THE VAMPIRE. WHEN HE BLED INTO THE SOIL WHERE HUNDREDS LAY DYING, THE PLAGUE TOOK ROOT."

THEY WERE **ANCIENT** THINGS, THE VAMPIRES, NOT MEANT FOR THE **MODERN** WORLD.

OVER EONS, THEY HAD BECOME **DIMINISHED,** LITTLE MORE THAN CARRION CREATURES. CORPSE EATERS. BUT I **WOKE** HIM...**HAIGUS,** AND THROUGH HIM, THE REST.

I HAVE LEARNED A **GREAT** DEAL ABOUT THEM SINCE THAT DAY.

AND DO YOU **TRULY** BELIEVE THAT THE PLAGUE BEGAN IN THAT SAME MOMENT...

...THAT SOMEHOW **YOU** CAUSED ALL OF THIS?

I DO.

THIS IS THE MAN YOU'VE CHOSEN TO **FOLLOW,** VANESSA.

THE **STORM** HAS WORSENED. WE NEED **EVERY** ABLE HAND ON DECK! BUT **GOD HELP** US **ALL**...

WHUMP

...THERE ARE **THINGS** OUT THERE.

WHAT DO YOU MEAN, "THINGS"?

SEE FOR YOURSELF, LORD BALTIMORE!

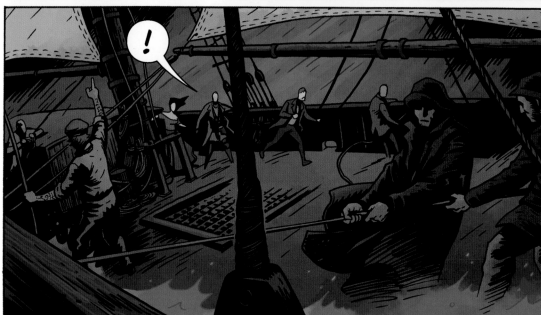

!

I SEE NOTHING!

THERE.

DEAR GOD.

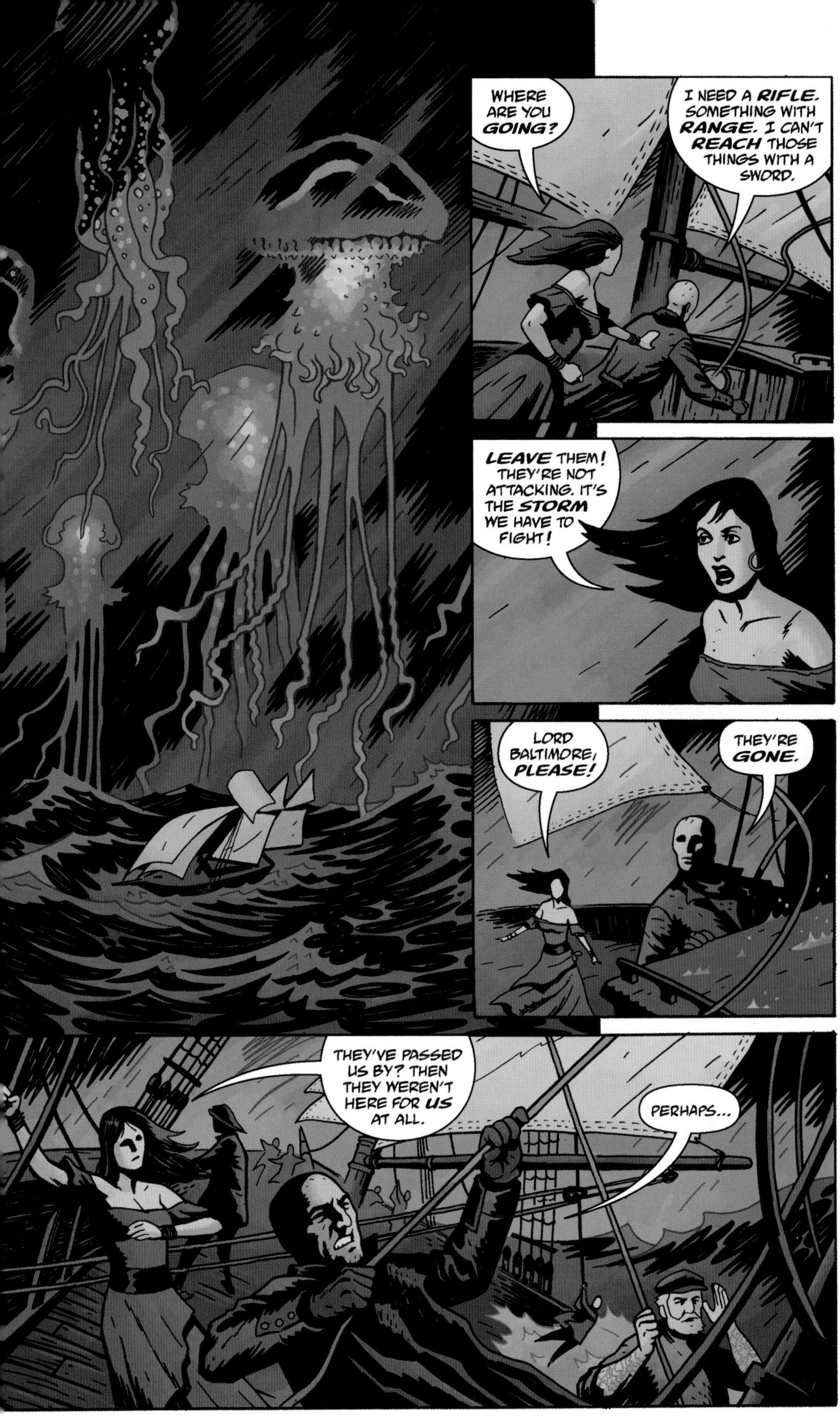
WHERE ARE YOU GOING?
I NEED A RIFLE. SOMETHING WITH RANGE. I CAN'T REACH THOSE THINGS WITH A SWORD.
LEAVE THEM! THEY'RE NOT ATTACKING. IT'S THE STORM WE HAVE TO FIGHT!
LORD BALTIMORE, PLEASE!
THEY'RE GONE.
THEY'VE PASSED US BY? THEN THEY WEREN'T HERE FOR US AT ALL.
PERHAPS...

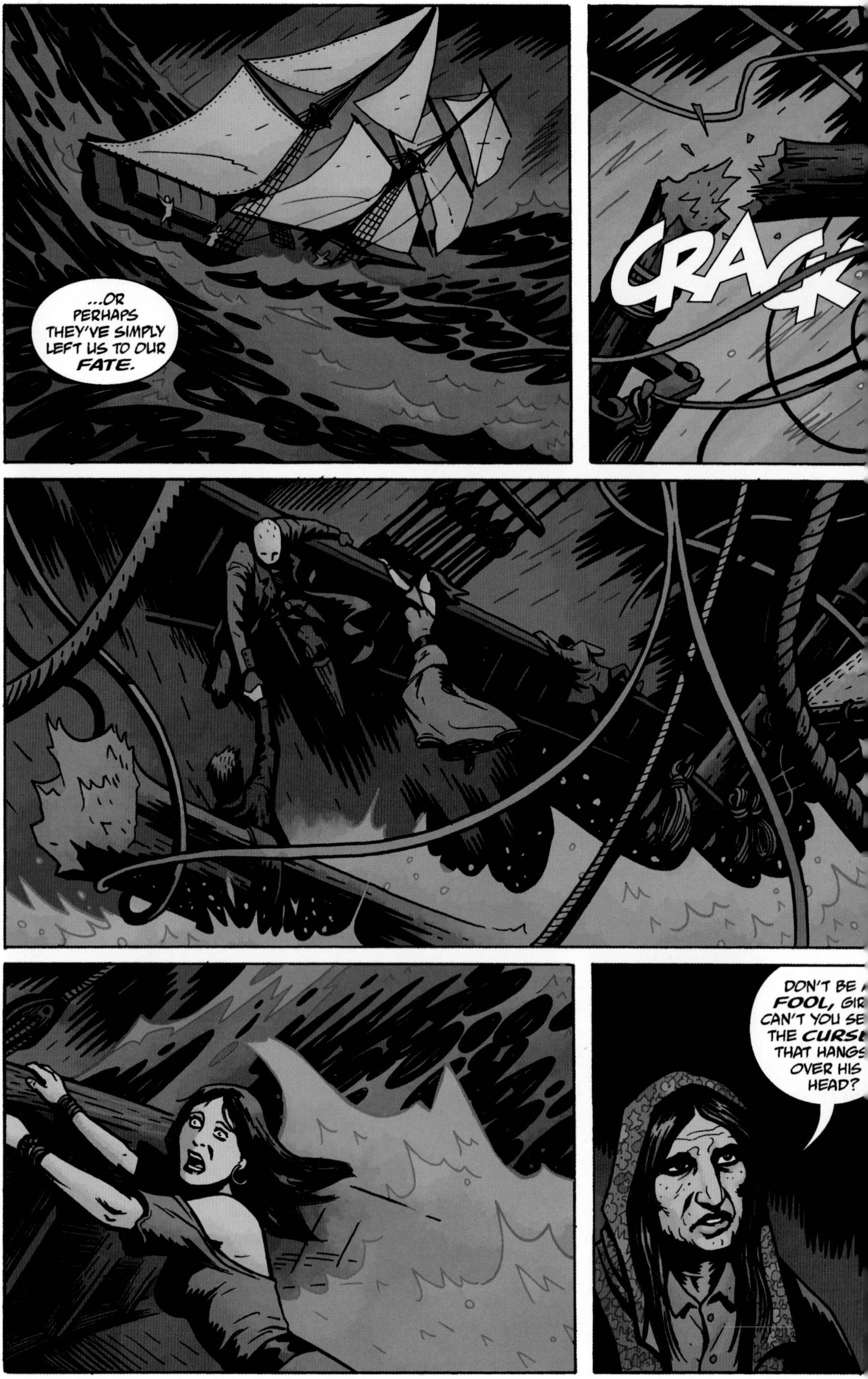
...OR PERHAPS THEY'VE SIMPLY LEFT US TO OUR FATE.
CRACK
DON'T BE FOOL, GIR CAN'T YOU SE THE CURS THAT HANGS OVER HIS HEAD?

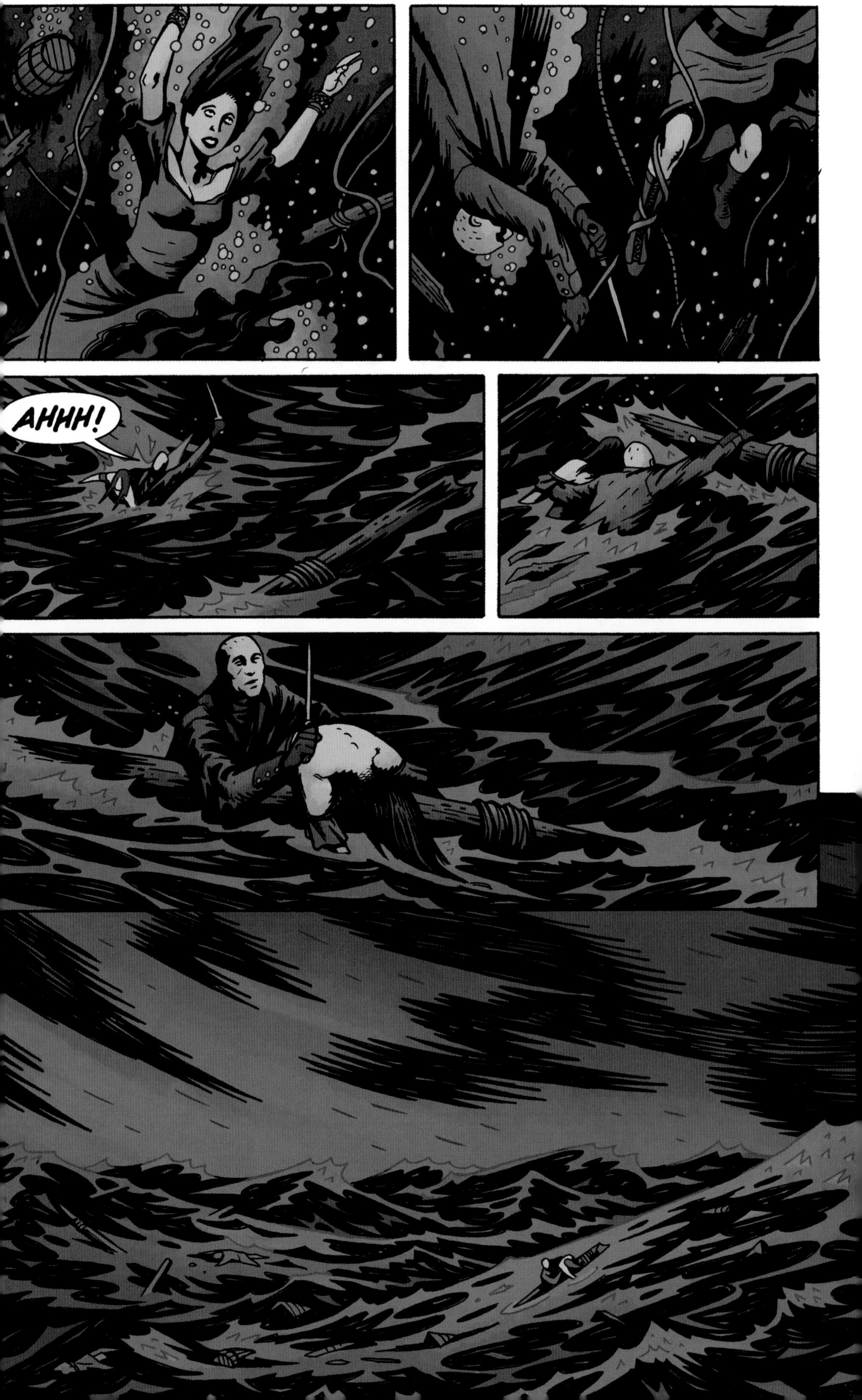
AHHH!

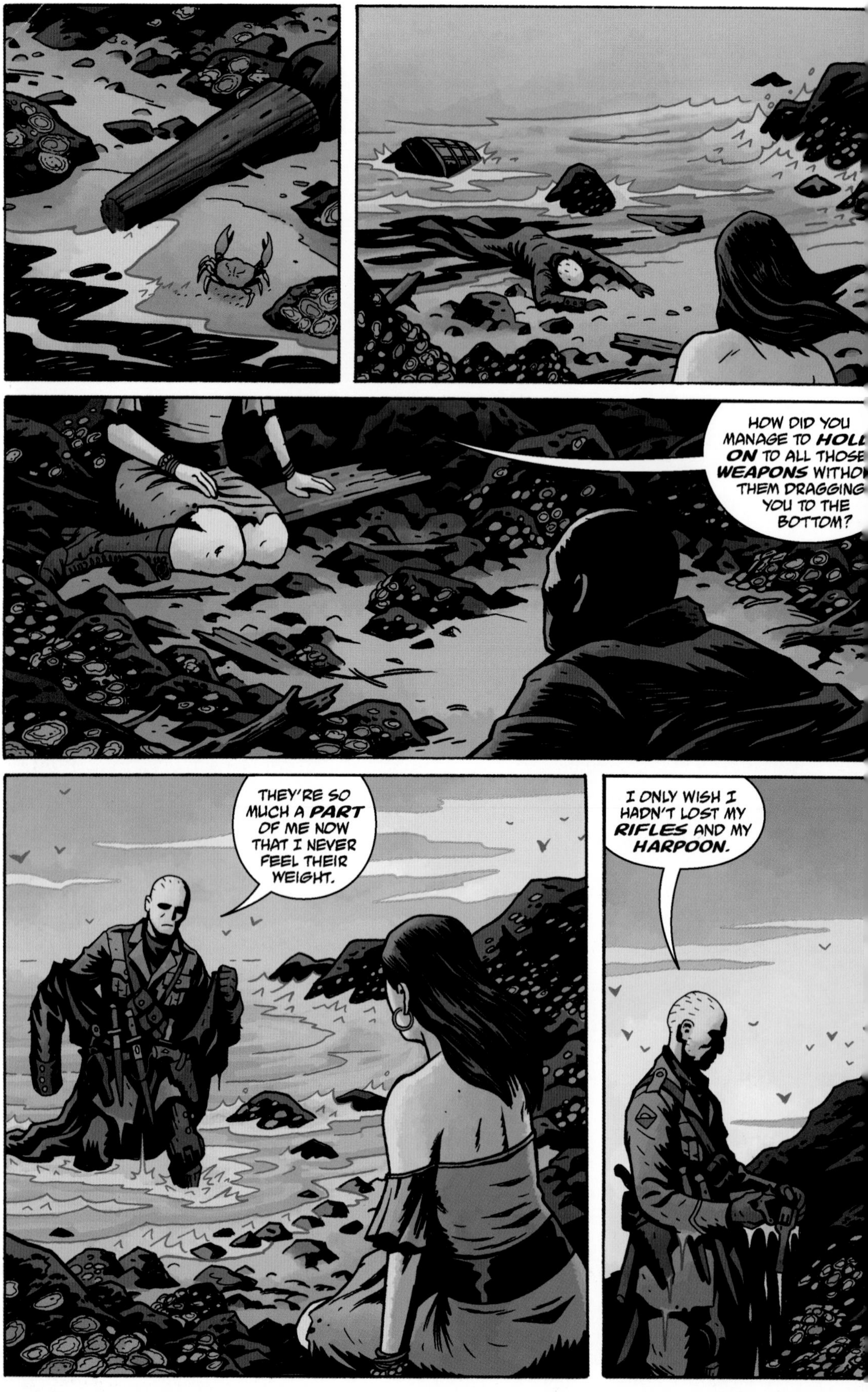
HOW DID YOU MANAGE TO HOL ON TO ALL THOSE WEAPONS WITHO THEM DRAGGING YOU TO THE BOTTOM?
THEY'RE SO MUCH A PART OF ME NOW THAT I NEVER FEEL THEIR WEIGHT.
I ONLY WISH I HADN'T LOST MY RIFLES AND MY HARPOON.

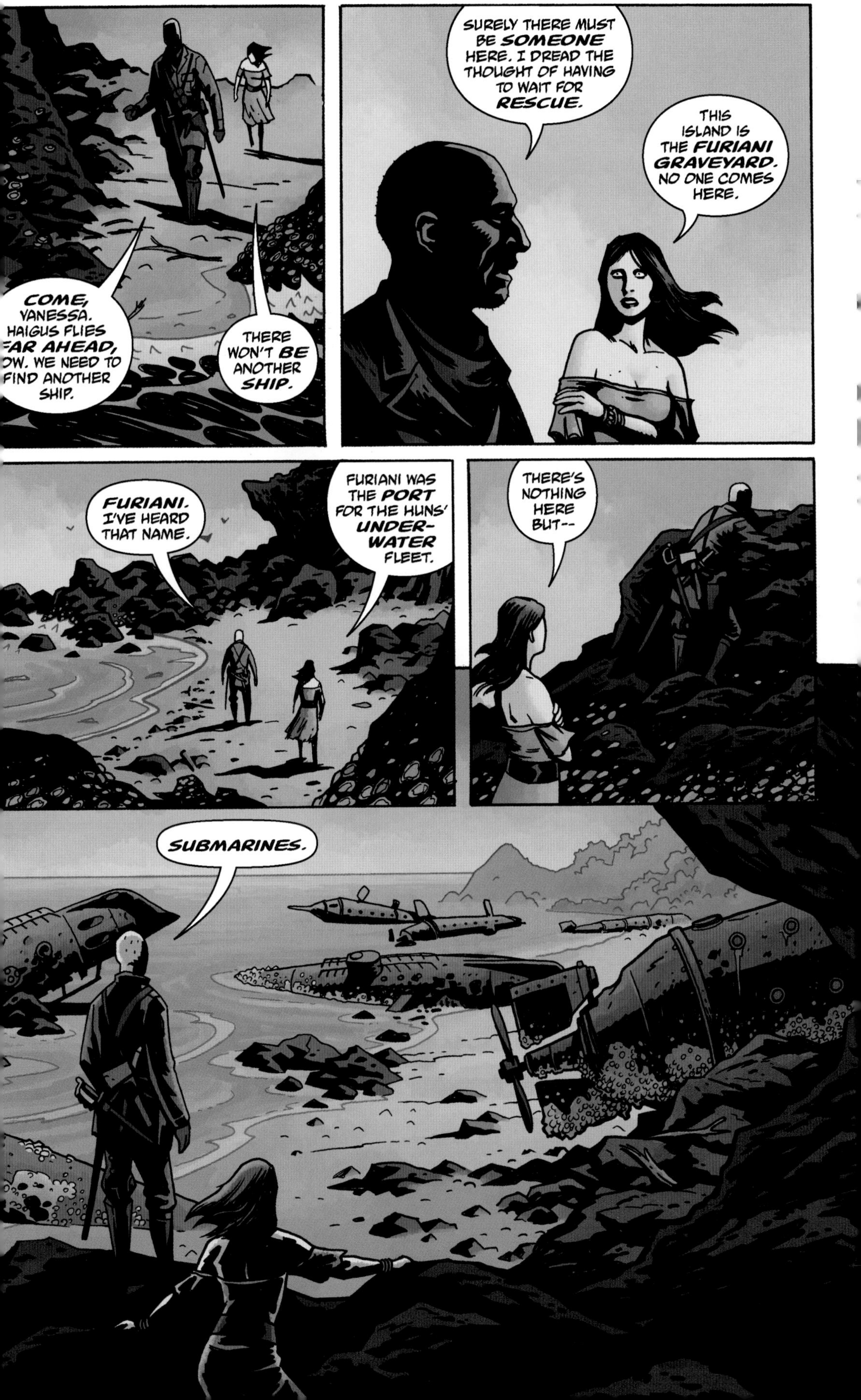
COME, VANESSA. HAIGUS FLIES
AR AHEAD,
OW. WE NEED TO FIND ANOTHER SHIP.
THERE WON'T BE ANOTHER SHIP.
SURELY THERE MUST BE SOMEONE HERE. I DREAD THE THOUGHT OF HAVING TO WAIT FOR RESCUE.
THIS ISLAND IS THE FURIANI GRAVEYARD. NO ONE COMES HERE.
FURIANI. I'VE HEARD THAT NAME.
FURIANI WAS THE PORT FOR THE HUNS' UNDER-WATER FLEET.
THERE'S NOTHING HERE BUT--
SUBMARINES.

SO MUCH FOR THE KAISER'S SECRET *UNDERWATER NAVY.*

WE SHOULD NOT BE HERE.

YOU FEEL WE'RE *INTRUDING?*

THEY SAY THIS ISLAND IS *HAUNTED* BY THE WAR'S *GHOSTS.*

OTHERS SAY THAT SOMETHING *EVIL* WAS HERE *BEFORE* THE WAR BEGAN, AND THAT'S WHY SO MANY *WRECKS* END UP HERE.

ARE YOU *WISHING,* NOW, THAT YOU HAD *LISTENED* TO YOUR GRANDMOTHER?

THERE IS A DIFFERENCE BETWEEN *CAUTION* AND *SUPERSTITION.* THAT WOMAN SEES EVIL *EVERYWHERE.*

THE WAY THE WORLD IS CHANGING, THAT MAY BE MORE *WISDOM* THAN MADNESS.

NOW, LET'S SEE WHAT *ELSE* HAS WASHED UP ON THESE SHORES.

I SUPPOSE *LIFEBO...* WOULD B... ASKING T... MUCH.

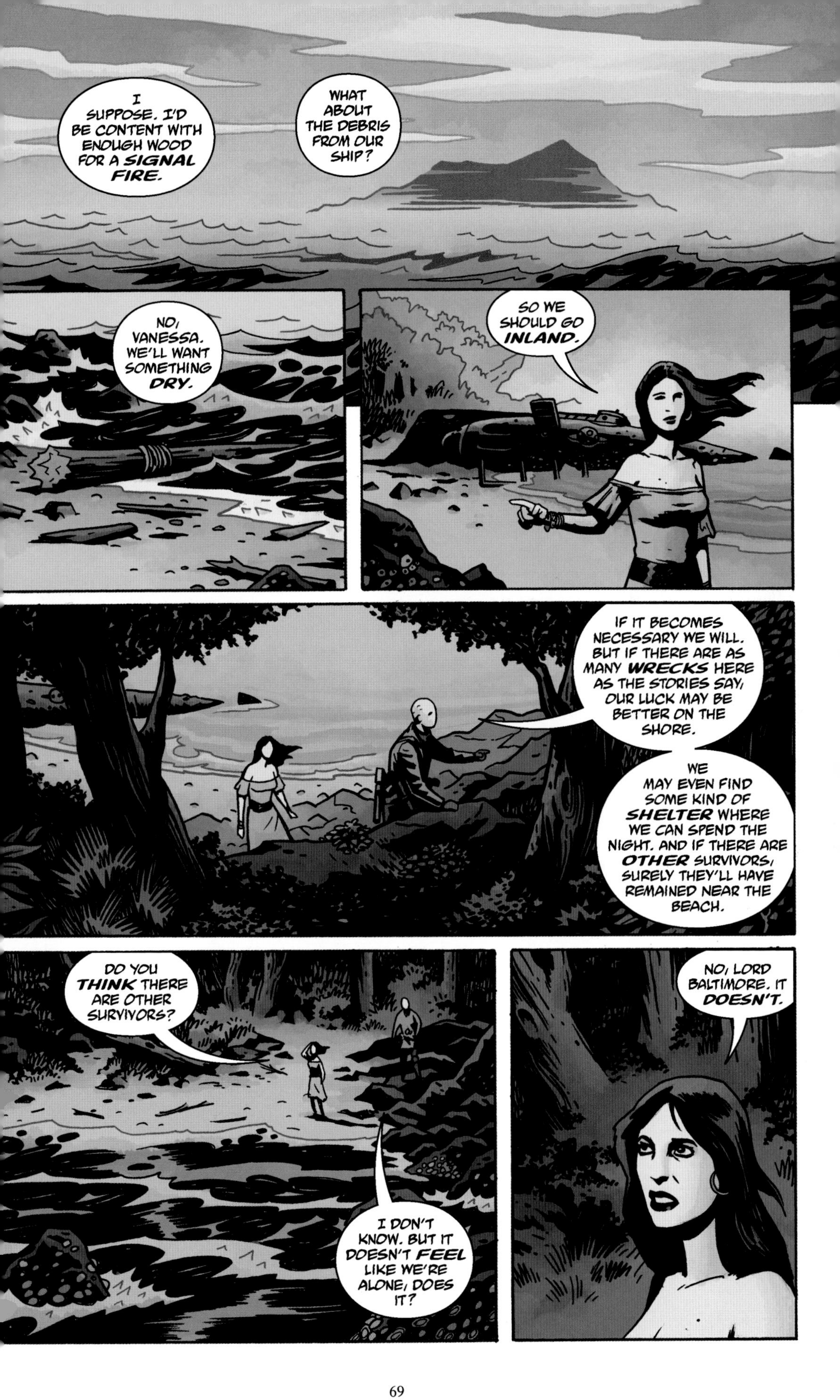
I SUPPOSE. I'D BE CONTENT WITH ENOUGH WOOD FOR A SIGNAL FIRE.
WHAT ABOUT THE DEBRIS FROM OUR SHIP?
NO, VANESSA. WE'LL WANT SOMETHING DRY.
SO WE SHOULD GO INLAND.
IF IT BECOMES NECESSARY WE WILL. BUT IF THERE ARE AS MANY WRECKS HERE AS THE STORIES SAY, OUR LUCK MAY BE BETTER ON THE SHORE.
WE MAY EVEN FIND SOME KIND OF SHELTER WHERE WE CAN SPEND THE NIGHT. AND IF THERE ARE OTHER SURVIVORS, SURELY THEY'LL HAVE REMAINED NEAR THE BEACH.
DO YOU THINK THERE ARE OTHER SURVIVORS?
I DON'T KNOW. BUT IT DOESN'T FEEL LIKE WE'RE ALONE, DOES IT?
NO, LORD BALTIMORE. IT DOESN'T.

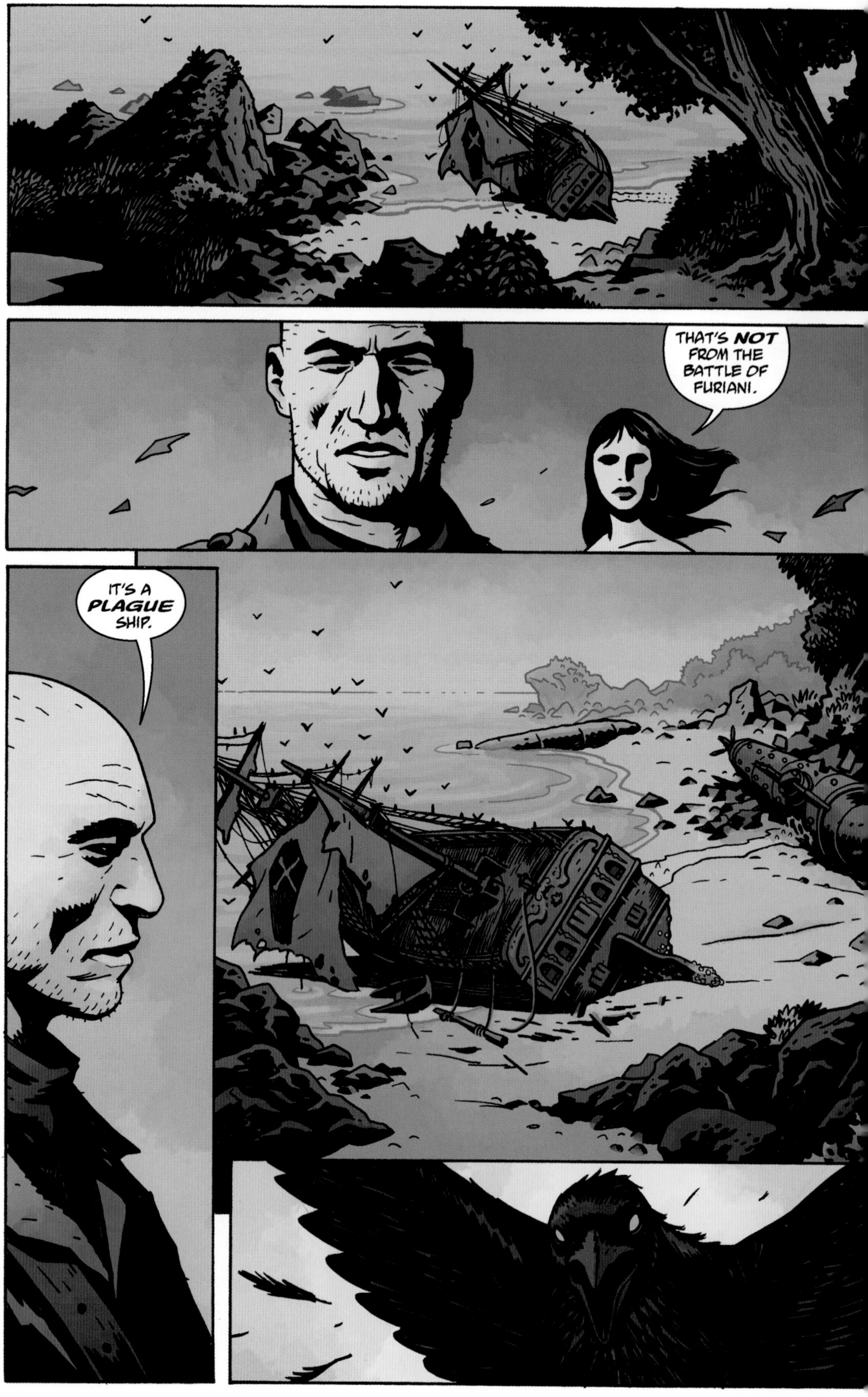
THAT'S NOT FROM THE BATTLE OF FURIANI.
IT'S A PLAGUE SHIP.

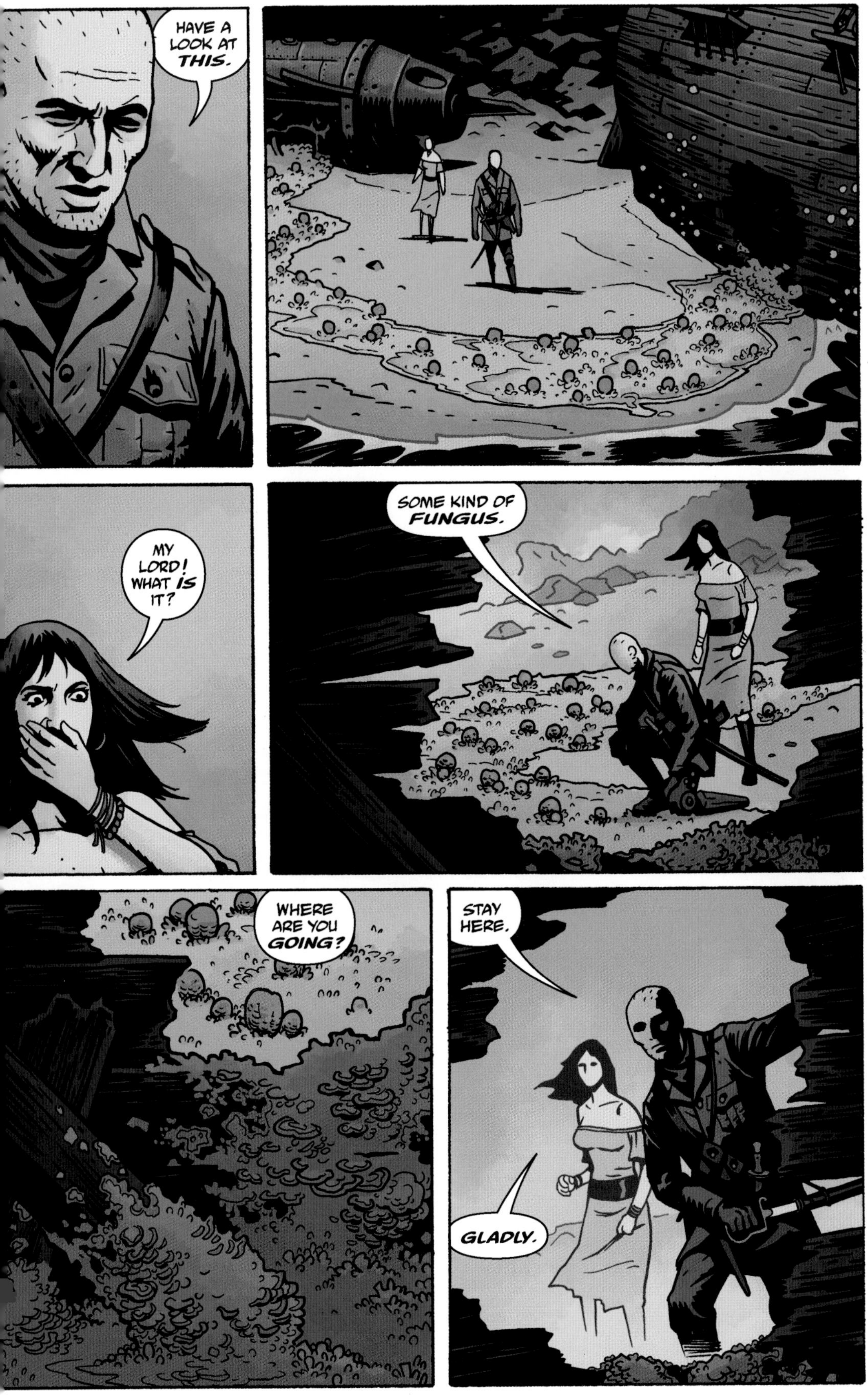
HAVE A LOOK AT THIS.
MY LORD! WHAT IS IT?
SOME KIND OF FUNGUS.
WHERE ARE YOU GOING?
STAY HERE.
GLADLY.

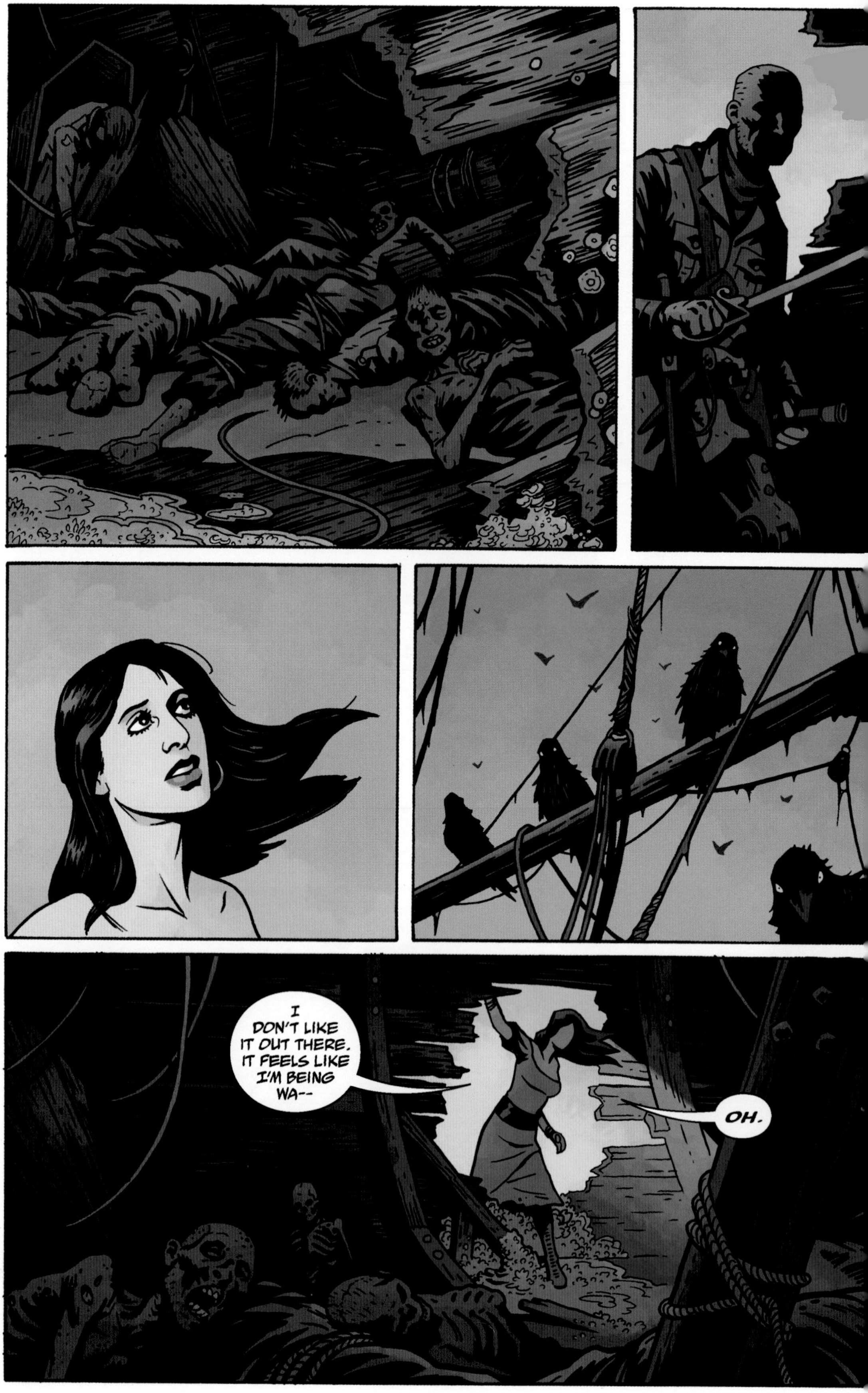

I DON'T LIKE IT OUT THERE. IT FEELS LIKE I'M BEING WA--
OH.

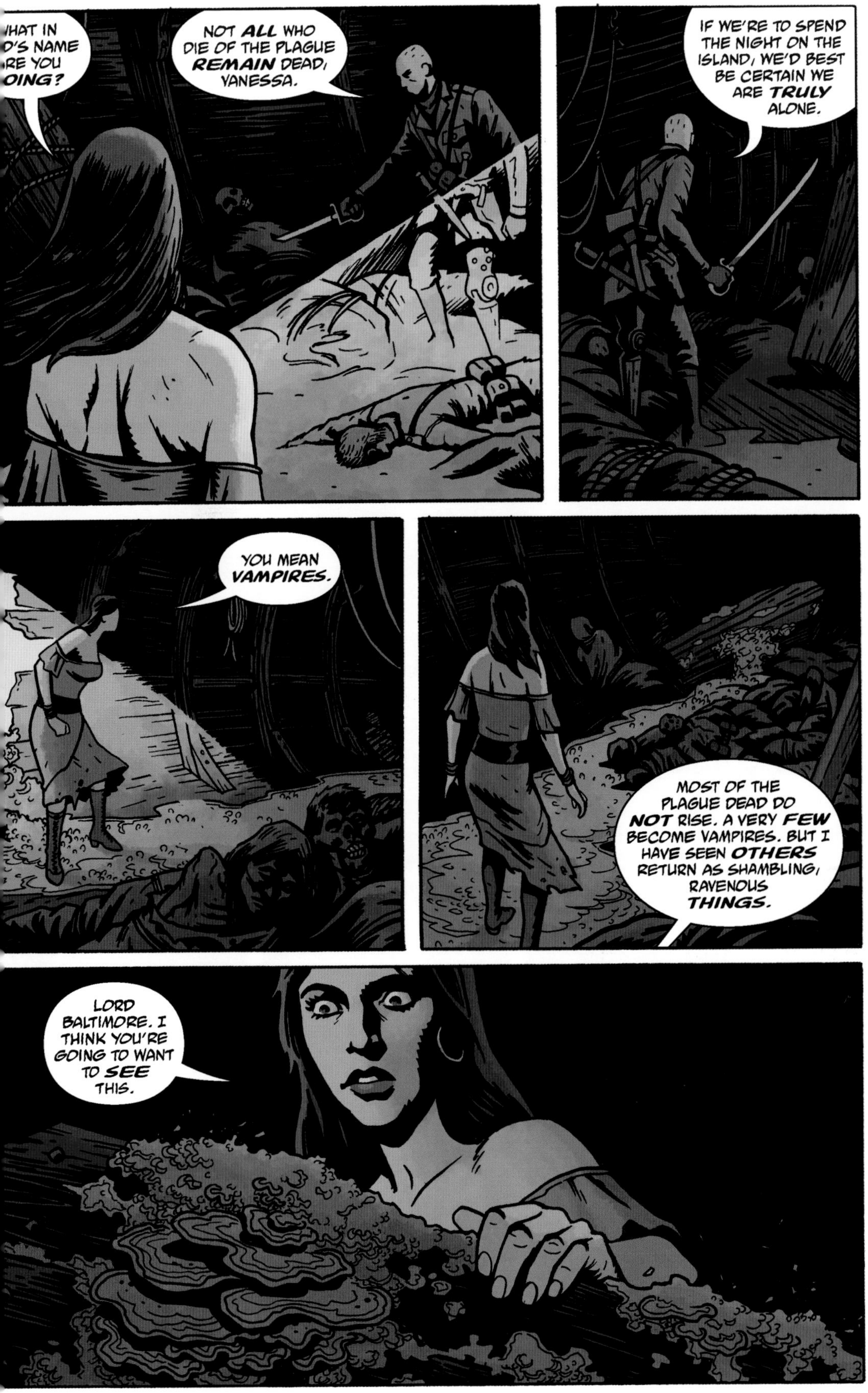
HAT IN D'S NAME RE YOU OING?
NOT ALL WHO DIE OF THE PLAGUE REMAIN DEAD, VANESSA.
IF WE'RE TO SPEND THE NIGHT ON THE ISLAND, WE'D BEST BE CERTAIN WE ARE TRULY ALONE.
YOU MEAN VAMPIRES.
MOST OF THE PLAGUE DEAD DO NOT RISE. A VERY FEW BECOME VAMPIRES. BUT I HAVE SEEN OTHERS RETURN AS SHAMBLING, RAVENOUS THINGS.
LORD BALTIMORE. I THINK YOU'RE GOING TO WANT TO SEE THIS.

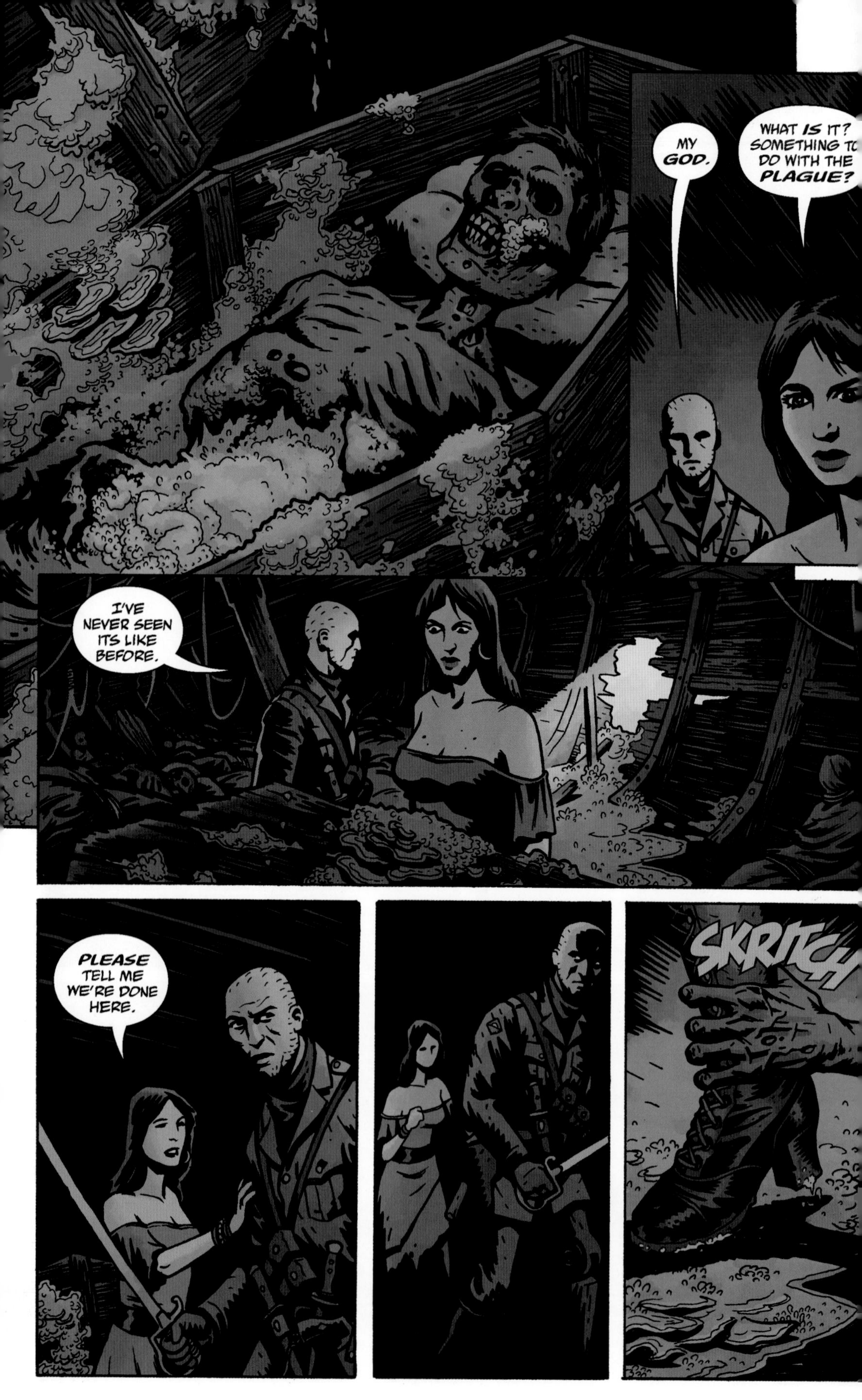
MY *GOD.*
WHAT *IS* IT? SOMETHING TO DO WITH THE ***PLAGUE?***
I'VE NEVER SEEN ITS LIKE BEFORE.
PLEASE TELL ME WE'RE DONE HERE.
SKRITCH

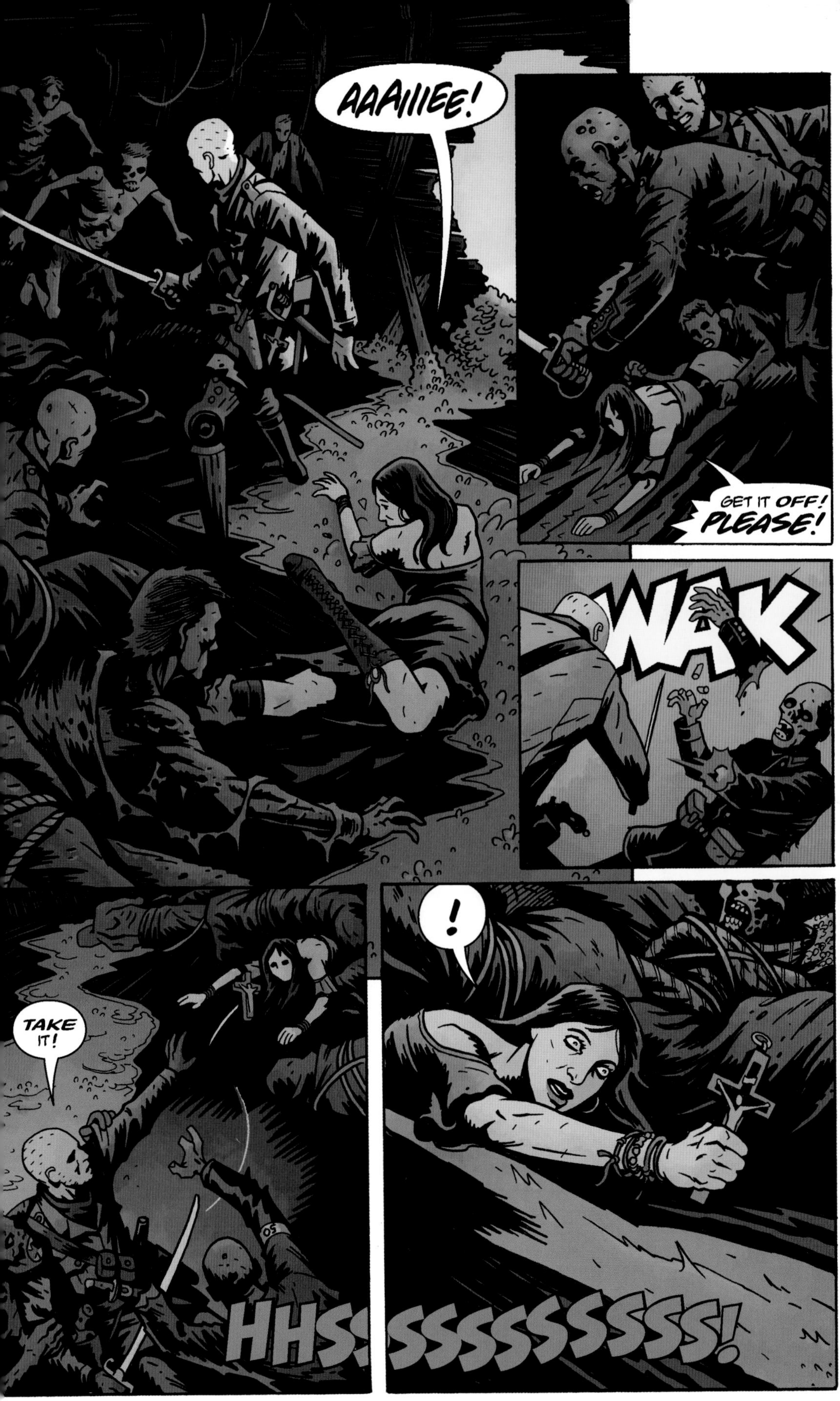
AAAIIIEE!
GET IT OFF! PLEASE!
WAK
TAKE IT!
!
HHSSSSSSSSSSSSS!

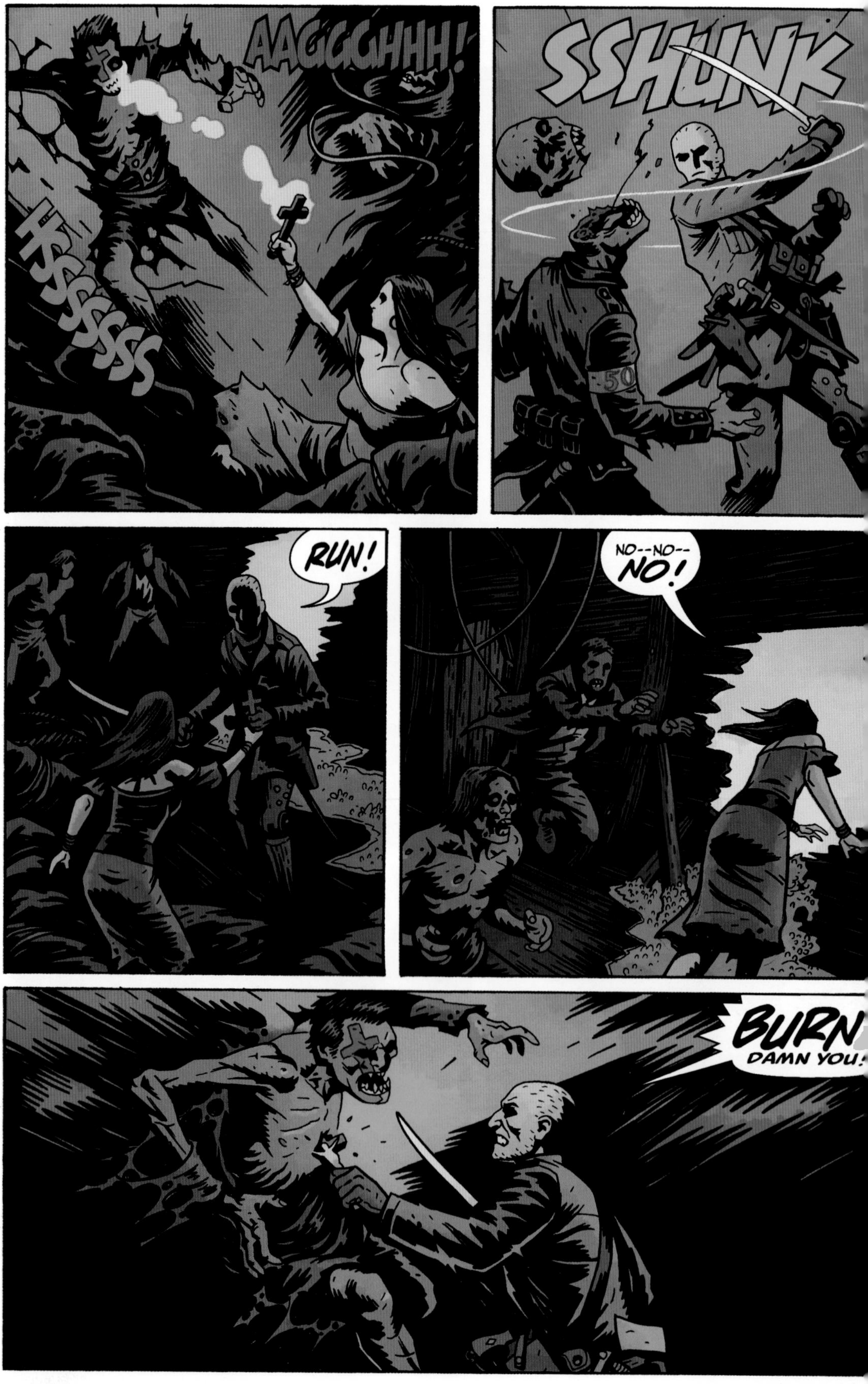
AAGGGHHH!
HSSSSSSS
SSHUNK
RUN!
NO--NO--
NO!
BURN
DAMN YOU!

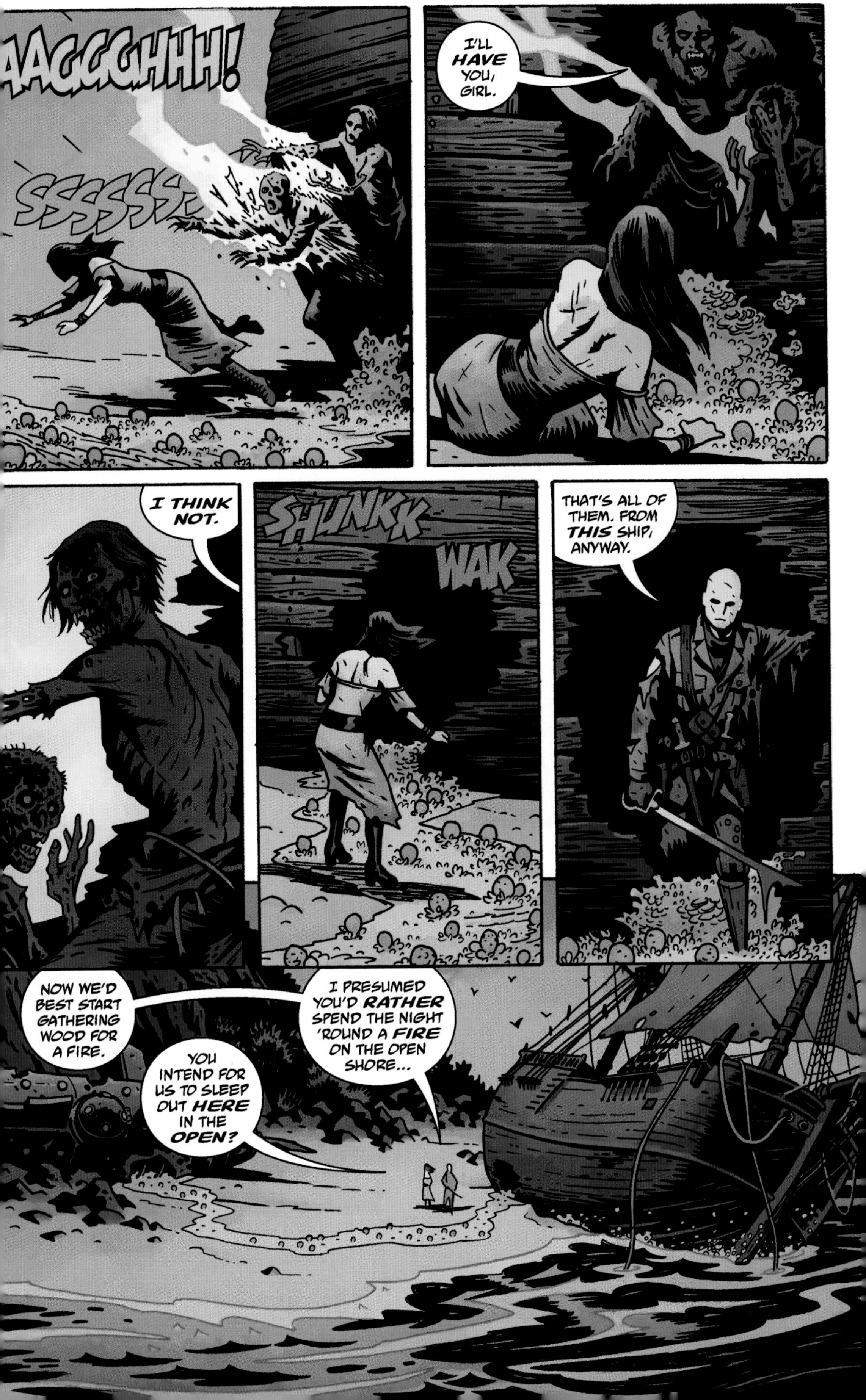
AAGGGHHH!
SSSSSS
I'LL HAVE YOU, GIRL.
I THINK NOT.
SHUNKK
WAK
THAT'S ALL OF THEM. FROM THIS SHIP, ANYWAY.
NOW WE'D BEST START GATHERING WOOD FOR A FIRE.
YOU INTEND FOR US TO SLEEP OUT HERE IN THE OPEN?
I PRESUMED YOU'D RATHER SPEND THE NIGHT 'ROUND A FIRE ON THE OPEN SHORE...

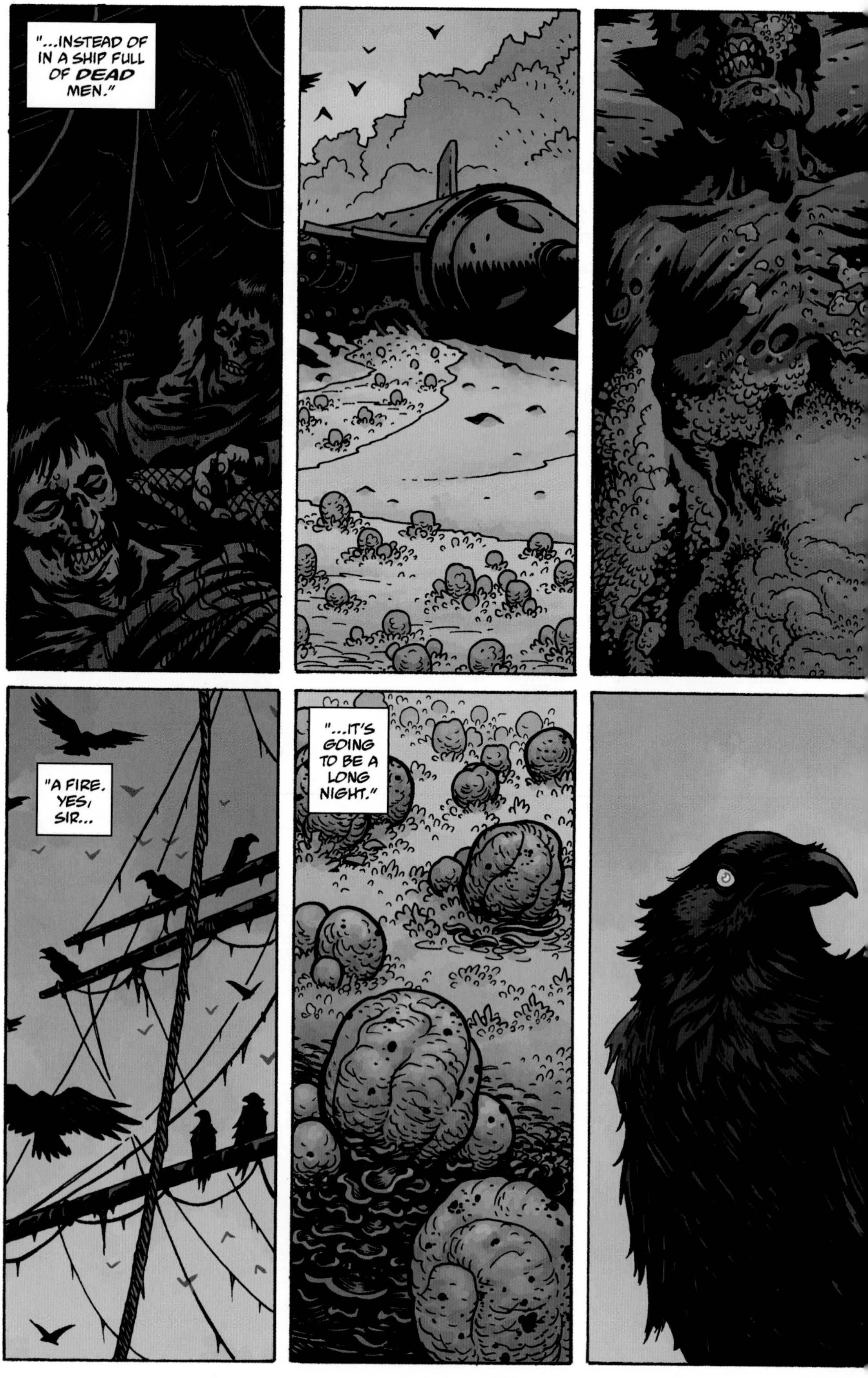
"...INSTEAD OF IN A SHIP FULL OF DEAD MEN."
"A FIRE. YES, SIR...
"...IT'S GOING TO BE A LONG NIGHT."

CHAPTER FOUR

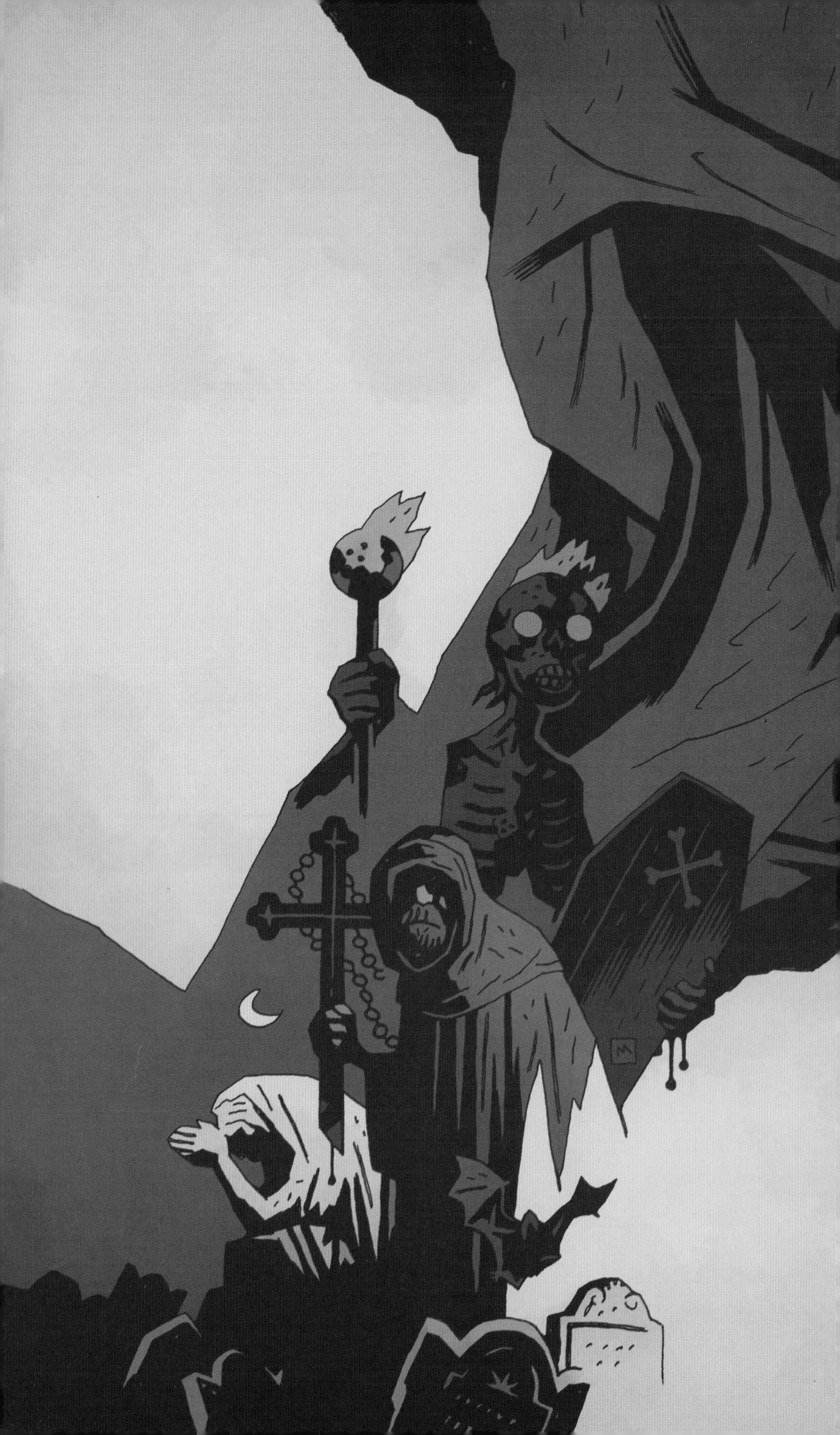

YOU TOLD ME THAT SAILORS THINK THIS ISLAND IS HAUNTED, BUT HOW STRONG IS THEIR FEAR? WILL THE SMOKE OF OUR FIRE BE ENOUGH TO DRAW THEM?

SOMEONE WILL COME, LORD BALTIMORE. THE SAILORS I'VE KNOWN WOULD NEVER IGNORE PEOPLE STRANDED BY A SHIPWRECK. NOT EVEN *HERE*.

"A FINE SENTIMENT, VANESSA. BUT FEAR CAN CRIPPLE THE STRONGEST OF MEN."

AND WHO IS TO SAY THAT THEY WILL THINK WHEN THEY SEE THE SMOKE FROM OUR FIRE. THEY MAY TELL THEMSELVES THERE ARE ONLY *GHOSTS* HERE. ONLY THE *DEAD*.

IF SO, IT WON'T BE LONG UNTIL THEY ARE RIGHT.

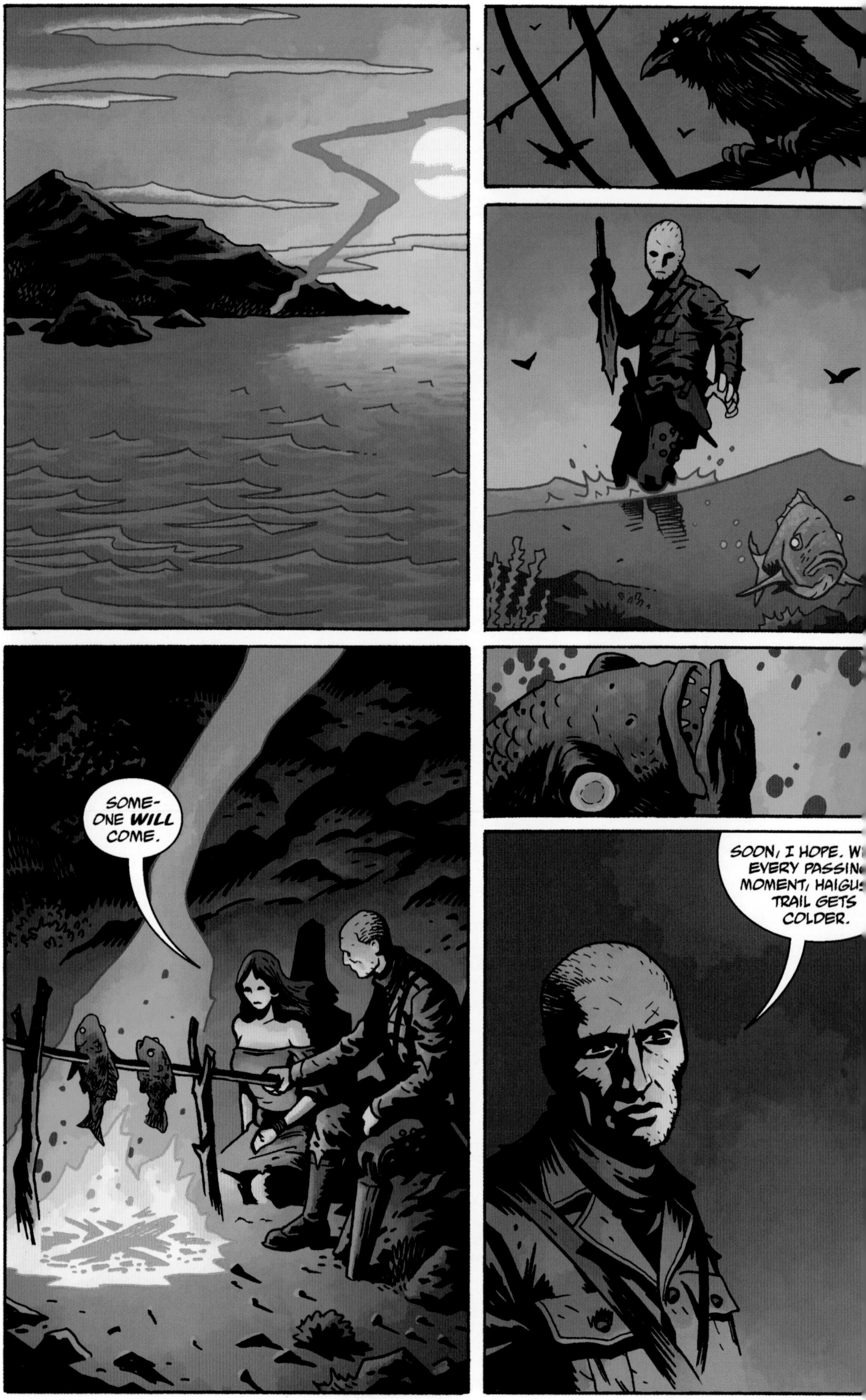
SOME-ONE WILL COME.
SOON, I HOPE. W
EVERY PASSIN
MOMENT, HAIGU
TRAIL GETS
COLDER.

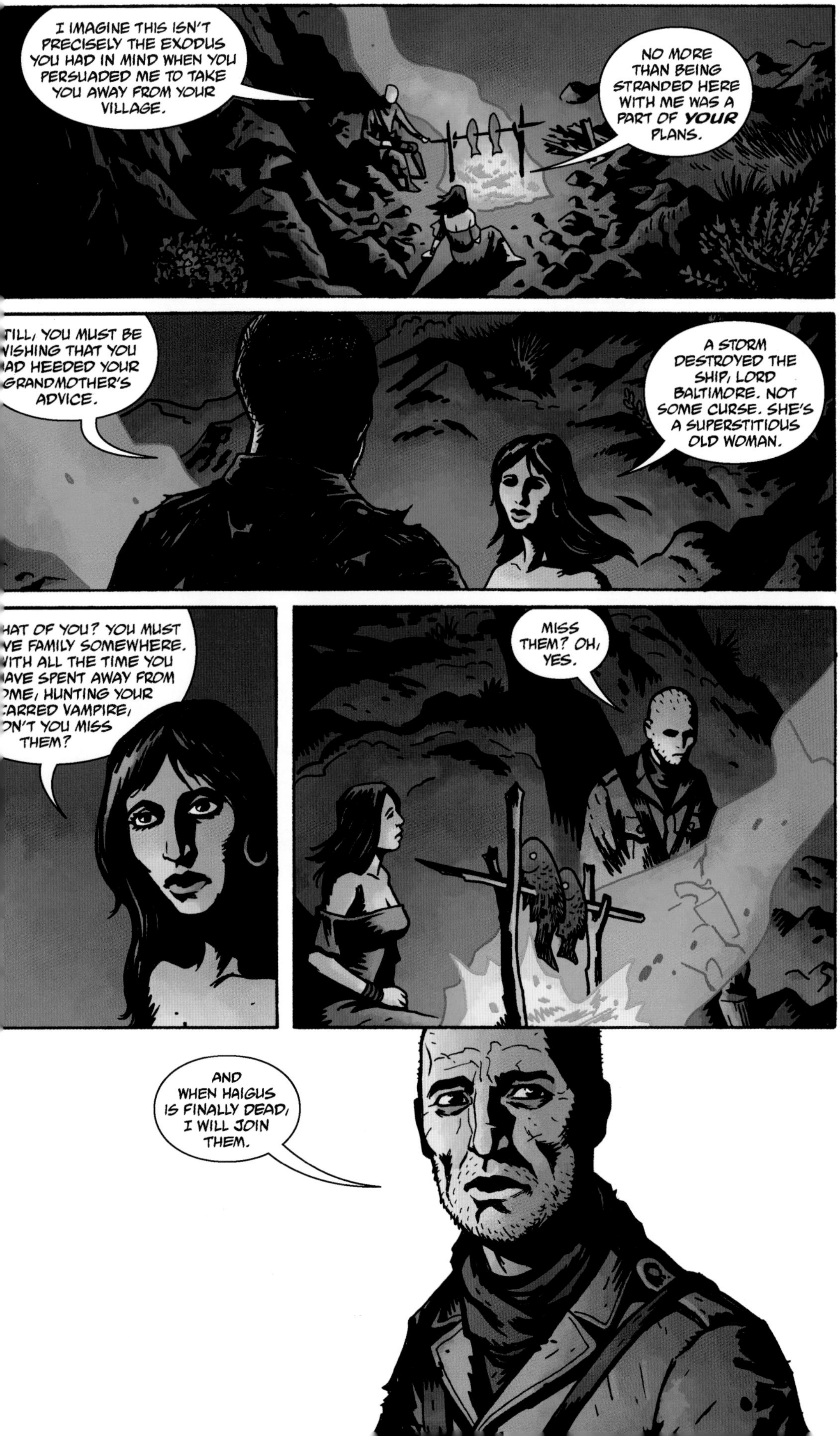
I IMAGINE THIS ISN'T PRECISELY THE EXODUS YOU HAD IN MIND WHEN YOU PERSUADED ME TO TAKE YOU AWAY FROM YOUR VILLAGE.
NO MORE THAN BEING STRANDED HERE WITH ME WAS A PART OF YOUR PLANS.
TILL, YOU MUST BE VISHING THAT YOU AD HEEDED YOUR GRANDMOTHER'S ADVICE.
A STORM DESTROYED THE SHIP, LORD BALTIMORE. NOT SOME CURSE. SHE'S A SUPERSTITIOUS OLD WOMAN.
HAT OF YOU? YOU MUST VE FAMILY SOMEWHERE. WITH ALL THE TIME YOU AVE SPENT AWAY FROM OME, HUNTING YOUR CARRED VAMPIRE, ON'T YOU MISS THEM?
MISS THEM? OH, YES.
AND WHEN HAIGUS IS FINALLY DEAD, I WILL JOIN THEM.

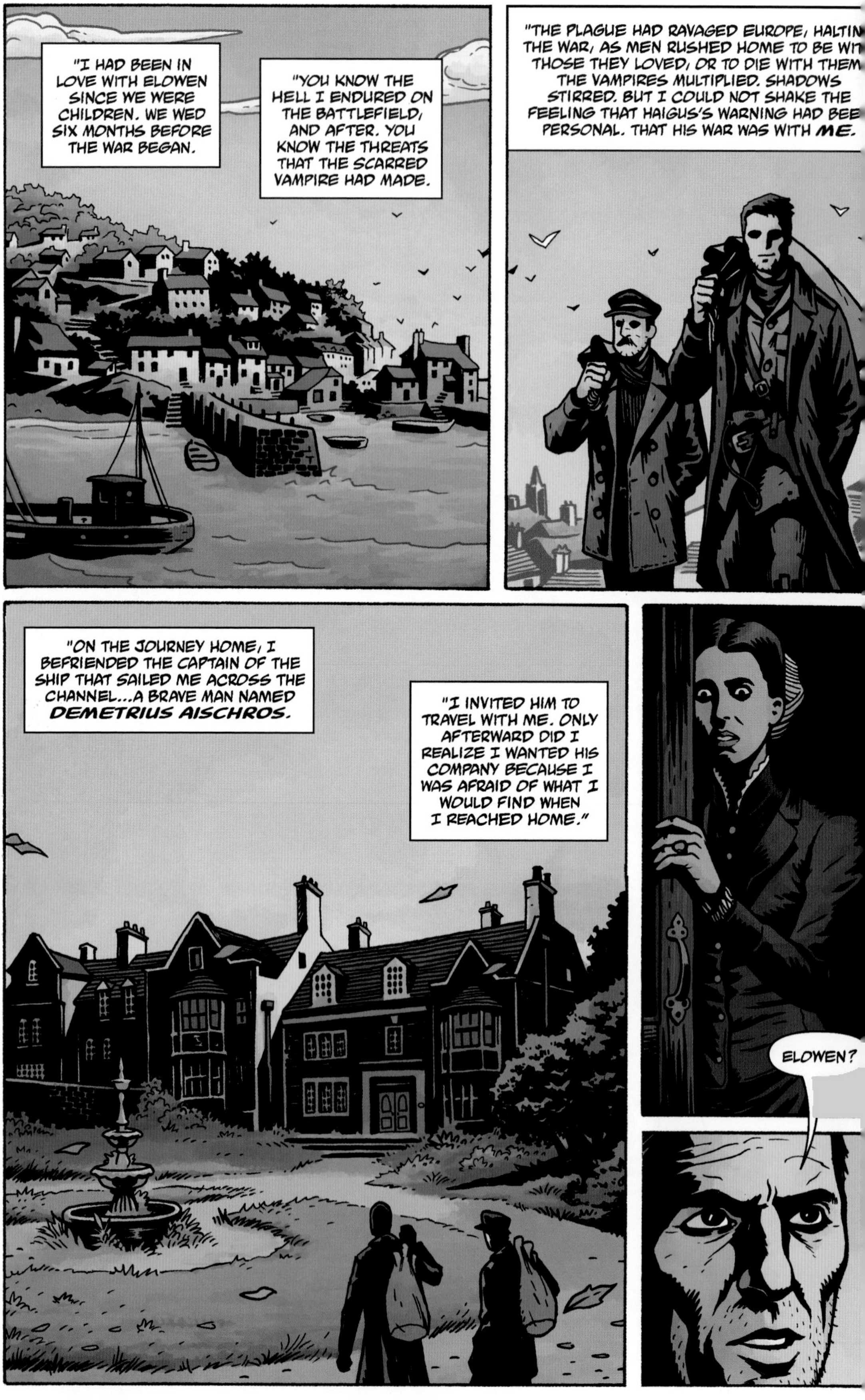
"I HAD BEEN IN LOVE WITH ELOWEN SINCE WE WERE CHILDREN. WE WED SIX MONTHS BEFORE THE WAR BEGAN.
"YOU KNOW THE HELL I ENDURED ON THE BATTLEFIELD, AND AFTER. YOU KNOW THE THREATS THAT THE SCARRED VAMPIRE HAD MADE.
"THE PLAGUE HAD RAVAGED EUROPE, HALTIN THE WAR, AS MEN RUSHED HOME TO BE WI THOSE THEY LOVED, OR TO DIE WITH THEM THE VAMPIRES MULTIPLIED. SHADOWS STIRRED. BUT I COULD NOT SHAKE THE FEELING THAT HAIGUS'S WARNING HAD BEE PERSONAL. THAT HIS WAR WAS WITH ME.
"ON THE JOURNEY HOME, I BEFRIENDED THE CAPTAIN OF THE SHIP THAT SAILED ME ACROSS THE CHANNEL...A BRAVE MAN NAMED DEMETRIUS AISCHROS.
"I INVITED HIM TO TRAVEL WITH ME. ONLY AFTERWARD DID I REALIZE I WANTED HIS COMPANY BECAUSE I WAS AFRAID OF WHAT I WOULD FIND WHEN I REACHED HOME."
ELOWEN?

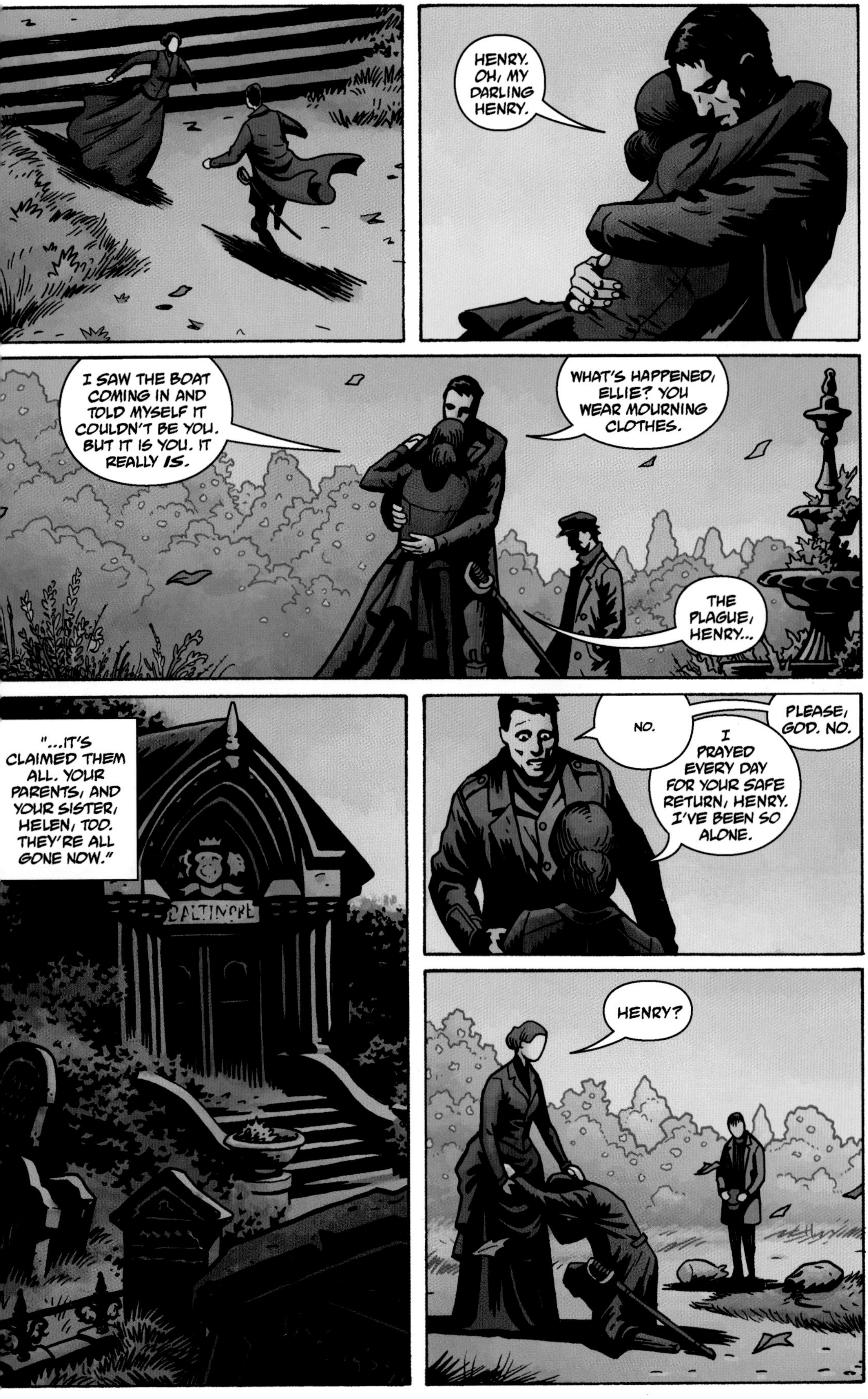
HENRY. OH, MY DARLING HENRY.
I SAW THE BOAT COMING IN AND TOLD MYSELF IT COULDN'T BE YOU. BUT IT IS YOU. IT REALLY IS.
WHAT'S HAPPENED, ELLIE? YOU WEAR MOURNING CLOTHES.
THE PLAGUE, HENRY...
"...IT'S CLAIMED THEM ALL. YOUR PARENTS, AND YOUR SISTER, HELEN, TOO. THEY'RE ALL GONE NOW."
NO.
PLEASE, GOD. NO.
I PRAYED EVERY DAY FOR YOUR SAFE RETURN, HENRY. I'VE BEEN SO ALONE.
HENRY?

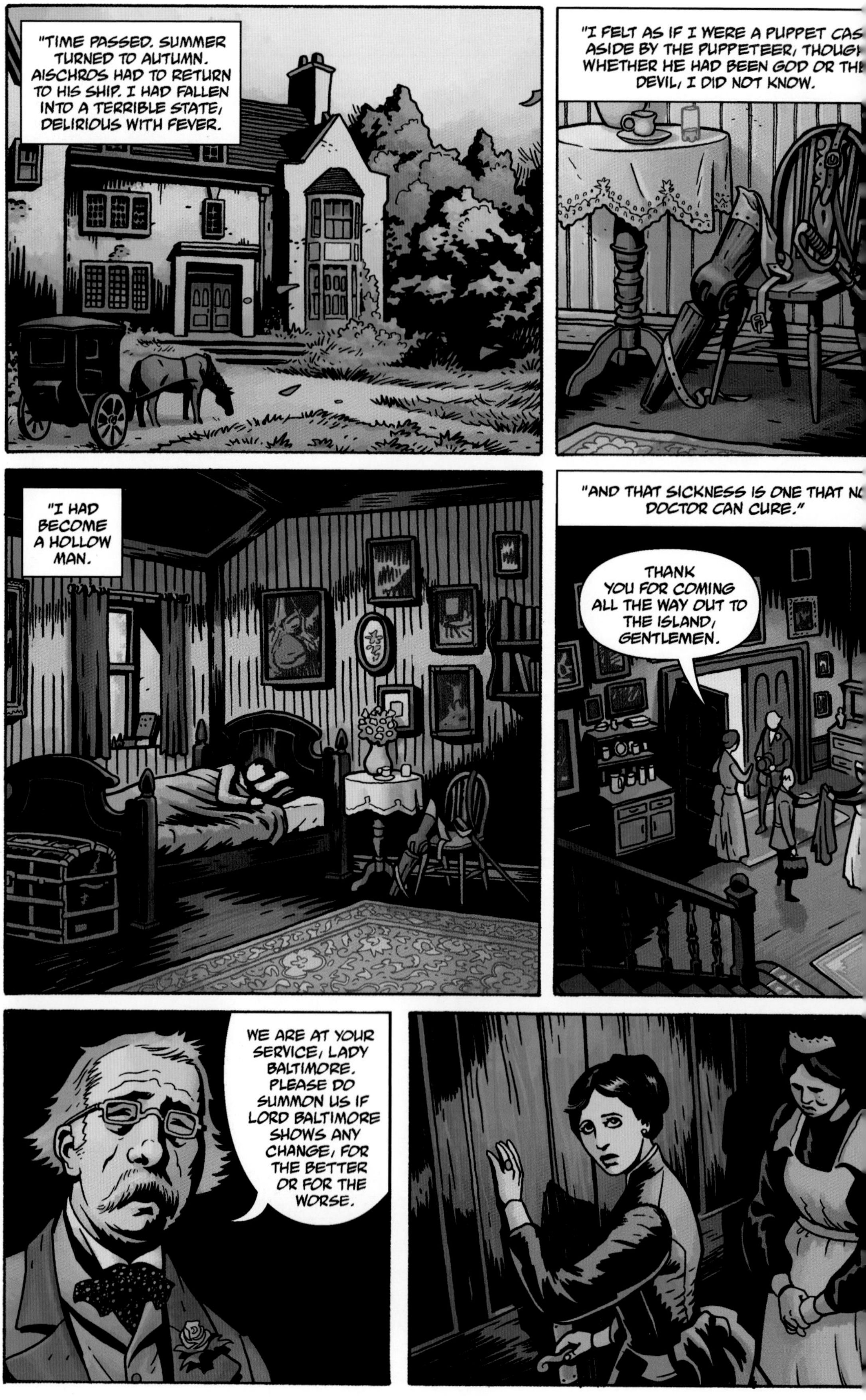
"TIME PASSED. SUMMER TURNED TO AUTUMN. AISCHROS HAD TO RETURN TO HIS SHIP. I HAD FALLEN INTO A TERRIBLE STATE, DELIRIOUS WITH FEVER.
"I FELT AS IF I WERE A PUPPET CAS ASIDE BY THE PUPPETEER, THOUGH WHETHER HE HAD BEEN GOD OR TH DEVIL, I DID NOT KNOW.
"I HAD BECOME A HOLLOW MAN.
"AND THAT SICKNESS IS ONE THAT N DOCTOR CAN CURE."
THANK YOU FOR COMING ALL THE WAY OUT TO THE ISLAND, GENTLEMEN.
WE ARE AT YOUR SERVICE, LADY BALTIMORE. PLEASE DO SUMMON US IF LORD BALTIMORE SHOWS ANY CHANGE, FOR THE BETTER OR FOR THE WORSE.

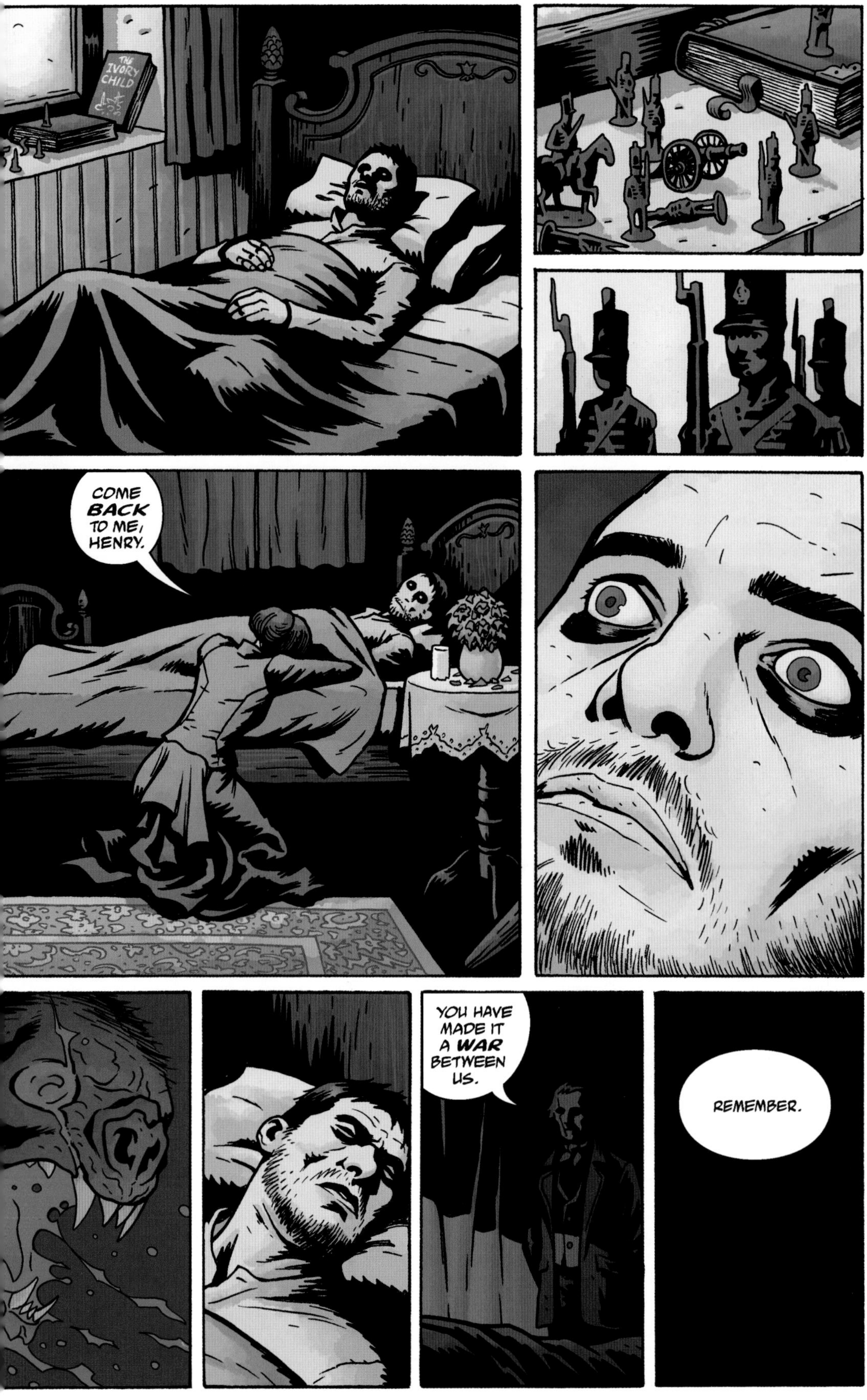
THE IVORY CHILD
COME BACK TO ME, HENRY.
YOU HAVE MADE IT A WAR BETWEEN US.
REMEMBER.

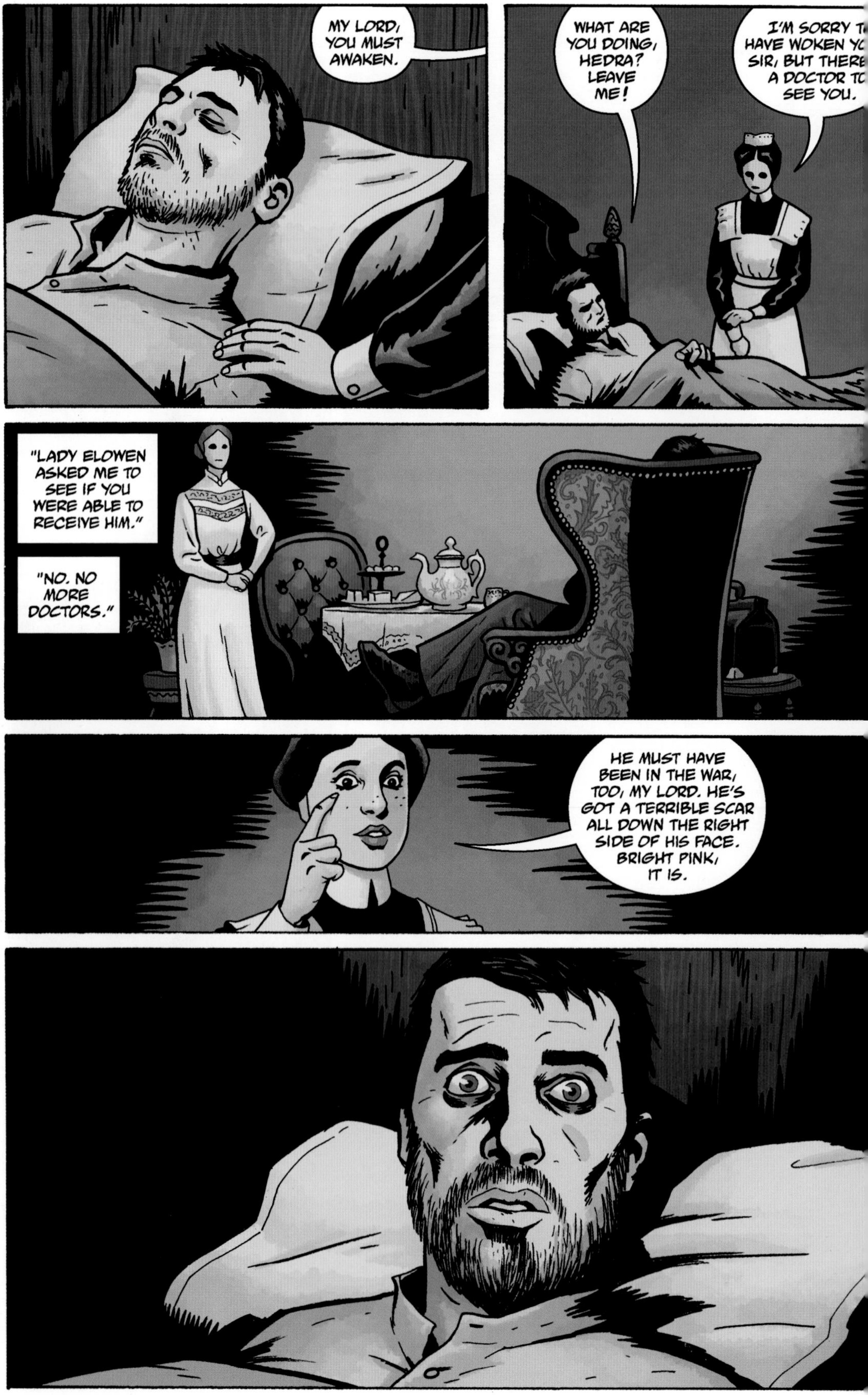

MY LORD, YOU MUST AWAKEN.
WHAT ARE YOU DOING, HEDRA? LEAVE ME!
I'M SORRY T HAVE WOKEN YO SIR, BUT THERE A DOCTOR TO SEE YOU.
"LADY ELOWEN ASKED ME TO SEE IF YOU WERE ABLE TO RECEIVE HIM."
"NO. NO MORE DOCTORS."
HE MUST HAVE BEEN IN THE WAR, TOO, MY LORD. HE'S GOT A TERRIBLE SCAR ALL DOWN THE RIGHT SIDE OF HIS FACE. BRIGHT PINK, IT IS.

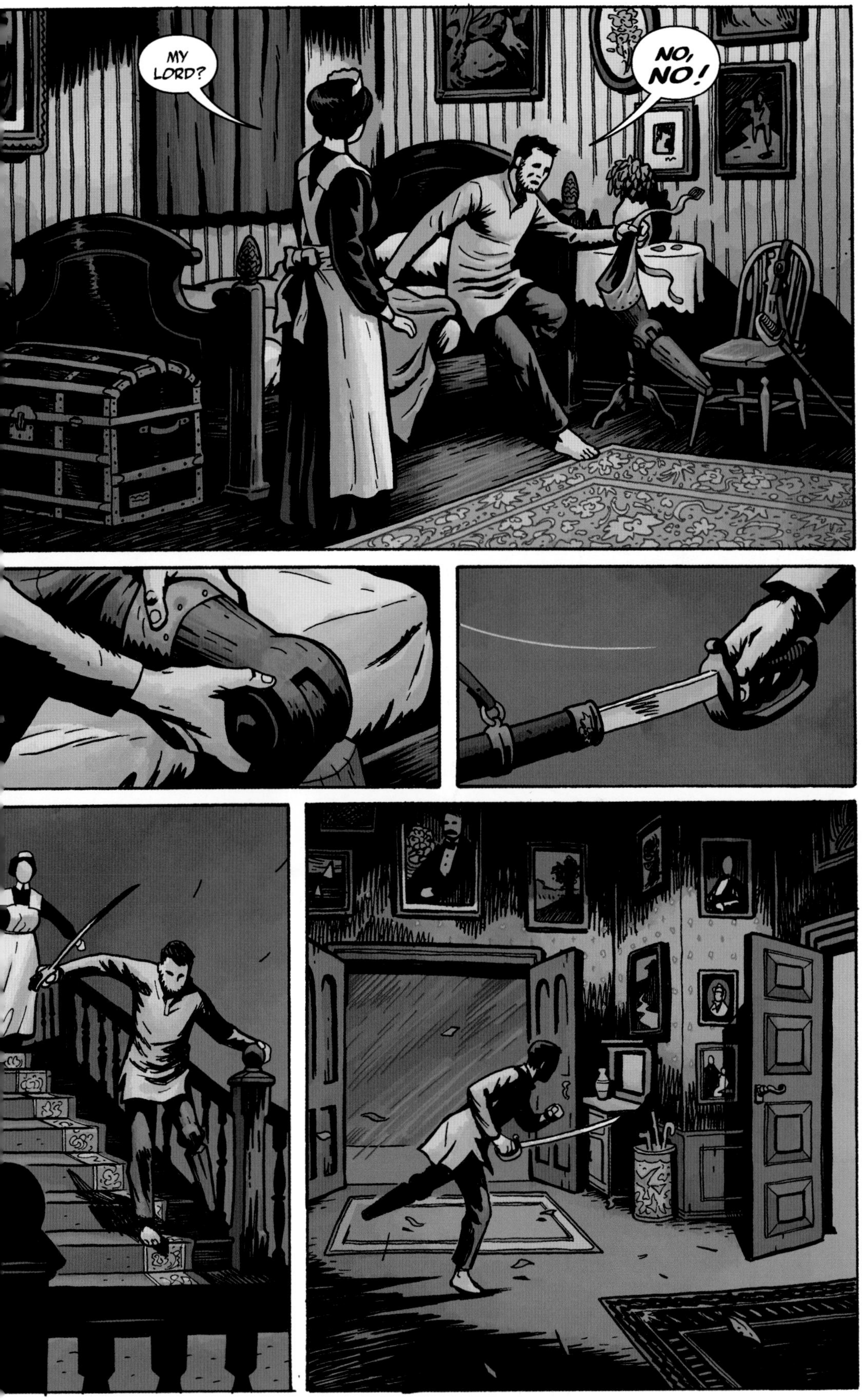
MY LORD?
NO, NO!

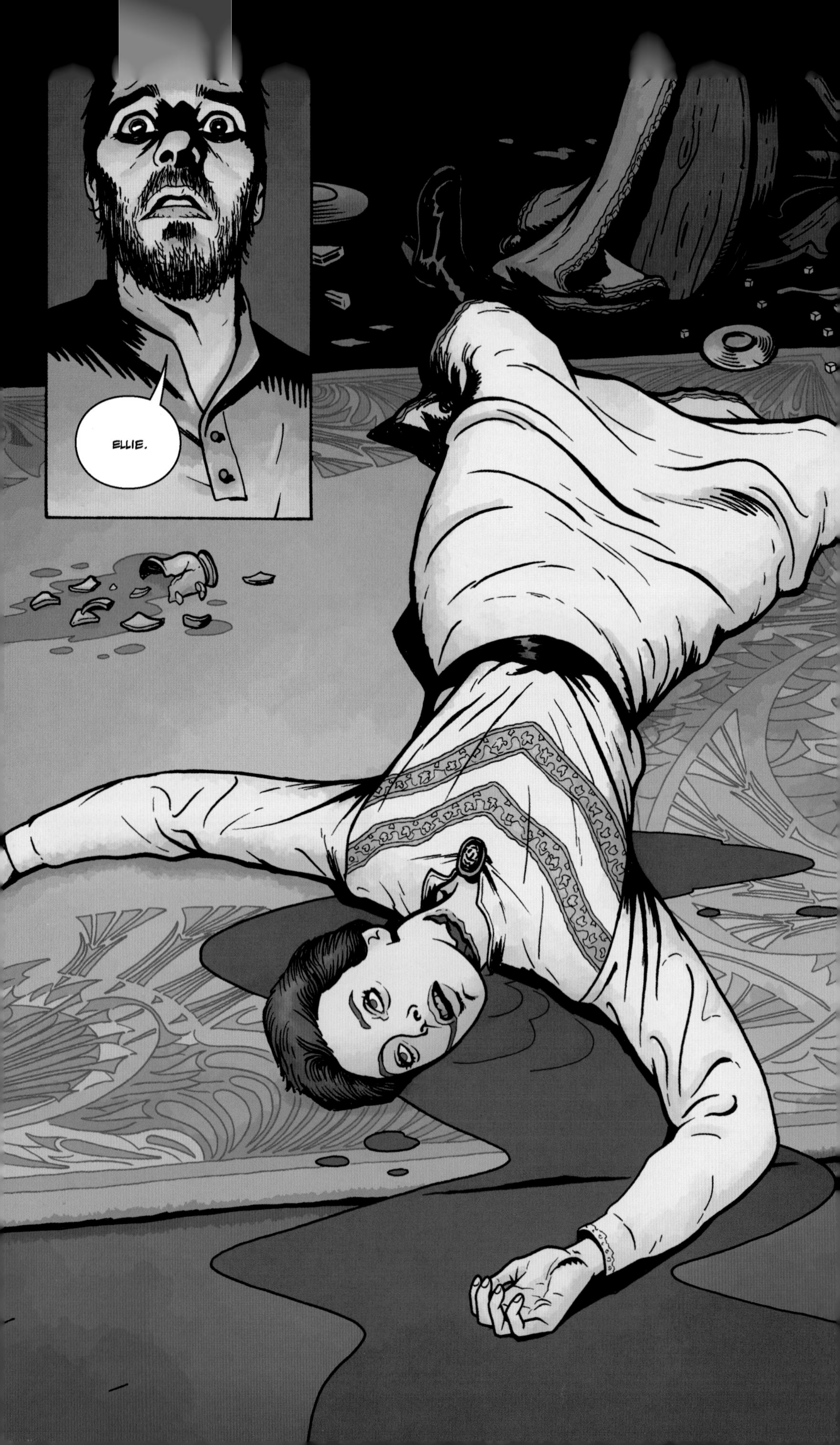
ELLIE.

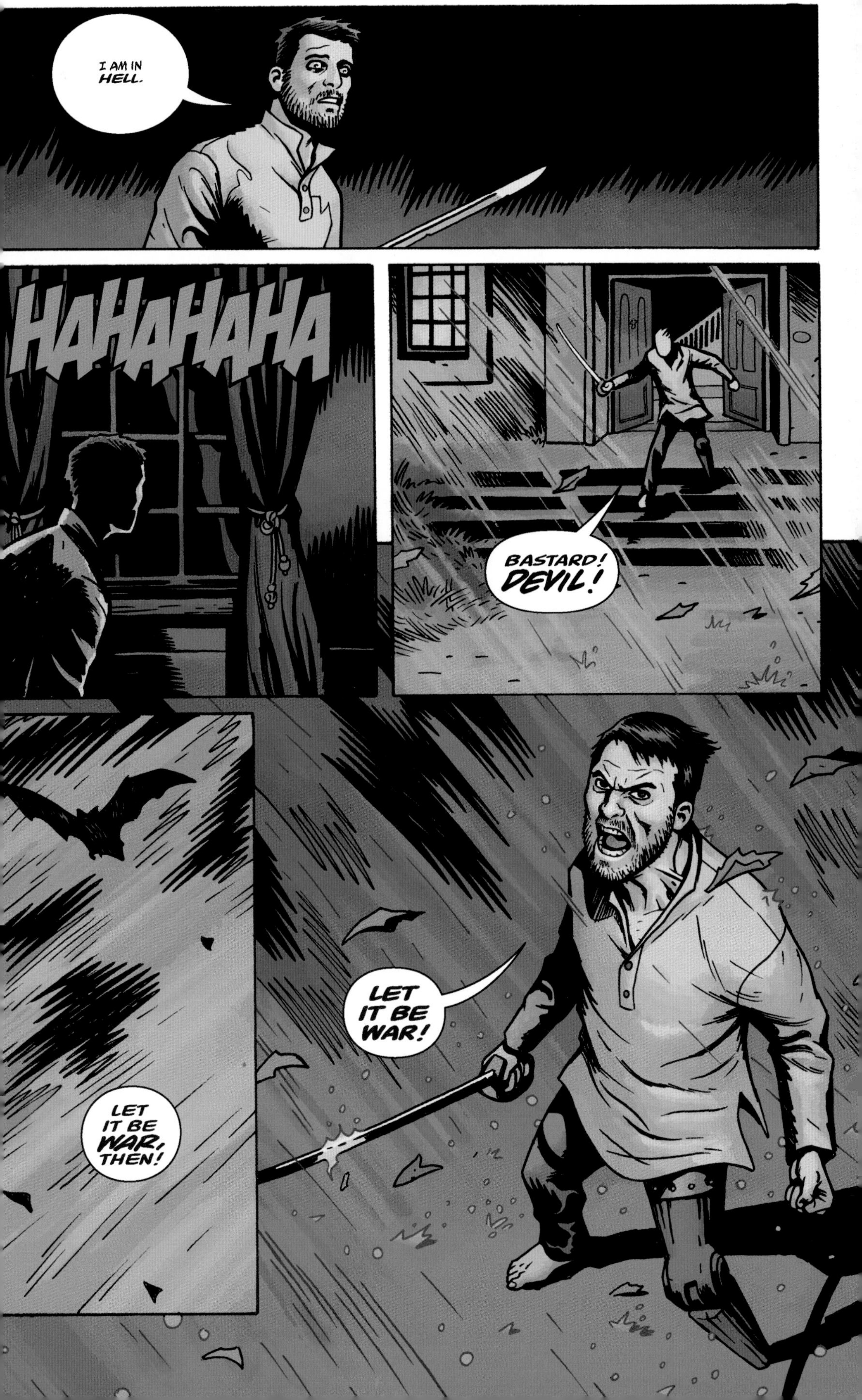
I AM IN HELL.
HAHAHAHA
BASTARD! DEVIL!
LET IT BE WAR!
LET IT BE WAR, THEN!

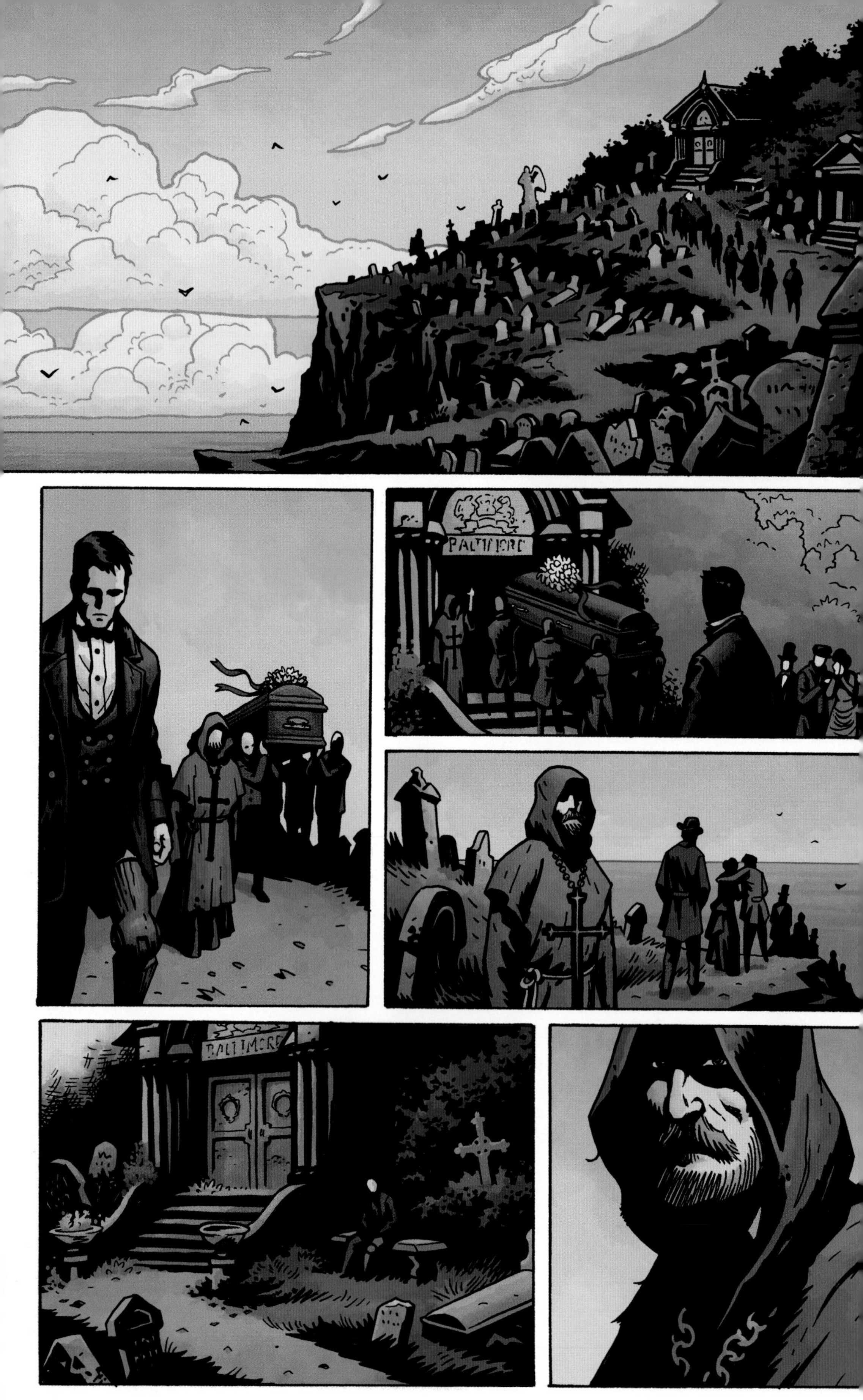
BALTIMORE

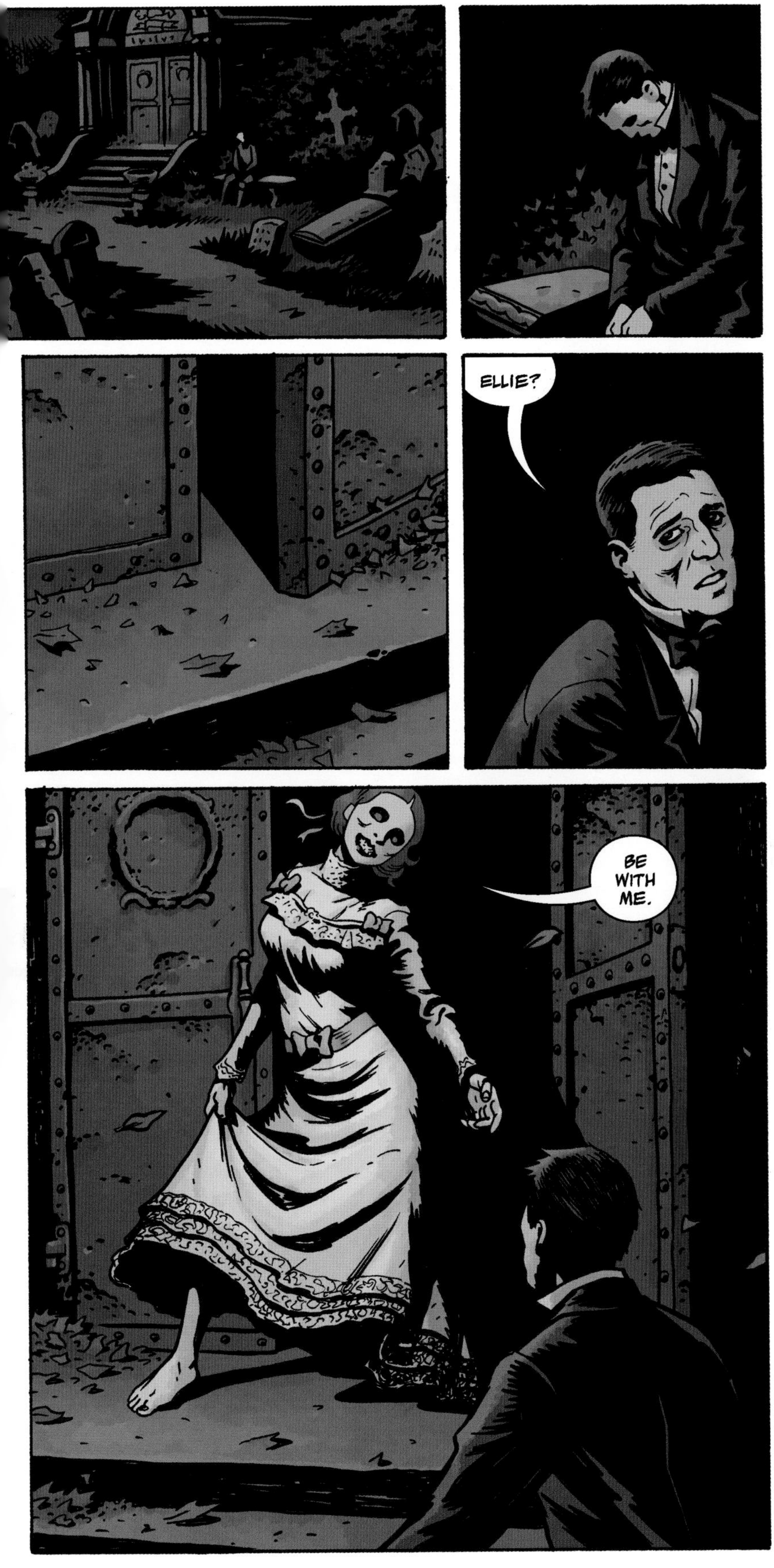
ELLIE?
BE WITH ME.

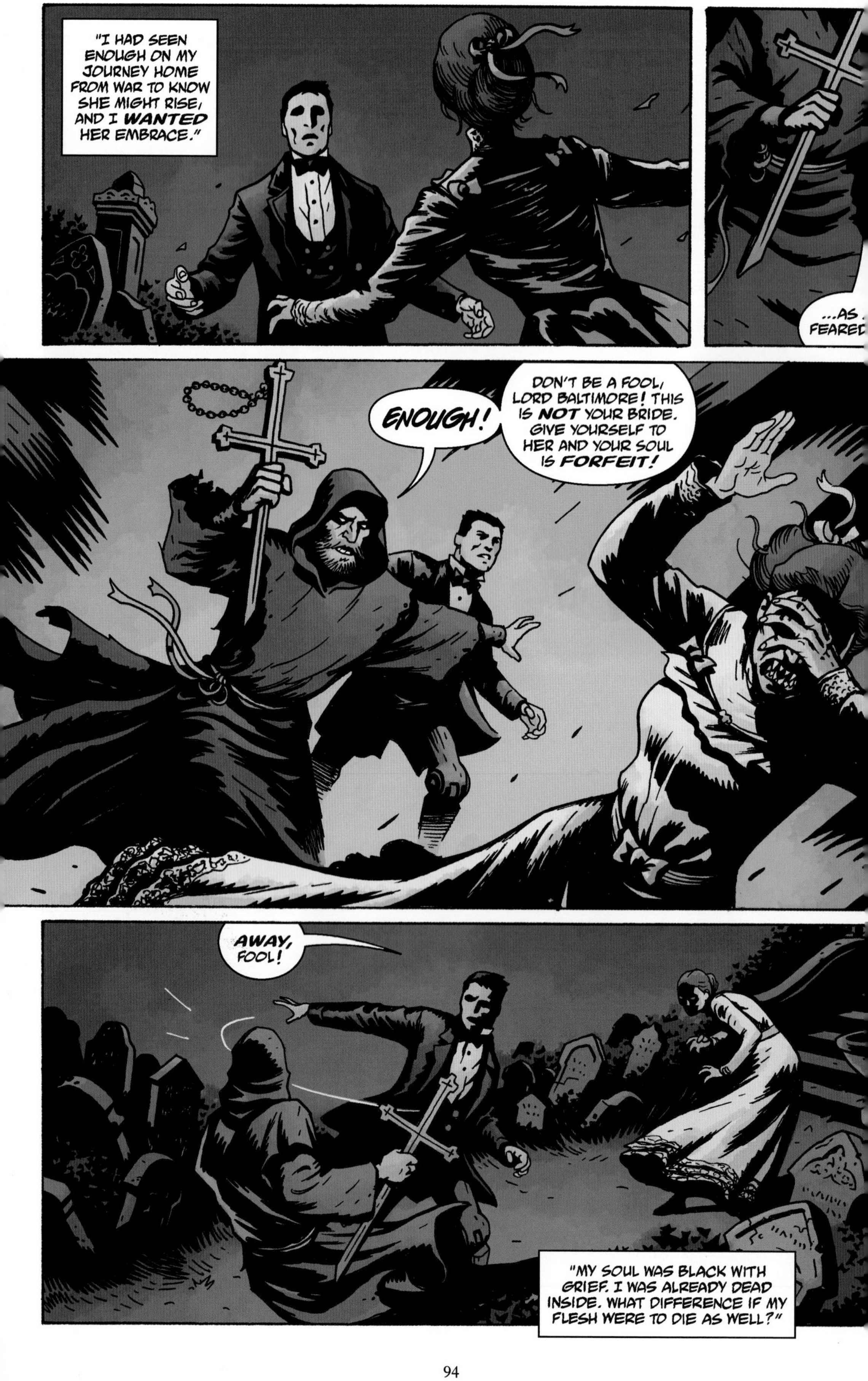
"I HAD SEEN ENOUGH ON MY JOURNEY HOME FROM WAR TO KNOW SHE MIGHT RISE, AND I WANTED HER EMBRACE."
...AS
FEARED
ENOUGH!
DON'T BE A FOOL, LORD BALTIMORE! THIS IS NOT YOUR BRIDE. GIVE YOURSELF TO HER AND YOUR SOUL IS FORFEIT!
AWAY, FOOL!
"MY SOUL WAS BLACK WITH GRIEF. I WAS ALREADY DEAD INSIDE. WHAT DIFFERENCE IF MY FLESH WERE TO DIE AS WELL?"

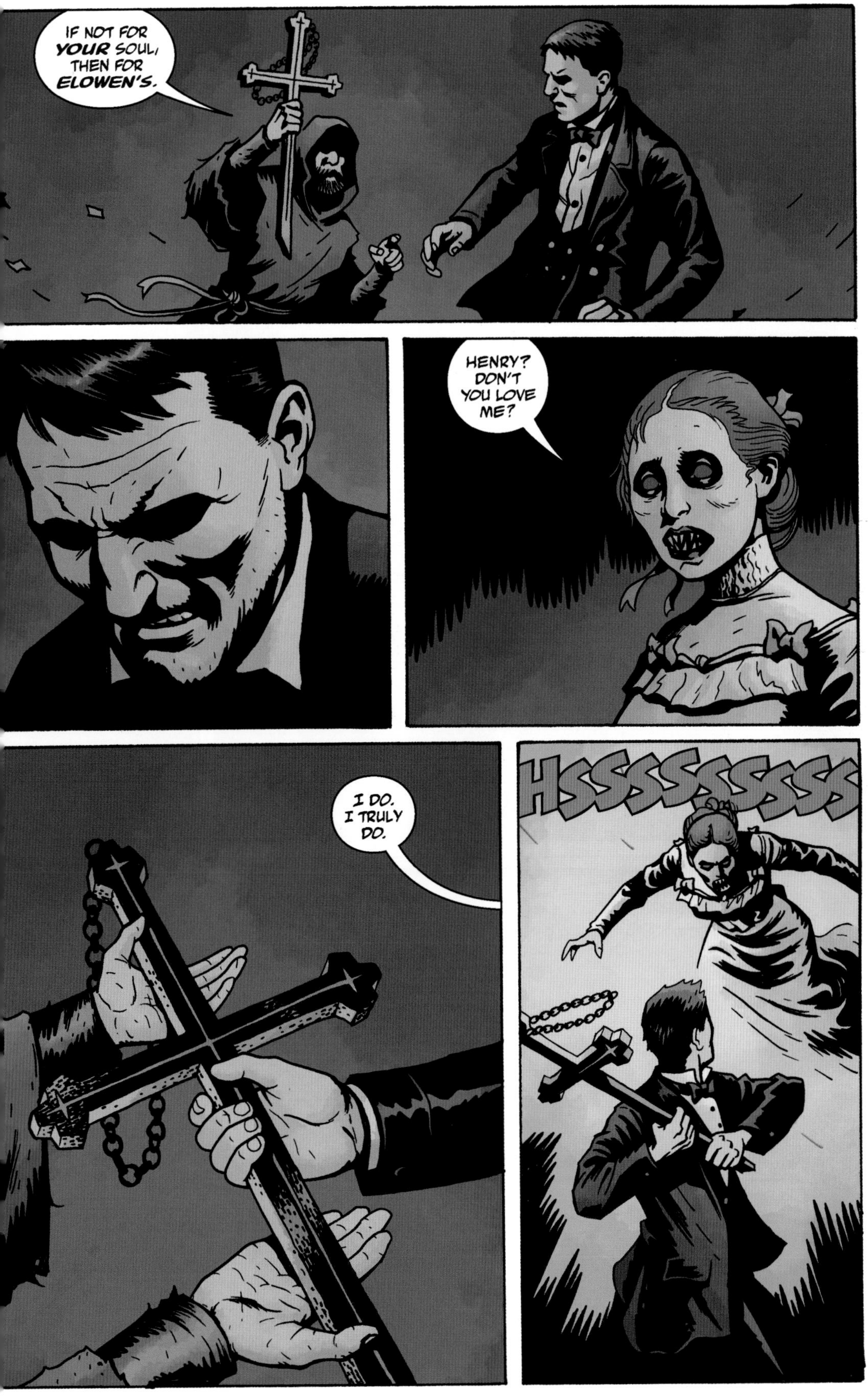
IF NOT FOR YOUR SOUL, THEN FOR ELOWEN'S.
HENRY? DON'T YOU LOVE ME?
I DO. I TRULY DO.
HSSSSSSSSS

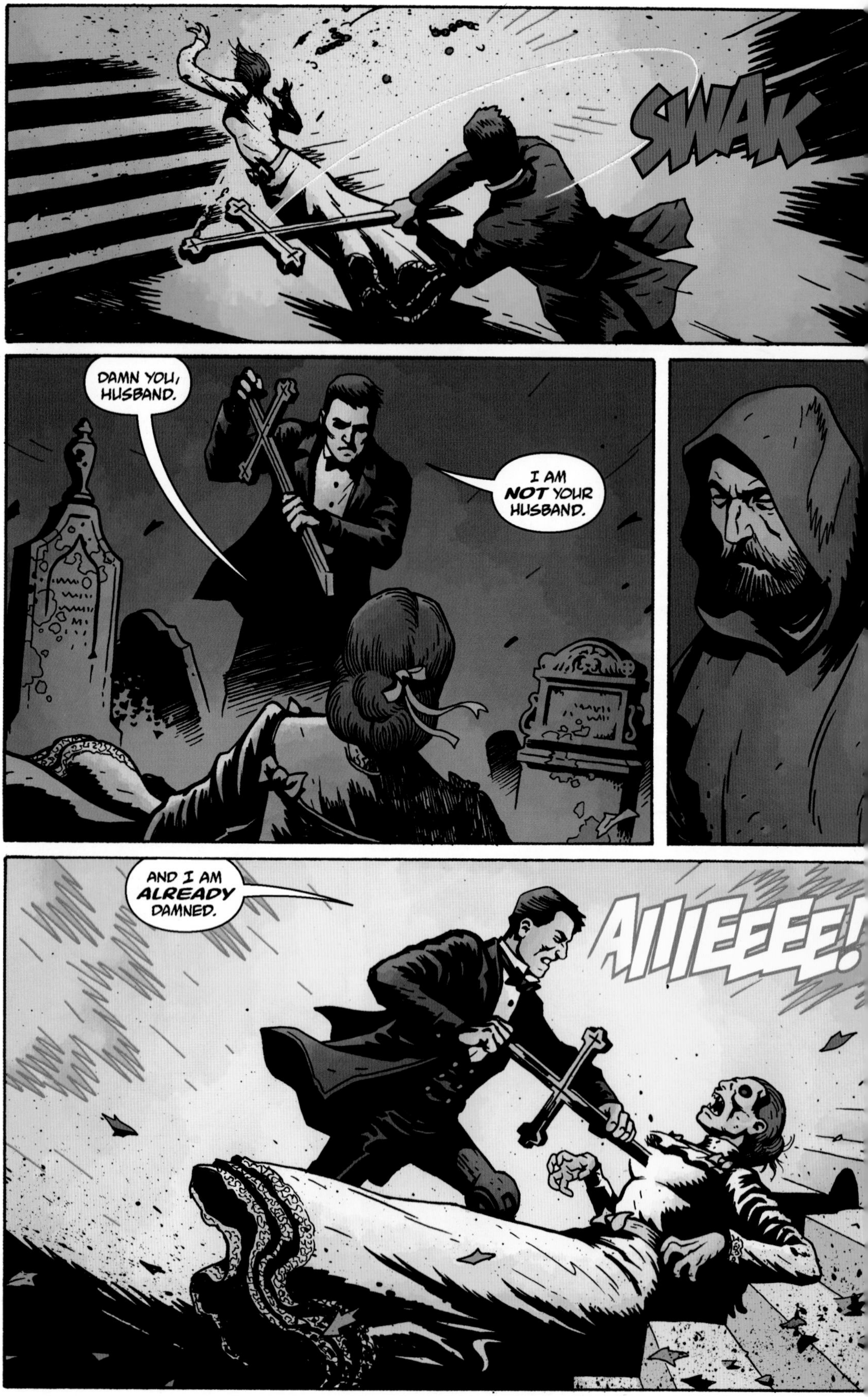
SWAK
DAMN YOU, HUSBAND.
I AM NOT YOUR HUSBAND.
AND I AM ALREADY DAMNED.
AIIEEEE!

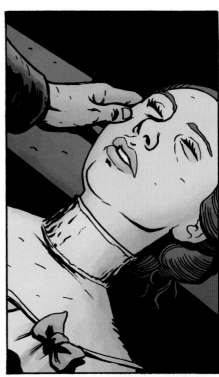

IT ISN'T OVER YET. THERE IS WORK STILL TO BE DONE IF YOU WISH FOR HER TRULY TO BE AT REST.

I HAVE SEEN MANY THINGS SINCE THIS PLAGUE BEGAN, MONK. I KNOW WHAT MUST BE DONE.

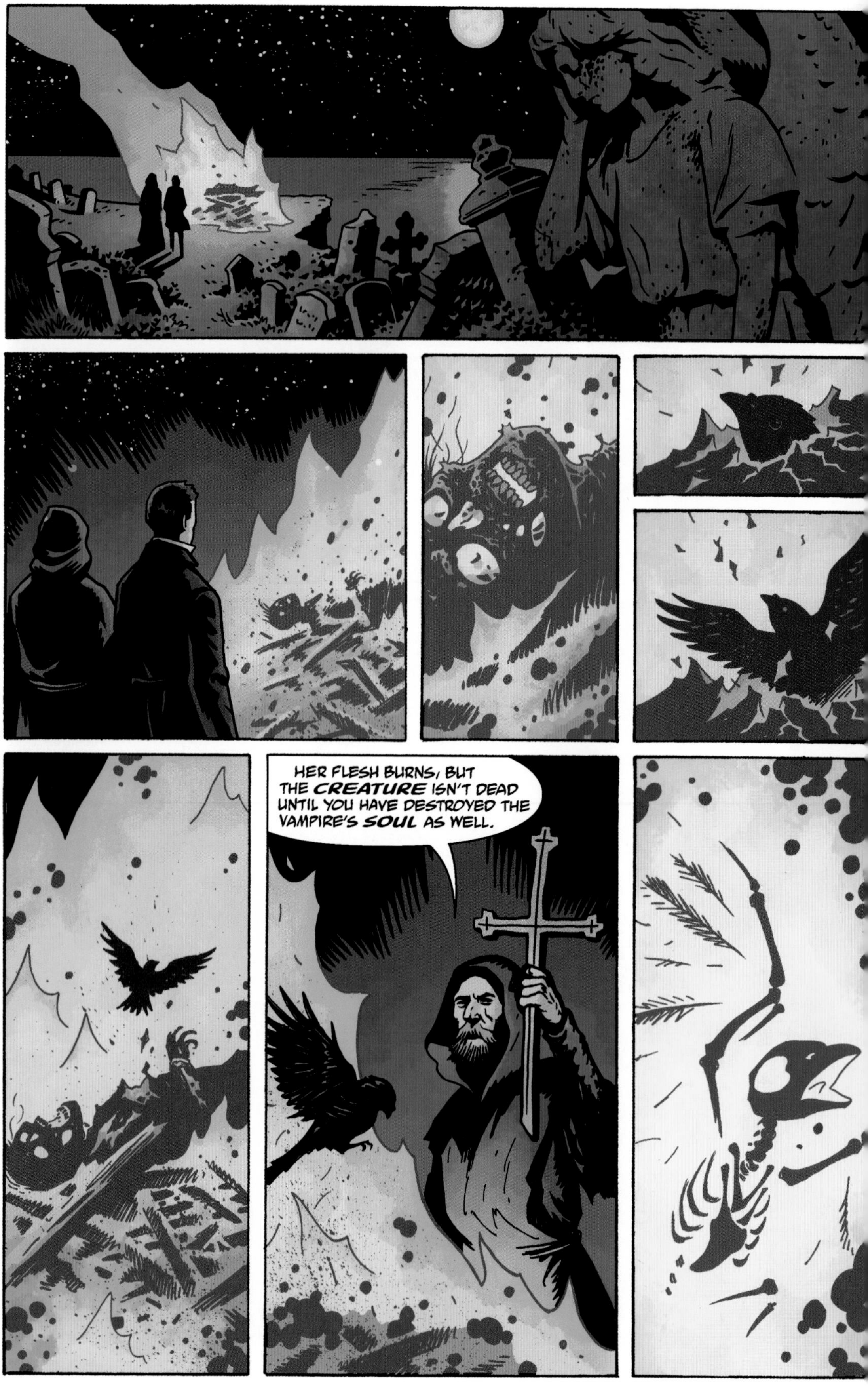
HER FLESH BURNS, BUT THE CREATURE ISN'T DEAD UNTIL YOU HAVE DESTROYED THE VAMPIRE'S SOUL AS WELL.

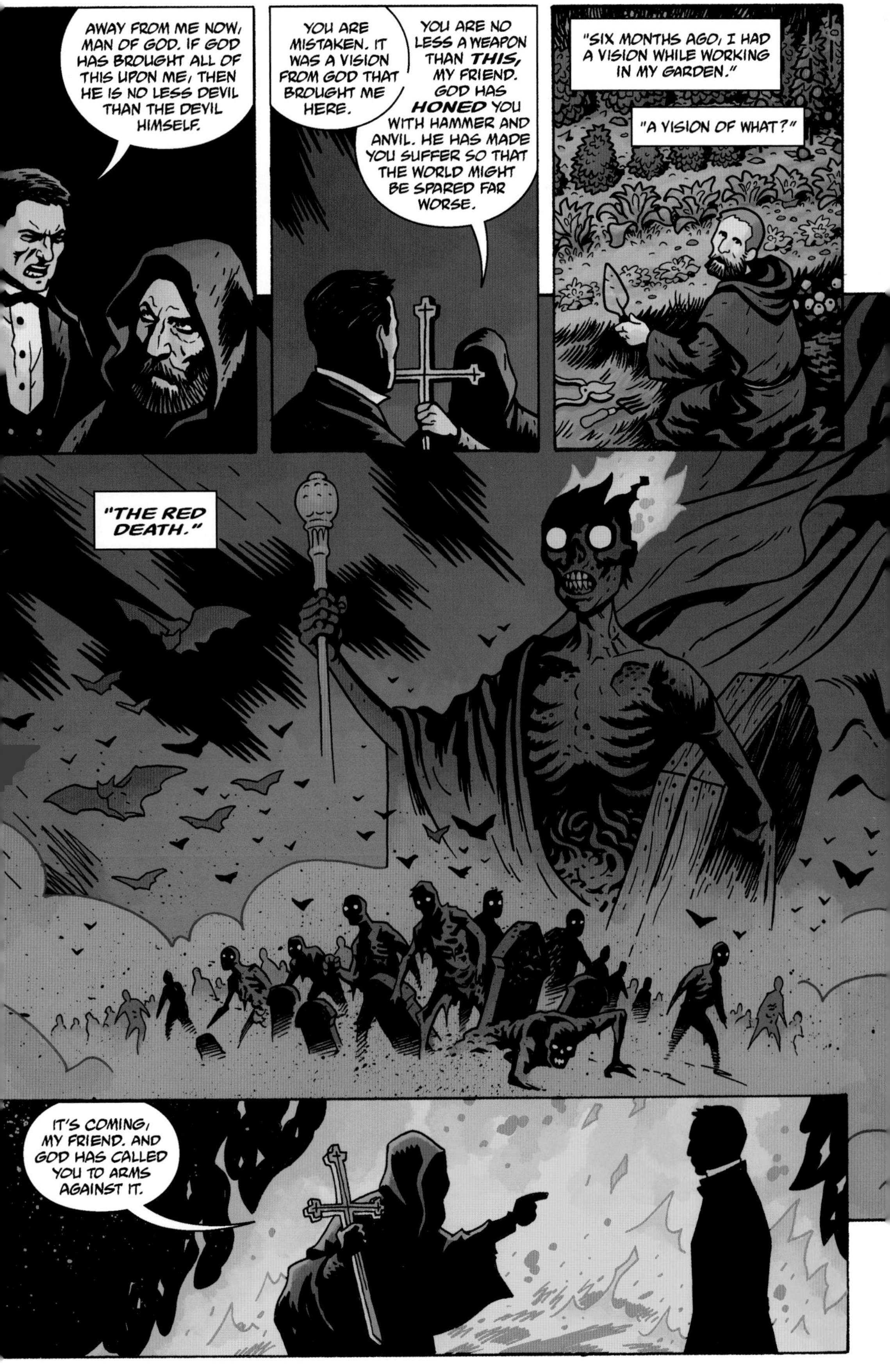
AWAY FROM ME NOW, MAN OF GOD. IF GOD HAS BROUGHT ALL OF THIS UPON ME, THEN HE IS NO LESS DEVIL THAN THE DEVIL HIMSELF.
YOU ARE MISTAKEN. IT WAS A VISION FROM GOD THAT BROUGHT ME HERE.
YOU ARE NO LESS A WEAPON THAN **THIS,** MY FRIEND. GOD HAS **HONED** YOU WITH HAMMER AND ANVIL. HE HAS MADE YOU SUFFER SO THAT THE WORLD MIGHT BE SPARED FAR WORSE.
"SIX MONTHS AGO, I HAD A VISION WHILE WORKING IN MY GARDEN."
"A VISION OF WHAT?"
"THE RED DEATH."
IT'S COMING, MY FRIEND. AND GOD HAS CALLED YOU TO ARMS AGAINST IT.

AND YOU HAVE BEEN FIGHTING AGAINST THIS RISING EVIL EVER SINCE.

I HAVE BEEN HUNTING THE MONSTER THAT KILLED MY WIFE. THAT IS MY SOLE PURPOSE. IF GOD HAS SOME *OTHER* MISSION, HE MUST FIND HIS *OWN* SOLDIERS.

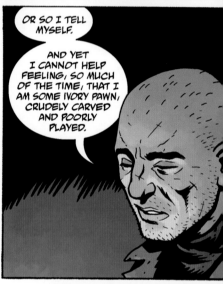

OR SO I TELL MYSELF.

AND YET I CANNOT HELP FEELING, SO MUCH OF THE TIME, THAT I AM SOME IVORY PAWN, CRUDELY CARVED AND POORLY PLAYED.

BUT SLEEP, NOW, VANESSA. WE'LL BE ALL RIGHT.

THERE ARE NO MORE ENEMIES HERE.

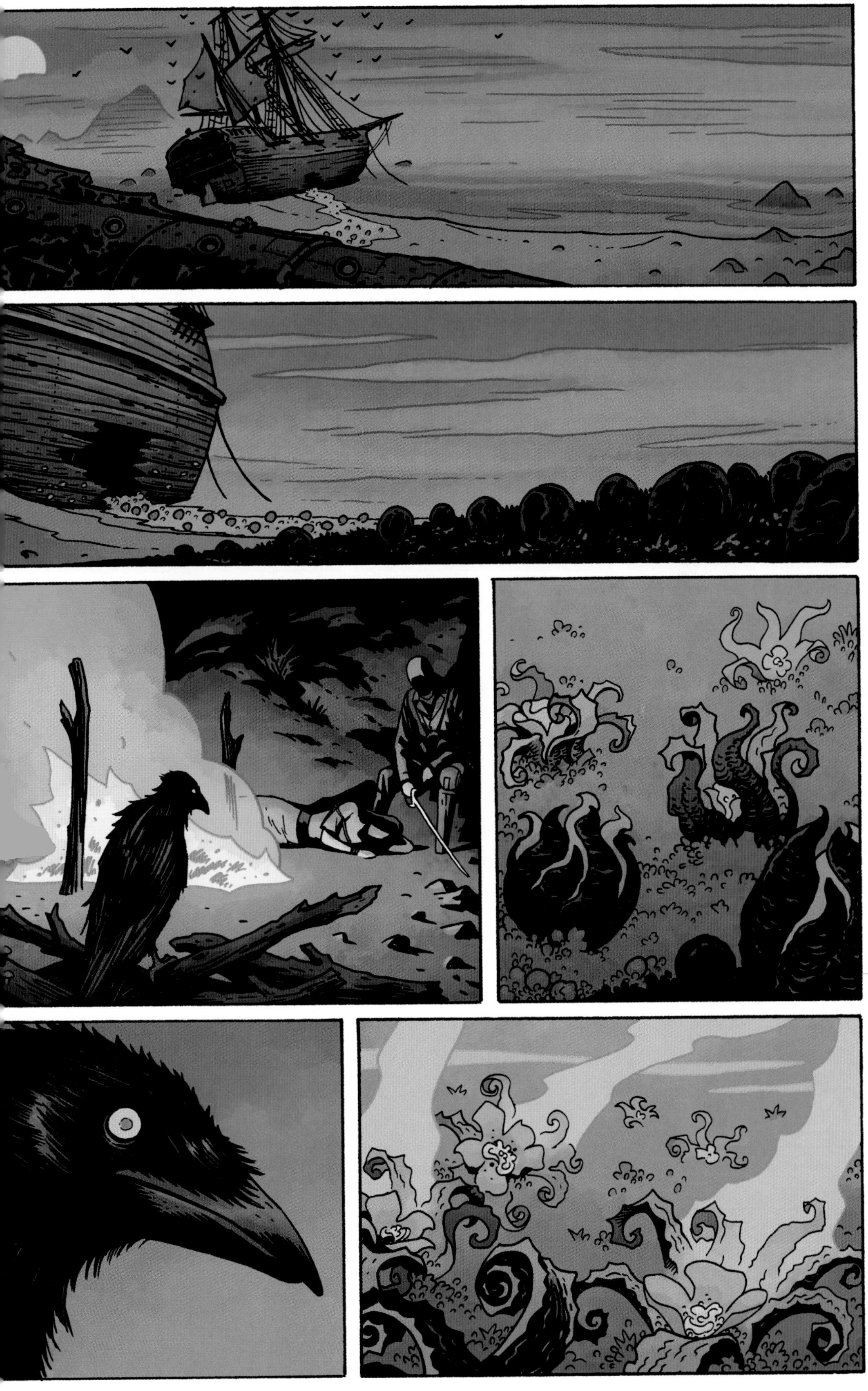

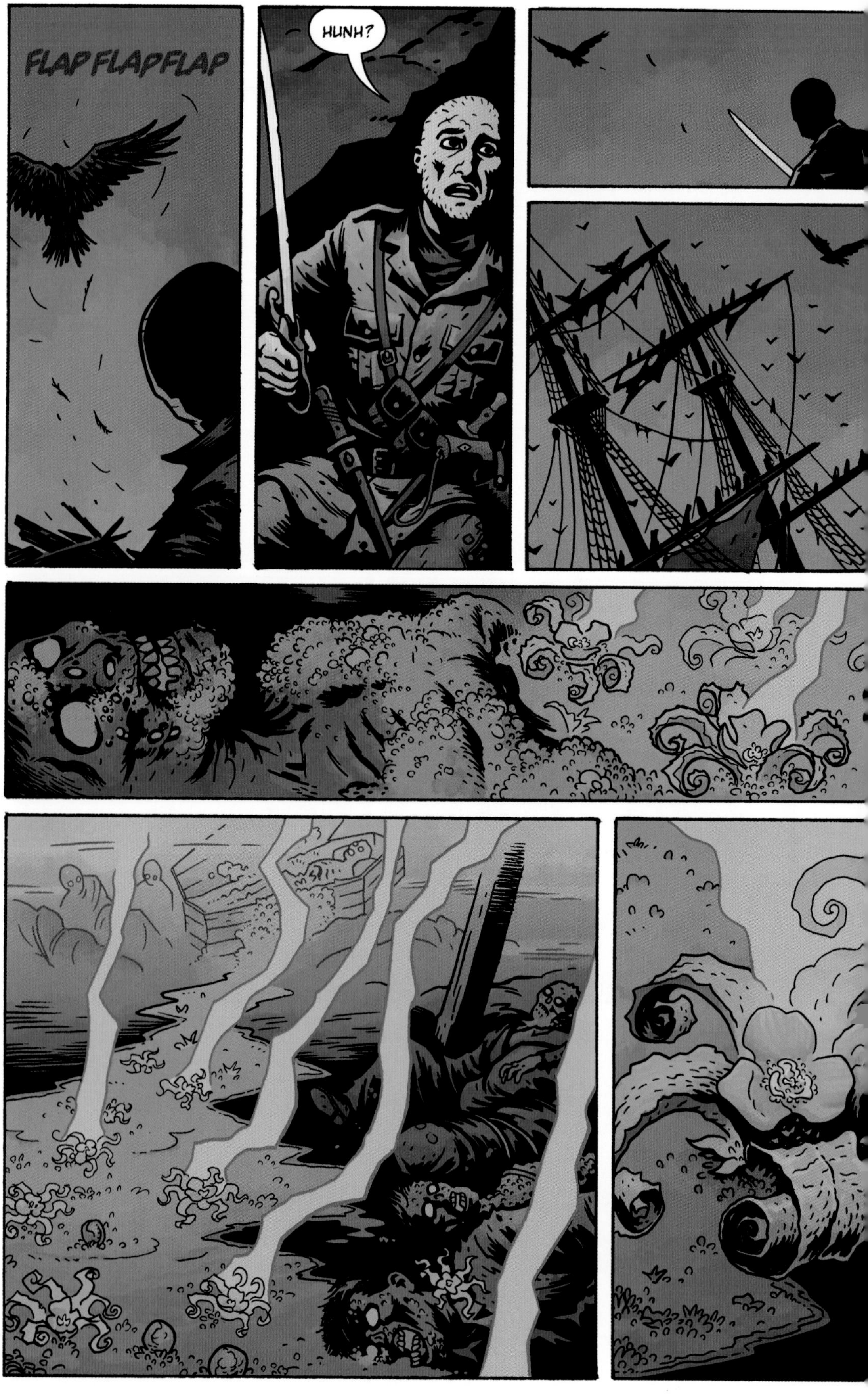
FLAP FLAP FLAP
HUNH?

CHAPTER FIVE

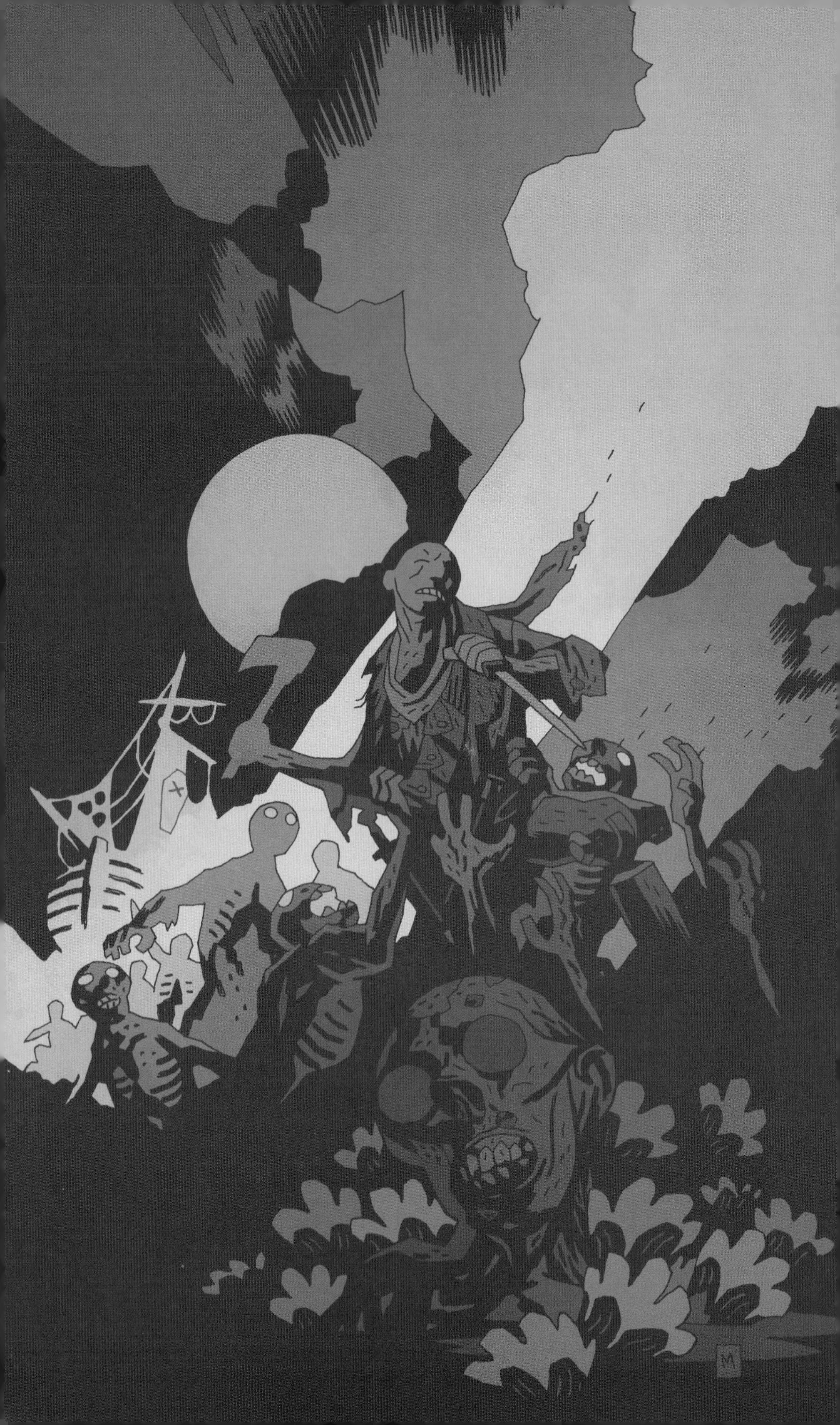

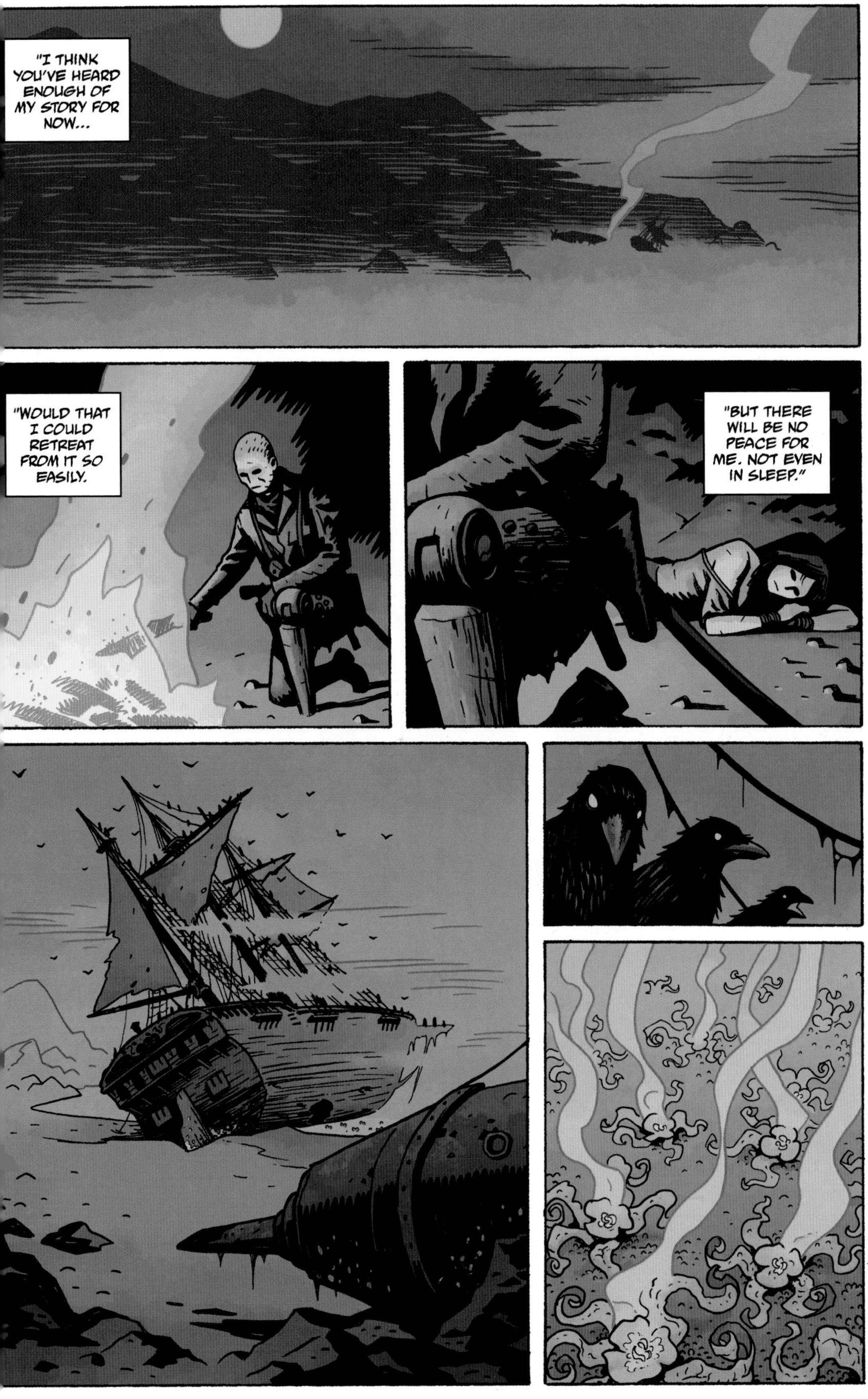
"I THINK YOU'VE HEARD ENOUGH OF MY STORY FOR NOW...
"WOULD THAT I COULD RETREAT FROM IT SO EASILY.
"BUT THERE WILL BE NO PEACE FOR ME. NOT EVEN IN SLEEP."

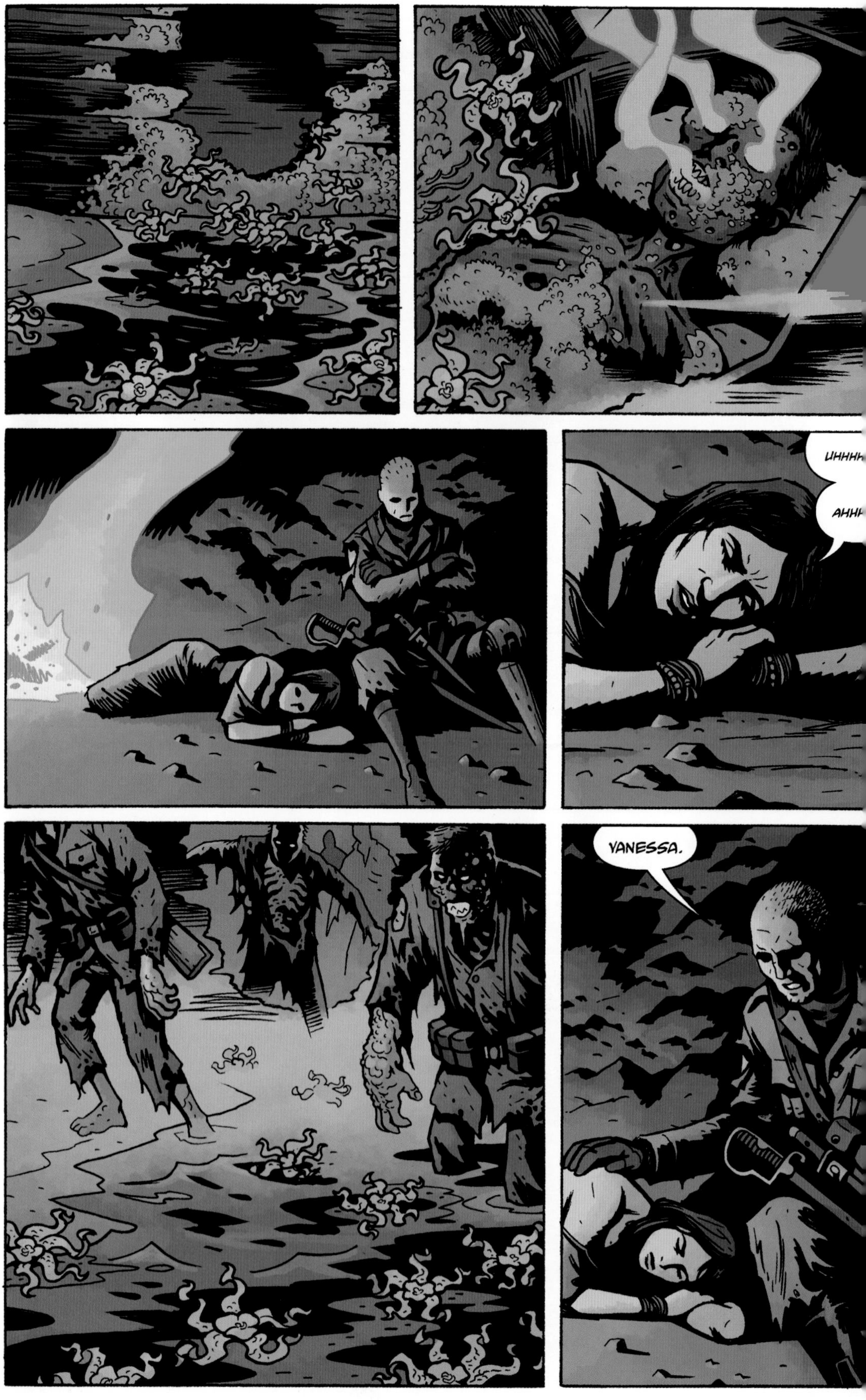
UHHHH
AHH
VANESSA.

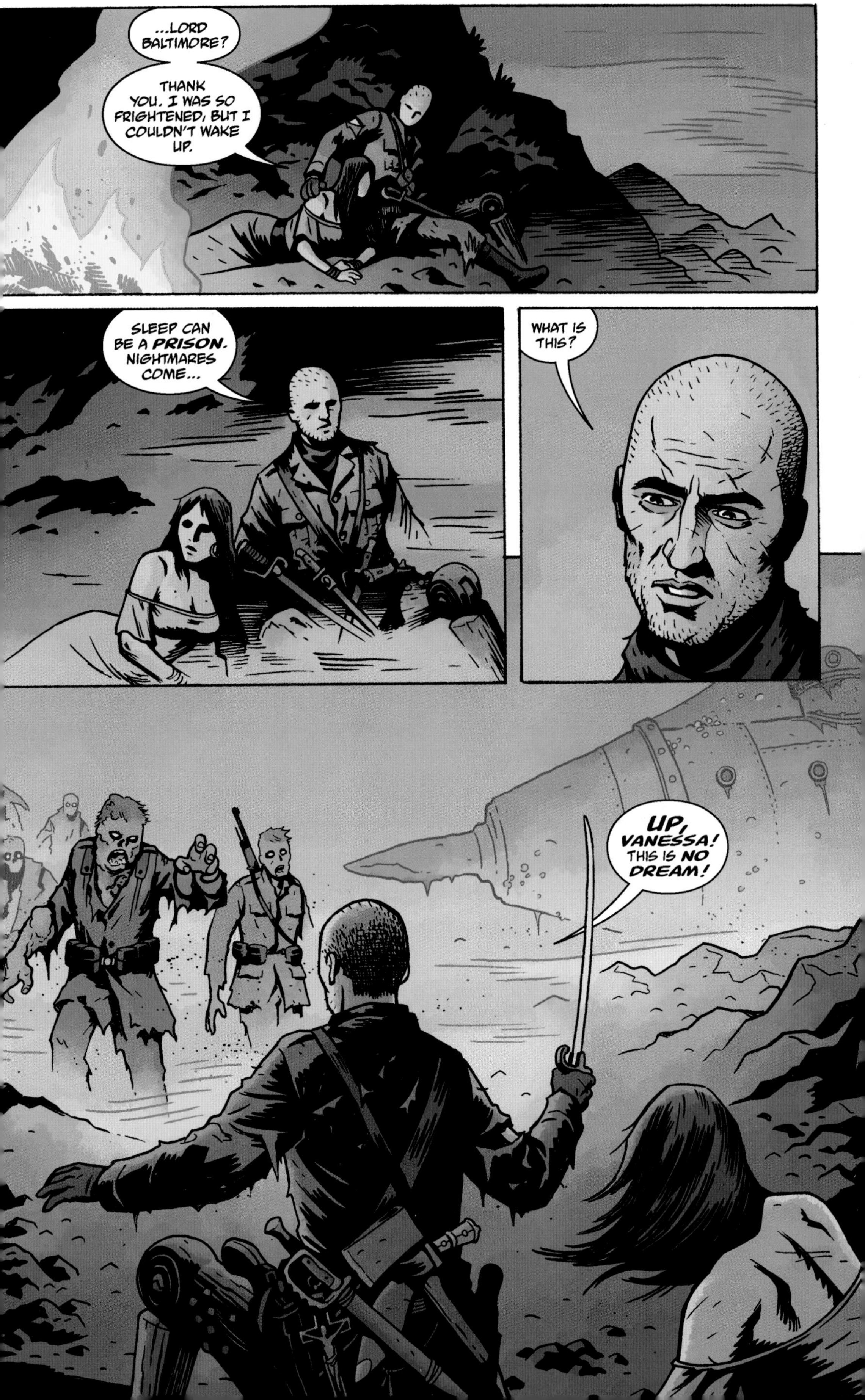
...LORD BALTIMORE?
THANK YOU. I WAS SO FRIGHTENED, BUT I COULDN'T WAKE UP.
SLEEP CAN BE A **PRISON**. NIGHTMARES COME...
WHAT IS THIS?
UP, VANESSA! THIS IS **NO DREAM!**

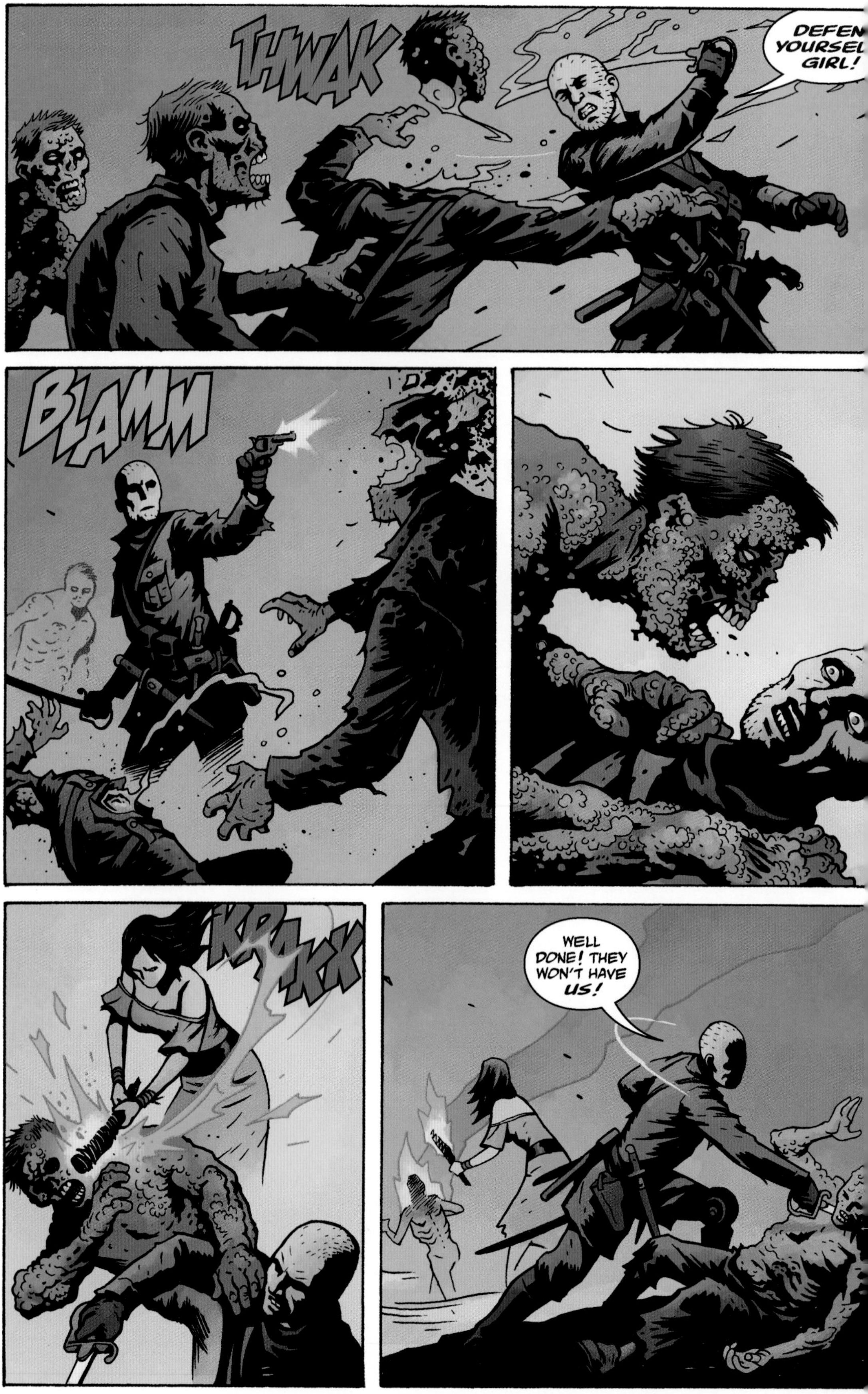
THWAK
DEFEN YOURSEL GIRL!
BLAMM
KRAKK
WELL DONE! THEY WON'T HAVE US!

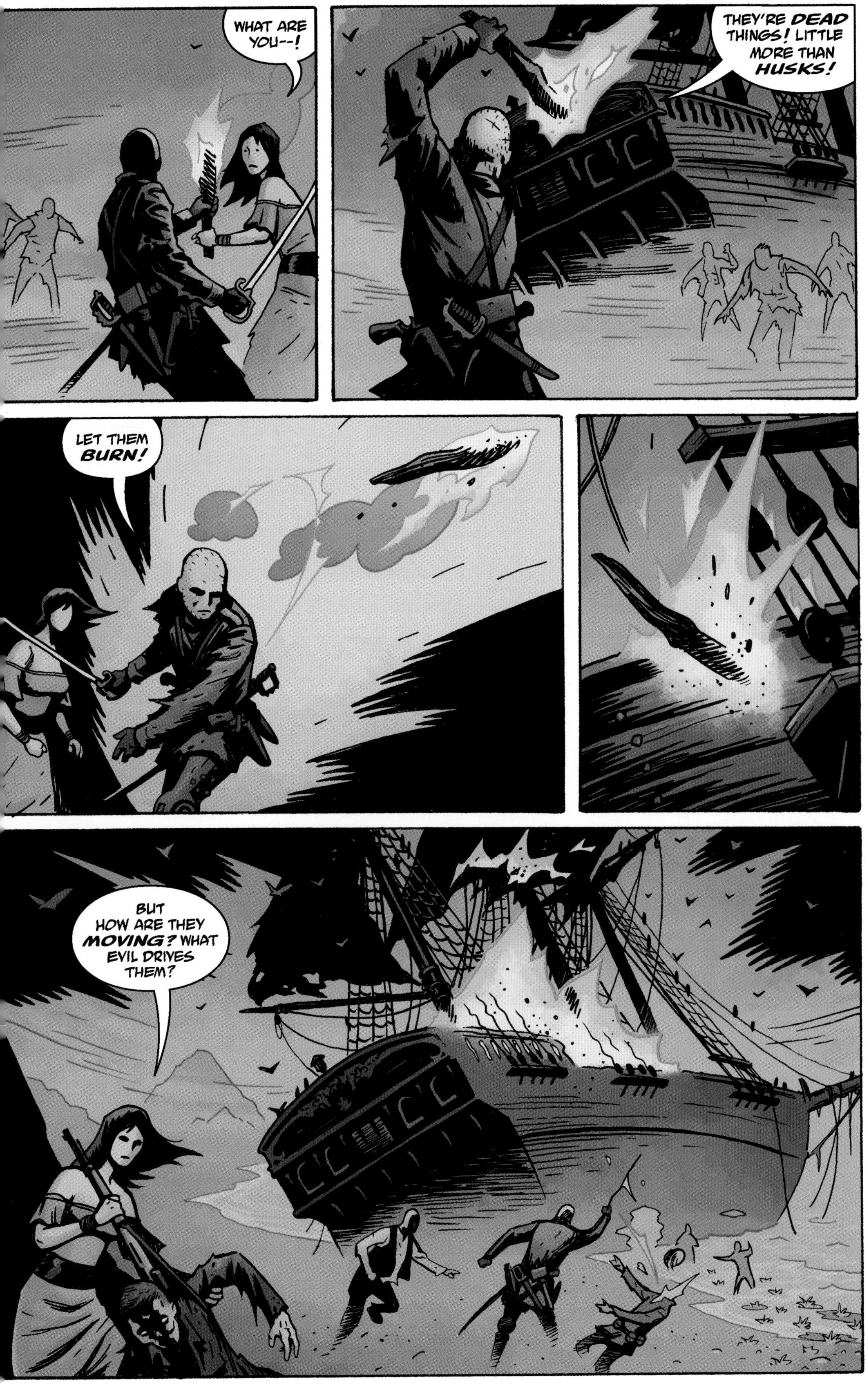
WHAT ARE YOU--!
THEY'RE DEAD THINGS! LITTLE MORE THAN HUSKS!
LET THEM BURN!
BUT HOW ARE THEY MOVING? WHAT EVIL DRIVES THEM?

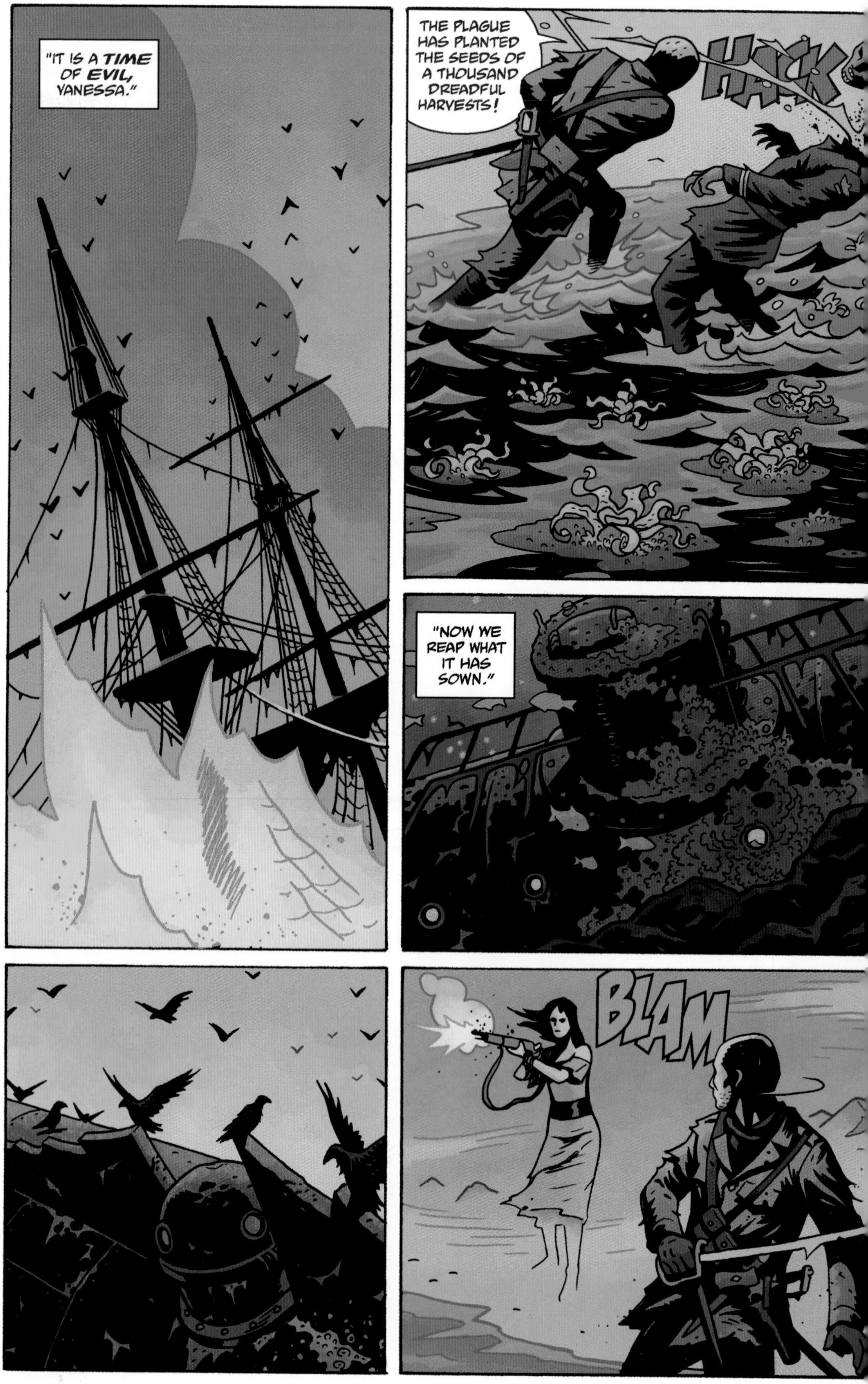

"IT IS A TIME OF EVIL, VANESSA."
THE PLAGUE HAS PLANTED THE SEEDS OF A THOUSAND DREADFUL HARVESTS!
HACK
"NOW WE REAP WHAT IT HAS SOWN."
BLAM

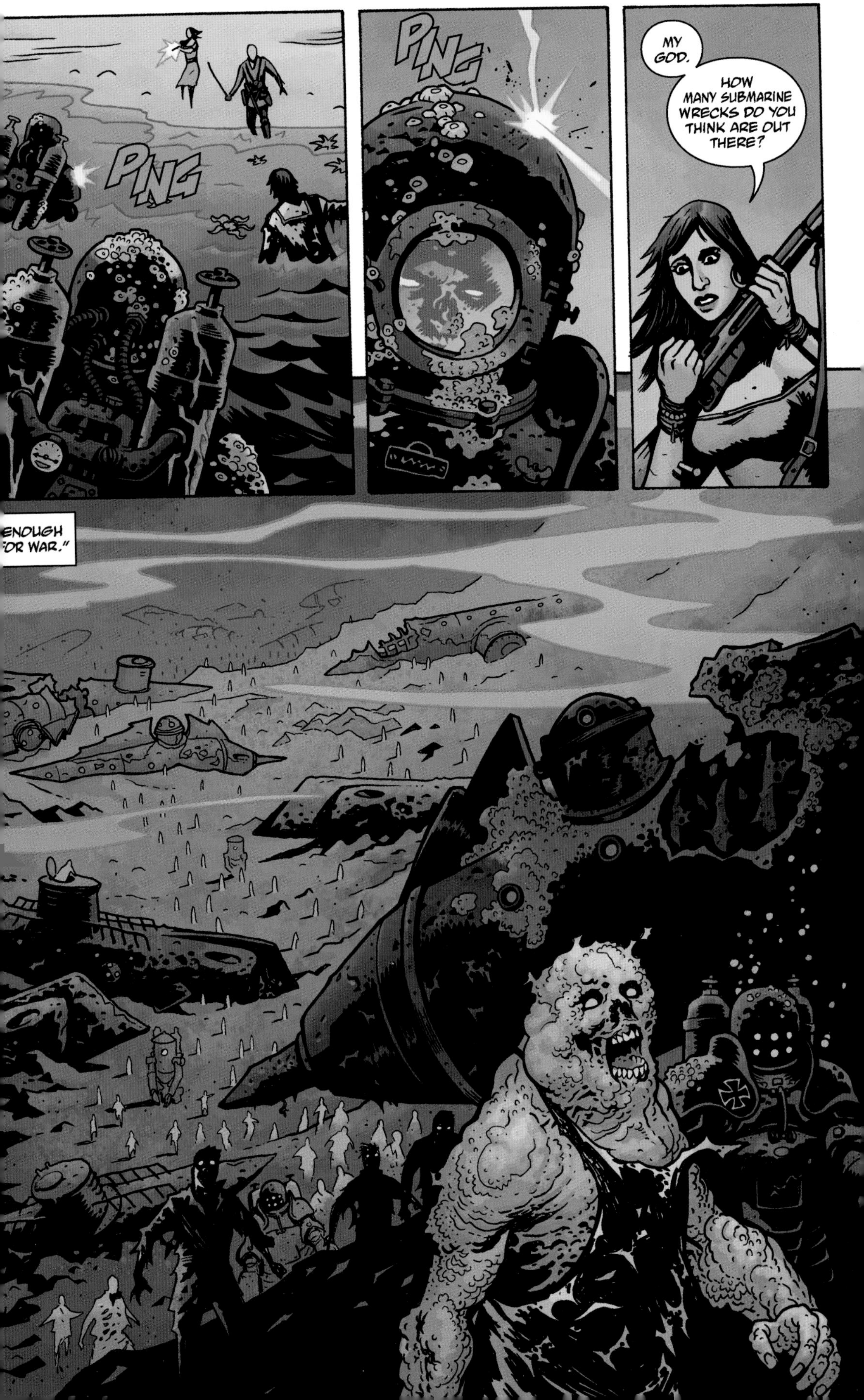
PING
PING
MY GOD.
HOW MANY SUBMARINE WRECKS DO YOU THINK ARE OUT THERE?
ENOUGH FOR WAR."

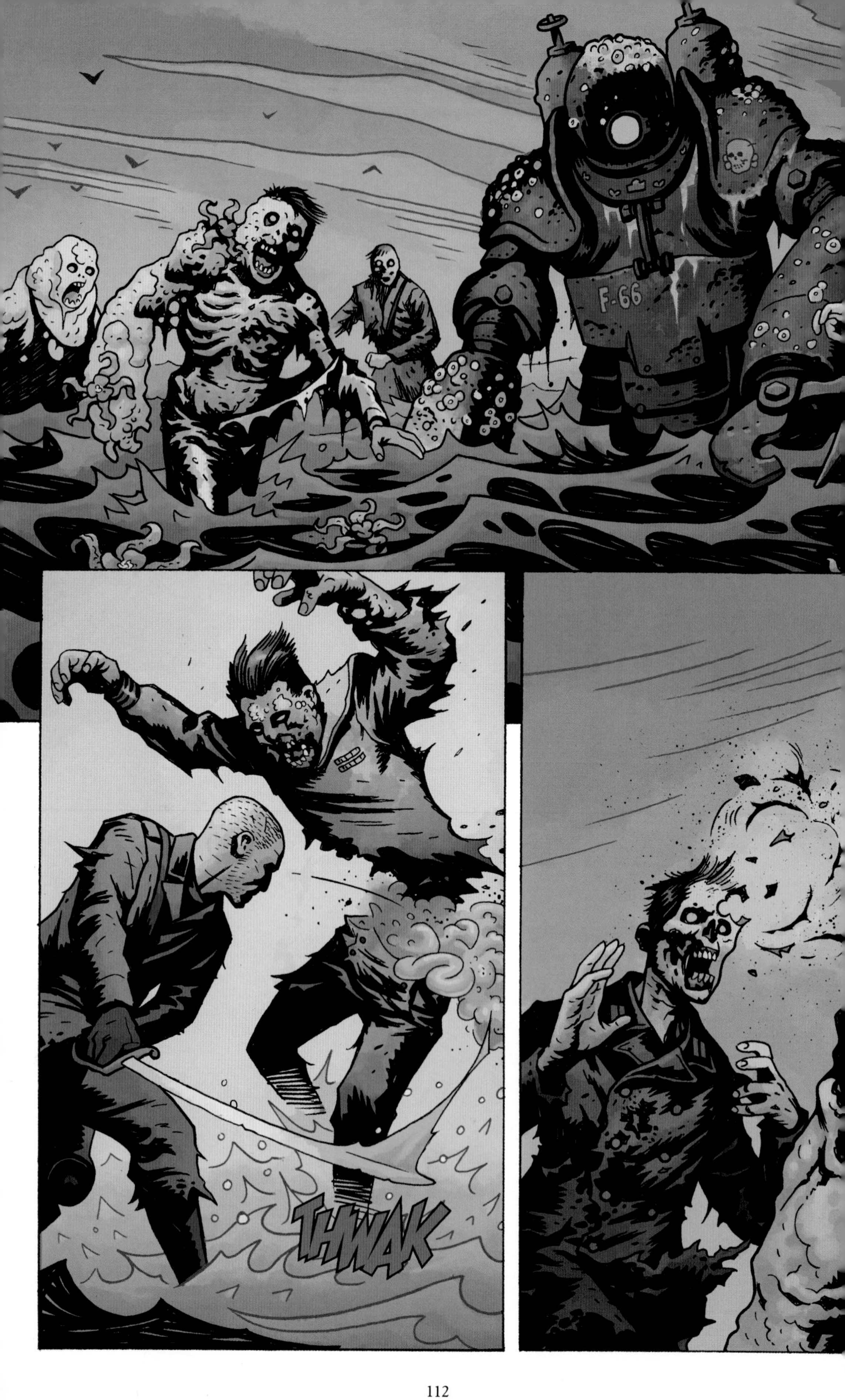
F-66
THWAK

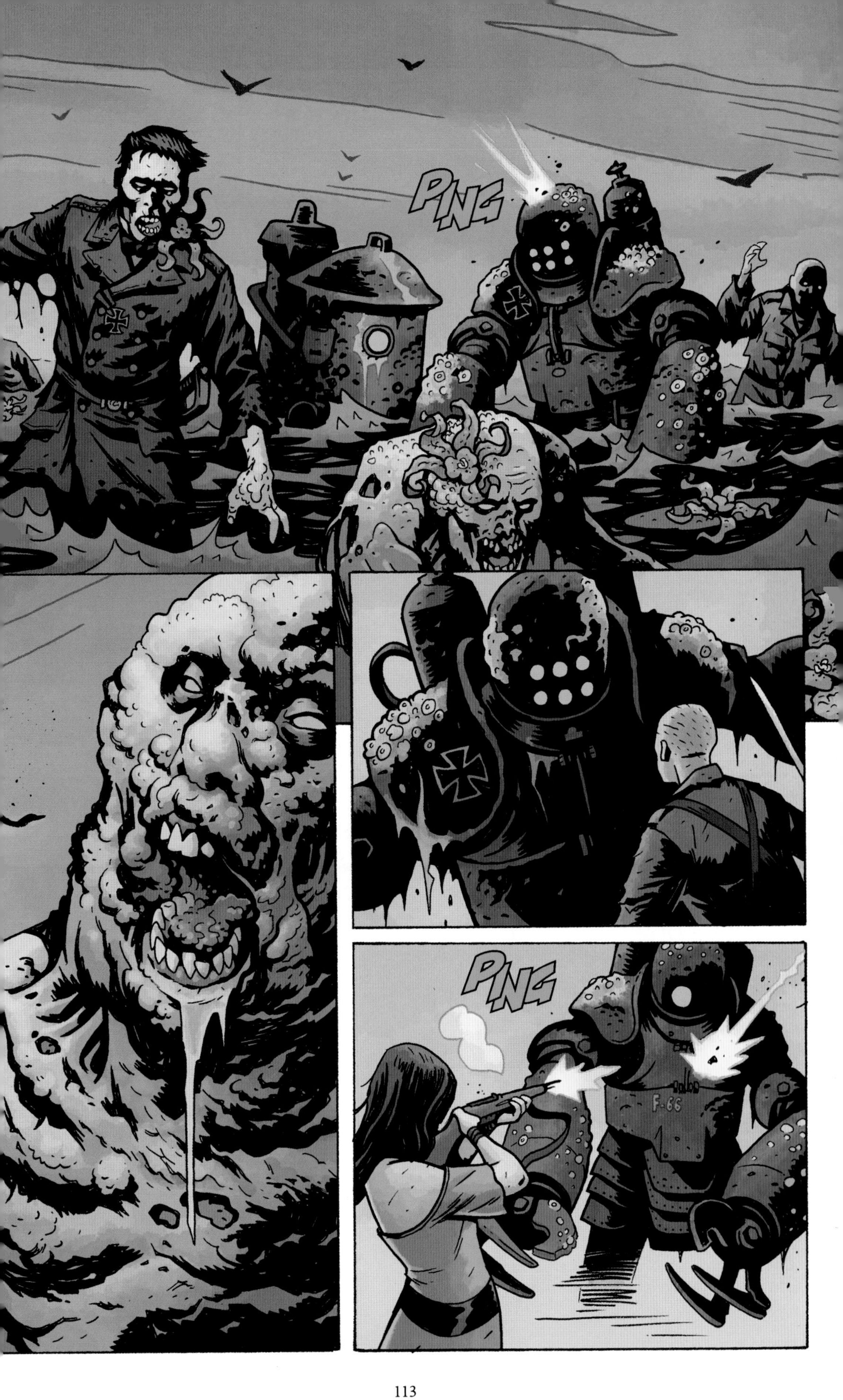
PING
PING
F-66

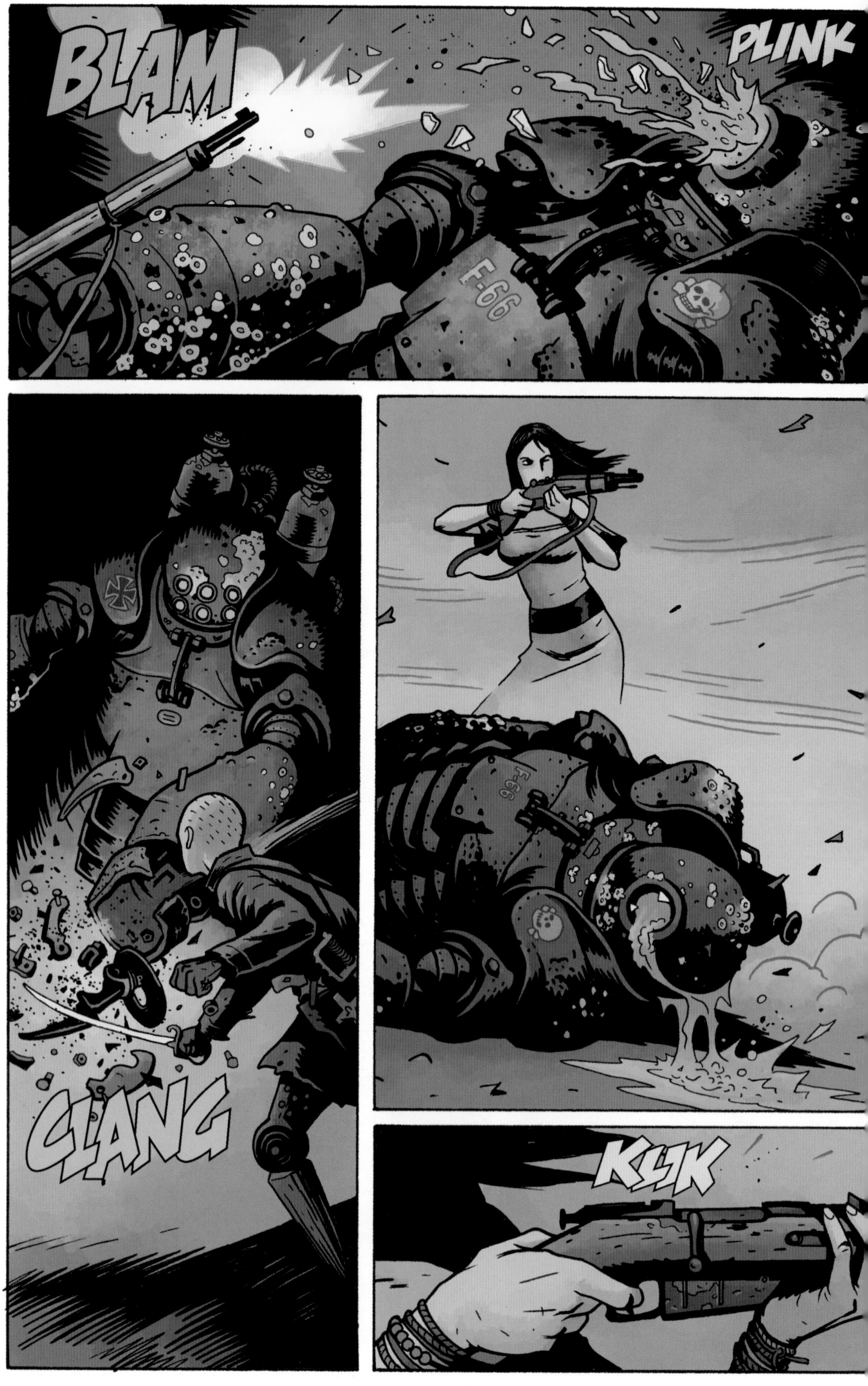
BLAM
PLINK
F-66
CLANG
F-66
KLIK

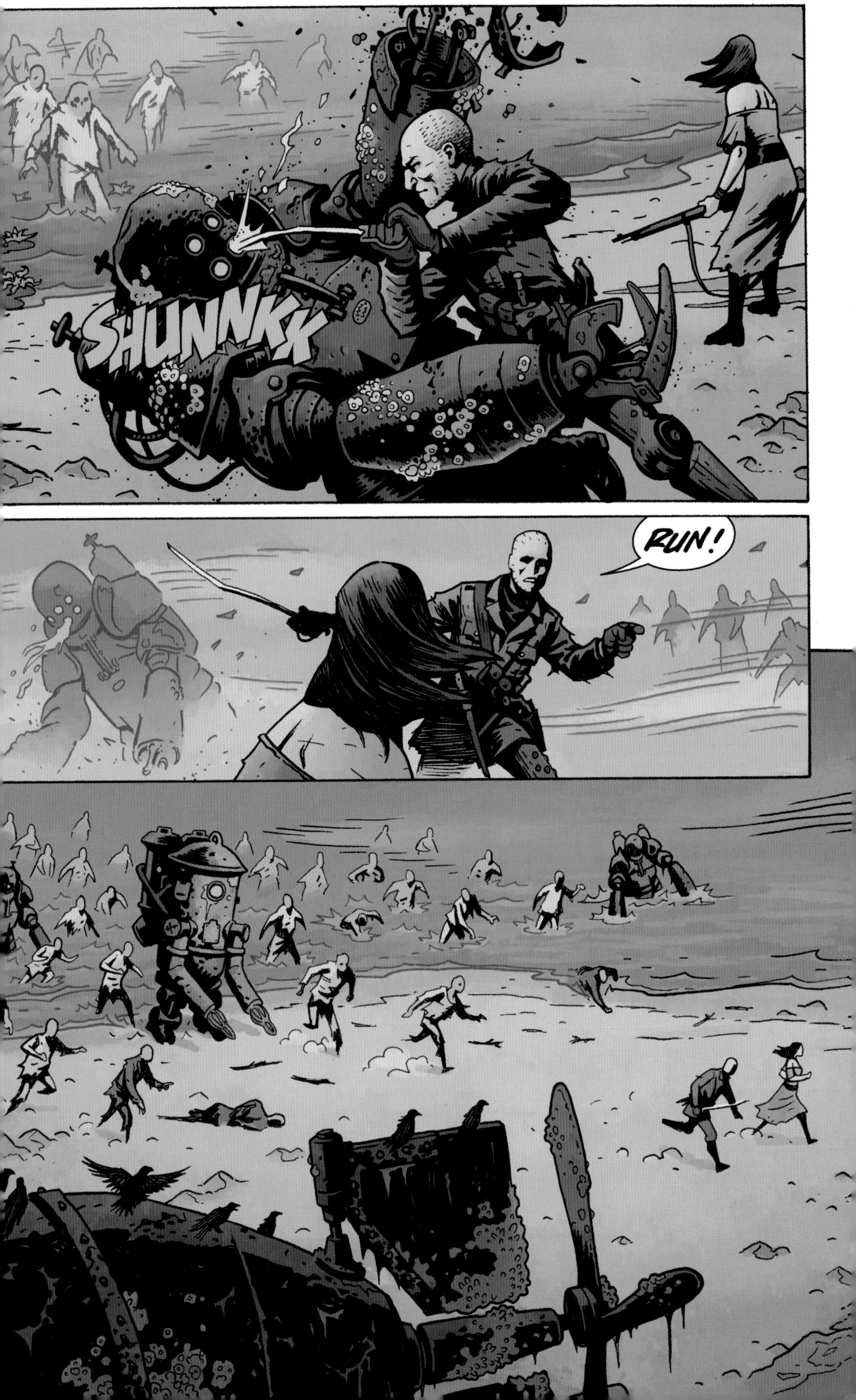
SHUNNKK
RUN!

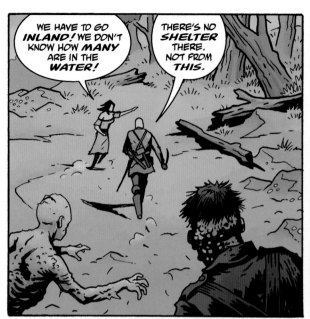

WE HAVE TO GO *INLAND!* WE DON'T KNOW HOW *MANY* ARE IN THE *WATER!*

THERE'S NO *SHELTER* THERE. NOT FROM *THIS.*

BUT MAYBE--!

YOU WANT TO TAKE SHELTER IN *THERE?* WHAT IF IT'S FILLED WITH THESE *THINGS?*

I DON'T THINK SO.

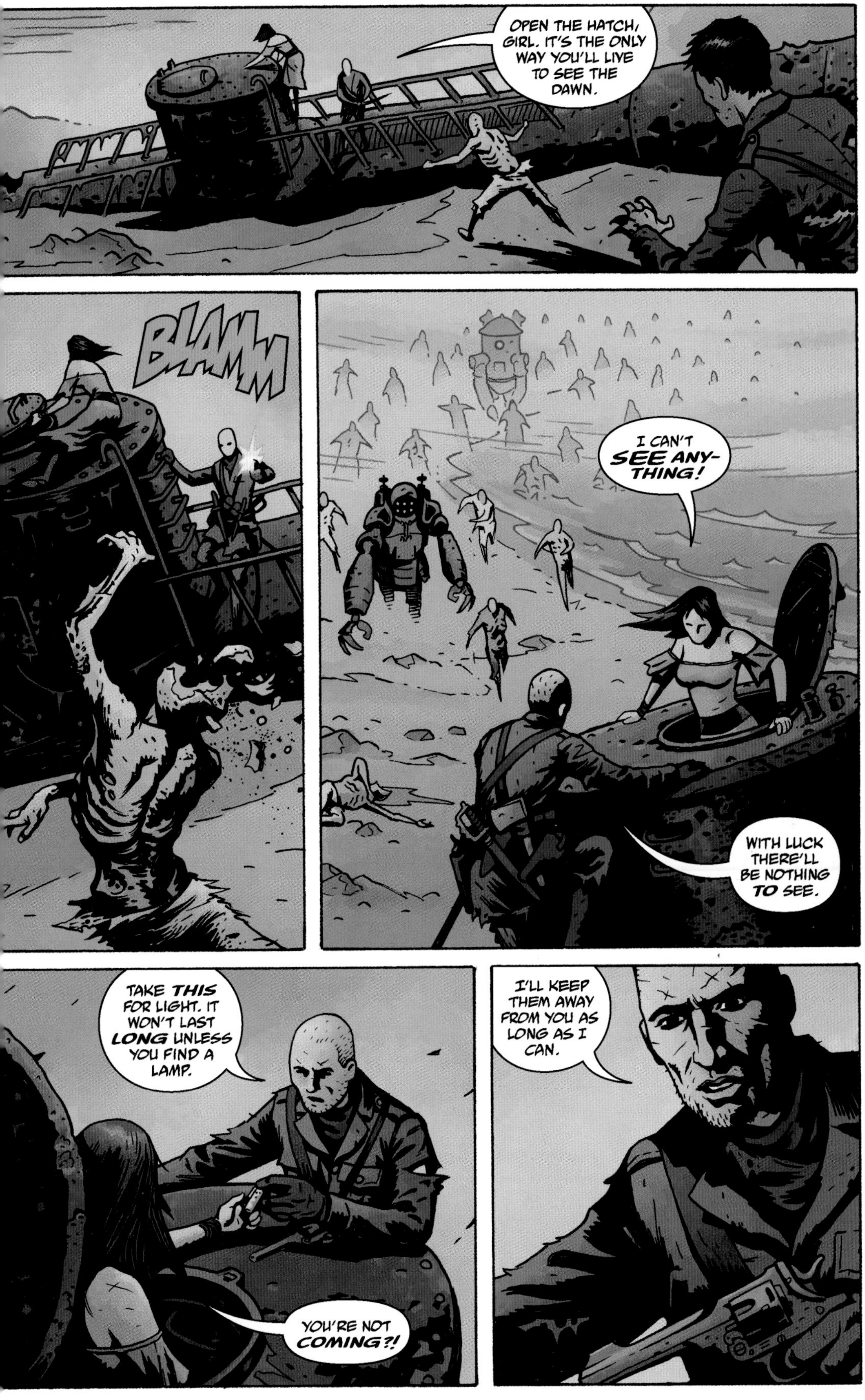
OPEN THE HATCH, GIRL. IT'S THE ONLY WAY YOU'LL LIVE TO SEE THE DAWN.
BLAMM
I CAN'T SEE ANY-THING!
WITH LUCK THERE'LL BE NOTHING TO SEE.
TAKE THIS FOR LIGHT. IT WON'T LAST LONG UNLESS YOU FIND A LAMP.
YOU'RE NOT COMING?!
I'LL KEEP THEM AWAY FROM YOU AS LONG AS I CAN.

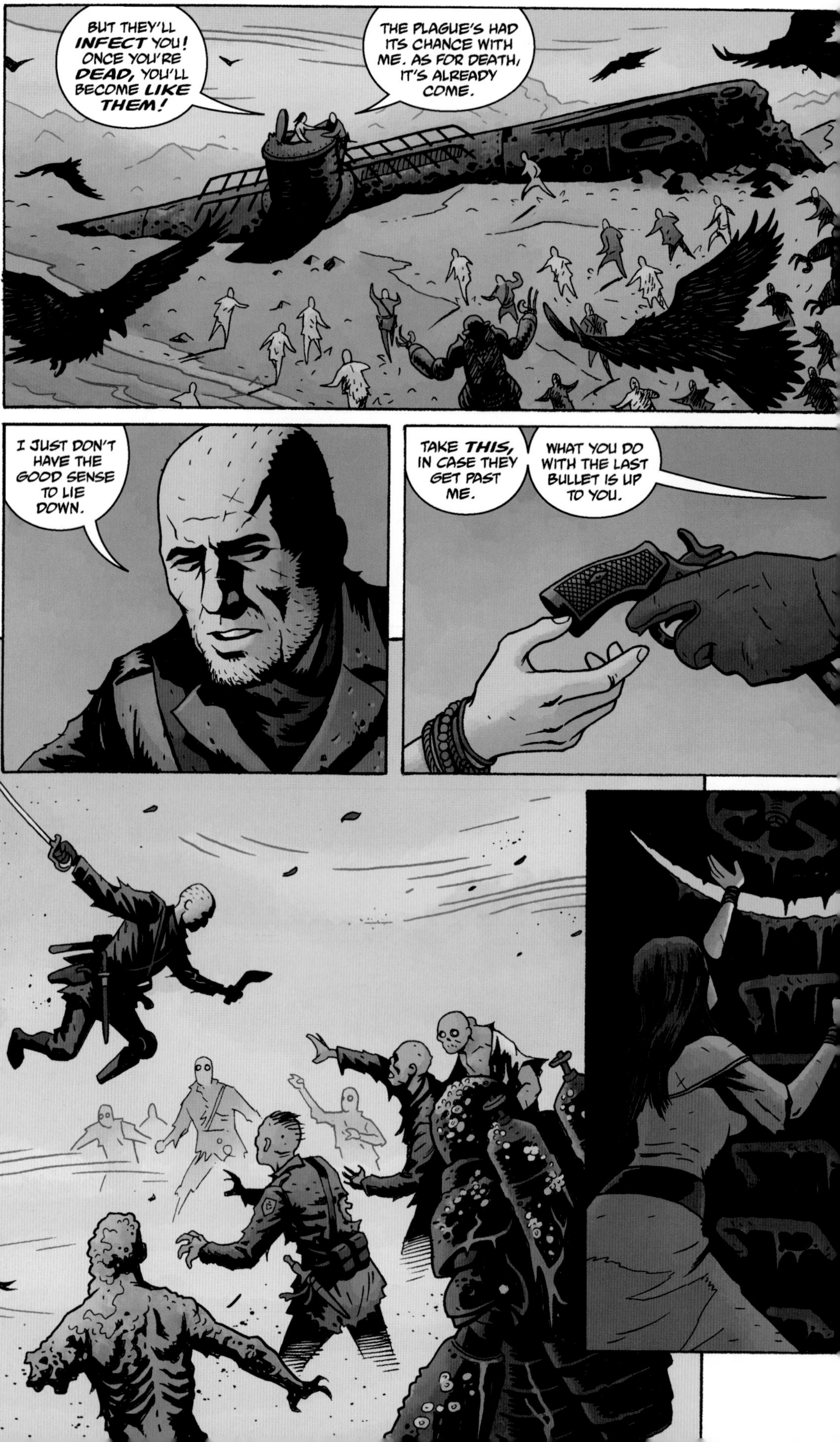
BUT THEY'LL INFECT YOU! ONCE YOU'RE DEAD, YOU'LL BECOME LIKE THEM!
THE PLAGUE'S HAD ITS CHANCE WITH ME. AS FOR DEATH, IT'S ALREADY COME.
I JUST DON'T HAVE THE GOOD SENSE TO LIE DOWN.
TAKE THIS, IN CASE THEY GET PAST ME.
WHAT YOU DO WITH THE LAST BULLET IS UP TO YOU.

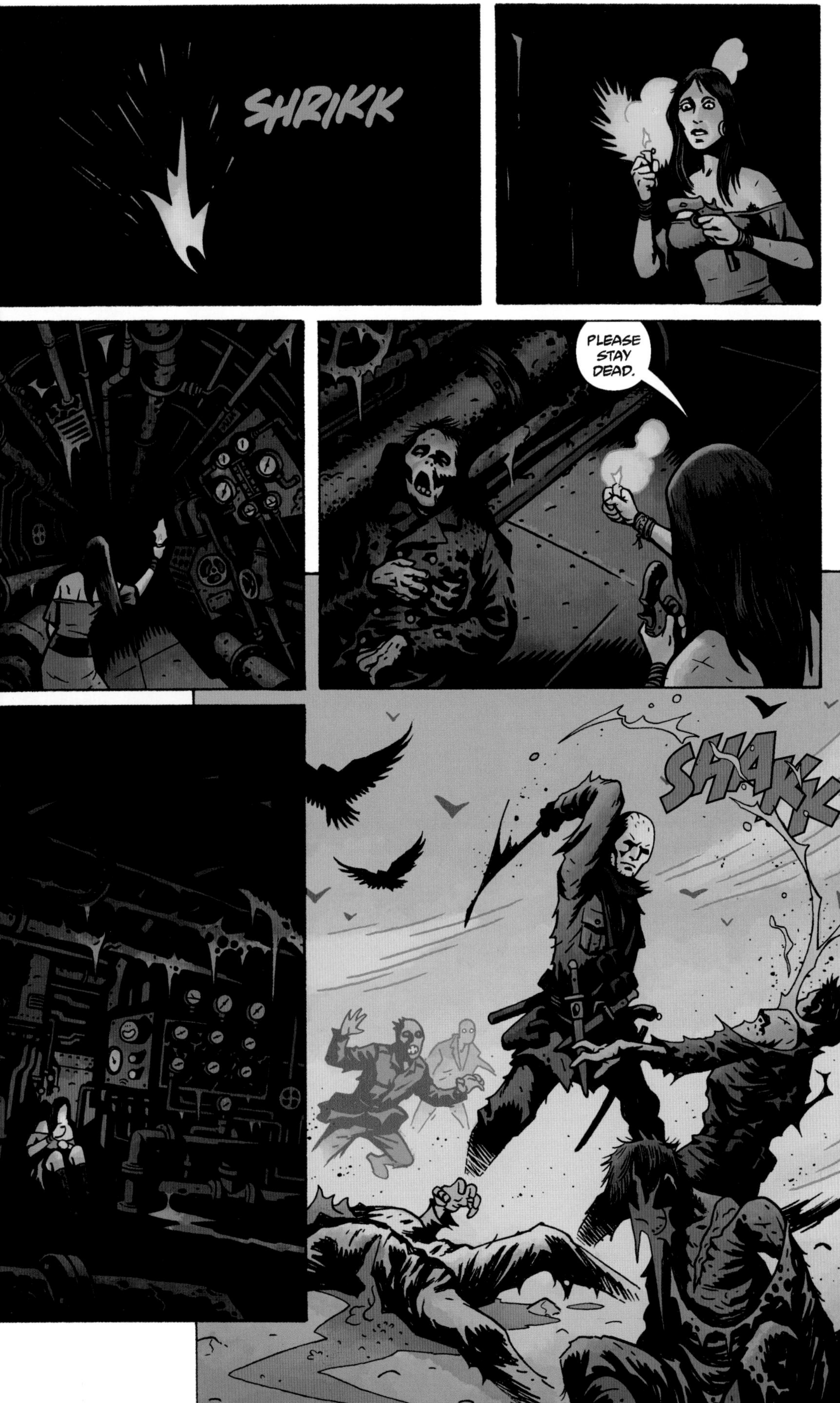
SHRIKK
PLEASE STAY DEAD.
SHAKK

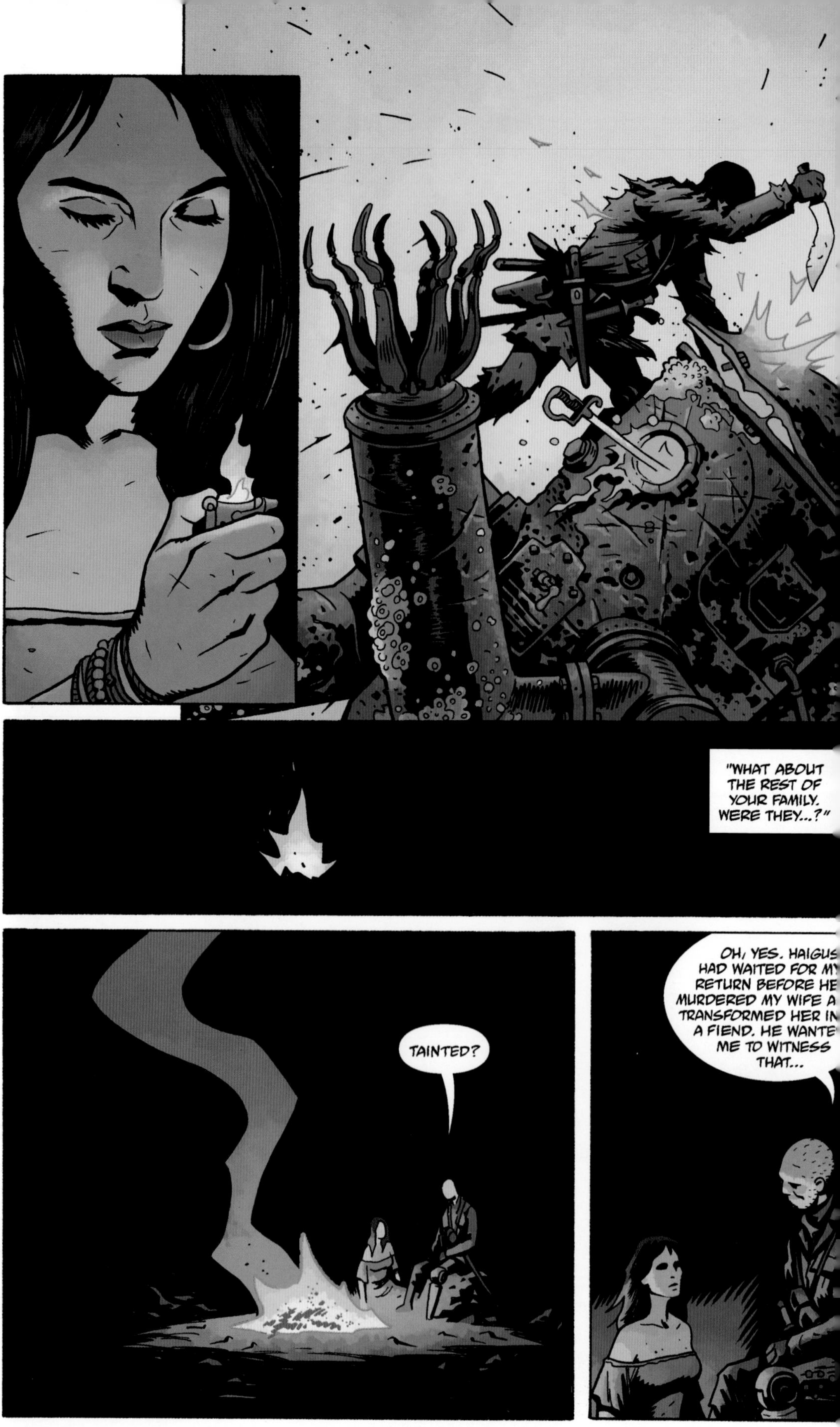
"WHAT ABOUT THE REST OF YOUR FAMILY. WERE THEY...?"
TAINTED?
OH, YES. HAIGUS HAD WAITED FOR MY RETURN BEFORE HE MURDERED MY WIFE A TRANSFORMED HER IN A FIEND. HE WANTE ME TO WITNESS THAT...

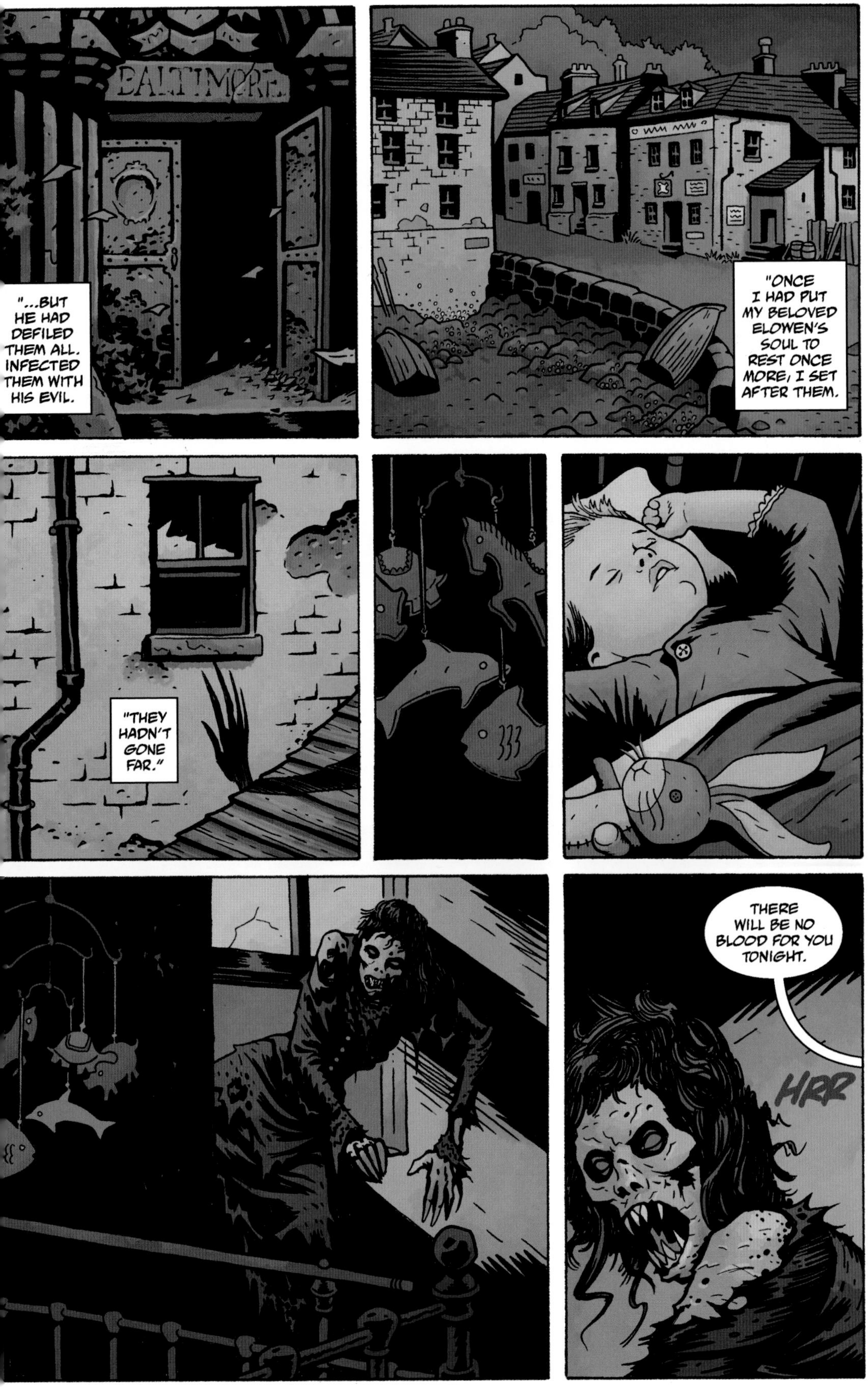

BALTIMORE
"...BUT HE HAD DEFILED THEM ALL. INFECTED THEM WITH HIS EVIL.
"ONCE I HAD PUT MY BELOVED ELOWEN'S SOUL TO REST ONCE MORE, I SET AFTER THEM.
"THEY HADN'T GONE FAR."
THERE WILL BE NO BLOOD FOR YOU TONIGHT.
HRR

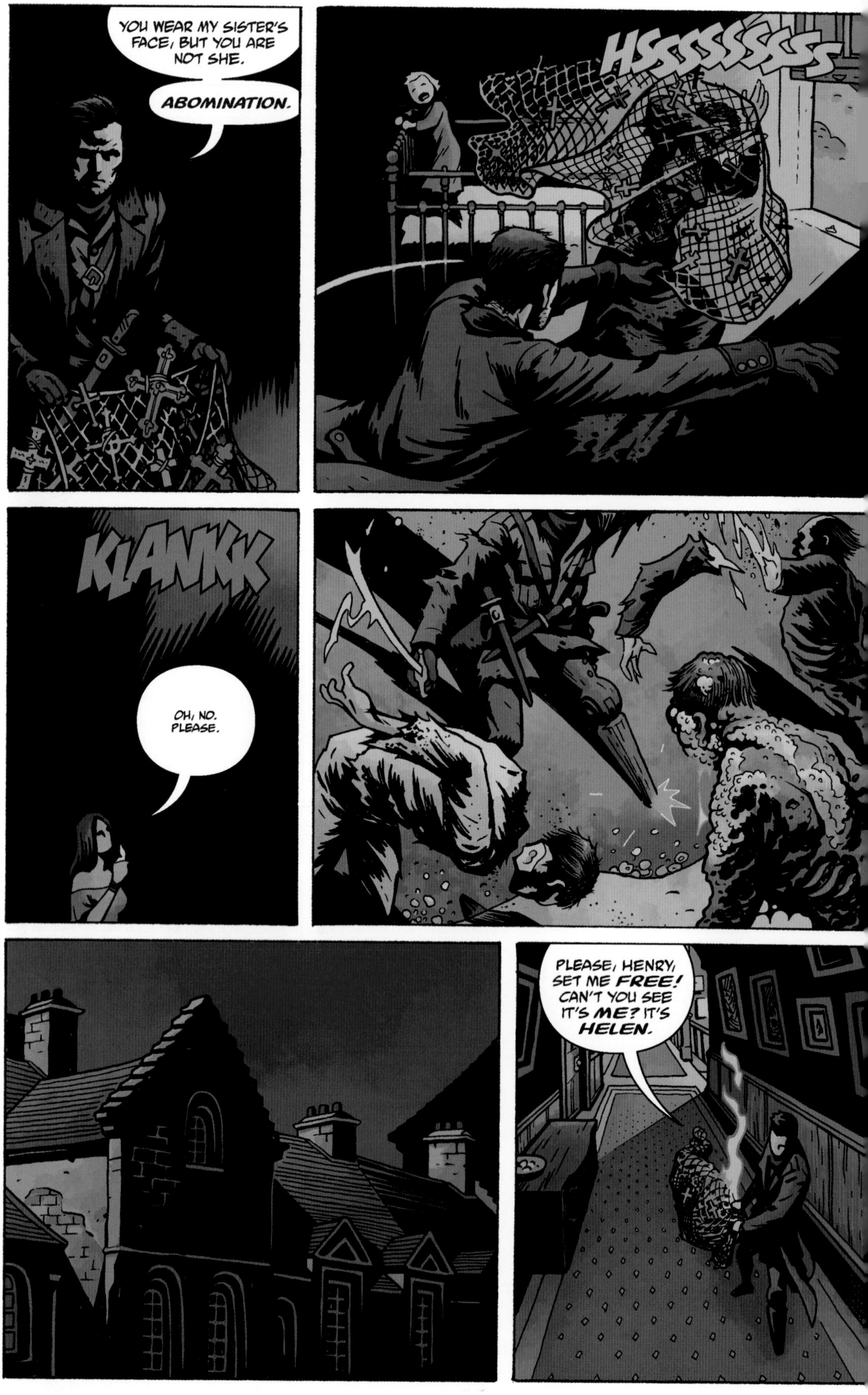
YOU WEAR MY SISTER'S FACE, BUT YOU ARE NOT SHE.
ABOMINATION.
HSSSSSSSS
KLANKK
OH, NO. PLEASE.
PLEASE, HENRY, SET ME FREE! CAN'T YOU SEE IT'S ME? IT'S HELEN.

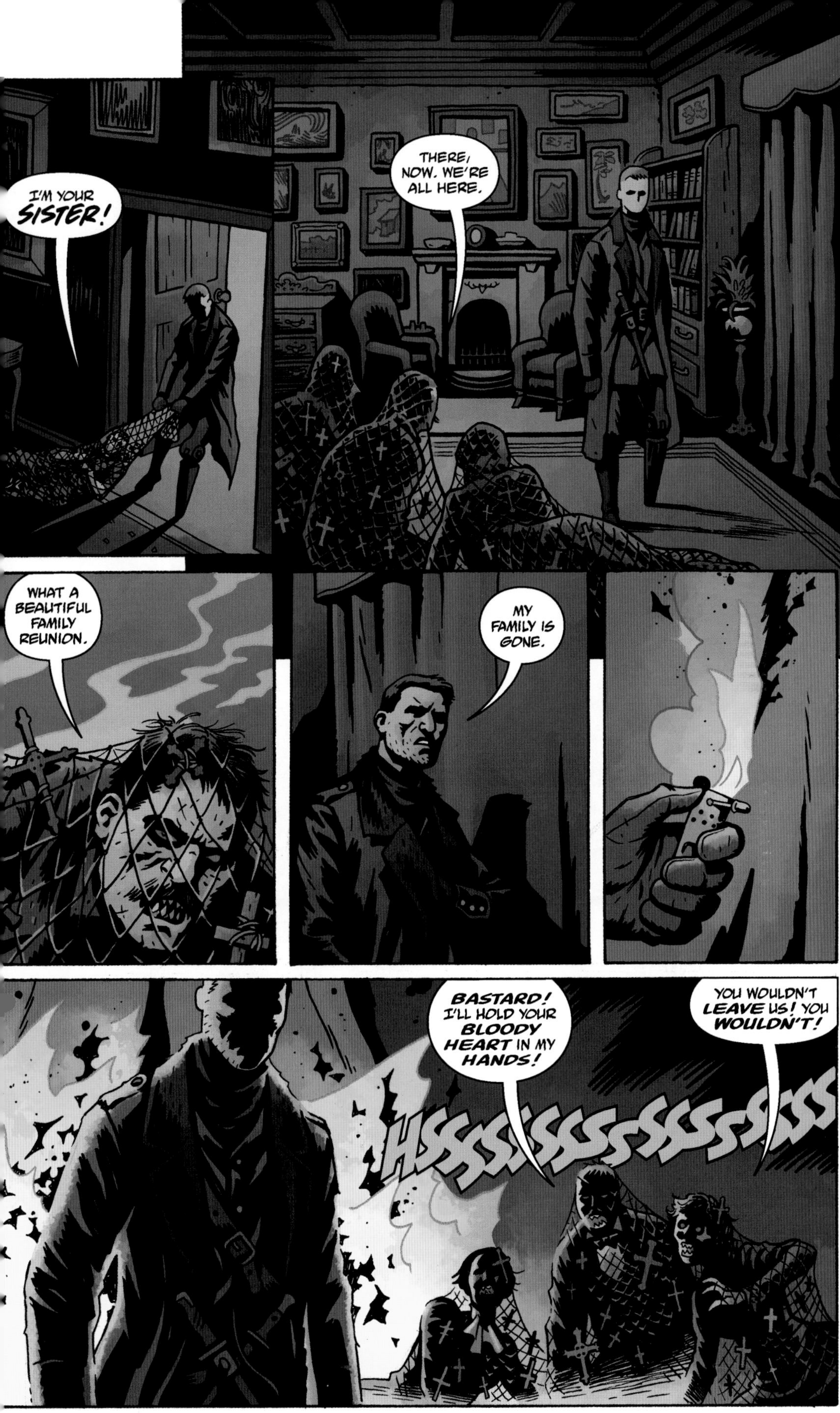
I'M YOUR SISTER!
THERE, NOW. WE'RE ALL HERE.
WHAT A BEAUTIFUL FAMILY REUNION.
MY FAMILY IS GONE.
BASTARD! I'LL HOLD YOUR BLOODY HEART IN MY HANDS!
YOU WOULDN'T LEAVE US! YOU WOULDN'T!
HSSSSSSSSSSSSSSS

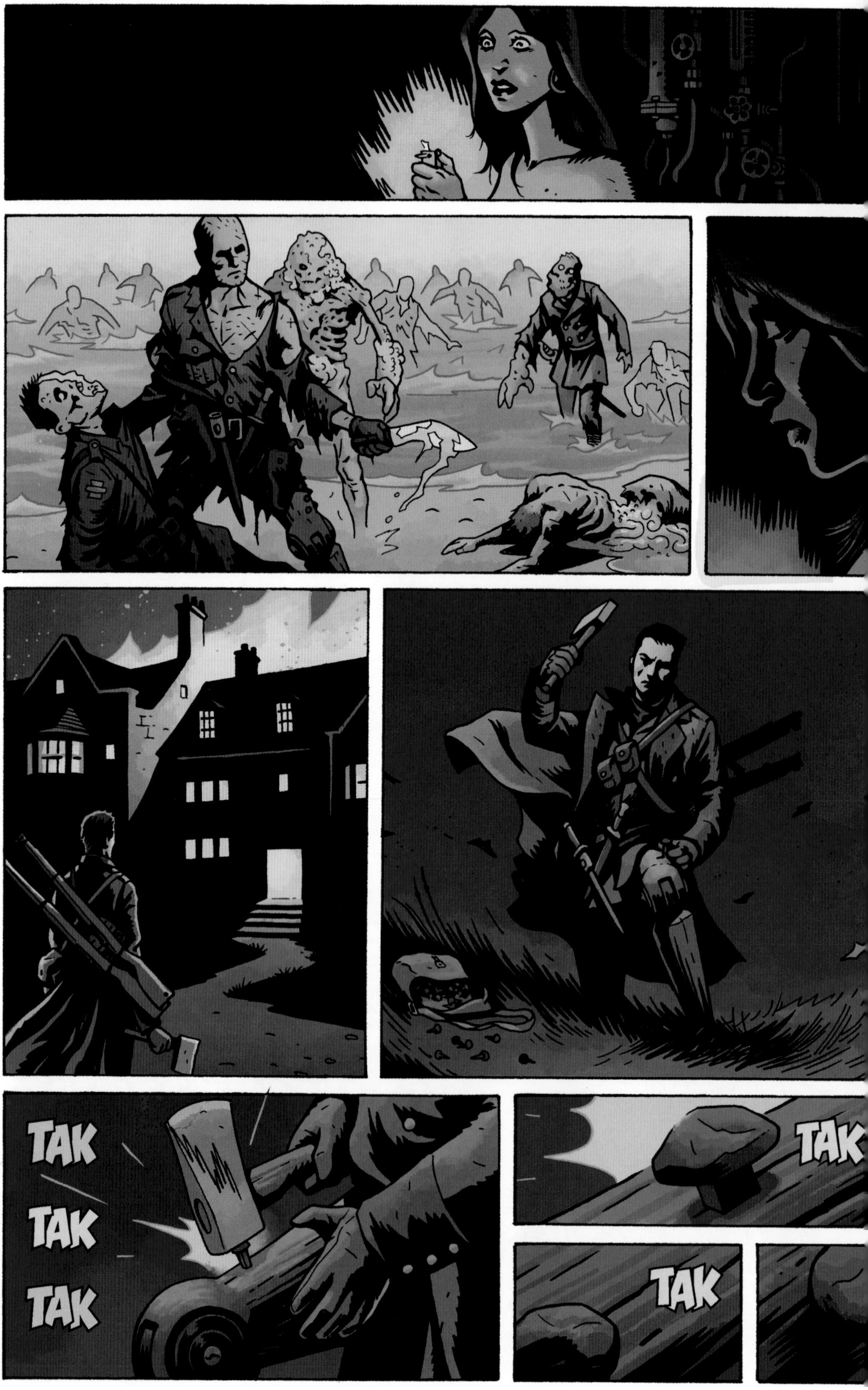
TAK
TAK
TAK
TAK
TAK

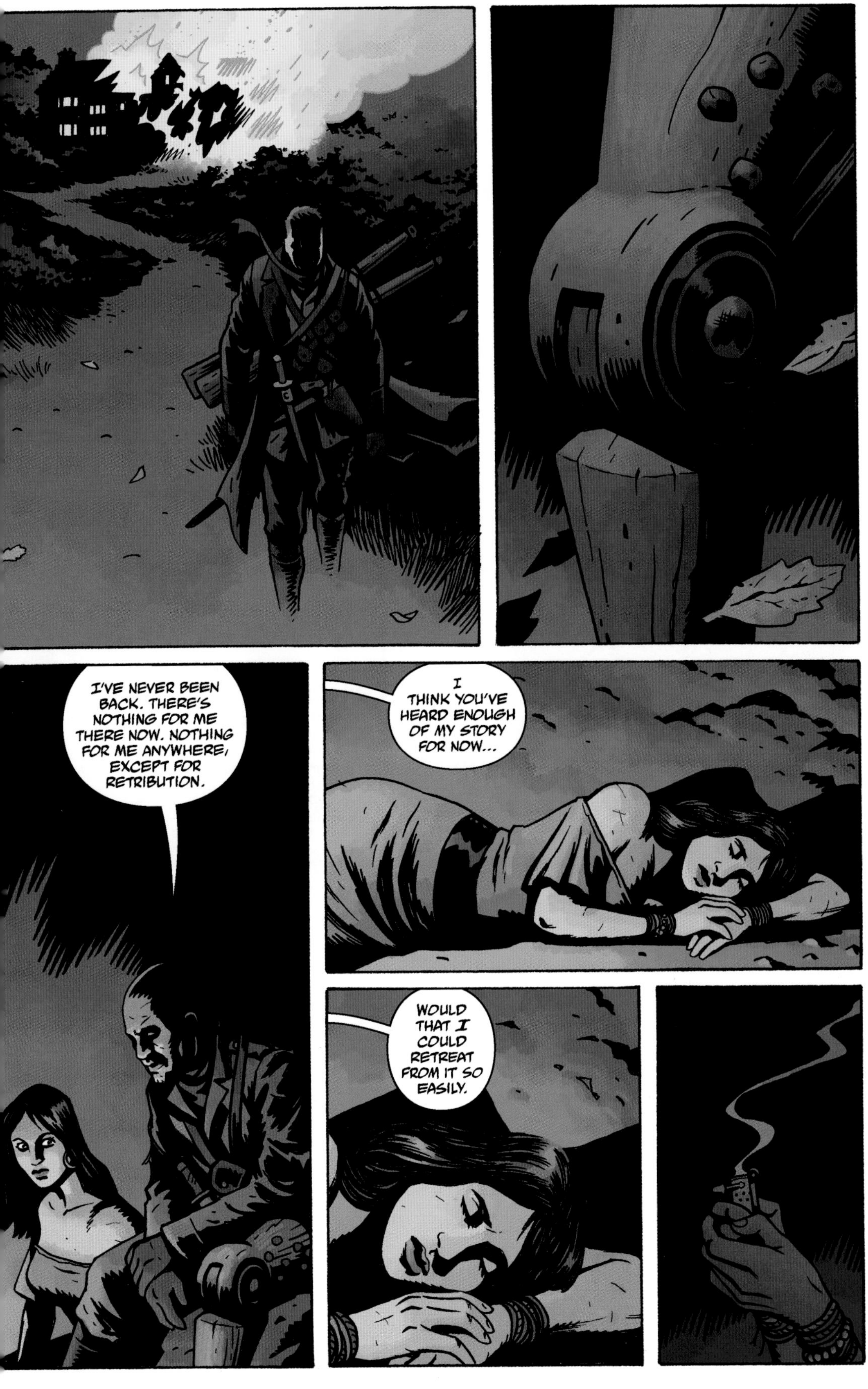
I'VE NEVER BEEN BACK. THERE'S NOTHING FOR ME THERE NOW. NOTHING FOR ME ANYWHERE, EXCEPT FOR RETRIBUTION.
I THINK YOU'VE HEARD ENOUGH OF MY STORY FOR NOW...
WOULD THAT I COULD RETREAT FROM IT SO EASILY.

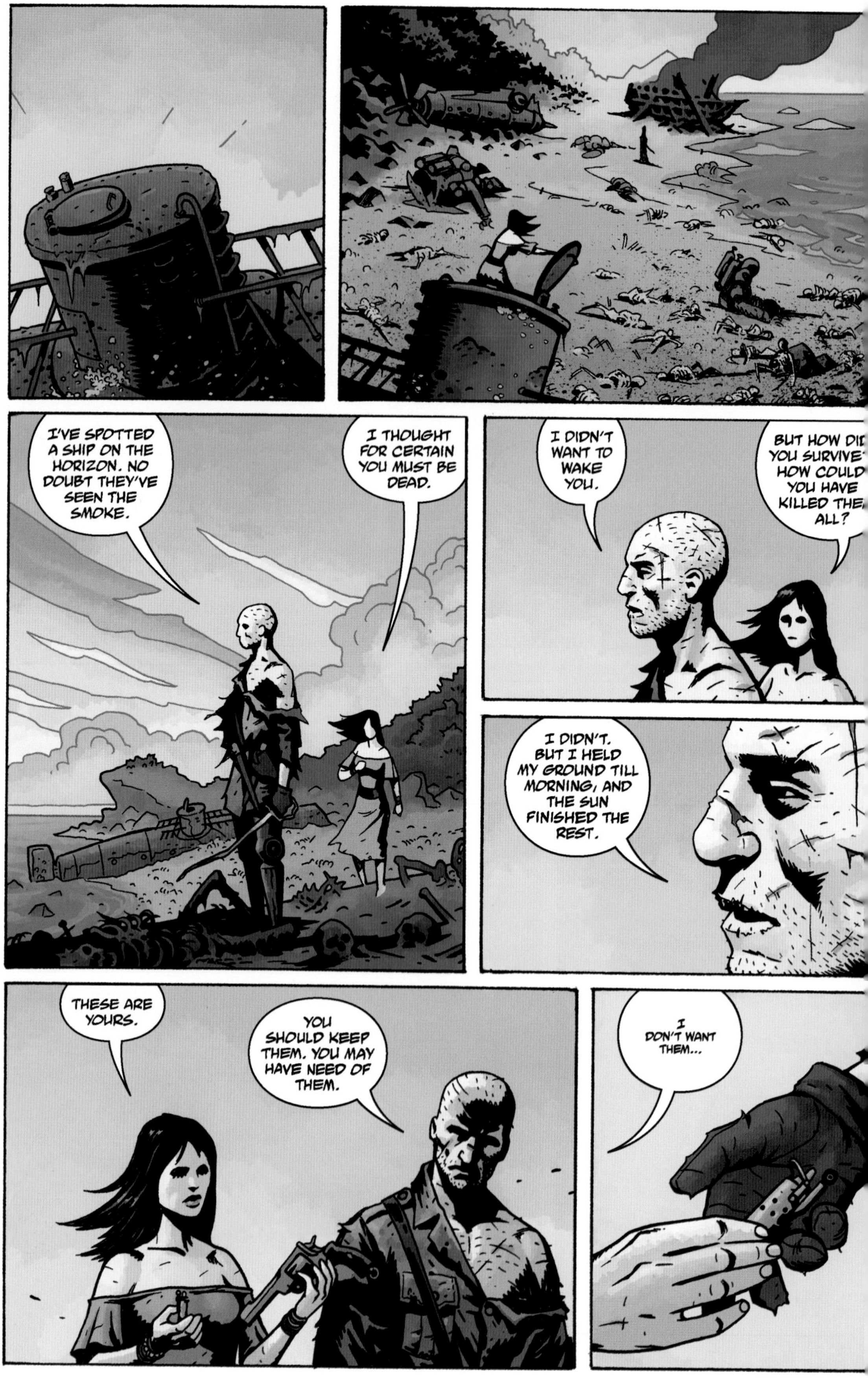
I'VE SPOTTED A SHIP ON THE HORIZON. NO DOUBT THEY'VE SEEN THE SMOKE.
I THOUGHT FOR CERTAIN YOU MUST BE DEAD.
I DIDN'T WANT TO WAKE YOU.
BUT HOW DI YOU SURVIVE HOW COULD YOU HAVE KILLED THE ALL?
I DIDN'T. BUT I HELD MY GROUND TILL MORNING, AND THE SUN FINISHED THE REST.
THESE ARE YOURS.
YOU SHOULD KEEP THEM. YOU MAY HAVE NEED OF THEM.
I DON'T WANT THEM...

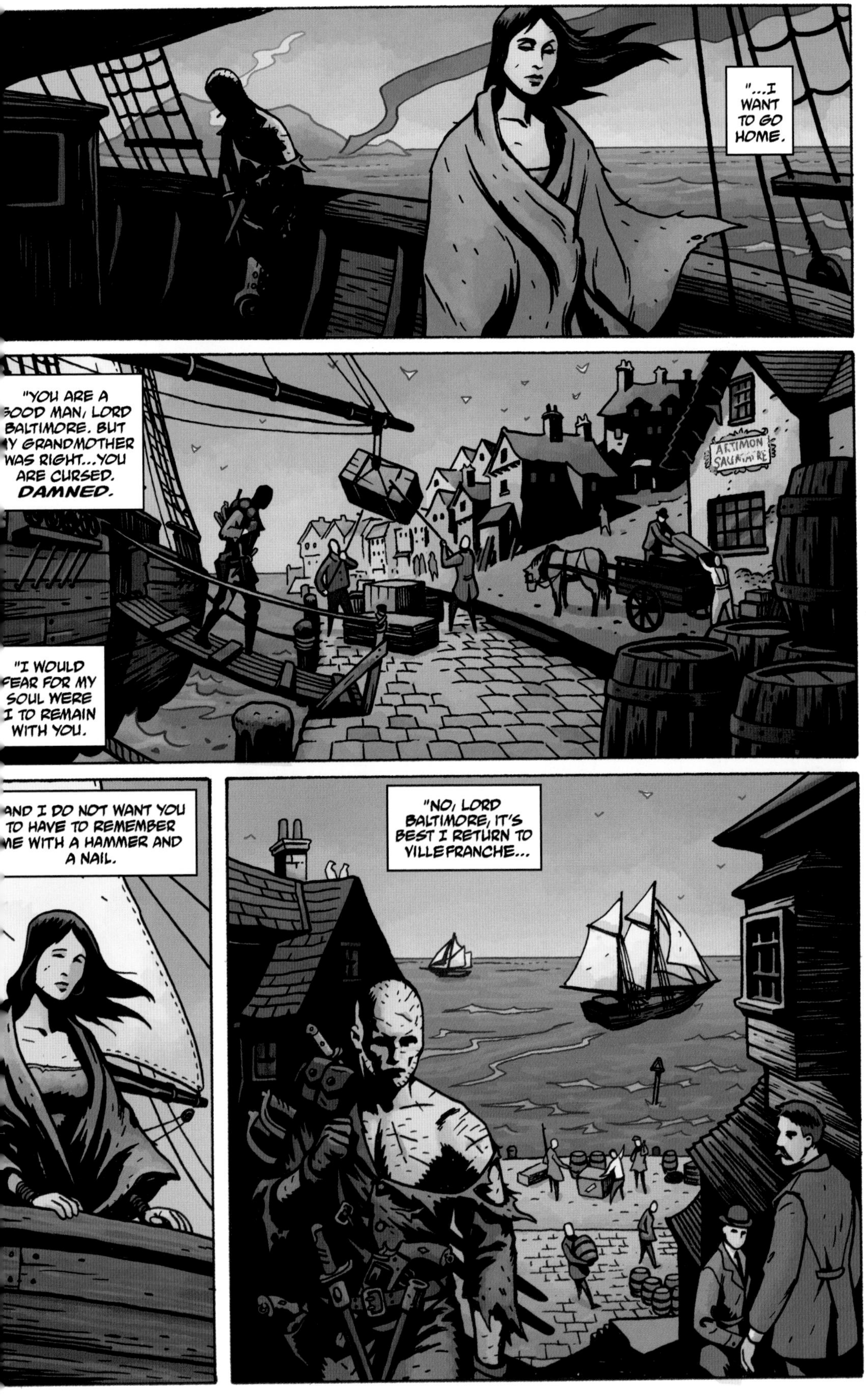

"...I WANT TO GO HOME.
"YOU ARE A GOOD MAN, LORD BALTIMORE. BUT MY GRANDMOTHER WAS RIGHT...YOU ARE CURSED. ***DAMNED.***
ARTIMON
"I WOULD FEAR FOR MY SOUL WERE I TO REMAIN WITH YOU.
AND I DO NOT WANT YOU TO HAVE TO REMEMBER ME WITH A HAMMER AND A NAIL.
"NO, LORD BALTIMORE, IT'S BEST I RETURN TO VILLEFRANCHE...

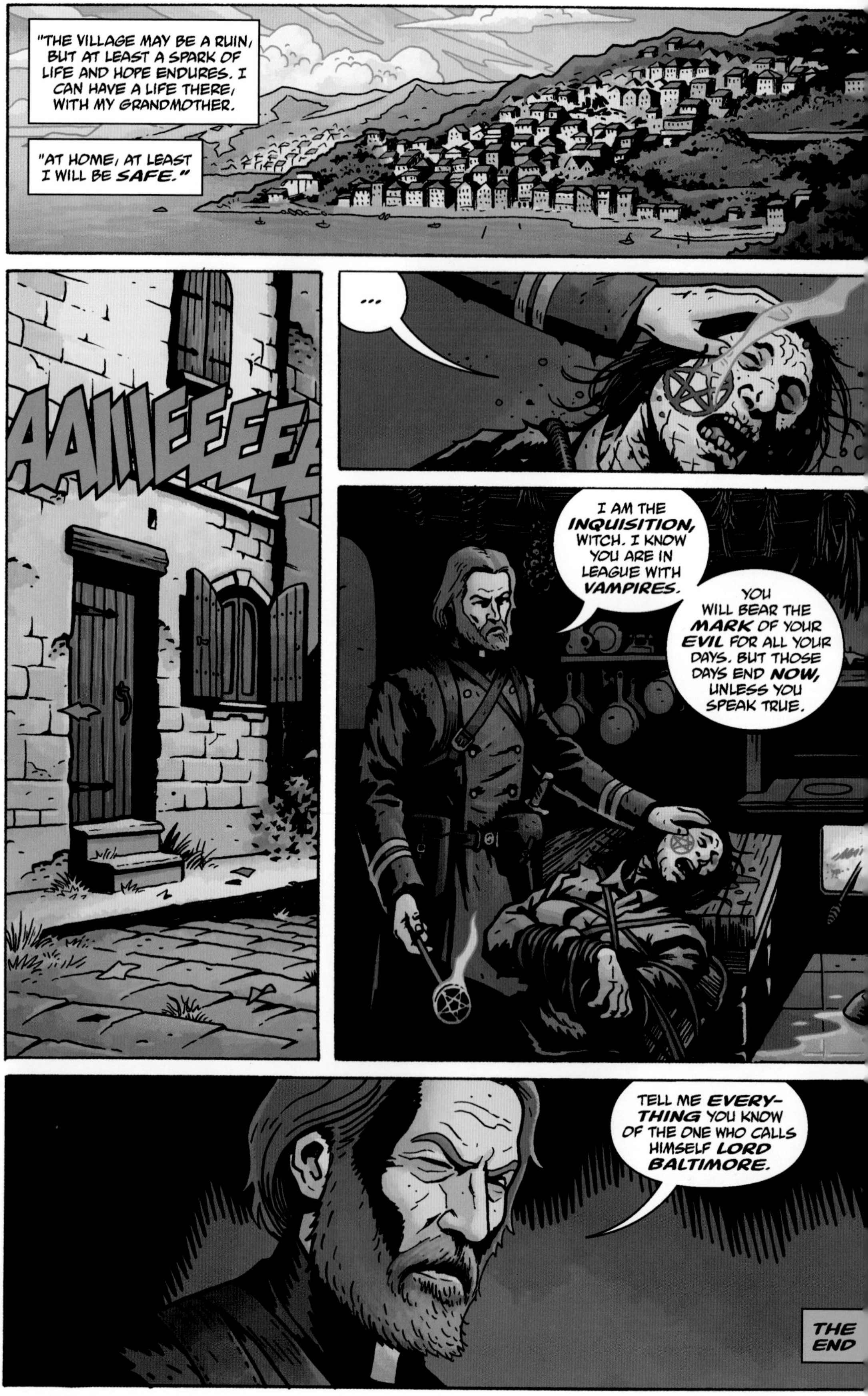
"THE VILLAGE MAY BE A RUIN, BUT AT LEAST A SPARK OF LIFE AND HOPE ENDURES. I CAN HAVE A LIFE THERE, WITH MY GRANDMOTHER.
"AT HOME, AT LEAST I WILL BE SAFE."
AAIIIEEEE
...
I AM THE INQUISITION, WITCH. I KNOW YOU ARE IN LEAGUE WITH VAMPIRES.
YOU WILL BEAR THE MARK OF YOUR EVIL FOR ALL YOUR DAYS. BUT THOSE DAYS END NOW, UNLESS YOU SPEAK TRUE.
TELL ME EVERY-THING YOU KNOW OF THE ONE WHO CALLS HIMSELF LORD BALTIMORE.
THE END

BALTIMORE™ THE PLAGUE SHIPS

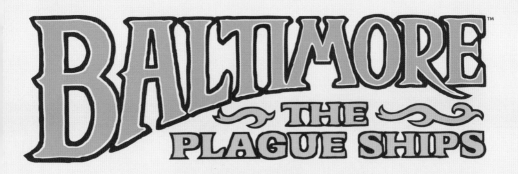

SKETCHBOOK

Notes by Ben Stenbeck

Some early "kite" sketches. They didn't really need any design work. Mike just wanted them to look like bats. Which is creepy enough.

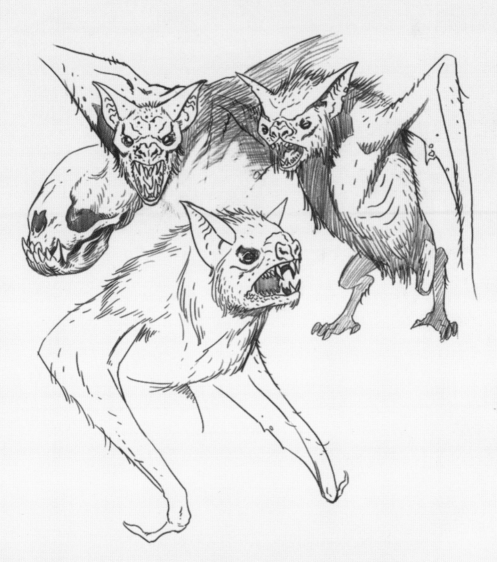

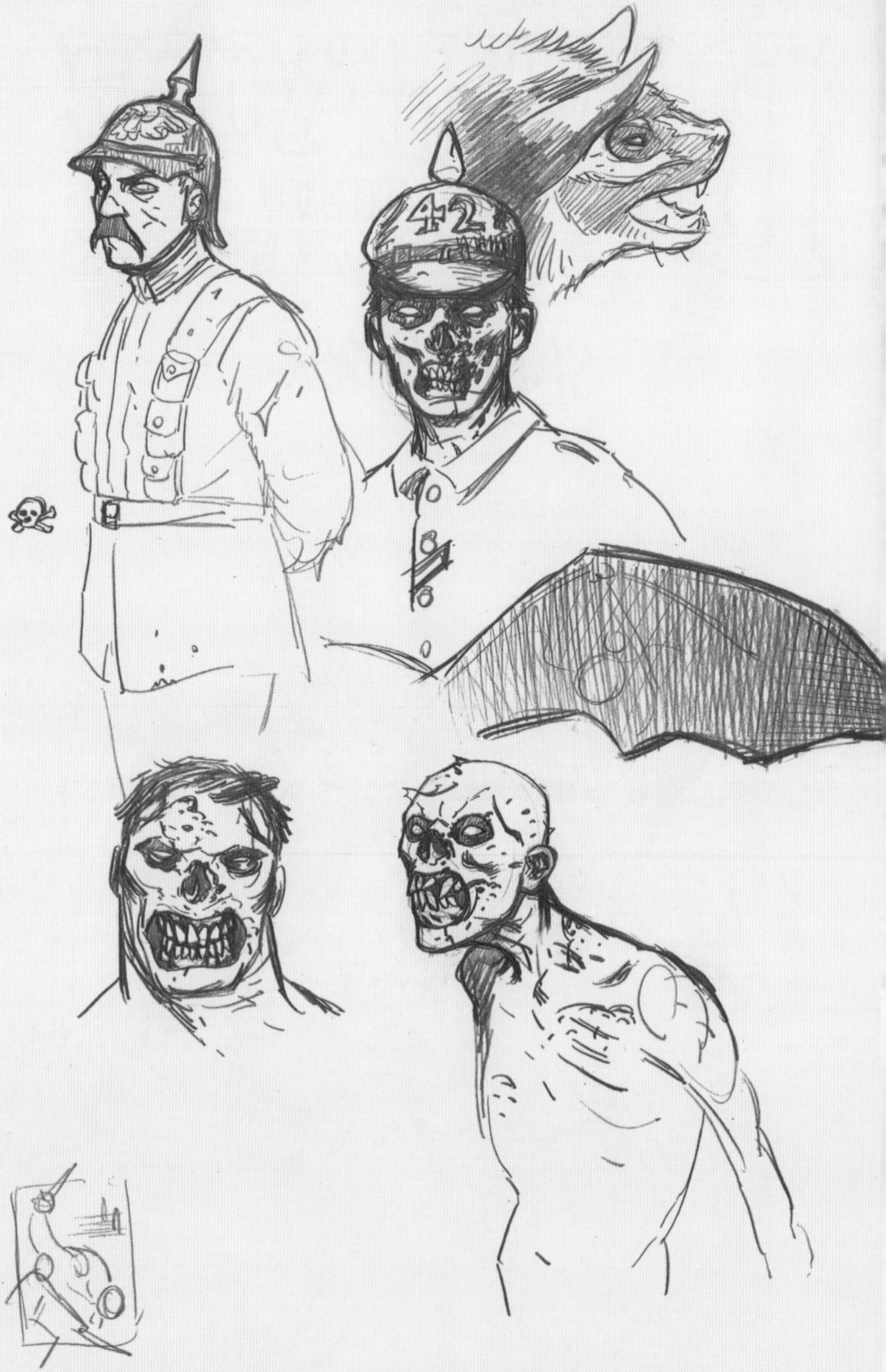
42

Following: new pinups done especially for this collection.

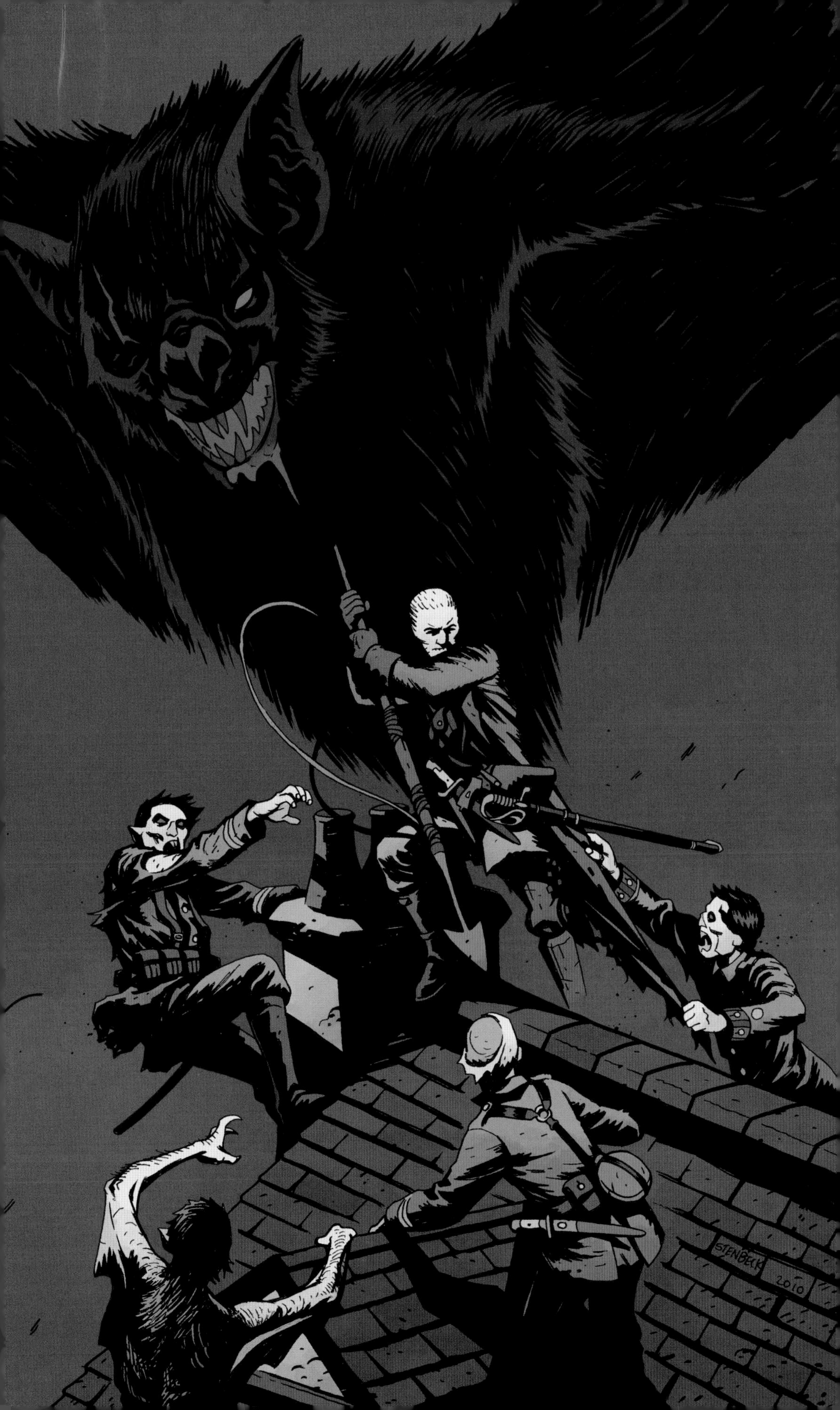
STENBECK
2010

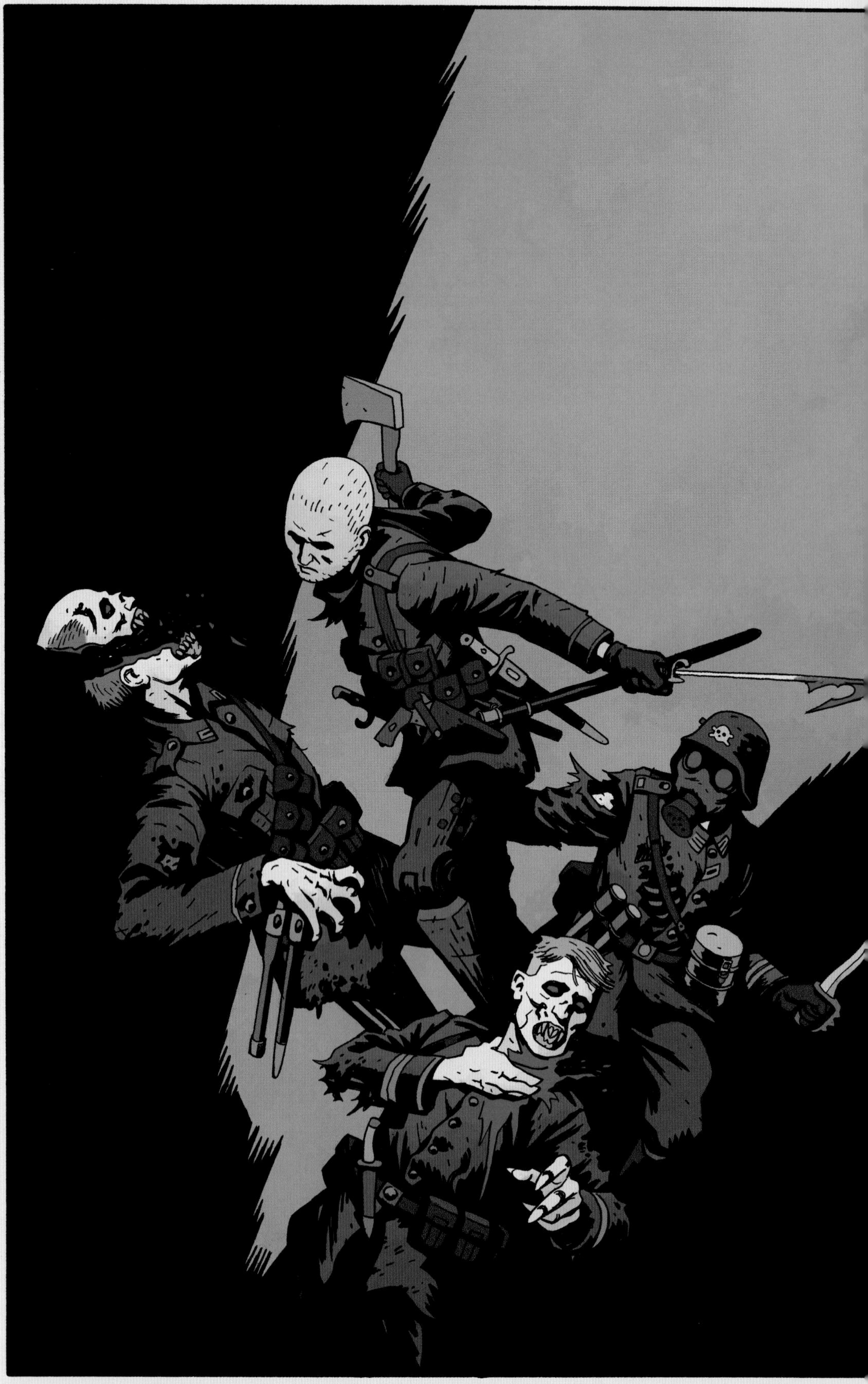

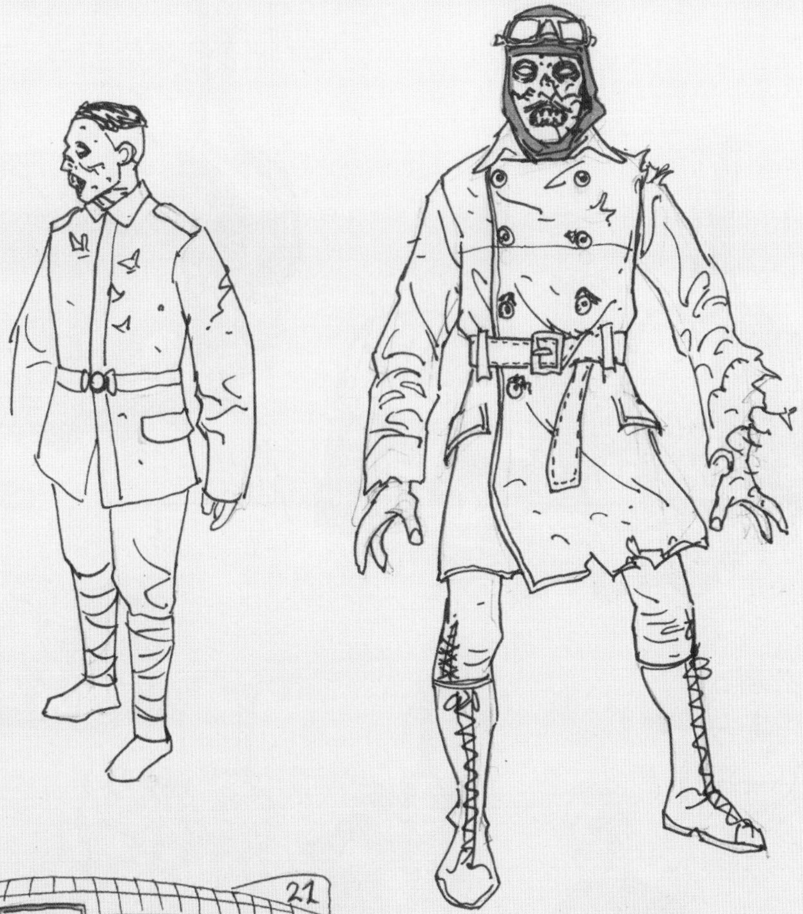

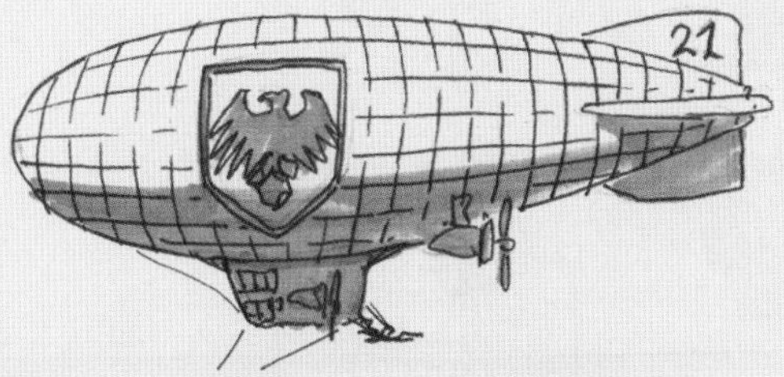
21

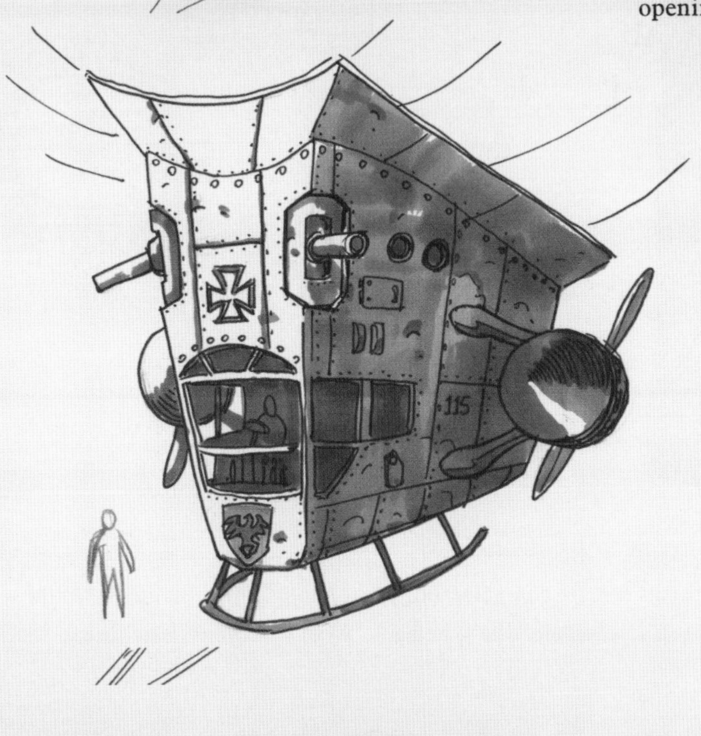
115

The blimp from the opening sequence.

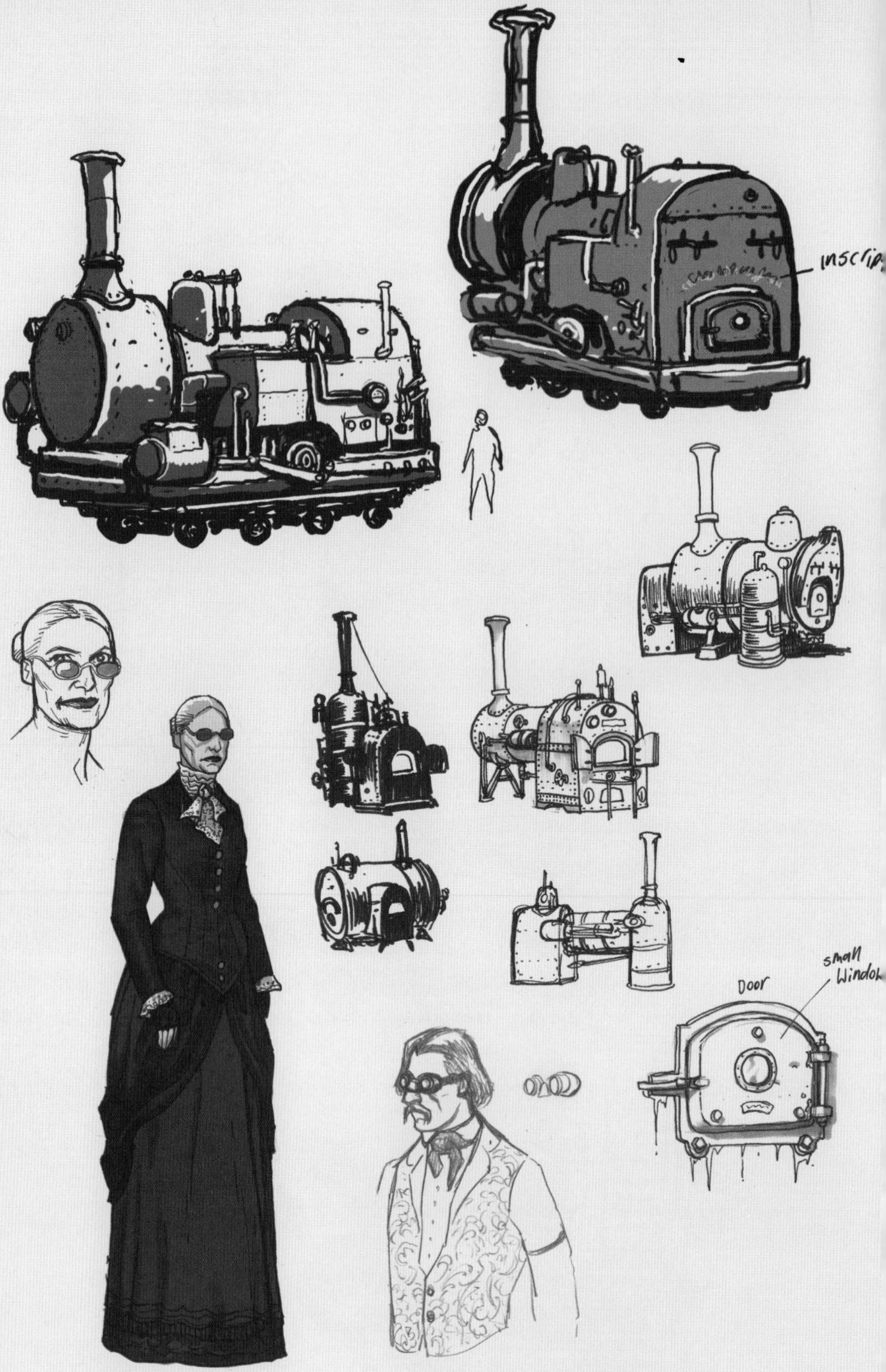
inscrip
Door
small
Windo

Fulcanelli was going to be a male character, but Mike thought the character would be more interesting as a female. She'll be back. With that weird machine.

Jellyfish things. We decided not to go too weird on their look. And I'm looking forward to drawing more of Judge Duvic. I think this was my first sketch of Baltimore.

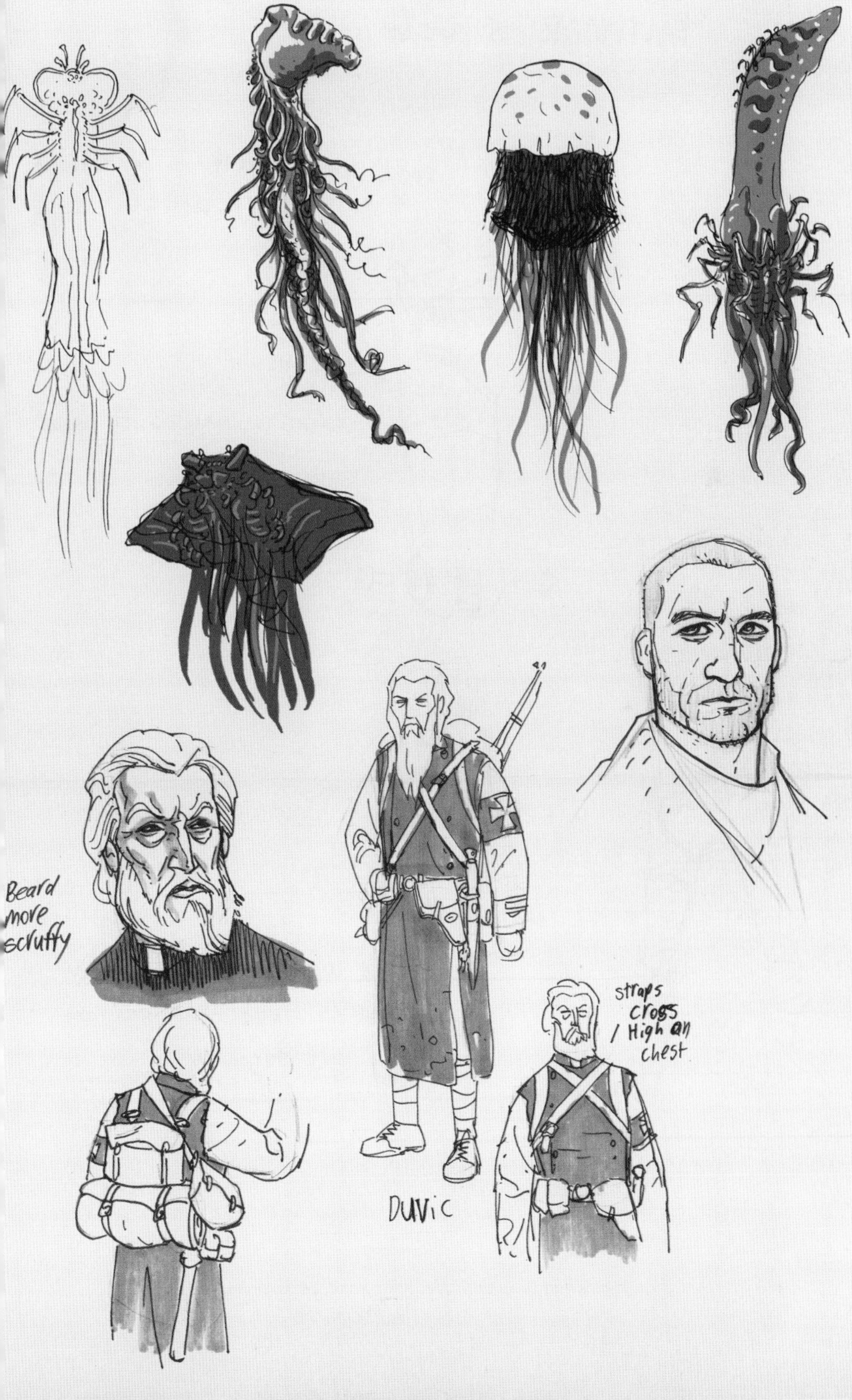
Beard more scruffy
DUVIC
straps cross / High on chest

BALTIMORE'S LEG

Some kind of belt to go around waist under clothes?

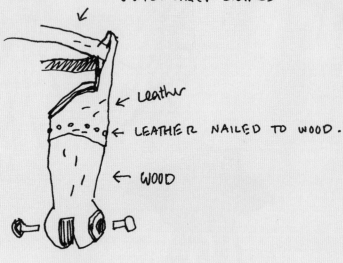

← Leather

← LEATHER NAILED TO WOOD.

← WOOD

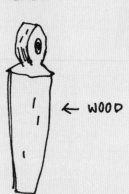

← WOOD

NO IDEA HOW IT ACTUALLY WORKS, but this is how it's put together.

Just as he's had to do with Hellboy's hand, Mike provides a mechanical guide for Baltimore's leg.

Layout for Page 14

Witch hand –
← Finger touching
water in bowl..
We need this to
clearly establish
color (red) in
water.

BLEED

Foreground misty -- Not too
much detail.

Vision is behind Baltimore - Baltimore
overlaps it --

TO SCOTT ALLIE - BEN STENBECK - CHRIS GOLDEN

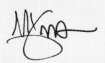

Page 22 was originally scripted to have more panels, but after seeing Ben's layout, Mike
sent this suggestion for simplifying it. The same layout was revisited again on page 99.
—Scott Allie

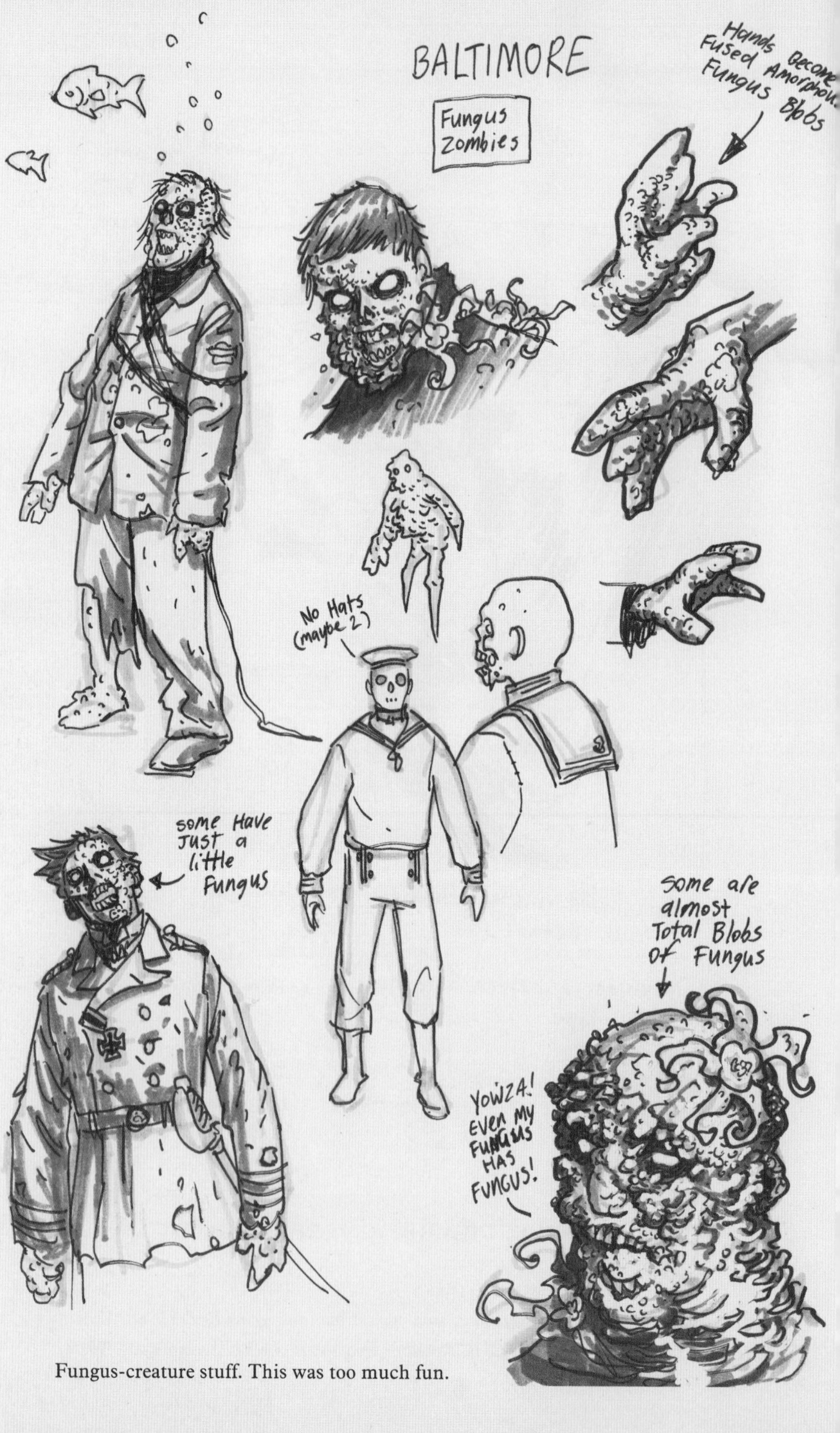

BALTIMORE
Fungus Zombies
Hands Become Fused Amorphous Fungus Blobs
No Hats (maybe 2)
some Have Just a little Fungus
Some are almost Total Blobs of Fungus
YOWZA! Even my Fungus Has Fungus!

Fungus-creature stuff. This was too much fun.

1
2
Dries
3
withers
and
cracks
4

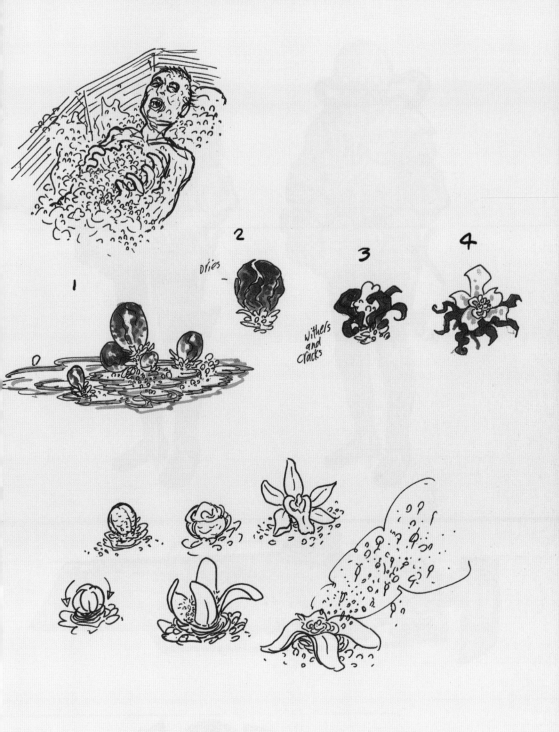

More preparation and design was done for the fungus zombies than any other part of the book.

Dive suits, for doing underwater stuff. This design wasn't clunky enough. So then I did the ones on the next page.

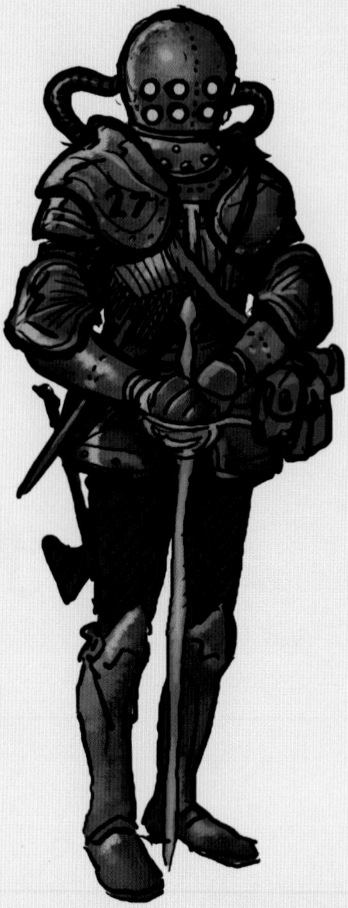
27

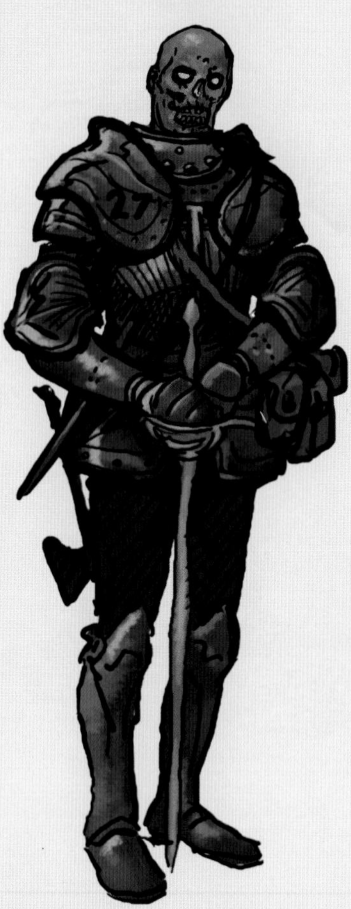
27

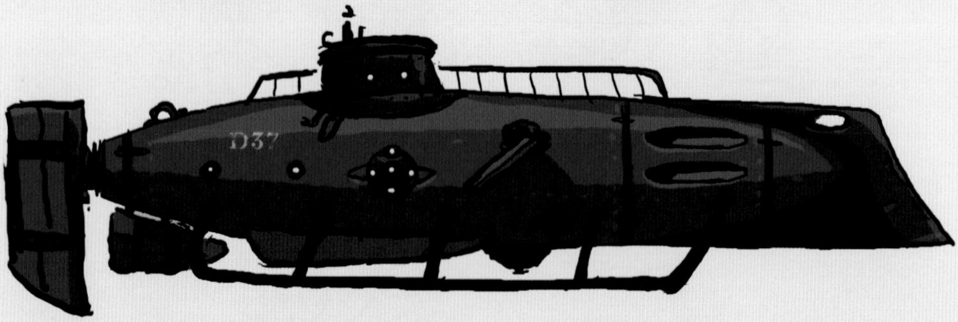
D37

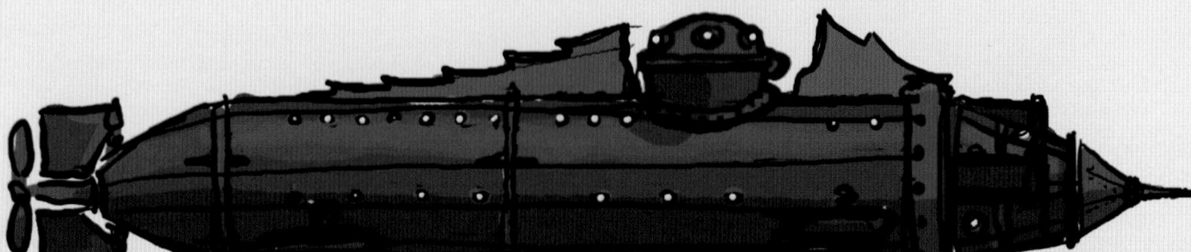

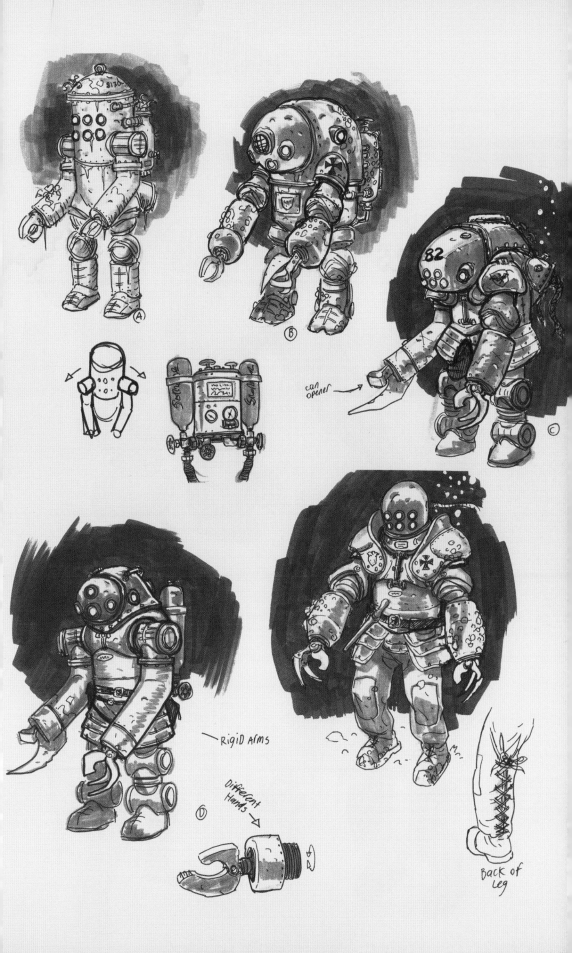

can opener

rigid arms

Different Hands

Back of Leg

Final designs and scale comparisons of the two different suits. Also a fungus zombie.

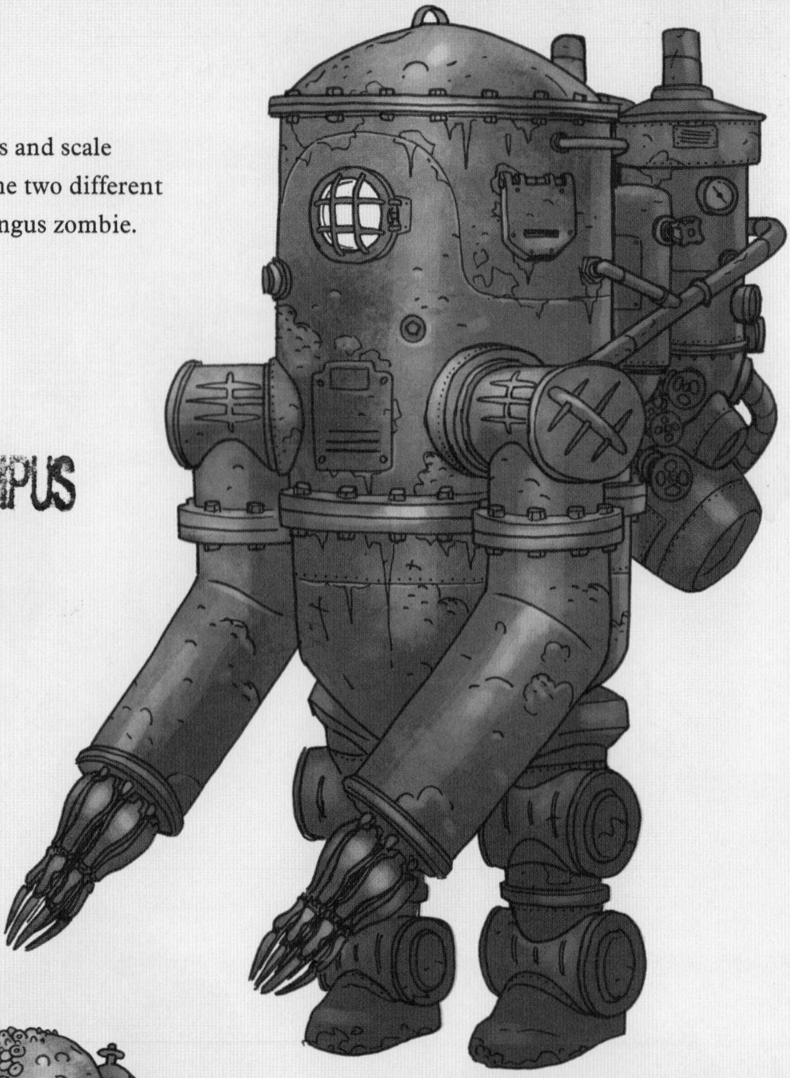

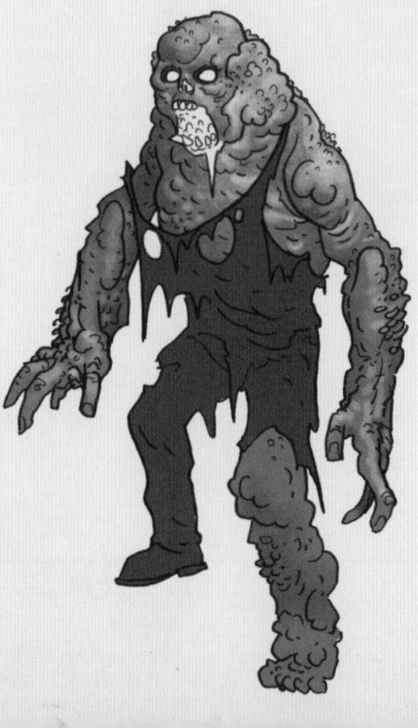

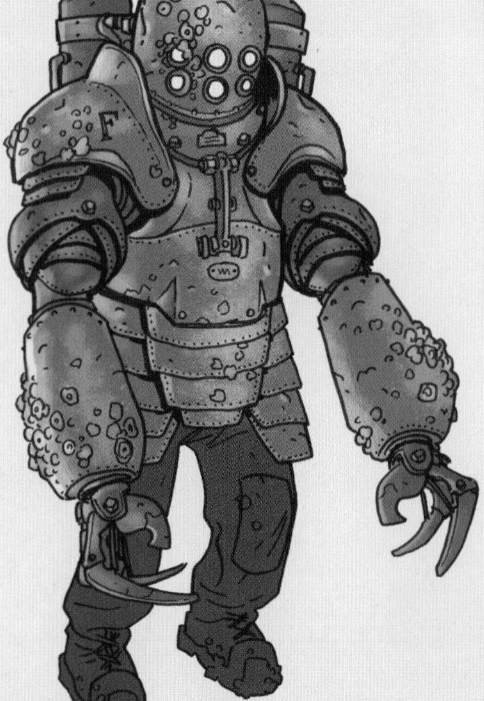
F

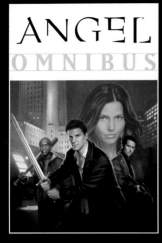

ANGEL OMNIBUS VOL. 1
Joss Whedon, Christopher Golden, and Tom Sniegoski

Angelus, the hunky, wildly popular vampire squeeze of Buffy Summers, has fled Sunnydale, and all the difficult emotional circumstances that go along with it, and set up shop as a paranormal investigator in Los Angeles. With the help of Sunnydale's favorite prom queen, Cordelia Chase, and demon-spawn wiseacre Doyle, Angel has his work cut out for him! Straight from the hit television series, follow Angel's exploits as he turns LA upside down. Includes the four-issue story written by Joss Whedon.

$24.99 | ISBN 978-1-59582-706-7

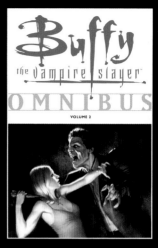

BUFFY THE VAMPIRE SLAYER OMNIBUS VOLUME 2
Christopher Golden, Ryan Sook, and others

As we follow the newly chosen Slayer from Los Angeles to Sunnydale and through her parents' divorce—with Dawn in tow—the souled vampire Angel makes his first appearance and the not-so-souled Spike and Drusilla cleave a bloody path toward the West Coast. This collection includes the critically acclaimed graphic novel *Ring of Fire* and the miniseries *A Stake to the Heart*, and reflects the Season 1 to Season 3 timeline of the cult-hit TV series.

$24.95 | ISBN 978-1-59307-826-3

THE GOON VOLUME 1: NOTHIN' BUT MISERY
Eric Powell

The Goon is a laugh-out-loud, action-packed romp through the streets of a town infested with zombies. An insane priest is building himself an army of the undead, and there's only one man who can put them in their place: the man they call Goon.

$16.99 | ISBN 978-1-59582-624-4

LIVING WITH THE DEAD
Mike Richardson and Ben Stenbeck

From the mind of Mike Richardson, creator of *The Mask* and *The Secret*, comes this hilariously frightening tale of Straw and Whip, two survivors of a global catastrophe who have lived through a plague that's left the world with seven billion brain-hungry zombies.

$9.95 | ISBN 978-1-59307-906-2

AVAILABLE AT YOUR LOCAL COMICS SHOP OR BOOKSTORE! • To find a comics shop in your area, call 1-888-266-4226.

For more information or to order direct visit darkhorse.com or call 1-800-862-0052 Mon.–Fri. 9 AM to 5 PM Pacific Time. Prices and availability subject to change without notice

DARK HORSE BOOKS *drawing on your nightmares*
DarkHorse.com

Angel™ & © 1998, 2011 Twentieth Century Fox Film Corporation. All rights reserved. Buffy the Vampire Slayer™ & © 1998, 2011 Twentieth Century Fox Film Corporation. All rights reserved. The Goon™ 2011 Eric Powell. Living with the Dead® © 2007 Dark Horse Comics, Inc. All rights reserved. Dark Horse Books® is a registered trademark of Dark Horse Comics, Inc.

HELLBOY

by MIKE MIGNOLA

HELLBOY LIBRARY EDITION VOLUME 1:
*SEED OF DESTRUCTION AND WAKE
THE DEVIL*
ISBN 978-1-59307-910-9 | $49.99

HELLBOY LIBRARY EDITION VOLUME 2:
*THE CHAINED COFFIN AND THE RIGHT
HAND OF DOOM*
ISBN 978-1-59307-989-5 | $49.99

HELLBOY LIBRARY EDITION VOLUME 3:
*CONQUEROR WORM AND
STRANGE PLACES*
ISBN 978-1-59582-352-6 | $49.99

HELLBOY LIBRARY EDITION VOLUME 4:
*THE CROOKED MAN AND THE
TROLL WITCH*
WITH RICHARD CORBEN AND OTHERS
ISBN 978-1-59582-658-9 | $49.99

SEED OF DESTRUCTION
WITH JOHN BYRNE
ISBN 978-1-59307-094-6 | $17.99

WAKE THE DEVIL
WITH DUNCAN FEGREDO
ISBN 978-1-59307-095-3 | $17.99

THE CHAINED COFFIN AND OTHERS
ISBN 978-1-59307-091-5 | $17.99

THE RIGHT HAND OF DOOM
ISBN 978-1-59307-093-9 | $17.99

CONQUEROR WORM
ISBN 978-1-59307-092-2 | $17.99

STRANGE PLACES
ISBN 978-1-59307-475-3 | $17.99

THE TROLL WITCH AND OTHERS
ISBN 978-1-59307-860-7 | $17.99

DARKNESS CALLS
WITH DUNCAN FEGREDO
ISBN 978-1-59307-896-6 | $19.99

THE WILD HUNT
WITH DUNCAN FEGREDO
ISBN 978-1-59582-352-6 | $19.99

THE CROOKED MAN AND OTHERS
WITH RICHARD CORBEN
ISBN 978-1-59582-477-6 | $17.99

THE BRIDE OF HELL AND OTHERS
WITH RICHARD CORBEN, KEVIN NOWLAN,
AND SCOTT HAMPTON
ISBN 978-1-59582-740-1 | $19.99

THE STORM AND THE FURY
ISBN 978-1-59582-827-9 | $19.99

HOUSE OF THE LIVING DEAD
WITH RICHARD CORBEN
ISBN 978-1-59582-757-9 | $14.99

THE ART OF HELLBOY
ISBN 978-1-59307-089-2 | $29.99

HELLBOY II: THE ART OF THE MOVIE
ISBN 978-1-59307-964-2 | $24.99

HELLBOY: THE COMPANION
ISBN 978-1-59307-655-9 | $14.99

HELLBOY: WEIRD TALES
VOLUME 1
ISBN 978-1-56971-622-9 | $17.99
VOLUME 2
ISBN 978-1-56971-953-4 | $17.99

HELLBOY: MASKS AND MONSTERS
WITH JAMES ROBINSON
AND SCOTT BENEFIEL
ISBN 978-1-59582-567-4 | $17.99

NOVELS

HELLBOY: EMERALD HELL
BY TOM PICCIRILLI
ISBN 978-1-59582-141-6 | $12.99

HELLBOY: THE ALL-SEEING EYE
BY MARK MORRIS
ISBN 978-1-59582-141-6 | $12.99

HELLBOY: THE FIRE WOLVES
BY TIM LEBBON
ISBN 978-1-59582-204-8 | $12.99

HELLBOY: THE ICE WOLVES
BY MARK CHADBOURN
ISBN 978-1-59582-205-5 | $12.99

SHORT STORIES
ILLUSTRATED BY MIKE MIGNOLA

HELLBOY: ODD JOBS
BY POPPY Z. BRITE, GREG RUCKA,
AND OTHERS
ISBN 978-1-56971-440-9 | $14.99

HELLBOY: ODDER JOBS
BY FRANK DARABONT, GUILLERMO
DEL TORO, AND OTHERS
ISBN 978-1-59307-226-1 | $14.99

HELLBOY: ODDEST JOBS
BY JOE R. LANSDALE, CHINA MIÉVILLE,
AND OTHERS
ISBN 978-1-59307-944-4 | $14.99

Prices and availability subject to change without notice.

AVAILABLE AT YOUR LOCAL COMICS SHOP OR BOOKSTORE! • To find a comics shop in your area, call 1-888-266-4226.
For more information or to order direct visit DarkHorse.com or call 1-800-862-0052 Mon.–Fri. 9 AM to 5 PM Pacific Time.
Prices and availability subject to change without notice.
Hellboy™ and © Mike Mignola. All rights reserved. Dark Horse Comics® and the Dark Horse logo are trademarks of Dark Horse Comics, Inc., registered in various categories and countries. All rights